"I'M WILLING TO HOLD THE WHOLE DAMN WORLD HOSTAGE!"

Commander Douglas Mawson picked up the microphone in the submarine's command center. He knew his men would do what he asked of them—mutiny. There was no other way he could save his wife and children, the wives and children of all his men. While his submarine was patrolling the Norwegian Sea, Palestinian terrorists had seized his crew's families, carrying them as hostages into Soviet-controlled territory. Now Douglas Mawson, Navy born and Navy bred, was making the loneliest decision of his life.

"This ship controls the start of nuclear war," he said. "We have that power, and *we* should use it."

COMMANDER MAWSON: HIS MUTINY COULD DESTROY THE WORLD

WARHEAD

WARHEAD

F. Robert Baker

BANTAM BOOKS
TORONTO · NEW YORK · LONDON

WARHEAD
A Bantam Book / July 1981

ISBN 0-553-14790-0

Published simultaneously in the United States and Canada

Bantam Books are published by Bantam Books, Inc. Its
trademark, consisting of the words "Bantam Books" and
the portrayal of a bantam, is Registered in U.S. Patent
and Trademark Office and in other countries. Marca Reg-
istrada. Bantam Books, Inc., 666 Fifth Avenue, New York,
New York 10103.

PRINTED IN THE UNITED STATES OF AMERICA

0 9 8 7 6 5 4 3 2 1

to my wife Terry,
friend, lover, colleague

Acknowledgements

The author wishes to thank Ray Towne of the McDonnell Douglas Corporation for his assistance in providing detailed information on the DC-10 aircraft. Pat Zaccardo was my typist, and she is much appreciated. Finally, I wish to thank Neal Burger, for it was due solely to his advice and encouragement that this book was begun.

The author has had certain classified information entrusted to him in his capacity as consultant to the defense industry. Having no wish to betray this trust or embarrass his associates, the author has deliberately obscured some of the military systems' capabilities and operational techniques disclosed in this work of fiction.

F. ROBERT BAKER

Chapter 1

Mathew Henry's flat at 32 Bunting Place had seen better days. Once the building had been quite fashionable, but London's sprawling industrialism had overtaken the street and now the large flats were divided into small units. Number 5 was on the third floor and consisted of nothing more than a large front room and a small alcove containing a bed and dresser. A dusty curtain separated the alcove from the room. Between the windows was a single stuffed chair with worn and stained fabric and a cheap filigreed iron floor lamp of the type popular in the 1930's. In the center of the room stood a plain table with two chairs. A dish sink stuck out from the wall opposite the door to the hall. Beside the sink stood an old-fashioned, waist-high bathtub covered by a large white enamel metal cover that served as a kitchen counter when the tub was not used for bathing. A row of open shelves over the sink and a two-burner gas plate completed the simple cooking facilities. Although Henry had lived here for almost three years, the room was empty of the ordinary accumulation of minor possessions that most people bring home over the years.

The metal cover to the bathtub stood against the wall. Henry was bending over the open tub in deep concentration, completely oblivious to the storm outside. Inside the tub, a short, squat, dark green bottle of Spanish champagne with a wide base was held firmly in a metal fixture clamped to the sides of the tub. A soft whirring sound came from the tub as Henry pressed the trigger of an electric hand drill and ap-

1

plied its diamond tip against the bottom of the glass bottle. Almost instantly, a foamy stream of wine gushed from the hole, covering the drill and running down Henry's hands to join the pool of champagne draining from the stained and chipped bottom of the tub. Henry removed the bottle from the clamp, being careful not to disturb either the label or the foil wrapping around the cork. Holding the bottle upright while the last of the wine drained out, Henry inspected his handiwork. Except for the weight and the small hole in the bottom, the bottle was indistinguishable from a full bottle of champagne.

Those drills made all the difference, thought Henry. Trust a German like Yonnie to find good drills. Yonnie knew her way about. He'd been right when he had sent word to cousin John in Ulster to use Yonnie to get them machine guns. Because of her, they'd been able to smuggle in enough guns to supply two new companies in County Armagh. They'll keep the damn British 3rd Brigade busy.

He smiled at the thought. Tomorrow he would finish this job to repay Yonnie for the support her group had given his. Then he'd be on his way to Ulster. At last! Three years in the bloody background was enough. His breath came faster, and his palms began to sweat as he thought of being with John in Armagh.

Calm down, he told himself. Better get on with it or you'll be up all night.

With that, he took the now-empty bottle to the table and put it beside the eleven others. Pulling the floor lamp over to the table, he sat down before a bottle-cutting machine he had bought at a crafts shop. He had been practicing with the apparatus over and over until he had become skilled in neatly slicing the bottom off even the thickest of bottles. He picked up the first bottle and placed it in the machine. Slowly rotating the bottle against the cutters, he scored the glass all the way around and slipped the loop of heating wire in the groove. After several seconds of careful alignment and adjustment of wire tension, he closed a switch with his left hand and saw the wire instantly glow red with heat as the electricity surged through it. The severed bottom fell into his waiting right hand. That was the part he liked the best. One instant the bottle was whole; the next it was not. There was a neatness and finality that pleased him.

Leaving the top half in the machine, he removed the

cutting wire and roughed up both surfaces of the cut with a small file. Reaching into one of several shoe cartons on the table, he took out a small Spanish 9-mm automatic pistol. From the same box, he picked up a full clip and inserted it in the pistol. Carefully keeping his finger away from the trigger, he pulled the slide back and chambered a round. From another carton, he took out a box of ammunition. Removing the clip from the pistol, he replaced the top round and reinserted the clip. Making sure the safety was off, he slipped the loaded and cocked gun together with a full spare clip into a plastic food bag and sealed the bag with a twist tie.

On an old but clean piece of tile, Henry carefully measured out two thin ribbons of epoxy superglue. Mixing them together with a spatula, he applied the glue to surfaces of both portions of the bottle. Being careful not to disturb the glue, he picked up the plastic bag containing the gun and inserted it in the upper portion of the bottle as far as it would go. Licking his lips in concentration, he picked up the bottom part of the bottle and slowly fitted it over the projecting butt of the pistol. Resting his wrist on the top of the bottle to steady his hand, he rotated the bottom until it was positioned exactly as when cut and pressed it slowly but forcefully against the upper portion. He pressed the two portions together and allowed the powerful glue to set up before removing the bottle from the machine and putting it into the empty champagne case under the table. Within an hour the glue would be completely cured, the bond only slightly weaker than the original glass, and the bottle ready for filling.

He leaned back in the hard chair and lit a cigarette, inhaling deeply. Good, he thought. The glue worked out fine. Must remember to rough up the glass.

Henry reached for the second bottle, whistling softly. He worked steadily into the night, his thoughts alternating between fantasies of heroic deeds in Ireland and plans for tomorrow. In five bottles he put five pistols and spare clips. In each of five more bottles he carefully fitted two fragmentation hand grenades, and in two additional bottles he put four 50-round boxes of extra ammunition. An hour after the twelfth bottle was finished, he carried the case over to the bathtub and began filling the bottles with ginger beer, using a small funnel inserted through the hole in the bottom. As each was filled, he sealed the hole with epoxy bonding putty used in auto body repair and set the bottle back into the champagne case. When all the bottles were filled, he carefully glued the surfaces of the cardboard top back in place.

He waited thirty minutes for the putty to set before turning off the lamp and going to the window. He slowly parted the faded curtain and intently searched the street below. The street was empty. The rain had stopped and the moon had come out. Henry picked up his keys from the dresser, put on an old sweater, and swung the heavy carton onto his shoulder. Out of the house, he walked to the corner and down two blocks to an old wooden Morris station wagon parked at the curb. He put the box in the back of the car and covered it with a blanket. On the sun visor over the driver's seat, the street light reflected off an employee plastic badge that read:

Heathrow Airport
All Service Areas
M.A. Henry
White's Flight Kitchens, Ltd.

Locking the rear doors, Henry walked quickly back to the flat. Although he thought he was too excited to do so, he fell asleep within a few minutes.

Some 400 miles to the north, the wind off the Norwegian Sea drove the rain before it, tearing at the upper slopes of the mountain Ben More Assynt in Scotland's northwest highlands. The chain link fence surrounding a low concrete structure at the summit of the mountain moaned as if to protest the violence of the stormy night. From atop one of the short steel towers projecting from the roof of the structure, a small dish antenna turned with almost imperceptible motion through a precise arc as it tracked one of several orbiting military satellites. Through the antenna poured countless pulses of electromagnetic energy in the endless combinations that make up the digital data stream by which computer systems talk to one another. The powerful gearing of the antenna mocked nature as it drove the dish against the wind without as much as one ten-thousandth of an inch variation in alignment. Below, protected by thick concrete, the racks of electronics were kept at an ideal temperature and humidity by a small but powerful air-conditioning unit.

The force of the storm was not lost on the machines,

however, for the signal generated by the whirling cups of the anemometer on one of the towers joined the data from the antenna and was carried down the mountain and across the intervening valleys by microwave links to the ridge above Loch Tiree on Dornoch Firth. There the data stream was reflected downward to a building on the shore at the head of a long wooden pier that was home to SubRon 42.

From beneath the building, thick coaxial cables carried the signals to the submarine tender *Cyrus A. Woods* which provided the forward support for the *Ohio*-class Trident missile submarines which made up SubRon 42. In the *Woods*, the coaxial cables were joined by other wire bundles, branching in every direction. One set led out from a junction box and dropped steeply in a swaying loop to disappear into the superstructure of the single submarine moored alongside.

The USS *Montana* was ugly. The ugliness was part of her, welded and hammered into her. Her superstructure, which rose sharply above the steeply sloping hull to enclose the twenty-four missile tubes, gave her an awkward, humped look. Her blunt bow was unexpectedly abrupt for her great width, making her appearance incomplete and overly thick. The nonreflecting black paint which covered her like a blanket made the details of her construction indistinct and added to the impression of a huge formless mass. The overall effect was one of brutish, unreasoning strength completely devoid of all beauty.

Lieutenant Junior Grade Tony Deville turned his head aside when a sudden gust of wind drove the rain into his face. He was leaning out over the coaming of the *Montana*'s bridge. Below him, just visible under the bow planes that stuck out on either side of the sail like, thick stubby wings, two enlisted men worked in an opening in the superstructure. The glare of the work light made their hands and faces unnaturally white against an almost invisible black hull.

The muscles of his stomach, hardened into thin bands by miles of running, pressed against the cold steel as Deville's thin and wiry body moved with the slow motion of the ship. He was alone on the small bridge and had been glad for the opportunity to put on his foul-weather gear and come topside. The *Montana* was his first submarine, and even after 13 months in her, he sometimes had difficulty accepting the orderly bustle and closeness created by 15 officers and 197 crew working and living in a steel cylinder 42 feet in diameter for 60 days at a time. That the cylinder was 560 feet long and was bigger than a World War II heavy cruiser did not seem to matter.

He frowned, his mouth twisting slightly from the effort of sorting out the complex feelings that surged through him at the thought of his wife Jan. Was it really any of his business what she did when he was gone, so long as she was there when he got back? So *what* if she was making it with Frank. She was doing that before he had met her. After all, *he* had moved in with *them*. But none of them were married then. And what about Jamie? Doesn't having a baby make it different?

For two years, the three students had lived together in a little cottage on the sand in San Diego's Mission Beach. He had one bedroom; they had the other. Sometimes when a Santa Ana blew the hot winds off the desert, he would lie in his bed and hear Jan's encouragements and moans come softly through the open windows while Frank made love to her. Frank, with his curly blond hair, tanned heavily muscled body, and easy self-assurance, seemed to Tony to be everything he was not. He envied Frank the way only a virgin male can. In the morning he would masturbate in the shower, hating both his weakness and his need, while he envisioned what he would do with Jan if Frank were gone. Then one day he came back from his NROTC summer cruise and Frank was gone. Dropped out of college and gone off to work on his cousin's cattle ranch. That night Jan came into his bed. The next day they rented out Frank's room.

In spite of Jan's hesitation and Navy regulations, they were secretly married that fall. After he received his commission and submarine training, he was assigned to the Blue Crew of the *Montana*, and they moved into a small house in Norfolk, Virginia. A year ago his son Jamie had been born and his world seemed complete. But now Frank was back. Jan had made no secret that he was coming down from a job in D.C. to spend weekends with her while Tony was at sea. What the hell should he do?

One of the enlisted men climbed out of the opening and stood on the narrow deck holding an electronic tester. The other switched off the work light.

"What did you find?" called Deville into the blackness.

"Nothing," shouted the man with the tester, his upturned

face appearing in the light from the *Woods'* deserted decks high above. "Ship's wiring and the shore cable check out OK. The problem's not ours, Mr. Deville."

"All right. Go tell the *Woods*. Then knock off," said Deville, stepping down from the coaming.

Still absorbed in himself, he pulled the bridge hatch open and climbed down the long ladder leading inside the narrow access trunk to the Control Room below. He put his back against the smooth, stainless-steel lining of the trunk and descended with practiced ease. Warm air, flavored with the distinctive smell of a warship, rose to meet him. Long before, he had decided the odor was a blend of fresh paint, warm electrical insulation, and food. He liked the smell.

Passing through the lower hatch, he paused at the base of the ladder and looked about him. Every possible cubic inch of space was crammed with equipment in this, the operational center of the vessel. To his left, in the forward port corner of the large compartment was the ship control center from which the movement of the *Montana* through the water was controlled. The large comfortable seats which looked exactly like the cockpit seats of an airplane, for the helmsman and planesmen, were empty. The complex array of lights on the main ballast control panel and on the hydraulic manifold outboard aft of the seats glowed red and yellow.

Deville glanced at the lights on the trim panel. All green. OK, he thought with pride. It had taken him almost a year to learn his way through the maze of equipment.

He turned to his right and looked past the companionway leading to the deck below at the consoles of the fire control center that extended in a long row down almost the entire length of the starboard side. Now the consoles from which the ship's defensive weapons were aimed and fired were mostly dark. The blank screens of the cathode-ray tube displays stared at him like dead eyes. Here and there he could make out the red-lighted words DISABLED and DEACTIVATED. His eyes swept the boards for any flashing green or yellow lights that would signal whether change in operational status had taken place while he was on the bridge. There were none.

He stripped off his foul weather gear and put his hand on the railing around the raised platform encircling the periscopes of the command center behind him. As he pulled off his boots he heard the JW sound-powered telephone in the navigation center buzz. He looked up just as Master Chief Quartermaster John Dacovak, who was working with a young enlisted man at the glass-topped plotting table, turned to him.

"Maneuvering room, sir," said the tall, middle-aged chief, holding the handset toward him.

Deville jerked the last boot free and hurried the few steps to the plotting table in the after starboard corner of the compartment.

"Officer of the deck," said Deville, taking the handset.

He recognized the voice of Lieutenant Lou Vetta, the Reactor Control Officer.

"Tony, I report reactor service is complete," said Vetta. "I've signed off the reactor service log, and we're ready for reactor cold start-up."

Remembering the required routine, Deville asked, "Reactor pre-start-up checklist complete?"

"Affirmative. The *Woods* is standing by to feed us power," replied Vetta.

"All right, Lou. Proceed with reactor cold start-up. Make the time twenty-one twenty-two," Deville concluded looking at the clock on the NAVDAC.

Deville hung up the phone and turned to make certain Dacovak was entering cold start-up in the quartermaster notebook just as Senior Chief Boatswain's Mate Paul Bronick ducked through the watertight door in the aft bulkhead from the missile compartment.

"All mooring lines doubled, sir, and the working party is all below," rumbled Bronick, his voice seeming to come from deep within his barrel chest. "Not that they needed any urging tonight. It's wet as hell up there."

"Tell me about it," laughed Deville, his face still wet with rain.

Then remembering he was doing double duty tonight as both the OOD and his normal duties as the *Montana*'s Electronic Countermeasures and Communications Officer, Deville said to Bronick, who was the Junior Officer of the Watch, "Chief, take the deck while I duck down to the comm center and check on our orders."

"Aye, aye, sir," said Bronick, nodding to Dacovak. In the flourescent lights, Bronick's close-cropped, graying hair appeared almost the same color as the deck.

As Deville made his way down the stairlike ladder, he discovered a new confidence rising in him. This was real.

This was him. At the moment, he was in command of the ship. At his order, men would come running to cast off and get underway. They would steer as he told them to steer. He could dive the boat or have her defensive weapons fired. He smiled at having to explain *that* to the captain. For a twenty-six year old, there was no other job like it. So why couldn't he kick Jan's ass instead of going along with her weird needs? He let her cut his balls off, goddamnit. If only he could keep this feeling of strength when he was with Jan!

The *Montana*, like all Trident missile submarines, had two crews. While one crew took the boat to sea for sixty days from Loch Tiree, the other was back in Norfolk, training and living with their families. Two months ago, when Tony Deville stepped down from the MAC jet that flew the Blue Crew home, he found Jan waiting for him at the fence with the other wives, holding Jamie. It was a beautiful southern evening in June. The faint odor of honeysuckle floated on the humid air. He could see tiny beads of perspiration above Jan's lip as he bent to kiss her. Her response had startled him. She kissed him back passionately, her tongue darting against the inside of his upper lip, her short thick body arching around Jamie to press her belly tightly against his genitals. He was surprised and somewhat embarrassed at this public display; he was glad their embrace was lost in the crush of bodies.

"Wheeeh. What was that all about?" he said, pushing her gently away. He took Jamie from her arms and looked down at her, vaguely annoyed.

"Nothing. I missed you, I guess," Jan answered and took hold of his free arm with both her hands. She stood up on her toes and gave him a quick kiss on the cheek. With his arm around her, they went off to collect his bag, looking for all the world like a Navy recruiting poster.

They shared the first joint while he cooked their steaks on the grimy gas grill that had come with the house. When he passed her a second joint to share, she begged off, saying she felt fine for now. By the time they went to bed, he was high and enjoying the effect the drug seemed to have on prolonging and intensifying their lovemaking. Later, his mind a mellow and satisfied blank, he lay with his leg over her naked body, the stiff black hairs of his calf mingling with the soft brown pelt of her pubic. He was just drifting off to sleep when, as if coming to a decision, she slid her body out from under his leg and sat up in their bed. As she lit a cigarette from the pack on the nightstand, she said, "I saw Frank while you were gone."

He twisted over on his side and looked up at her. The flare of the match in the darkness of the room burned the image of her at that moment forever in his memory: her bare back up against the headboard, her lips pursed over the end of the cigarette, her large breasts lifted to press against her raised knees as she inhaled deeply. Her vulva protruded shamelessly from between her legs.

Exhaling, she said, "I don't know how it happened. It just happened. He called me about a week after you'd gone. Said he got the number from Ellen Morgan. He said he was in Norfolk on business and why didn't we all get together."

He rolled over on his back away from her and stared at the ceiling, dreading what was coming.

"I told him to come out," she continued. "I didn't tell him you weren't here. I was afraid he wouldn't come. I mean, I hadn't seen him or anything since he dropped out that summer. I just wanted to see him, that's all. He came out that evening. I fixed him some dinner and we sat around talking about the days at the beach. We smoked some grass, and, I don't know, we were upstairs making it. And it was good. Just like before. Like he'd never been away."

He started to get up to get away from her words but everything was happening in slow motion. He tried to concentrate on what it all meant and what he felt. His mind wanted to drift with the moment, to be a spectator rather than a participant. In his effort to focus his attention, he moaned, "Oh, Jan." It came out sounding as if he were calling for his mother.

She reached out to him, putting her hand on his bare shoulder. Tears welled up in her eyes.

"But I love you. I love you both. Oh, God," she sobbed, "help me, Tony. Please help me." She threw herself across him, burying her face in his chest.

His mind was reeling, filled with conflicting emotions that flowed within him and fought for supremacy. Through the drug-created haze, one thought came clear to him. If he rejected her now, if he put her down for what she had done, she would take his son and go to Frank. He would lose everything. Instinctively, he put a protective arm over her shoulders. As her sobs racked her body and her tears fell to run glistening down the thick hairs on his chest, anger drained from him. The press of her body restrained him emotionally as well as physically.

"Shh, it's all right, honey. It's all right," he muttered forgivingly, as if to an errant child. "We'll work it out." He kissed her hair, stroking the small of her back with his free hand.

He felt her cheek move against his chest in response, and as his hand moved downward onto the soft pillowy mounds of her buttocks, he felt an erection begin. She turned her head, her mouth seeking his. Just before their lips met, he looked into her eyes. But whether he saw gratitude or triumph his confused mind could not determine.

When he awoke in the morning, he knew he had trapped himself. He threw on his running gear, anxious to be out in the open. He ran the first mile hard and fast until the blood pounded in his ears and his breathing came in great sobs. Then he slowed the pace as he felt himself begin to loosen up and ran his usual eight-minute mile for the next ten. As always when he ran, he began to relax and think more clearly than at any other time. But as much as he thought about it, he could see no way out. Two days later, when Jan took Jamie and went to Frank to "get her head straight," Tony began running mornings and evenings.

His break came three weeks later when it was announced that the *Montana* Blue Crew had won the Fleet Achievement Award for the year. When Jan called, he told her that the Navy was picking up the air fare for the families of the Blue Crew to visit Europe. The next day Jan was back, excitedly planning their two week holiday and making arrangements to leave Jamie with her parents in Wisconsin. Tony was content, but he knew she had made no promises for the future.

And now it's over, he thought, as he pushed open the door to the communications center. Tomorrow she's flying straight back to Frank, and I'm going to sea for two months. Damn her to hell, anyway.

He walked to his desk in the center of the small compartment containing all of the *Montana*'s communication systems. Racks of electronic equipment covered the space along the bulkheads from deck to overhead, extending even over the low door through which he had just entered. The duty radioman sprawled in front of one of the room's consoles reading. He was listening casually to the constant stream of CW traffic that came softly from a speaker above him. The old-fashioned Morse code telegraph key looked oddly out of place beside the computer terminal keyboard and CRT display on the console. The forward end of the compartment was taken up by the new, acoustic-secure-data-link system and the code computer. Deville reached into a desk drawer and took out the letter he had begun to Jan. The hell with it, he thought and threw it in the waste container against the bulkhead. The sound of the high-speed printer of the code computer starting up startled him even though he was expecting it. As the duty radioman came out of his chair, Deville said, "I'll get it. Find out how they're coming on the land line."

Deville walked over to the code computer and stared down at the printer. Already several folds of paper were lying in the basket behind the terminal. These were the *Montana*'s operational orders. Picking up the incoming message log, he made the required entries as the high-speed printer fell silent.

The duty radioman hung up the phone and said, "They've found the problem, sir. Should be about ten more minutes."

"OK, tell the JOOD I'll be with the commander," said Deville. He scooped up the completed message from the basket and went out.

Lieutenant Commander Harry Edelstone, the Executive Officer, was sprawled in a wardroom chair smoking a large briar pipe when Deville walked in. Around him, in identical chairs grouped at the after end of the long narrow compartment, other officers of the Blue Crew sat in similar attitudes of relaxation. Conversation among the small group had finally begun to slow as each man's interest in his own as well as his fellow officers' holiday stories waned.

Deville handed the message to Edelstone, saying, "Orders, sir." Edelstone grunted as he heaved himself up into a sitting position, put on a pair of reading glasses from the end table beside him, and scanned the message.

"Tell me again, Deville," said Edelstone in mock sarcasm, "how is it that your damn computer can talk to Norfolk and I got to get wet going to the head shed to talk to The Old Man forty fucking miles away."

Although Edelstone was childless, his thoughts as he read the orders were just like those of a mother getting a large family ready for an outing. His job was to provide the captain with a ship and crew that in all respects were capable of carrying out whatever duty might be assigned to them. His mind began, once again, to grapple with the hundreds of details concerning getting the ship ready for sea. The off-duty crew members had been coming aboard all day. Realizing that many of them would be too excited or too broke after spending two weeks abroad with their families to think of eating before coming aboard, he had ordered an open galley so that they might fix themselves some food between scheduled meals, something rarely done in port. The last of the crew should be aboard anytime now, Edelstone thought. They'll be coming back on the last liberty bus from the pubs in Dornoch. All the officers were aboard except The Old Man. All stores except ordinance and perishables were aboard. He turned to Deville. "How's the reactor service going?"

"Completed, sir. We began cold start-up at twenty-one twenty-two."

"Good. It says here our primary launch area is Sigma Twenty-Seven, so we'll be getting underway about fourteen hundred. On the way out we'll conduct tests of the acoustic digital-data link. The code name is Pilot Fish. How about that? Looks like they finally got the seabed transceiver net working."

Heaving himself up out of the chair, he handed the message back to Deville and announced to the wardroom in general, "We begin loading perishables at oh eight-thirty and ordinance at oh nine hundred. The captain comes aboard at oh nine-thirty for a briefing on the *Woods* at ten-thirty. By the time we finish that, I want everything settled down, including the men's telephoning to their families. That goes for officers, too. I guess most of the families are taking the afternoon Pan World flight out of Heathrow. My wife is."

"Mine too, sir," said Deville. Several other officers mumbled agreement.

"That's it, then. I'm turning in. See you in the morning."

The wardroom's "Good-night, Commander" followed him out the door.

Some miles to the south, the wind hurled the heavy rain hard against small glass panes making up the dormer windows of the master bedroom of an old but sturdy lakeside cottage on the shore of Loch Ness. The thick wooden frames rattled with each gust. During the day, the room was bright and cheerful; now, however, the drapes were pulled to shut out the storm and the room was warmly lit by lamps that flanked a large and comfortable bed. Directly across the room from the bed stood a small, mantelless, soapstone fireplace. Commander Douglas Mawson squatted before it, stoking the hotly burning coals. A pair of faded blue pajamas covered his tall and lean frame. The firelight accentuated his ruddy complexion and reflected the warmth of his deeply set blue eyes.

He was utterly relaxed and lost in thought which, for him, was not unusual. Mawson had the ability of concentrating his entire consciousness on whatever he was doing at the time. All other problems were submerged to an unconscious level so that unneeded thought rarely intruded upon the task at hand. His mind, however, would continue to consider the submerged problems without any awareness on his part. He was, thus, often able to come up with solutions to apparently new problems that were seemingly spontaneous, causing others to think of him as a young genius. He thought otherwise and considered himself to possess only a trick mind not worthy of the compliments he received.

Sailing and the sea had always been part of Mawson's life. To begin with, there was never a time that a Mawson wasn't serving as an officer in the U.S. Navy. The Mawson family and the Navy had been joined when young Tobias Mawson signed on as a midshipman with Captain John Peck Rathbun on the Continental sloop *Providence*, June 19, 1777, for a wage of twelve dollars per month. Tobias was lucky. He served under captains who took prizes. After the war, Tobias took his prize money, bought a house in Providence, and a share in a merchant ship that he captained. For generations since, the Mawsons who did not serve in the Navy served either on the Mawson Line ships or in the numerous other Mawson family businesses ashore. As his father before him, Doug Mawson had no need to work for a living. The income from his share of the family businesses far exceeded his Navy pay and allowances.

A sudden flare of flame as the newly added coal caught fire reminded him of when he had first lit the fireplace that afternoon. They had gotten properly soaked when caught out on the lake on the small sailboat that came with the cottage.

A squall had roared off the mountain, and it had been a close thing to prevent the little boat from being knocked down. Robbie and Kathy were great. One quick shout to get down and stay down in the bottom of the boat was enough. Robbie had even thrown a protective arm over the shoulders of his nine-year-old sister. For eleven, Robbie handles himself well in an emergency, Mawson thought.

Satisfied with the fire, he started to rise just as his wife Barbara opened the door and came in carrying a half-full bottle of Otard in her left hand with two snifter glasses sticking out from between her fingers. She was tall, and the long, fitted robe she was wearing over her nightgown flowed smoothly over her hips and down her long legs, giving only a hint of the fullness of her well-proportioned breasts. Her long honey-colored hair fell over both sides of her shoulders, framing her tanned face. At thirty-six Barbara was just beginning to show the lines of an active woman who spent a good deal of her time on the water.

Mawson turned and went towards her as she closed the door. Seeing the slight movement of her breasts beneath the folds of the robe, he felt familiar pleasurable stirrings within him. He smiled as he recalled that he had seen those perfect breasts before he had seen her face or even known her name.

It was during the summer of his second year at the Academy. Mawson had come home to his parents' summer place in Newport for two weeks at the end of his cadet cruise to sail in the Northeast Collegiate Snipe Championship Race. He was sailing a new boat that his father and he had built during the spring holidays. He was just coming up on the windward mark on a starboard tack. Ahead and to windward was the lead Snipe. They were well out in front of the rest of the fleet. Two boats alone on the sparkling water. His was the faster. He was overtaking the other boat but could not headreach on it due to the skill of the other sailor, who was totally hidden behind the sail.

As he came up on the stern of the old Snipe, he heard a heavy thud and saw the thin mast whip forward from the force of a blow. A small water-logged piece of timber came sliding out from beneath the stained counter. The boat luffed up and away from him slightly, and he saw the white T-shirt on the faceless torso now visible under the sail whipped off to reveal a beautiful pair of breasts that disappeared just as quickly as the girl bent down to stuff the shirt somewhere below her feet.

Forgetting the race entirely, as he shot past, he watched fascinated as she jammed her foot down hard, yanked up the centerboard, and fell off around the mark. As he rounded to windward of her, she turned without making any move to cover herself and shouted, "Throw me your shirt!"

"What?" he shouted stupidly, stunned by the unexpected pleasure of seeing the sunlight playing on her splendid breasts.

"Your shirt, damn it! I've got a leak in the centerboard trunk."

He put his knee over the tiller, pulled off his shirt, and threw it to her across the few feet of water that separated them. Concentrating once again on sailing, he moved past her and later crossed the line to win. She took second, finishing a few seconds behind him. Although he looked for her as soon as he could break away from the group of well-wishers, she was lost in the mob of people at the dinghy dock.

He did not see her again until that night when he stood beside her on the yacht club dance floor. He was presented with the first place cup, and she received the pewter plate for second place. Throughout the commodore's long-winded speech, he felt awkward and was too embarrassed to look at her directly, yet he desperately wanted to talk to her before she disappeared into the regatta crowd filling the clubhouse. He need not have worried. The instant they stepped away from the microphone, she turned and put her hand on his arm.

"You can buy me a drink now and tell me about yourself," she said with sparkling eyes. "After all, you know far more about me than I know about you."

He grinned and without thinking about it covered her hand with his and led her off toward the bar. That was the beginning. They were married two days after his graduation from the Academy.

Barbara turned from the door. "Kids are fast asleep," she said. "Nothing bothers those two." Noticing Mawson's expression as he took the bottle and glasses from her, she said, "You've got that smile again."

"I was just thinking of the first time I saw you," he said, moving to the bed and putting the glasses down on the nightstand.

"Well, I hate to snipe at you," she said, "but that was a long time ago."

"That's really bad," Mawson said with mock disgust. "You've gotten so good at puns that I can hardly keep abreast of you." A grin spread over his face.

"Ugh," she grunted through an equally wide grin. "Pour the booze, sailor, and get into bed."

Picking up a small journal from the nightstand on her side, Barbara slipped out of the robe and got under the covers, sliding over toward his side of the bed.

Mawson poured two fingers of brandy into each glass. He handed one to Barbara and put the other down on the nightstand while he got into bed beside her. He turned, picked up a journal identical to the one Barbara was holding and settled back against the pillows. Barbara leaned back close beside him, her hair falling across his left shoulder, opened her journal to the thick, felt bookmark that Kathy had made, and took a sip of brandy. Mawson opened his journal to a thin piece of finely sanded and polished wood covered with vague symbols that Robbie imagined were Indian carvings, and began reading aloud.

"Saturday, 5 April. At sea," he read. "I've half made up my mind to sell *Tranquility* and have John Barry up in Boothbay build us a new boat with a more modern rig and underbody."

"Oh, no!" exclaimed Barbara. "I love *Tranquility*, even if she is a gut buster."

Mawson took a sip of his brandy and waited.

"Of course, a better galley and more light below would be nice," added Barbara. "Just what kind of rig did you have in mind?"

"Funny you should ask," he said and began to read again.

It was an old and much-cherished routine. Over the years the reading and discussion of their journals to one another had become an important part of their marriage, one that they both enjoyed and looked forward to. No matter how pressing the social calendar, or how foreign the location, they would find a time and place to lie down somewhere as they lay now with their heads together reading to one another of their thoughts and feelings experienced when they were apart.

It had begun in desperation. Mawson was commissioned

in June 1965 and had applied for submarine school in New London. His request was denied, and after a three-week honeymoon in Maine on *Tranquility*, he was ordered to a river patrol squadron in Viet Nam. Being separated from Barbara after only three weeks caused him to give serious thoughts to resigning his commission as soon as possible. When he sought advice, his father, then a rear admiral, had first questioned him in great detail as to the precise nature of his reason for not wanting to serve in Viet Nam. Once over this hurdle, his father said that separation, however painful now, would not diminish the love that he and Barbara felt for each other, provided they shared the significant emotional experiences received when they were apart. For that reason, he said, most Navy families were great letter writers, as he well knew.

Mawson's father did say, almost as an afterthought, that a man cannot serve two masters. If Mawson did not believe he could put duty before family, he had better resign now lest he someday find himself trapped in a conflict that he could not resolve with honor. When he told Barbara of what his father had said, she had come up with the idea of keeping a journal while they were apart, rather than letters, since letters would be forgotten by the time they would see each other.

And so they read to each other, speaking softly of their thoughts and feelings while the storm lashed the wild highlands all around them and their children slept soundly in the next room.

Finally, Mawson said sleepily, "I'm done," and closed his journal.

"I've only got one more," Barbara replied and began reading: "June 5, Thursday. At home. Driving back from the commissary this afternoon, a car passed us with a bumper sticker that read 'Honk if you're horny.' I started blowing the horn like mad as soon as the car was past. Robbie and Kathy thought I was nuts and demanded to know why. 'No reason,' I told them. 'Just something your father would want me to do if he were here.' "

With that, Barbara closed her journal and reaching under the blankets, slid her right hand inside Mawson's pajama bottoms. Mawson slowly arched his back as a wave of pleasure surged upward from his groin. With his left arm around her shoulders, he turned Barbara toward him and sought her half-parted lips with his. As her breasts pressed against his chest, he felt her reach up and turn off the light. The journals fell to the floor, forgotten, their purpose accomplished. Seconds later they were joined by his pajamas and her nightgown.

Chapter 2

Lieutenant Ross Wallstrom, the Combat Systems Officer, rested his arms on the bridge coaming and looked down at the working party on the foredeck. An Academy ring hung heavily on one finger as he clasped his hands before him. On one side of the ring, the raised numerals 1972 were worn from his habit of twisting the ring when deep in thought.

He stood in a corner of the narrow bridge, tall and relaxed, the tan of his crisp khaki uniform contrasting with the deeper browns of his smooth skin. From beneath the peak of his cap, his rich amber eyes mirrored the gold of his cap device.

He was an uncommonly handsome man. The kind whose appearance alone wins from most people an interest and acceptance at first sight. Although he enjoyed and, perhaps, even depended upon creating this reaction in people he met, he had not the slightest conceit about his looks. To him, his appearance was only a part of the uniqueness he felt about himself. A uniqueness he thought marked him for a special role in life.

He inhaled deeply, tasting the cool morning air and feeling the warmth of the first probing rays of the sun as it climbed above the highlands into a clear sky. It was going to be a warm day. Then, as he watched Chief Bronick directing the installation of the ordinance-loading rails, old doubts began to assail him. God, I hate beginning new assignments, he thought. Each time you've got to start all over again. And you've got to be so damn careful. You can create a situation in the beginning that takes a long time, if ever, to work out.

Unconsciously, his right hand went to the ring and slowly began twisting it back and forth. Why the hell do you do it? he wondered. You work your ass off to push yourself ahead and then, when you're out there in front of everyone, you wish you were back in the pack, unnoticed. You and your special feelings. Special shit. You're just another over-educated, middle-class nigger wondering where the hell he really belongs. His thoughts were interrupted by the bridge 1 MC squawk box as the boatswain's call screeched out.

"The smoking lamp is out. The smoking lamp is out. Prepare to receive live ordinance through the forward logistics hatch. Set condition Yoke. Set condition Yoke."

Wallstrom looked intently at the foredeck, mentally checking the preparations. He could see Lieutenant Junior Grade Paul Schrader, the First Lieutenant, standing beside the talker, and he knew Lieutenant Dave Rossman, the Ordinance Officer, was below with Senior Chief Torpedoman Jackson. This was as good a place as any for him since he would have nothing to do unless something went wrong. They would be taking aboard only enough defensive missiles to replace those sent over to the *Woods* earlier. Even so, they were sufficient to sink a Russian fleet. The missiles were not particularly sensitive and, in fact, would merely break apart if dropped; but let one of the boosters filled with solid propellant catch fire and the flames of hell would break loose. In the unlikely event that something did go wrong on the foredeck, he could be down there in three seconds. If an accident happened below, the best route to the loading area was through the control room below him.

Reaching down, he picked up the sound-powered handset for the JC circuit:

"Foredeck and logistics trunk. Bridge."

"Foredeck, aye, aye."

"Logistics trunk, aye, aye."

"Foredeck and logistics trunk. Bridge. Tell Mr. Schrader and Mr. Rossman that Lieutenant Wallstrom is on the bridge."

As he hung up the phone, a young signalman came up through the hatch and hoisted the red signal flag Bravo on the dismountable mast at the after end of the bridge. Looking up, Wallstrom saw an identical signal being run up the yardarm of the *Woods*. At the same time, the movement of a cargo boom on the *Woods* caught his eye as the first of the missiles swung out high above the *Montana*.

The missile hung there for a moment, its outline made

indistinct by the blue-gray camouflage painting. Wallstrom squinted his eyes against the glare of the bright sky and waited expectantly, hardly daring to believe what he saw. Hot damn! A Mark Two Tomahawk! Mawson really had endorsed his tactical plan completely. And after only one meeting. Endorsed, hell! That plan was radically different from current thinking. Mawson must have sold it all the way up the line for that beautiful bird to be hanging there. Suddenly he felt a lot better. Alllrrright! It's gonna be fine . . . fine . . . fine, he thought, his natural ebullience, for the moment, overcoming his acquired reserve.

The missile dropped slowly to the *Montana*'s deck. A working party guided it into position above the handling cradle on the spidery rails that angled steeply down toward the deck and disappeared into the open hatch of the logistics trunk. Chief Bronick, gauging the slight motion of the *Montana* carefully, held out his arm ready to signal the winch operator who was watching from his perch high above on the *Woods*. Judging the moment exactly, Bronick signalled the winch operator as the 18,000-ton *Montana* moved upward toward the one-ton missile. At the signal, the winch operator dropped the missile the last few inches into the waiting cradle and slacked off the hoist.

The working party swarmed over the bird, securing it to the cradle and casting loose the sling from the *Woods*. Bronick climbed up and swiftly but thoroughly inspected the restraining straps. Satisfied, he jumped down and looked at Lieutenant Schrader, who nodded.

"Stand by below," said Bronick to the talker beside him. Turning to the operator of the electric winch bolted to the deck beneath the rails, Bronick said, "Slack off and ease the load."

The winch drum began to turn. Slowly the long missile moved down the rails toward the darkly shadowed hatch opening. Below, Lieutenant Rossman stood beside Chief Dan Jackson and watched the circle of blue sky visible through the hatch disappear as the blunt nose of the missile entered the angled logistics trunk. They stood in the center of the crew's upper berthing space, normally their lounge. All around them rose double-tiered berths with the curtains tied back to reveal neatly made bunks.

Now the chairs and tables of the lounge were pushed against the after bulkhead to make room for the rails running down from the logistics trunk. Beside the rails, a section of the deck had been removed and temporary safety lines installed. Similar sections had been removed from the lower two decks so that the missile could be lowered directly to the ordnance test and service compartment below.

As the missile came abreast of him, Rossman noticed the elongated protective cover sealing the openings through which the folded wings deployed.

"What the hell?" he exclaimed as he ducked his head to see the underside of the missile. Seeing the large cover over the raised engine air inlet, he said to the talker beside him, "Avast slacking. Hold the load."

"Foredeck. Logistics trunk. Avast slacking. Hold the load," repeated the talker into the phone.

"Logistics trunk. Foredeck. Aye, aye."

The missile's sliding descent stopped.

Turning to Jackson, Rossman said, "Chief, this is a Mark Two. Look at the larger wings and the fan jet intake. It's for a loiter mission. We can't use it. How'd it get on the *Woods*?"

"According to Mr. Edelstone, sir, four were flown in two days ago on the captain's personal requisition."

"The captain requested surface ship missiles? What the hell's going on?" asked Rossman guiltily, realizing that he had not checked the ordinance loading manifest as he normally would because, instead, he had taken the time to call his family in London.

"I'm sorry, Mr. Rossman. Honest to God. I thought you knew. Mr. Edelstone told me we'd be loading 'em but for me not to talk about it. Somethin' about it being a welcome aboard surprise for Mr. Wallstrom."

"Well, he isn't the only one surprised. That's what I get for living in the back. I never hear anything," said Rossman philosophically.

"Beg pardon, sir?"

"Never mind. It's an old New York Jewish joke."

"I didn't know you're a New Yorker, Mr. Rossman," said Jackson with an innocent expression.

"Very funny, Chief. That's two I owe you," grinned Rossman who genuinely liked Jackson's outspoken good humor. Turning to the talker, he said, "Slack off and ease the load. Jackson, let me see the manifest."

The missile resumed its descent until its center was at

deck level with its nose projecting through the deck opening
into the lower berthing space below. The working party attached a sling to the center of balance and ran the cable
from the deck winch through a snatch block suspended from
the overhead and attached it to the sling. The rails were
moved apart and the tail of the missile swung downward
through the opening in the deck as the cable was slacked off.
The missile, now horizontal, was then slowly lowered through
the deck.

Something about Rossman's reaction kept nagging at
Jackson as he watched the missile descend. Then it came to
him. Shit, he thought. I clean forgot about Poley.

"Mr. Rossman. I'm goin' below to check on the loading
and stowage sequence."

As Rossman nodded, Jackson turned and ran lightly
down the ladder leading below. He passed through the
deserted berthing space, which was identical to the one
above, down a second ladder, and emerged in the ordinance
test and service compartment.

The compartment was wide, extending almost the entire
width of the hull. Below it, in the very bottom of the ship,
was the magazine. These two spaces, together with the two
berthing spaces above, formed the forward-most compart-
ments of the submarine. On the other side of the watertight
bulkhead were the bow tanks and, beyond them, the sea.

The center of the compartment was taken up with the
ordinance checkout stands surrounded by racks of electronic
equipment. Against the forward bulkhead stood a computer
that could pinpoint the location and cause of a malfunction
in any of the systems of the various defensive weapons carried by the *Montana*. Ready racks in which the weapons were
stored while waiting to be loaded into the torpedo tubes filled
the space between the checkout stands and the outer bulkheads of the compartment on either side. Overhead tracks
with portable electric hoists encircled the room and led to a
watertight scuttle in the center of the after bulkhead. On the
other side of the bulkhead lay the torpedo room, which years
before had been relocated from the bows of submarines.

The torpedo room was so named more from tradition
than function. Although propeller-driven, steam-powered
Mark 48 torpedos were among the weapons stored on the
ready racks, most of the *Montana*'s defensive weapons were
guided missiles of one type or another. The old-fashioned

steam torpedo was carried only for use against other submarines. Rocket-powered missiles were far more effective against surface ships.

Jackson went up to First Class Torpedoman's Mate James Poley who was standing at the watch desk near the watertight door leading to the torpedo room. Through the open door, the inboard ends of the starboard bank of three torpedo tubes were visible. The tubes, which angled back from the side of the hull, were covered with pipes and valves, making them appear like sections of a giant clarinet. Out of sight were three more torpedo tubes on the portside of the ship.

"Poley," said Jackson, "we're taking on four Mark Two Tomahawks. Load three of 'em in Tubes One, Three, and Five. Put the fourth in a ready rack. After the Mark Two's, I'll be sendin' down six standard Tomahawks. Put a couple of 'em in Tubes Two and Four and the rest in the ready racks. Ya got all that?"

"Sure," answered Poley, looking up from the notebook in which he had recorded Jackson's orders.

"Did you really get the word, or are we gonna reload when the skipper comes aboard?"

"What I gave you is the Old Man's own mix, smart ass. After the last Tomahawk, you'll be gettin' six SIAM's. Put 'em all in the ready racks next to the Harpoons. Leave the single Mark Forty-eight in Tube Six. Any questions?"

"Yeah. One. What the hell's goin' on? What're we doin' with Mark Two's? We gotta stick a dish antenna outta the water to use 'em. When we do that, we're gonna get Red aircraft like flies on dog shi . . ." Poley stopped in midsentence as the next thought struck him. He felt a sudden, sharp shiver spread across his lower back, as if someone had dashed a thimbleful of ice water on his bare spine.

"Jeeezus H. Kee-rist in a handbasket! That's what them fuckin' SIAM's are for! The Old Man is fixin' ta launch an over-the-horizon Tomahawk attack usin' them Mark Two's for linkup and jammin'. When those Russian fly boys spot the antenna, the Cap'n's gonna bet our ass on shootin' 'em down with the SIAM's 'fore they get close enough to zap us. Shit almighty. That's attack boat crap. What happened to play it deep and play it cool?"

"I'd say we just changed our tactics," said Jackson softly, putting a hand on Poley's shoulder.

Ignoring the hand, Poley turned away from Jackson toward the working party who were staring at them. "Load that sucker in Tube One 'fore I kick your sweet, young asses old Navy style," barked Poley.

Turning back to Jackson, he said, "OK, I'll try anything once. 'Specially if the Old Man has the conn. But I'm telling ya, if it comes down to it and those self-initiating antiaircraft mothers don't anti them Russki aircraft, I ain't reenlistin' no more."

Poley, who was even more thickly built than Jackson and had no neck at all, broke out in a huge, grin, pleased with his own joke. His heavily larded cheeks lifted in delight, almost closing his small eyes. A thin trail of tobacco juice started from the corner of his mouth as high-pitched laughter exploded from him to fill the compartment and echo off the steel bulkheads. He spit into an old No. 10 can on the deck.

"Amen, brother," murmured Jackson, shaking his head and starting toward the ladder to rejoin Lieutenant Rossman.

A mile away, Commander Mawson slowed his speeding Morgan as it crested the hill above the base at Loch Tiree. He drank in the scene that burst into view before him. Like a Carl Evers painting, the *Woods* and *Montana* floated on the sparkling waters, seemingly trapped by the green hills that all but enclosed the little loch. The long wooden pier was a brown smear leading to the brilliant white of the concrete parking lot. Silvery metal roofs on the shoreside buildings shimmered and danced in the waves of heat raised by the sunlight.

He guided the car down the road and stopped at the guard gate in the perimeter fence. Returning the Marine sentry's salute, he said, "There'll be a man coming by this afternoon to take this car back to the garage in Dornoch. Will you see that he gets in and out all right?"

"Yes, sir, Captain. I'll take care of it," replied the sentry, already reaching for the phone to pass the word to the quarterdecks of the *Woods* as Mawson drove off.

Mawson pulled the car into a vacant parking space at the pierhead. The two ships lay directly before him. The *Woods*, with her covered decks containing empty cabins that sometimes housed the submarine crews, towered over the long squat shape of the *Montana*. Seeing a missile being swung out from the side of the *Woods*, he wondered how many of his officers had been caught by his instructions to Edelstone last night. He smiled. After a year together, Edelstone was finally getting used to his methods; he had only sputtered once over being told not to go into any details of the Plan of the Day during officers call this morning. Edelstone was a damn fine XO. The best. He always carefully explained exactly what was needed from every department head. Today, he would not. Instead, each officer would have to personally dig out the details of the day's activities. After two weeks off with their families, all of them were bound to be a little loose, with their minds half ashore and half aboard, including himself. The best way to tighten them up was to create opportunities for each individual to become personally aware of any slackness in himself. For the kind officers he had aboard, that alone would be all that would be necessary to get the individual's thoughts concentrated fully on the ship. Mawson looked proudly at the *Montana* and the figures who moved about her foredeck and gangway, loading missiles and perishable stores. Together they were the best in the U.S. Navy and that meant the best in the whole fouled-up world.

Leaving his bag in the passenger's seat, he picked up his briefcase and slid out of the little car. He squared his cap over his eyes and strode down the pier towards the gangway leading upward to the quarterdeck of the *Woods*. Word of his coming passed quickly from the *Woods* to the *Montana*. It was as if the approach of the captain caused a switch to be thrown, turning on a dynamo. Suddenly, there was an awakening. Energy began flowing through the ship that moments before had been alive, but dormant and without purpose.

Mawson sat at the desk of his day cabin going through the inevitable paper work that had accumulated during his absence. Edelstone stood beside him, a pipe stuck squarely into the side of his mouth. Its smoke curled upward toward the overhead to be whisked quickly away by the air-conditioning system. That Edelstone smoked at all in Mawson's cabin was a measure of the unusual compatibility between the two men. Mawson, although a nonsmoker himself, found the aroma of Edelstone's tobacco pleasant and vaguely reminiscent of his father. The XO, an inveterate smoker, was never so happy as when his teeth were clenched tightly on the stem of a lighted pipe.

Mawson worked his way through the sheaf of papers

with his usual efficiency. Some he put aside with only a glance; some he read carefully before signing them; and some he discussed briefly with Edelstone. Finishing the last one, he leaned back in his chair and asked, "That it?"

"Just about," replied Edelstone, gathering up the signed papers from the desk. "Reactor service was completed during the first watch and we're critical again with steam on the line." Edelstone took off his glasses and, with long practice, folded them with one hand and put them into the case in his shirt pocket. Before speaking again, he took the pipe from his mouth. "Lieutenant Wallstrom's waiting to report in to you, and you're on with Captain Brewer at ten-thirty. We're loading ordnance and perishables now and will be ready to proceed as planned." Edelstone thought for a moment before adding, "That's it, Captain."

"Mawson stood up. "Everyone get back OK?"

"Yes, sir. Everyone was aboard by midnight and sober to boot. Except for Poley," Edelstone added with a grin, "who had to be encouraged by the watch to stop singing."

Mawson smiled and shook his head. "What would we do without Poley? He's our only tie to the old days when most sailors were both rowdy and single. Which reminds me. Any family problems?"

"None that I know of. From what Dacovak tells me, flight two thirty-one out of Heathrow this afternoon is almost a charter flight it's got so many *Montanas* aboard. Harriet's on it."

"I know. Barbara told me she and Harriet were flying home together."

Mawson started to steer Edelstone toward the door. "How was Cornwall? You find any relatives?"

Edelstone smiled. "Only in the cemetery. It was too far back to find any living cousins this first trip. Not that we cared. It was fun just tramping through the countryside. My ancestors were just an excuse."

"They always are," chuckled Mawson. He turned to Edelstone, "As usual, Harry, you've done a hell of a good job. Leave me alone with Wallstrom now, but come by at ten-twenty or so and we'll all go up to Captain Brewer's briefing."

"Yes, sir." As Edelstone turned to go, a knock sounded on the cabin door.

"Come," called Mawson.

The door opened and Lieutenant Wallstrom entered the cabin. Seeing Edelstone coming toward him, he said in greeting, "Commander."

Edelstone smiled and said as he passed, "I'll see you in half an hour."

Puzzled, Wallstrom looked toward Mawson who smiled and held out his hand.

"Welcome aboard, Lieutenant. We're going to Captain Brewer's operations briefing in a half hour," said Mawson warmly, taking Wallstrom's outstretched hand in both of his. "Sorry I couldn't be there when you reported in to Norfolk, but I was up in Newport at the War College. We ran your tactics through the WARS computer with no less than the CNO, Admiral Sauer himself, looking on. Coffee?"

"Yes, thank you, sir," replied Wallstrom, following Mawson to the buffet that stood against the mahogany-paneled bulkhead separating the day cabin from Mawson's sleeping cabin.

Mawson set his own cup down and picked up the heavy Navy carafe. Wallstrom took a clean cup from the stack at the back of the buffet and placed it beside Mawson's. Mawson began pouring. It was amazing, Wallstrom thought. Because of Mawson, it was happening just like his father and grandfather said it must happen. Wallstrom's mind went back many years as he watched the brown liquid swirling against the white of his cup.

His father and grandfather. They were a pair. Always impressing upon him his role in life. And why not? He was standing here because they worked hard and saved to move the family up another notch. He knew about duty long before entering Annapolis.

Now, because of Mawson, it was all beginning to happen. Wallstrom felt a wave of affection surge through him toward this man standing so close beside him who, without having met him, had not only raised him from the obscurity of the *Dolphin*'s wardroom, but had championed his ideas at the very highest levels of Navy command.

The stream of coffee stopped. The cup was half full. Wallstrom tore his mind away from his inner thoughts and picked up the cup.

His emotions, however, were still with him as he said genuinely and somewhat self-consciously, "Captain, I want to thank you for all you've done for me. Jumping me up to this billet was a great compliment, but pushing my ideas all the way to the CNO has done more for my career than I could ever have done on my own. I hope I don't let you down."

Mawson waved Wallstrom into a chair beside the desk and resumed his own seat.

"You won't let me or anyone else down. If you're worried about your tactics failing, forget it. They'll succeed just as your paper predicts. And if for some reason they don't, then the failure will be due to events that no tactical plan can envision."

Mawson leaned forward in the chair and held Wallstrom's eyes with his.

"If you're worried about your performance as second officer of this boat, good. You should be. From what I hear you're already making your first mistake. And you're going to make a lot more because that's the price we all pay for doing something for the first time. But know this. In matters concerning this boat, I'll back you all the way, all the time. If I don't like what you're doing, I'll call you in for a private talk, but that's it. If it's any consolation to you, I don't think failure is in you. I believe you have the best command potential of any junior officer I have ever met. And that opinion is based upon what others have said about you. Because it's the oldest attack submarine in the fleet, you may have felt buried in the *Dolphin*, but the selection system was working just the same. So don't thank me. It was only a question of time. If I hadn't pulled you out, some other captain would have. The Navy's system may not be perfect, but it's survived fools and presidents for over two hundred years. Having recognized your talents, it was my duty to assist you toward command."

Still holding Wallstrom's eyes, Mawson leaned back in the chair, folded his hands behind his head, and smiled. "It was also my pleasure. What's the use of having the name of Mawson if you can't work the system your own way occasionally?"

Wallstrom was confused. He had never met anyone quite as direct and frank as Mawson. Mawson wanted him, that was clear. But did Mawson like him? Suddenly, he wasn't sure.

"You said I was making my first mistake, sir?" Wallstrom said stiffly.

"Relax, Ross. It's not terminal," said Mawson, sitting up.

"I made the same mistake when Tulley took me on as Exec in the *Adams*. From what Edelstone tells me, you're laying back to get a feel for things. That's a reasonable approach, but it won't work. You've got four lieutenants and almost half the crew of this boat reporting to you. You've got to come on strong from the beginning and keep pouring it on. This is a tight crew. You've got to force your way in. Otherwise they'll just flow right around you as if you weren't there. Do you understand what I'm saying?"

Wallstrom began to relax. This was a subject to which he had given considerable thought and one in which he had first-hand experience.

"Yes, sir. I understand exactly what you're saying. But with all respect, Captain, I don't agree. As far as I can determine, none of the officers and few of the men reporting to me have ever served under a black officer. My experience has been that even today most whites are just as prepared to reject a black in an authority position as they are to accept him, which, I suppose, is a form of equality. I think it depends mostly on how well they know him. By coming on strong initially, particularly if I act only through the four division heads, I believe I risk turning off men needlessly. Don't misunderstand me. I'm not running a popularity contest. I'm going to turn off some individuals no matter what I do. It's just that I think there'll be fewer rejections if I work from the bottom up, one division at a time. It's not so much a question of laying back as it is a question of timing."

"The racial thing?" reflected Mawson, looking at Wallstrom with increased interest. "You're probably right. I was thinking in terms of my own experience, which may not apply here. Where do you want to begin?"

"I thought I'd start with Dave Rossman and Chief Jackson since their division contains the most old-Navy types."

Mawson laughed. "I can't imagine a man with strong prejudices against anything being able to cope with Jackson for long. Still, it's as good a place to begin as any. By the way, how is your family's relocation going?"

"Fine, Captain. Nancy and the kids are in Los Angeles visiting my parents while the furniture is en route. They'll be in Norfolk next week."

"Good," said Mawson, moving his chair closer to the desk. "I want to go over the launch sequences. Launch of the Trident missiles, of course, remains unchanged. We'll get the strategic target assignments when we arrive in our launch area, Sigma Twenty-Seven. The standard offensive missile countdown to launch still holds. Right?"

"Yes, sir."

"Now, about the defensive missiles launch sequence. Do you agree with the tube loading mix I ordered?"

"Yes, sir, I do. But I've been thinking about changing the plan itself to take advantage of the specifics of our operational orders. If I may suggest, I believe we could gain a significant increase in target range at time of launch," said Wallstrom, taking some papers from the file folder he was holding.

"Good. I was chewing on the same thing," said Mawson reaching into his briefcase open on the desk. Underneath the journal he had read to Barbara last night, he found a lined pad containing several pages of notes and calculations. "Target range at launch is a function of several operational factors. Here, see if you agree that these are the most significant," said Mawson, his voice reflecting the intellectual excitement he always felt when tackling a new problem.

Captain Roger Brewer's quarters were on the 03 deck of the *Woods* in the after end of the bridge structure. The day cabin was large and comfortably furnished, as became the commanding officer of SubRon 42. Mawson, Edelstone, and Wallstrom were seated in leather chairs beside the old oak desk that almost hid Brewer, who was of average height and small boned.

Lieutenant Commander Jess Jacobs, SubRon 42 Operations Officer, stood with a pointer before a large chart covering the entire forward bulkhead of the cabin. The curtains that normally hid the chart were pulled back to reveal the details of the world's northernmost seas.

Stretching across the very top of the chart were the Russian home waters of the Kara and Barents Seas. The light-blue coloring of the waters contrasted with the yellow tones of the land masses and showed that much of these waters were less than six hundred feet deep and were, therefore, too dangerous for Trident missile submarine operations. The entire left-hand side of the chart was taken up with the abysmally deep water of the Arctic Ocean surrounding the North Pole. A jagged red line showed the multi-year limit of the polar ice cap.

Toward the right-hand side of the chart, the low-lying Kola Peninsula, containing a large Soviet naval base at Murmansk, reached downward as if suspended from the overhead. The jagged coast of Norway filled the right-hand side of the chart until it ended in the North Sea and the coastline of Scotland. The coasts of Iceland and Greenland filled the bottom of the chart. The islands of Spitzbergen and Jan Mayen stood out clearly in the deep waters of the Norwegian and Greenland Seas. At various places, intelligence information was plotted on clear acetate overlays pinned to the chart.

Jacobs cleared his throat. "Since your last patrol, Soviet-American relations are little changed. Traditional political tensions continue. Soviet military excursions into Afghanistan and, particularly, in Africa, using Cuban and local nationals, continue to provide the primary potential cause for near-term American military action. The long-term picture is not so clear since Soviet military activity in Africa is expected to increase now that their naval base at Assab, Ethiopia, is fully operational, including the airstrip. In other words, gentlemen, nothing new.

"Of more immediate concern is the relocation of the high-frequency direction-finding station from Kolguyev Island to the Kanin Peninsula on the mainland. With the recent addition of two DF stations on peaks in the islands of Franz Josef Land, this relocation provides the Soviets with the capability for obtaining extremely accurate line-of-bearings on transmission from anywhere in the northern portions of the Norwegian Sea. The stations on Novaya Land continue to cover the southern regions of the Norwegian Sea, with the usual penalties in accuracy. Electronic emission control is still the name of the game, gentlemen. If you lose lock on the extremely low-frequency, or ELF, strategic command system, reestablish contact using either a satellite relay or the new seabed acoustic digital-data link.

"Further, we also now believe that three military satellites launched over the past six months into polar orbits by the Soviets are part of a rudimentary system for detecting and tracking deeply submerged submarines by sensing disturbances in the earth's electric field. This initial capability appears unable to accomplish the detection function and is not sufficiently accurate to provide a firing bearing. However, if they get a fix on you by other means, we believe the system is probably capable of locking onto your wake and providing continuous, near real-time disclosure of your track. Again, the name of the game is to prevent initial detection by more traditional means. Maintaining deep submergence and electronic silence continues to be your best defense against detection.

"One last surface consideration. The aircraft carrier *Riga* and a *Kresta II*-class antisubmarine warfare cruiser have been in Murmansk for the past seventeen days. We believe they will put to sea within fifty-four hours with at least two additional escorts. We have no information on either their destination or probable track. When we get the information, we'll feed it to you."

Jacobs took a drink of coffee and looked around at the three officers seated before him. "If there are no questions on the surface situation, I'll move on to the underwater."

There being none, Jacobs nodded to an ensign from his department who moved quietly down the side of the cabin and drew curtains over the ports. Jacobs dimmed the cabin lights and pushed a button. Behind the charts, lights came on to reveal the features of the ocean floor beneath the area covered by the chart.

The effect was dramatic. Land masses remained yellow in color, but the blues and whites of the sea surface were replaced by cool shades of green that blended and darkened according to the depth of the water. The Barents and Kara Seas glowed light green in color and formed a huge shallow plain. At the base of the Barents Sea, the Nansen Fracture zone slashed diagonally across the chart from Tromsø, Norway, to the coast of Greenland like a deep trench. The North Pole itself lay among a series of serrated ridges separating the almost black-shaded Abyssal Plains under the arctic ice cap. Yellow splashes of color pricked the greens of the sea floor wherever islands rose above the surface.

Jacobs, now silhouetted against the wall of light, resumed speaking.

"As you know, your primary launch area is Sigma Twenty-Seven off Jan Mayen Island."

A small lighted arrow, projected from the flashlight held in Jacob's hand, appeared on the display just west of the island.

"No change in Soviet operational capabilities affecting this area has been detected since your last patrol. Your first alternate launch area is Gamma Nine off Cape Platten on the island of North East Land."

The little arrow of light jumped almost a thousand miles closer to Russian home waters.

"The Soviets now have large acoustic sonar arrays deployed on the seabed around Franz Josef Land. The system is controlled from Bukhta Tikhaya on Hooker Island and is fully operational. However, we believe these arrays are oriented for monitoring the Barents Sea and the Svalbard, rather than the Arctic Ocean. Therefore, make your approach to Gamma Nine at a depth of at least six hundred feet, following the Nansen Fracture zone. Do not cut the corner short and cross the Yermak Plateau or you will be detected.

"Your second alternate launch area is Delta Three off Tromsø, Norway. We recommend you use the Vesteralen Trough close in shore for your approach rather than the shorter route through the Barents Trough in order to avoid the sonar arrays on Franz Josef.

"Now for the last two items. The attack submarine *Tustin* will be transiting Sigma Twenty-Seven on 6 August at approximately fifteen-twenty. No other friendly submarines are scheduled to transit any of your launch areas. You may assume that any other contacts are hostile.

"Finally," Jacobs said as he turned toward his audience, his smile appearing ghoulish in the strange light, "in cooperation with the Royal Navy we have set up a test range for the seabed acoustic data-link system. The code name for the test is Pilot Fish. The range extends from Wick here in Scotland to Sumburgh Head in the Shetland Islands. The shipboard portion of the test is straightforward and is a continuation of the tests performed during the last Blue Crew patrol. We have two civilian contractor representatives standing by to go over the test plan and procedures with the commander and Lieutenant Wallstrom after this meeting. Any questions?"

Mawson turned and looked at Edelstone and Wallstrom, both of whom shook their heads in reply. Mawson shook his own head.

"No. You covered all my questions. Damn fine briefing, Jess."

"Doug, I'd like a word with you, if you please," said Captain Brewer. "That's all, gentlemen. Good luck."

Mawson turned to Brewer as the others left. Bright daylight flooded the cabin as the ensign opened the curtains and went out. Brewer lit a cigar from the humidor on the desk and leaned forward with his elbows resting on the green, leather-bound desk pad.

"Doug, I don't like the new tactics. I endorsed your request to take them up the line because I believed they deserved consideration by our best brains. Well, they got that, and they're approved. But my objections still stand. I agree that they increase the probability of surviving the first attack on the boat. In most operational areas, there will be sufficient time before a second attack can be mounted to permit both launch of the Tridents and successful withdrawal of the boat. In our operational areas, right on the doorstep of the Soviet's major antisubmarine units, that time interval won't exist. You'd get the Tridents off, but that's all. You'd never make it out of there. They'd pinpoint you with the first attack and get you on the second. Damn it, Doug. Wallstrom's tactics are simply a two-step kamikaze attack. I wish you'd wait until the second series of Outlaw Shark tests are completed this winter. That means holding off for one, maybe two, more patrols. What d'you say?"

Mawson inhaled deeply and, lost in thought, exhaled loudly. "Roger, there's no argument about the fact that the tactics decrease the probability of surviving the second attack by major ASW units if it follows immediately after the first. We went all over that at Newport with the CNO. It all comes down to the size of the second attacking force. If it's large, we're in trouble. If it's small, then our Harpoon missiles can handle it at ranges of up to sixty miles."

Brewer interrupted. "And that's the one area where you got garbage out of the computer. There's no way of guessing the size and make of the second ASW force. That's what I'm talking about. It's a toss up. It could just as well be big as little. And as far as having the CNO there, who're you kidding, Doug? Admiral Sauer's been a friend of your father for years. Of course he'd come up to Newport."

"OK, OK," said Mawson, his face growing dead serious. "You're pushing pretty hard, Roger. Forget Newport. There's no answer to probabilistic situations except gut feeling. My guts tell me the Soviets can't get their act together when it comes to a shooting war. It would be the first time out for them. Any second attack they mount any would be disorganized and committed piecemeal. I'd destroy them in detail with

Harpoons, particularly in their home waters, where confusion would be the greatest. That's what I believe, and I'm willing to bet my boat and my ass on it."

"Take it easy. Take it easy. I had to ask," said Brewer, startled at the heat of Mawson's response. "As Jess said a few moments ago, the situation is perfectly normal. The odds are this patrol will be no more exciting than any of the others. But if the balloon does go up while you're out there, I wanted to get that off my conscience. OK, Doug?"

"Sure, Rog," said Mawson, relaxing. "I think I just unloaded some of the things I couldn't say back at the Pentagon onto you."

"I understand," said Brewer. Then, moving onto safer ground, he said, "All the families get squared away for their returns?"

"As far as we know. From what Harry tells me, most of the dependents, including Barbara and the kids, are going back on Pan World this evening. Apparently everyone had a great time ashore and made it back aboard without any problems. What more can you ask of Navy men?"

"Not a hell of a lot," said Brewer smiling and standing up. Holding out his hand, he said, "Well, good luck to you, Doug."

"Thanks, Rog. See you in a couple of months." Mawson shook Brewer's hand and went out into the sunshine.

Brewer stared at the door long after Mawson had left. The younger man's attitude bothered him. There was an undefinable line between the normal combative spirit of the commanding officer of a Trident missile submarine and excessive aggressiveness. The same rule held true for initiative. Initiative in a commanding officer was absolutely necessary to success, but too much was bad. How much was too much? Mawson certainly showed initiative in getting Wallstrom's plan accepted. Was that indicative of some flaw in Mawson?

Brewer stood up, walked to a port, and gazed down at the *Montana*. The soothing, everyday sounds of the working parties drifted up to him. Nonsense, he thought. I've known Doug for years. He's a fine officer from a fine family, as solid as they come. You just had to look at his relationship with Barbara and the kids to see that.

Reassured, he turned back to his desk. His mind picked up the routine thoughts of his professional life and he forgot about Mawson. Later, he would curse himself for doing so.

Chapter 3

Jan Deville turned her shoulder and slipped under the shower. Inclining her head slightly to keep the cap covering her hair clear of the spray, she clutched her arms across her breasts and let the stream play over her neck and back. The warm water flowed down over her body, glistening in the soft light and splashing against the expensive Italian-marble tiles and heavy, gold-plated fixtures of the large shower stall. The fine, downy soft, brown hairs covering the small of her back ran together in two wavy lines and disappeared into the cleft between her buttocks.

Not yet fully awake, although it was well past noon, she turned and dropped her arms. The full force of the water now beat against her breasts. Her hips undulated in unconscious response to the stimulation of her skin. Her nipples hardened. Without thinking about it, she took the soap in her hand and began washing her genitals.

As she idly soaped herself, the heady events of the past twenty-four hours mingled with the erotic sensations rising from between her legs and ran pleasantly through her mind. Yesterday she had been Jan Nobody. Then she had dropped her packages in the hotel lobby and met Martin in a scene right out of an old Fred Astaire movie. Last night they had dinner in the fanciest restaurant she had ever been in and then went on to a casino, where she won over two hundred pounds that Martin had let her keep. Now, here she was in Martin's suite. It was only ten floors above the hotel room she and Tony had shared, but a whole different world.

Martin really knows how to do it, she thought. If we can get it on in Washington the way we got it on here. And all because I dropped those gifts for Tony's family! Serves him right. I told him I didn't want to shop for all that shit.

Turning off the water, Jan pushed open the shower door and dried herself with a large towel. She tore off the shower cap and with a shake of her head let her long hair fall about her in a chestnut cascade. Jan turned to admire herself in the mirror. Her complexion was fair and still radiated the healthy glow of her childhood on a Wisconsin dairy farm.

Jan liked what she saw and smiled as she recalled that Frank had once said admiringly that from her tits to her knees she was all cunt. It was the greatest compliment anyone had ever paid her. That is, until she met Martin. She stood thinking about the differences between Martin and Frank. Compared to Martin, Frank was a mere boy. Tony did not enter her mind at all.

As she bent over to dry her legs, she noticed a series of tiny red welts high up on the inside of her thighs. She felt a rush of pleasure as she recalled how these marks got there. Her vagina tightened involuntarily with a spasm of anticipation. She wanted Martin again. Right now.

A discrete knock on the closed door startled her. As it opened, Martin's leonine head appeared around the edge.

"So you are up? Do you mind if I come in?"

"No, of course not," said Jan, looking at him in the mirror.

Martin Schlosser entered the bathroom. He was just under six feet tall and looked every inch the wealthy West German industrialist that he was. At fifty-eight, his once-blond hair was pure silver and brought a measure of distinction to the rather heavy features of his large head. His trim, conservatively cut, dark-gray suit and vest completed the picture of a successful and powerful businessman.

Taking the towel from Jan's suddenly trembling hands, he parted her hair and kissed her on the back of her neck.

"The porter has brought up all your bags, and I was able to get your ticket transferred to First Class. So now we sit together," said Schlosser, with only a slight accent.

Sitting down on the toilet seat, he began drying the few drops of water that remained on Jan's back. Beautiful, Schlosser thought, as he gazed at the fine hairs on her back made even softer by the recent washing. Like a fawn, he thought as he bent and put his lips against her skin just above the cleft of her buttocks. Her body smelled clean and fresh; her skin, warm and soft.

Watching in the mirror, Jan felt her knees go weak from excitement. His mouth was moving lower. She felt his hand on her shoulder, pressing her down. Her knees bent as she grabbed the sink for support.

"Oh, yes," she moaned bending forward.

As he stood up and bent to kiss her on the mouth, she felt a rush of exquisite pain as his fingers slipped deep between her buttocks and pinched the tender skin of her anus.

Frantic with desire, she tore at his belt buckle, pulling his pants and shorts down with quick, chopping motions of her hands. Taking his swollen penis in one hand, she pulled him down on top of her as she sank to her back on the wet rug. The last orgasm of her life occurred before Martin entered her.

Across the city in Uxbridge, Henry paused before the open door and gave his room one last look. He was taking nothing with him except the usual work clothes he wore. Of course, the bottle cutter, diamond drill, and empty cartridge boxes would all be found eventually and could be used against him. For some time he had puzzled over different schemes for disposing of them. In the end, he decided the risk of taking them out of the room far outweighed the risk of simply leaving them. By the time they were discovered, he would be in Ireland and well on his way to Ulster. Seeing nothing amiss, Henry stepped into the hall and pulled the door closed behind him. For the last time, he turned the key in the dead bolt before starting down the stairs.

The hand-held transreceiver lying on the floor of the nondescript house painter's van parked across the street from 32 Bunting Place gave off a shrill, whistling sound. Detective Sergeant Austin Goodson, who tended to corpulence, leaned over with difficulty in the cramped confines of the small van and raised the radio to his ear.

He was bored. They did not have much to go on. The message from military intelligence in Belfast had said only that the address 32 Bunting Place had come up in one of their investigations. It could mean anything. Or nothing. But it was enough to get Goodson out of the Yard and into the van.

"Goodson here," he said without taking his eyes from the steps and doorway visible through the peephole concealed in the truck's side.

"No, he's not come down yet. Perhaps he works the evening shift? If he does, he should be coming along soon."

At that moment, Henry emerged from the doorway. Goodson depressed the switch button he held in his free hand

and started the 16-mm camera that was focused on the entrance.

"He's just coming out now. Camera's running. I don't recognize him, Inspector. He's wearing work clothes and he's not carrying anything. Any change in the drill?" asked Goodson.

He listened to the inspector's reply. Then he answered, "Right, then. I'll be in with the film directly," as Henry turned at the bottom of the steps and walked out of view.

Walking away from the apartment, Henry felt excitement well up within him. At last it had begun. Only with the greatest of efforts was he able to restrain himself from running. He was barely able to hold his pace to that of any man on his way to work and was sorely tempted to look behind him to see if he were being followed. Take it easy, he told himself. You've been coming this way for three years. No one's ever followed you before. Why should you be followed today? Only you know that today's different.

Still, when he stopped to pet the big tabby sitting on its customary lower step of the last house on the street, he could not resist taking a long look back down the row of flats. Seeing nothing out of the ordinary, Henry lit a cigarette and began to relax as he retraced his path of last night. At the old Morris, he pulled open the door and slid behind the wheel with only a glance toward the back to see that the case of champagne bottles was undisturbed. Just before he drove off, he reached up and took his badge from the visor and clipped it to his shirt pocket.

Ten minutes later he was whistling softly to himself as he backed the Morris into an empty spot along the curb. If he believed in good omens, this was it. The transfer of the champagne bottles from the Morris to the White's truck was most critical. It was the one time when he was obviously doing something that was not only against the rules but out of the ordinary. To make the transfer, he had selected a quiet street just off his route from White's to Heathrow. Twice before he had made trial runs of the transfer: pulling his truck up alongside the parked Morris, jumping out quickly but not too hastily, unlocking and opening the back door of the Morris, and pretending to remove a box and carry it back to the truck. At no time had he been seen or questioned. The spot was perfect and he was here. His fears had proven groundless, and he exulted in a smooth mission. So far, so good, he thought.

This feeling of confidence was still with him when he entered the side door of a large, drab building that was White's Flight Kitchens Ltd. Old Harry, the doorkeeper, glanced up as he passed.

"Aye there, Henry. Mr. Wilkes says for you to be sure and check the board."

His confidence evaporated and the sour taste of bile rose in his throat. The board! he thought in near panic. Wilkes can't have changed the flight assignments. Not today.

He hurried down the hall to the assignment board where his fears were confirmed. Jerry Potter had Flight 231. What the hell was he going to do? First off, you've got to calm down, he told himself. Fingers shaking with emotion, he forced himself to slowly take out and light a cigarette. Inhaling deeply, he began to relax by sheer will power.

He had to get the assignments changed. But how? By switching with Jerry Potter, that's how, he thought. It would cost him ten quid, but it was the one way to get Jerry to agree. The bloke was always short of money. He felt his confidence returning as he hurried off down the hall to look for Jerry.

As expected, for ten pounds Potter agreed to let Henry take his route, but only if Mr. Wilkes approved.

"I hain't gonna lose me job for no ten quid," Potter had declared. So off the two of them went to find Mr. Wilkes.

Wilkes was bending over a large food mixer in the center of the kitchen when Henry and Potter found him. Parts of the machine were spread out on the floor, the black grease making dirty smudges on the scrupulously clean tile. Henry, his nerves stretched almost to the breaking point, waited for Mr. Wilkes to finish talking to the mechanic kneeling before the machine.

"Yes, what is it?" said Wilkes distractedly. "I don't know how Mr. White expects me to dispatch vans and see to the repair of these filthy machines."

"Mr. Wilkes, I'd like to change routes with Potter today," said Henry simply.

"Change routes? Why should you want to do that?" asked Wilkes, looking at Henry for the first time.

"I've been servicing Pan World Flight two thirty-one for

over a month now, and there's a stewardess I've been trying to get to come out with me. I've got this gift for her, sir."

"A stewardess. I mean really, Henry!" exclaimed Wilkes. "All the routes are scrambled. Ryder's mother is ill and Mr. White allowed him to start his holiday early. I can't. . . ."

"Potter doesn't mind," interrupted Henry. Then prodding Potter with his elbow, "Do you, Jerry?"

"No, I don't mind, Mr. Wilkes. They's all the same to me," responded Potter sincerely.

Wilkes looked at the two young men and pondered his decision.

"Oh, very well. I suppose boys must be boys," said Wilkes finally, and shrugged his approval.

An hour later, Henry slowly backed his lift van toward the open galley service door in the right side of the huge Pan World Airways DC-10 aircraft that was Flight 231.

Satisfied with the positioning, Henry opened the driver's door and walked around onto a small platform containing the lift controls. With the movement of a single lever, the body of the van rose up on powerful hydraulic scissors to the level of the open service doorway. The interior lights of the aircraft glowed dimly in the late afternoon sunlight reflecting off the polished aluminum surfaces of the galley. With one last adjustment, Henry released the lever and stepped through the doorway. A quick look around confirmed that, as expected, none of the cabin attendants were yet aboard.

Good, thought Henry as he rolled up the door forming the back of the van. The case of champagne stood in the center of the opening where he had hastily placed it: a cardboard carton, alien among the neat aluminum food containers. It could have been sticky having to explain its presence to the stewardesses working in the galley.

Balancing the carton on his hip, he reached down with a free hand and opened the door of a small storage locker in the outboard portion of the galley structure. With a small cry that was almost a moan, he bent down and shoved the box deep into the locker.

He rose and entered the van as he began to transfer the food containers, Henry felt the tension drain from him. Whatever happens now, he thought, was Yonnie and her group's problem. He'd done his part exactly as planned. By God, I've earned the right to be with cousin John in Armagh. As he pulled the door down over the now-empty van and stepped to the lift controls, he glanced up and noticed shadowy figures watching from behind the smoked glass windows of the international passenger lounge. Hard luck on you people, he thought, as he put the van in gear and drove off.

Doris Dacovak turned from the window where she had been standing idly watching the orderly bustle taking place below. The area was crowded with passengers who had been cleared through passport control. Three-year-old Ginny, Doris' youngest child, came bursting out of the crowd chased by her eight-year-old brother, Paul. Both children were crying. Doris reached out and gently but firmly grabbed a child in each of her large hands.

"Stop it. For the last time. Stop it," Doris said in a voice more harsh than she felt. "Paul, stay away from her."

"She kicked me," Paul protested.

"He hit me," interjected Ginny.

"I don't care who did what. Just stay away from each other. We're going aboard the plane soon. Paul, go find your brothers."

Doris took Ginny in her arms and threaded her way back to their seats. The kids need a nap, she thought. And why not? They had been up at dawn. She smiled fondly and with no little pride. Between her five and Phyllis' six, they were a little army. Besides, they had gotten to the airport much too early.

Doris put Ginny down. They had reached their seats which stood in the midst of a small clearing surrounded by hand luggage, toy bags, and the grilled wall of the international passenger waiting area. As she straightened up, a familiar face on the far side of the grill caught her attention.

"Phyllis, look, There's Jan Deville," Doris said, dropping into a seat beside her sister. "This time she's got a man old enough to be her father."

Phyllis Jackson twisted around in her seat and looked out through the grillwork.

"Where?"

"There. Just behind that older woman wearing the hat with the red cherries."

Phyllis saw Jan standing close beside Schlosser, her hip against his thigh as they waited in one of the passport control lines. Phyllis' darkly pretty face hardened.

"Whore," she exclaimed in a voice totally devoid of any

sympathy. "Dumb broad's got everything going for her and she's screwing it all away. I've got no use for a bitch that slips out on her man."

"Well, she's coming up in the world. He looks like an ambassador or something. That suit must have cost a fortune, don't you think?" asked Doris conversationally.

As they watched, they both noticed Jan's hand, which was almost but not quite hidden by the raincoat over Schlosser's arm, slide upward under his suit coat. Phyllis turned to Doris, her eyes flashing. The two sisters were not, however, the only witnesses to Jan's intimate action.

Barbara Mawson stood talking to Harriet Edelstone while they waited in the passport control line a few yards behind and to the right of where Jan and Schlosser stood. Trying to be fair, she had almost decided they were not traveling together when the movement of Jan's hand convinced her otherwise.

For the moment, all thoughts of the pleasant lunch she and Harriet had shared were driven from Barbara's mind. She slapped the passports she was holding in her right hand against the palm of her left hand in exasperation. Robbie, standing in front of her, turned his head at the sound.

"Oh, why doesn't he divorce her?" asked Barbara, turning to Harriet. She explained, "I'm talking about Jan Deville."

"I know. I noticed them when we first got in line. Are you sure they're together?" asked Harriet, who had not seen Jan's gesture.

"I'd say they are as together as a man and a woman can be," laughed Barbara, recovering her humor. "Jan's behavior bothers me less than Tony's acceptance of it. He must know he's going to be judged as either immature or weak of character. Neither of which is going to help his career."

"I think he puts up with her because he's afraid of losing their little boy."

"I suppose so," said Barbara, still watching Jan and Schlosser as they passed through the control point and entered an unmarked door that Barbara knew led to a VIP lounge. "Maybe the problem will resolve itself," she continued. "Maybe Jan will go away and leave the boy with Tony." Later she was to recall those words with horror.

* * *

Yonnie Trupp was uncomfortably warm. Small beads of perspiration ran down from the hairs of her unshaven armpits. At the small of her back, her slip was already soaked through. Yet she felt cold. She always felt like this before an operation. Last year while waiting in the car outside that bank in Stuttgart, she had shivered with a cold sweat that bathed her body. Her thin, almost bloodless lips lifted slightly as she recalled with pleasure how easily they had kidnapped the director of the bank. The ransom had made this operation possible. Saayed may be excitable, she thought, but he plans well. Good planning is everything. Luck plays a part, certainly, but even good fortune cannot overcome a bad plan.

As she sat in the international passenger lounge within view of the passport control point, no one would have suspected her of being a terrorist. She wore a two-piece brown outfit of light-weight tweed. Her blond hair was pulled back and gathered in a bun that was just visible beneath the wide brim of a tan hat. On her feet she wore a pair of heavy, brown walking shoes. Except for the quick, intense movements of her eyes, she appeared to be a placid, European domestic en route to join her employer. Which, in fact, was exactly what the papers she carried were designed to make any inquiring authority believe.

Yonnie looked up from the small book she was pretending to read. Her eyes opened slightly. Saayed Qabrestan, the leader of their group, was just leaving the passport check point, his thin torso almost bowed from the weight of the camera equipment which festooned his neck. He walked with quick, small steps directly past a couple standing before an unmarked door. As Qabrestan passed, the man turned to pull open the door for his female companion, revealing his face. Yonnie's stomach muscles contracted involuntarily. Martin Schlosser! That man was Martin Schlosser.

Before kidnapping the bank director, they had considered several other industralists. Martin Schlosser had been her choice. Schlosser had fought in the Wehrmacht to keep Hitler in power. Now his factories turned out armoured cars and guns that kept the Palestinian people subject to the will of the Western capitalists. She looked at Schlosser with hatred. He lived in luxury with his wife and grown children around him. His grandchildren grew fat while Palestinian children died from contaminated water within sight of new gambling casinos and hotels. If fate would only deliver him and his juicy companion to her. If only those two were on Flight 231!

Yonnie broke off staring as the door closed behind Schlosser. With a quick glance toward Qabrestan as he passed, she noted that he had seen her. By reaching up and adjusting her hat, she signaled that the other three members of their team had arrived and passed her without incident. Had they not arrived, she would have scratched her knee.

Qabrestan continued on his way without making any sign that he had seen Yonnie. To anyone who might notice, he seemed like any other Middle Eastern student among a sea of them from all countries. A thin smile appeared on Yonnie's mouth. Qabrestan was a very experienced freedom fighter, having operated in both Israel and West Germany as well as his native Iran. The image of him sitting meekly in a class, attentive to the ramblings of some naïve professor, amused her as much as her tightly stretched nerves would allow. What do universities know of the gut-wrenching realities of class struggle? she thought.

Yonnie, herself the last surviving member of a once very active German Red Terrorist group, had met Qabrestan several years before. He had fled Iran for West Germany after the Communist *Tudeh* cell to which he belonged had been outlawed by the revolutionary council. With him, Qabrestan had brought three trusted members of the Palestinian fedayeen. The two brothers Hamed Jadayel and Mahmud Jadayel were Egyptians, but born of Palestinian parents. The third freedom fighter, Abdulla bin Salim, was a true Palestinian who had been raised in a refugee camp in Jordan. All were dedicated Marxists, totally committed to bringing a Communist Palestine into being.

Yonnie glanced at her watch. At least thirty-five minutes before they called the flight. It's just as well that I'm last to board, she thought. That way I can follow the plan and perhaps see if Herr Schlosser is coming with us. She shivered slightly as she returned to her book and pretended to read. Her mind was a swirl of half-completed thoughts and memories that chased each other endlessly. The tension within her made the effort to maintain a relaxed and calm appearance almost unbearable. This is the part she dreaded: the time going so slowly. It seemed an eternity before the loudspeaker announced that Pan World Flight 231 was ready for boarding.

Yonnie delayed standing up in order to continue watching for Schlosser. She decided he was not coming out and was in the middle of rising from her seat when the door opened and Jan appeared, laughing and half turning to Schlosser. Suddenly Yonnie was completely calm. They *are* coming with us. I knew it. They are mine, she thought as she fell in behind them for the walk to the gate.

Jan sank down into the left-hand window seat in the very front of the First Class cabin, thankful to be away from what she imagined to be the disapproving eyes of Barbara Mawson and Harriet Edelstone. That was close, Jan thought with relief. For a time she was afraid they were going to meet; at one point Barbara actually waved at her. But then a surge in the crowd carried them ahead into the plane and safely away from the two women, who were now seated behind her and Martin.

Oh, why can't they leave me alone, thought Jan, recalling her panic at seeing Barbara's greeting. It was all so perfect and, now, those goddamned wardroom wives. They were everywhere. Always so nice on the outside while inside they were putting her down. Fuck 'em. I got what I want and nothing's going to spoil it, she decided defiantly as she gazed out the window.

She turned to Schlosser as he sat down in the aisle seat beside her and gave him her most radiant smile.

"Will you show me Washington the way you showed me London?" she said, her voice almost purring with double meaning.

Schlosser leaned toward her, his mouth close to her ear, his hand on her arm.

"My dear, I am going to show you things you did not know existed. I assure you, you will enjoy them all immensely."

As he squeezed her arm, she turned and they both smiled as if conspirators in some secret plot.

"But who will I be?" asked Jan, "How will you explain me?"

Schlosser thought for a second, his hand to his chin. Then the conspirator's smile returned.

"You will be my daughter. That will make everything even more exciting. Do you think you could speak with an accent?"

"I don't know. I've never tried."

"Well, you try it here during this flight. Try to speak as I do. If you enjoy our little game, we will continue when we land. What do you think?"

"Out of sight," laughed Jan in a mock German accent.

Schlosser laughed with her. This one makes me feel twenty again, he thought.

Pan World Airlines Purser Carol Moore had a cold. She felt terrible and, as she stood in the forward galley and checked through the flight manifest, she longed to be in bed in her little apartment in Alexandria. She sneezed into another tissue, her golden hair flying about the brown gabardine collar of her trim uniform.

"Oh, hell," she said to no one in particular. "One more like that and I'll stab myself with the pen."

Just then the passenger agent in charge of loading the flight came through the open door from the jetway.

"Hello, Carol. You're just about loaded. How do you tally?"

"All but six are on board. We've got an awful lot of women and children with strange tickets. What's going on?"

"Right. Dependents of your fighting Navy going home. They came over two weeks ago on Flight seven oh nine. I don't know what's going on. Why don't you ask them?"

"I think I will," said Carol just as the last few passengers boarded.

Carol stepped to the side of the open door. She picked up the phone, told the pilot the last of the passengers were boarded, and requested permission to close the loading door. She nodded as the pilot's voice in her ear grunted consent. Carol followed the agent to the door and helped swing it closed. Just before she turned the large handle that sealed the door, the agent's voice came to her.

"Cheerio. Take care of your cold, love."

Feeling the handle slip into the locked position, Carol turned, clipboard in hand, and made her way down the aisle toward the after galley to finish giving out the rest-period assignments.

Saayed Qabrestan sat in an aisle seat just forward of the after galley in the Economy Class section. The other members of the team were scattered in other areas of Economy

Class. He had given much thought to the seating arrangement. It would be best if they were all seated near the center galley so that they could move as one when the time came. But to do so the tickets would have had to be bought as a block, which was too risky. The coordination problem due to the different distances from the galley would have to be accepted; whoever was most distant would start first.

Qabrestan unbuckled his seat belt and stepped back to the galley for a drink of water. When he turned into the galley area searching for the water fountain, he came upon five stewardesses talking by the serving counter. Carol turned to him as he came up, leaving the others to discuss the schedule.

"May I help you?"

"Yes, please. I was looking for some water," said Qabrestan. He saw a pretty face framed in blond hair, but as he noticed her slightly reddened nose and fluid eyes, he thought, she's been crying.

"I'll get you some," said Carol, turning to the counter and drawing some water into a paper cup from a spigot.

Just as she was about to put the cup into Qabrestan's outstretched hand, Carol suddenly sneezed. Her left hand flew upward to cover her mouth. The contents of the cup, jolted by the quick spasm that racked her body, partially spilled out over Qabrestan's hand to run down his wrist and arm.

"I'm awfully sorry," said Carol, dabbing at his arm with a tissue snatched from the counter. "I've got a really bad cold it seems."

Qabrestan looked at her without smiling.

"It is nothing. No harm was done," he said, drinking what was left in the cup as he turned and went back to his seat.

Carol felt a shiver run up her spine as she turned back to the group. Those eyes, she thought. Cold and friendless. I wouldn't like to make him angry. Or maybe I did. I sure hope not.

Hearing the warning gong from the cockpit, Carol returned to her departure station in First Class. As she walked up the aisle, she felt the plane being pushed back away from the gate. By the time she finished checking her passengers' seat belts, the plane was moving down the hardstand toward the taxiway leading to the end of the active runway.

Finishing the required demonstrations of emergency procedures, Carol dropped wearily into a crew seat beside the center galley and fastened her seat belt. Thankful for being seated, if only for a few minutes, she let her mind dwell quietly and happily on being home in a few hours. The sound of engines winding up to full power broke into her thoughts. She turned her head and instinctively looked toward the galley to make sure everything was secure. She sensed the plane turn onto the end of the runway and begin its takeoff roll. The sound of the engines rose to a roar, and their thrust forced her back in the hard seat. The plane rotated sharply; a second later the wheels left the ground. She heard the hydraulics squeal as first the wheels were retracted and then the flaps started up.

A few seats in front of Carol, Barbara Mawson leaned forward and took her journal from the pocket of the seat before her and dropped the small table from its raised position. Beside her, Harriet Edelstone saw the motion and opened the hardbound novel resting in her lap. Barbara opened the journal to the half-filled page indicated by Kathy's bookmark. She took up her pen and began the first of many entries she would make before she saw her husband again:

> "August 4, Monday. Aboard Pan World Flight
> 231. We are airborne and I think of you. . . ."

Doug Mawson stood on the crowded bridge of the *Montana* and waited patiently. It had been two or three seconds since he had decided they would clear the Scottish fishing trawler crossing ahead from their starboard bow and could return to base course. Lieutenant Junior Grade George Robare, the *Montana*'s navigator standing before him, had the conn and was at the same time vastly less experienced than he, and so was far more cautious. Which was as it should be, thought Mawson. Interesting, here's a rare chance to actually measure experience in terms of the difference in the time between our decisions. Mawson began a mental count . . . three, four, five, six. Just as he was about to count seven, Robare bent forward to the watertight squawk box under the coaming.

"Come left to course oh four zero."

"Come left to course oh four zero, aye," said the box as the helmsman below repeated the order.

So, Mawson thought, in this case, fifteen years experience is worth exactly seven seconds. That could make a difference. Particularly when running on the surface as they were now.

Mawson pulled the collar of his bridge jacket closer around his neck as a gust of wind probed his clothes for entrance. Bathed in sunlight, the coast of Scotland was visible off to port. Blowing from the North Sea, the wind stole the warmth from the sun. He disliked running on the surface at any time, much less along a coast. The *Montana*'s proper element was the depths of the sea, for on the surface she was especially vulnerable to collision and Soviet tracking systems. And, since most of her hull was submerged, she had very little reserve buoyancy for a ship her size.

When he had first read the orders, Mawson had been impressed. No less than two Royal Navy frigates had been assigned to escort the *Montana* over the test range. The British must be very interested in the new system to assign two frigates, which are always in very short supply. The HMS *Reward* and *Norham*: they should be coming into radar range anytime now.

Just then the squawk box in front of Robare came to life.

"Bridge. CIC," said the voice of Lieutenant Terry McKenna, the CIC officer and oceanographer. "Two surface vessels bearing one two seven. Range sixteen thousand and closing. Speed twenty-three."

Robare leaned forward and depressed the talk switch.

"Bridge. Aye. Aye."

Robare turned and glanced at Mawson to make certain his captain had heard the report. Mawson nodded and turned to raise his binoculars along the reported bearing just as the starboard lookout shouted.

"Warship one two five, sixteen thousand."

Good report, thought Mawson as he sought the ships. Must remember to compliment McKenna when I get below. That man could have just repeated the CIC report, which he no doubt heard. Instead, he reported the contact was a warship which CIC did not know. There they are, he thought, as the upper works of the leading vessel came in to view. With that huge bedspring antenna, she couldn't be anything but a Royal Navy frigate.

Mawson lowered his glasses and leaned over to the squawk box beside him.

"CIC. Captain here. The vessels bearing one two seven

are our escorts. Report when range is five hundred. Report all range and bearings below five hundred."

"CIC. Aye. Aye."

Mawson turned to the starboard lookout.

"The warship bearing one two five is one of two escorts. Do not report their range unless below five hundred."

Mawson watched the sleek hulls of the two Royal Navy ships come up over the horizon. The leading frigate altered course slightly to come up on the starboard side of the *Montana*. The second vessel increased speed and curved away slightly to come up on the port side from astern.

"The HMS *Reward* is coming up to starboard, sir. The frigate to port is the HMS *Norham*," said Robare, cradling the recognition book in his arms.

"Very well," said Mawson as he watched the show the two frigate captains were putting on for his benefit.

As if attached by some unseen framework, the two ships curved in toward the *Montana* at high speed, their wakes forming concentric white lines of churning water. Mawson watched in fascination as the two frigates came dashing up from astern. Surely they'll overshoot; they've come too far, thought Mawson. And, at the last possible instant, both ships slowed suddenly and took station on either quarter exactly five hundred yards from the *Montana*.

Oh, well done, thought Mawson smiling. A combined operation with the U.S. Navy always brought out the best in any Royal Navy captain. They all took it as a challenge, as if still smarting from the single-ship engagements they had lost two hundred years ago.

"Bridge. CIC. Escort taking up station. Range five hundred."

"Very well," said Mawson reaching for the UHF handset.

"Pilot Fish to Escort Leader," said Mawson speaking into the handset of the short range radio.

"Escort Leader to Pilot Fish. Go ahead," said a very British voice in Mawson's ear.

"Good afternoon, Captain. It is reassuring to see the seamanlike smartness of the Royal Navy endures in this changing world," said Mawson, looking across to his unseen counterpart on the bridge of *Reward*.

Mawson had deliberately issued an invitation to an ancient game of one-upmanship between warship captains. He wondered what form of reply his counterpart would make. The British captain could not compliment the handling of the *Montana* since she had not deviated from her course, nor could he compliment her appearance since she looked much like a large club being towed through the water. That was exactly why Mawson had chosen his particular opening.

"Escort Leader to Pilot Fish. Good afternoon to you, Captain. We endure because the United States Navy has assumed the lion's share of the responsibility for this world."

Mawson chuckled. Lion's share indeed. He was ready, however.

"Pilot Fish to Escort Leader. We may have the lion's share, but unlike you, sir, we have no reward."

"Escort Leader to Pilot Fish. Well said, sir. I am overcome by a superior force. How may we assist you before retiring in disorder?"

"Pilot Fish to Escort Leader. If you will maintain station on me, I will submerge and leave it to you to keep me safe while my head is down. I will give you the final course as we come up on the test range. Over."

"Escort Leader to Pilot Fish. Roger. Standing by for final course change."

"Captain. Navigator. We are twelve minutes from the beginning of the test range. Final course over range is oh three three."

"Very well," said Mawson, holding down the talk switch.

"Test Control. This is the Captain. Are you ready to begin the run?"

"Test Control. Aye. Aye. Captain," came Wallstrom's deep, baritone voice. "Communications has lock-up signals on both the accoustic range and the satellite. Standing by to commence the run."

"Very well," concluded Mawson picking up the handset.

"Pilot Fish to Escort Leader, I am diving now. Course change in eleven minutes."

"Escort Leader to Pilot Fish. Roger. We will watch over you."

"Clear the bridge," commanded Mawson as the watch started tumbling below.

With one final sweeping look around the horizon, Mawson pushed the diving alarm and yelled into the squawk box, "Dive! Dive!"

Mawson turned and jumped down the hatch, shutting

and dogging its cover behind him. Before he reached the bottom of the long ladder, Dacovak, standing at the main ballast control panel, shouted:

"Straight board!"

The *Montana* angled downward and sank toward her element like a repentant seeking salvation. Within seconds, all that could be seen from the escorts was a single dish antenna, moving inexorably across the surface of the sea.

Chapter 4

Yonnie Trupp looked up. The FASTEN SEAT BELT light above her had gone out. Her arm trembled with excitement as she looked at her watch. Wait two minutes after the sign went off, Saayed had said. Then whoever was farthest from the center galley would start up the aisle. Saayed was farthest. At 6:18 he would stand up and begin making his way forward. When she saw him pass in the opposite aisle, she would stand and start forward. Beneath her clothes, sweat drenched her hard young body.

She waited, turning away from the portly, middle-aged businessman in the aisle seat beside her to gaze out the window at the right wing. Totally absorbed, she heard the sound of her heartbeat loud in her ears.

6:18 exactly. She turned from the window and looked across to the opposite aisle. The man beside her looked up from the papers in his lap.

"Hi. I'm Ralph Albertson from Minneapolis. You been on vacation?" he said pleasantly.

Yonnie, concentrating on spotting Qabrestan among the few passengers who were beginning to stand up, automatically shook her head in response to the question. For several heartbeats, time seemed suspended. Then Qabrestan came into view, walking slowly but purposely up the aisle with Mahmud a few steps behind.

Yonnie stood up, slipping her bag onto her shoulder.

"Entschuldigung sie, bitte," mumbled Yonnie as she

stepped past the still-smiling Albertson. Turning, she made her way along the aisle that angled upward as the plane climbed to cruising altitude. As she came into the center Economy Class cabin, Abdulla's face appeared briefly over the top of a seat. When she passed, he stood up and followed behind her. A few steps farther and she saw Hamed fall into step behind Qabrestan and Mahmud in the other aisle. It was working. They were well grouped. The center galley is just ahead, she thought with excitement as she stepped around a young woman getting something out of the overhead rack.

Yonnie came abreast of the galley and looked quickly across the plane. Saayed and Mahmud had already turned the corner from the other aisle. She sensed Abdulla close behind her. Four stewardesses were in the galley preparing drink carts. As planned, Yonnie dropped to her knees before the locker in which Henry was to have hidden the champagne case. Would it be there? As she pulled open the locker door, one of the stewardesses noticed her.

"Hey, what's going on . . . ?" began the stewardess. But she got no further as the four men closed in around the startled girls.

Yonnie's frantically groping hand felt the cardboard carton.

"It's here," she grunted with triumph.

Bending forward until her head was level with the low locker, Yonnie pulled at the carton with all her strength. Out slid the case onto the rust-colored carpet. Yonnie rose back onto her knees and grabbed a corner of the carton with her left hand. With her right, she tore open the partially glued top.

Rows of champagne bottles glistened darkly in the light from the overhead. Two stewardesses saw the bottles.

"Stop that! What're you doing?" said one.

The other reached for the telephone hanging inside the galley. Saayed tore the instrument from her grasp and pushed her viciously out of the galley area. She fell heavily against the passenger loading door across the aisle. The others pushed the remaining stewardesses out of the way as Yonnie took the first bottle from the case and smashed it against the hard corner of the galley partition. A plastic bag containing a pistol and spare clip tumbled out.

Yonnie tore open the plastic with her fingernails and handed the gun and clip to Saayed, who turned to cover their actions. Yonnie's breath came in great sobs. They had to arm themselves quickly and disperse. By the time she had smashed the last of the bottles and deposited the spare ammunition in her bag, her fingers were bleeding from several small cuts.

Yonnie stood up beside the others. For an instant her eyes met Qabrestan's. His normally expressionless eyes were alight with a strange, insane fire. Then she looked at the brothers and Abdulla. Like Qabrestan, excitement danced in their eyes. In each right hand, they held the small but heavy automatics that had been loaded and cocked by Henry. In their left hands, each held a grenade.

With a loud yell that startled them all, Qabrestan pulled the safety pin from the grenade with the little finger of his right hand. Jumping behind the dazed stewardess who had just gotten to her feet, Qabrestan slammed his right arm across her chest pulling her close to him and clapped the grenade hard against her left temple. He felt the almost fainting stewardess sag against him.

"Grenade! Grenade!" shouted Qabrestan, shoving the stewardess ahead of him through the curtain that opened into the left aisle of the First Class cabin.

Abdulla and the brothers pulled the pins on their grenades and ran back down the aisles into the Economy Class cabins, screaming as they went. Yonnie pulled the pin on her grenade with her right middle finger and ran forward into First Class along the right aisle. Holding the grenade above her head for all to see, she yelled at the top of her voice: "Down! Down! Everybody down! Grenade! Grenade! Everybody down!"

When she reached the First Class galley at the front of the cabin, she turned and faced the passengers, sweeping her pistol from side to side for all to see. With a quick glance over her right shoulder, she noted that Qabrestan had also reached the galley and had the stewardesses under control. Looking back into the cabin, she saw that most of the passengers were staring at her with frightened expressions. Surprisingly, a few continued their activities oblivious to what was happening around them. Yonnie had to do something. She must have total control.

"Attention! Attention! We are taking over the aircraft!" Yonnie shouted. Her English, usually almost accent free, was now heavily slurred with German pronounciation due to her anxiety.

A few rows from where Yonnie stood, Sam Samson of Fort Worth sat in an aisle seat beside his wife, Eunice. They had dined well, lingering over a second bottle of good Rhine wine before boarding the flight. Eunice had had very little of the second bottle; Sam drank most of it.

When Yonnie rushed by him, Sam had been totally absorbed in a mystery novel by his favorite author. Eunice, however, saw Yonnie and grabbed Sam's arm in fright. Looking in the direction of Eunice's stare, Sam saw what seemed to be an angry young woman shouting in some strange language. He stood up and started for Yonnie.

"Now look heah, miss," declared Sam, his string tie swinging as he waggled his finger at Yonnie. "Ah don't rightly know what y'all think . . ."

The staccato crack of the shot sounded flat and oddly abrupt in the heavily sound-proofed cabin. An expression of disbelief spread over Sam's face. He half turned back toward Eunice, who watched frozen with horror as Sam's shirtfront blossomed into a sticky red mass. The scream trapped in Eunice's throat burst forth as Sam took a single, halting step toward her before reeling sideways to fall across the lap of a well-dressed male passenger in the center section of seats.

Except for Eunice's soul-wrenching sobs, there was complete silence in the cabin. Everyone was looking at Yonnie now.

Carol Moore was setting an ice bucket down on a beverage cart just as Qabrestan shoved his hostage stewardess ahead of him into the first-class galley.

"Your keys. Your keys to the cockpit. One of you has them. Get out the keys or your passengers die!" Qabrestan screamed at them.

Why, that's the man I spilled water on, thought Carol. She stared at his pistol and grenade. They're real! she thought, and so she reached into her uniform pocket and took out her keys. With trembling hands, she found the key to the cockpit and held it out to Qabrestan.

Just then, Yonnie's shot rang out. Carol spun around as though shot herself. From behind, Qabrestan threw his arm over Carol's chest. She felt the steel of the grenade cold against the skin of her neck.

"You two. Out. Out!" shouted Qabrestan, gesturing with his pistol.

"You open it," he said to Carol viciously, twisting her around to face the cockpit door.

Unable to look down, Carol groped for the lock with her key. She felt faint. Oh God, where is the lock? Finding it at last, she slipped in the key and turned the mechanism. As the door came unlatched, Qabrestan shoved Carol hard from behind, banging the door open. Unable to stop herself, Carol flew forward against the flight engineer's seat. Her fall unchecked, she sprawled onto the cockpit deck. The heads of the flight crew snapped around; the surprise was complete.

Pete Worthington, the pilot, started to move his thumb toward the microphone button on the control wheel.

"No, no. Don't move a finger!" screamed Qabrestan, jumping to Worthington's side and pressing the muzzle of the gun against his temple.

Worthington lifted his thumb from the wheel.

"All right. Take it easy," said Worthington in a calm voice as he eased himself back slightly in the seat, his head forced over at an angle by the pressure of the gun.

"Take off your headsets and unplug them," commanded Qabrestan. "You. Put your keys in my pocket and leave us," he ordered Carol.

Carol got up slowly and did as he asked. Qabrestan followed her to the door, three pairs of headsets over his arm, snapped the lock after her and moved to the empty observer's seat behind Worthington.

"Come to a heading of two-thirty. Set the power for maximum cruise. Don't play games. I understand air navigation."

Putting the pistol in his lap, Qabrestan took the safety pin from around his little finger where he had been wearing it and carefully reinserted it in the grenade. He put the grenade in his coat pocket and flexed the cramped muscles of his left hand. Taking a cigarette from the pack in his shirt pocket, he lit up. He leaned back in the seat and picked up the pistol.

Qabrestan looked around him. As Worthington turned the plane to the southwest, the late afternoon sunlight flooding the small cockpit moved from dead ahead to the right and shone through the clear-view window at the copilot's shoulder. The copilot was hunched over readjusting the navigational instruments to the new course. The flight engineer, on Qabrestan's right, was similarly engaged in setting the thrust of the engines to obtain the greatest possible range.

No one spoke. Here at the very front of the aircraft, the

vibration of the engines and sound of the air rushing over the skin of the plane were all far behind them. The soft, whispering swish of the thin, cold air being thrust aside by the narrow nose of the plane was the only sound heard.

Qabrestan began to grow calmer. He glanced over his left shoulder and was reassured to see the coast of France far below. The worst was over.

Selecting the landing site and working out the details of the flight to get there had been the hardest part of the plan. They needed a place to land where they would be safe from any rescue attempt for the two or three days it would take to meet their demands. They also needed a place that could provide food and water for several hundred persons. Not only that, but when they found a site, how could he make certain the pilots were flying to it and not somewhere else. The decision that he and the brothers would go to the United States after they kidnapped the German banker had helped a lot. With America's casual attitude toward internal travel by foreigners, anything was possible.

An article on Ethiopia in *Time* magazine gave them the perfect landing site. Qabrestan was able to learn basic navigation by taking evening courses in small boat navigation given by the U.S. Coast Guard Auxiliary. After those he sent away for a mail order course in air navigation advertised in a magazine. He did not fully understand the subject, but he did know enough to give directions and prevent the pilot from tricking him.

His thoughts were interrupted by a question from Worthington.

"Where we going? The Azores?"

"No. When you have the Lisbon beacon at two-hundred-and-seventy degrees relative, you will come to a heading to take us to Omega coordinates BH798 and AE979 which is at thirteen degrees north latitude and forty-two degrees, forty-five minutes east longitude."

Russ Conrad, the copilot, turned to Qabrestan.

"Forty-two degrees east longitude?" he repeated incredulously. "We're at zero longitude now, that's a helluva long ways away."

"Yes, but that is the only place we can land safely. If we are not over it at dawn, we will destroy this plane and everyone in it. Do you understand that?" snarled Qabrestan poking his pistol toward Conrad's face.

"I gottcha. No tricks," said Worthington. Then turning to Conrad and the flight engineer, he added, "Charlie, Russ. I'm serious. No tricks. Do like the man says."

Charlie Wall, the flight engineer, nodded. Conrad continued to stare at Qabrestan for a moment before turning back to the plane's flight computer to enter the new destination.

Barbara Mawson had just settled down to writing in her journal when she heard someone shouting and looked up. With a sharp intake of breath and a sudden increase in her heartbeat, she looked past Harriet to see a man shoving a stewardess up the aisle. Then she saw a young woman on the opposite side of the plane waving a small pistol and holding what looked like a hand grenade over her head. The kids! Instinctively, she leaned forward to the space between the two seats before her. Her mind was racing, but years of sailing were paying off. Barbara had found from experience that she could act and think things through at the same time. Up or down, she thought. Better up. The area under the seats is wide open. If the grenade goes off on the deck, it'll spray the entire floor area.

"Emergency," hissed Barbara from between the seats. "Kathy, get down on the seat. Robbie, lie down over her. Get all of you on the cushions and don't move. There may be an explosion so hold on." With that, she reached through the opening and pulled up the middle armrest from between her two children.

Both did as they were told, Robbie doing his best to cover his sister with his body.

"Why do you suppose they picked this flight to hijack?" asked Harriet in a whisper. "My God," she continued, her voice trembling slightly, "could they have known that all of us *Montanas* would be on board?"

Without taking her eyes off of Yonnie Trupp, Barbara whispered, "I don't know. But if they don't know what they've caught, then we don't want to tell them. If you get a chance, pass the word to keep quiet about who we are."

They fell silent as Yonnie edged through the first row of center section seats to their side of the plane. Reaching the left aisle, she stopped in front of Martin Schlosser, who, she knew, was familiar with hand grenades.

"Hold out your right hand," she commanded, carefully keeping the grenade out of reach.

Schlosser hesitantly extended his right hand, searching Yonnie's face for some clue as to what was coming.

"Farther," demanded Yonnie, giving no hint she knew who he was.

Schlosser extended his right hand to arm's length. Yonnie passed her right hand with the pistol over his open palm and let the grenade safety pin she had been holding around her middle finger drop. Schlosser instinctively closed his hand over the pin.

Twisting around to bring her gun hand out of reach, Yonnie shoved her left hand holding the grenade in front of Schlosser's face. Startled, Schlosser recoiled in his seat.

"Insert the pin," said Yonnie with a short laugh at Schlosser's discomfort. "Be careful, my hand is very tired."

Without looking up, Schlosser took her hand in his and slowly rotated it to bring the hole for the safety pin into view. Jan watched, afraid to look at Yonnie.

"Release your grip slightly," said Schlosser evenly. "The holes are not aligned."

As Yonnie relaxed her pressure a bit, the holes came into line. Schlosser slid the pin home.

"*Fertig!*" he exclaimed.

"Up! Up! Everybody up!" shouted Yonnie. "All adults will move to the rear of the aircraft. The children will stay here. Move!" she said, gesturing to Schlosser and Jan.

Schlosser stood up and, with unconscious good manners, waited for Jan to slide out of the seat before following her down the aisle toward the rear of the plane. Jan looked straight ahead as she passed Harriet and Barbara, pretending not to see them.

"You people there. Come over to this side and start back," Yonnie called to a group of passengers milling about in the far aisle.

Then, turning back she gestured toward the remaining passengers seated in front of Harriet and Barbara.

"You stay here," she said to Carol Moore, motioning the other two stewardesses to go aft. As Yonnie followed up the aisle, she noticed Kathy and Robbie lying on the seat. Yonnie looked from Harriet to Barbara who were standing.

"Which of you is the mother of these children?" demanded Yonnie.

"I am," answered Barbara.

"You stay here and keep all children quiet," ordered

Yonnie. Gesturing toward Harriet with the gun, she said, "You join the others in the rear of the plane."

Harriet gave Barbara a long look and joined the passengers streaming aft. Children, carrying playthings and clothes, began appearing in the far aisle, dazed and subdued, urged forward by Abdulla in the after cabin. Barbara stood up and with a glance at Yonnie, who seemed to have no objections, went to them. Carol followed.

"Hi. Why don't you sit over there with my kids," she said, trying to steer the children away from the boots sticking out in the aisle. God, that body's going to be a problem, thought Barbara.

A new problem occurred to her as she recognized Allen Olsen, Junior, son of the ship control officer. Behind young Allen she saw more *Montana* children. That female terrorist may be smart enough to wonder why so many different children all know me. I'll have to beat them to it, she thought.

"Hello everybody," she announced in a loud voice. "My name is Mrs. Mawson. I'm going to help take care of you. I'll show you where the bathrooms are and get you some dinner. Right now, just sit down where you can. When we're all here, we'll find everyone a seat."

As she concluded, he saw Doris Dacovak standing with the last of the children just inside the curtain to the First Class cabin. Barbara went to her.

"I'm Barbara Mawson," she said taking Doris' hand and squeezing it twice.

"Doris Dacovak," the taller woman answered without the slightest hint of recognition. "I'm a nurse. They said I could help with the children."

"I'm Carol Moore," said the stewardess, looking around the crowded cabin. "We'll have to double up the little ones."

"Good idea," Barbara said. Then turning to Doris, "Let's ask if we can move the body."

"Body!" exclaimed Doris.

"Yes, one of the passengers was shot. I think he's dead," Barbara said, nodding in the direction of a small knot of children staring down at the body wedged between the seats at the forward end of the cabin.

Barbara and Doris approached Yonnie, who was standing in the forward end of the cabin with her back against the side of the plane.

"What is it?" Yonnie demanded.

Barbara hesitated. "We'd like to put the body in a lavatory," Doris stated.

"All right," said Yonnie.

"Food," asked Barbara, finding her voice. "Can we serve them dinner?"

"Yes. Yes. I don't care about that. Eat, drink, just don't interfere," said Yonnie.

Barbara settled the children while Doris dragged the body out of sight.

Captain Worthington straightened up from the control panel and twisted around in his seat.

"Lisbon bears ninety degrees left."

"Take a heading for your first way point. Stay on the airway."

"We can't fly an airway without a flight plan. We'll run into somebody. Let me talk to the control center and get us clearance for any place you want," pleaded the pilot.

"No!" Saayed leaped out of his seat and pressed his gun against the back of Worthington's head. "Do not lie to me. We are being tracked on radar right now. They know we are not on your flight plan. They will clear everyone out of our way, and you know it."

"All right. All right. I'm not trying to trick you. I'm just trying to keep us from getting killed. Can I at least change to an altitude for eastbound flights?"

"Yes, but slowly. No tricks."

"I wouldn't think of it," said Worthington and turned to Conrad. "Give me a heading, Charlie."

Conrad leaned forward and punched the buttons on the front of the computer control display unit.

Chapter 5

At 6:27 the air traffic controller at the radar control center outside of London suddenly bent over and peered more closely at the situation developing on the screen before him. Reflecting sudden tension, he licked his lips, which appeared blue and bloodless in the greenish light from the screen. The radar pip that was Pan World Flight 231 had just begun moving southwest while continuing to climb. Two other pips that represented inbound aircraft were now directly in the path of Flight 231.

"Pan World two three one. We have you turning left. Do you wish a new clearance?"

He waited, watching the screen intently. No response came. He repeated the message. Still no response. He would have to vector the other aircraft to keep clear.

"Air France seven four five. Traffic eleven o'clock, southwest bound Pan World two three one climbing out of sixteen thousand. Turn right to oh two four."

"Air France. Turning right to oh two four," came the prompt reply.

"Iberian niner three. Traffic one o'clock, southwest bound Pan World two three one out of sixteen thousand. Turn left to three four four. Continue descent."

"Iberian niner three. Turning left to three four four. Continuing descent," came the Spanish pilot's voice in his ear.

"Pan World two three one. We have you heading two three zero out of seventeen hundred. Do you have an emergency?"

Again he waited, watching the pip move closer to the edge of the screen with every sweep of the set. Hearing no reply, he reached forward and changed radio frequencies while repeating the message. Still no response. The pip was almost to the edge of the screen. He pushed a small button on his console. Moments later, his supervisor appeared at his side.

"Pan World two three one has taken a wide deviation to the southwest from his flight plan. I can't raise him on any frequency. I don't like it. What d'you think?"

"You know what I think. Hijacking. Keep clearing his path. I'll alert Brest that we'll be handing him off to them. If they can't raise him and he continues his present course, I'll declare a hijacking alert."

"Right," said the controller, as he watched Flight 231 continue to move along a course that would take him out over the English Channel toward the Bay of Biscay.

Twelve minutes later, when the radar control center at

Brest, France, was unable to raise Flight 231 and confirmed its continued course to the southwest, the supervisor notified his chief that a hijacking appeared to be in progress. The chief immediately telephoned first Pan World Operations at Heathrow, then Scotland Yard headquarters in London, and finally the Home Ministry.

A young Foreign Service officer, who had duty that evening in the political section at the United States embassy in London, turned reluctantly from a conversation with his officemate when his phone rang.

"Edward Graves here," he said unenthusiastically.

"This is Paul Depiensky," said the voice on the other end of the line. "I'm Operations Director of Pan World Airlines here in London. British radar control center at Leith Hill has just informed us that our Flight two three one out of Heathrow for Washington appears to have been hijacked. The flight is far off course and does not respond to radio calls. We also have been unable to raise them on any company frequencies. I have just declared the flight hijacked and am making formal request for the government's assistance in tracking the aircraft and recovering the passengers after it lands."

"I understand." Graves glanced at his watch. "Mr. Depiensky, would you hold for a moment? I want to get your message to Ambassador Balston before he leaves for an engagement. Then I'll come back and get the details from you."

Graves turned to his colleague.

"Charles. Pan World Airlines Flight two thirty-one out of Heathrow for Washington appears to have been hijacked. Would you please inform the ambassador and the duty defense attaché for me while I get the details?"

Charles reached for the telephone on his desk while Graves resumed his conversation.

"What time did the flight take off and in what direction is it presently headed?" began Graves, pulling a pad toward him.

When he hung up, Graves turned to Charles questioningly.

"The ambassador is waiting for you in his dressing room. How many on board the airplane?"

"Two hundred and eighty-three," Graves said as he headed for the door.

* * *

Raymond Balston continued dressing in front of a wardrobe built into the small room while he heard the hijacking report. The defense attaché, a seasoned army officer, stood in the doorway leading to the ambassador's bedroom.

"No idea why they picked this particular flight or where they're headed?" asked Balston, while he finished tying his black tie.

"No, sir. They're working on getting us a passenger list now," answered Graves.

Satisfied with his appearance, Balston turned to the two men.

"Graves, pass everything we have on to Washington immediately. As soon as you have a passenger list, send it along also. Call the Home Ministry and attempt to work directly with whatever investigating agency of theirs is handling the case. Scotland Yard, I should think. We need to know who the hijackers are and where they may be headed as soon as possible. Remember, pass all information directly to Washington. Do not wait until I've seen it. Send it and tell me afterward."

Balston picked up a dinner jacket that had been laid out for him and slipped it on. Graves stepped forward to assist him. Turning toward the attaché, Balston said,

"Major, inform Defense directly. I think it would be a good idea to have the aircraft's flight tracked, if possible." Then, looking at both men, "Have I forgotten anything, gentlemen?"

"Mr. Ambassador," said the Major, "if I may suggest, sir, it would be most helpful to know the types of weapons aboard and how many hijackers we are dealing with. Perhaps Mr. Graves could attempt to have the British determine that."

"Good point. See if you can find out, Graves," said Balston. Then, looking directly at Graves, "If, God forbid, the situation changes for the worse, inform me immediately wherever I am. Thank you, gentlemen."

Sergeant Goodson stood waiting in front of the door to No. 5. It would be wrong to accuse him of being angry. He was much too experienced a man for that. Annoyed would be a better description of his feelings at this moment. He had waited three hours for his film to come back from the laboratory, and then running the film for the inspector had been anticlimactic. All he had to show were some very clear pictures of a young man coming out of a building. As the inspector himself said, there wasn't anything remarkable about the entire sequence. He made a note to have still photos made from the frames showing the three best views of Henry. He had put the film away and was about to go home to have dinner with his family for the first time in a week when the inspector called him back in with news of the hijacking.

It had taken an hour to find a magistrate and obtain a search warrant. Now the landlady can't get her bloody key to fit the flaming lock, Goodson thought impatiently. Henry, of course, would have had it changed.

"Here, let me have a go," Goodson said to the slovenly woman, taking a ring of master keys from his pocket.

On the fifth attempt, Goodson felt the key turn in the lock. He pushed the door open and entered the musty room. When he saw the bottle cutter on the table, his good humor returned. Here now, that's something, he thought.

Goodson searched the lodgings quickly and professionally. He found the empty cartridge box and three unopened bottles of champagne that Henry had purchased as insurance against breaking a bottle during the cutting. In a dresser drawer, he found a stack of paycheck receipts from White's Flight Kitchen. Along the sides and bottom of one of the empty shoe cartons, he found an interesting checkered pattern of grease stains.

Grenades, Goodson thought as he made his way downstairs to make his report from the landlady's telephone. That's what made those marks. Grenades. Of course, he temporized, the laboratory will have to analyze the grease to be certain, but it was hand grenades.

He was positive the hijackers were armed with pistols and grenades smuggled aboard in champagne bottles by Henry, who worked for an airline food caterer. The fact that Henry made no attempt to hide any of the preparations in his flat meant that he was already on his way out of the country.

Within minutes of receiving Goodson's report, the inspector, as instructed by the Home Office, passed the information directly to Graves at the American Embassy.

Chapter 6

Lieutenant Commander Duke Rodgers leaned forward over the paper napkin spread out on the side of his Pentagon desk. Turning his head, he took a huge bite out of the cheeseburger he held in his left hand. Mustard and mayonnaise oozed from between the buns and ran down his fingers to drip on the napkin. Cold. Stone damn cold, he thought disgustedly as he hungrily took another bite.

Carefully keeping both his mouth and his left hand away from the pages of neat typing on the desk before him, he put down the light-blue pencil he was holding and with his right hand groped for a second napkin. I'm getting too old for this crap, he thought. Man cannot live by cold, soggy bread alone. Three years is enough. I'm going back to sea, he decided as he picked up the pencil and resumed correcting the next-to-final draft of the talking paper in front of him.

For the hundredth time he comforted himself with the fantasy that he would hand in his request for transfer together with this paper. He would not, of course. Being an action officer in OP-6, the Plans, Policy, and Operations section of the Office of the Chief of Naval Operations, was the most important assignment he had ever held. Even if it was also the most nerve-racking. Well, that was the price of playing big league ball. Where else, he thought philosophically, could an unknown lieutenant commander give military advice to the President of the United States? Not that he personally advised the President; that was the job of the Joint Chiefs of Staff.

His job was to do the thinking in his specialty, and that, in turn, was eventually passed to the Joint Chiefs by the Chief of Naval Operations, the military head of the Navy. Even though there were several levels of command between him and the CNO, when it came to questions of politico-naval matters involving the Middle East, it was his thinking, his basic logic, that became the Navy's formal position. The echelons above him served as a group of progressively hard-nosed critics to make sure that his answer was the right one. They always made changes in his work, but so far they had never rejected his basic approach to a solution. In that sense, it was Rodgers' ideas that were recommended to the President. Unfortunately, because the rest of the world did not work or sleep the same hours as he, the job raised hell with his family and social life. As his wife once said when he began to make love to her one night, she knew that some dingbat somewhere was doing his damndest to make her life miserable before morning.

Rogers looked up as a female chief yeoman knocked lightly on the entrance to the cubicle that was his office.

"Sir, briefing at fifteen hundred in The Tank on this," she said, extending a small, folded note toward him.

"Thank you," Rodgers replied, absently taking the note.

The typed words from his boss, Rear Admiral Anderson, the Deputy Chief of Naval Operations and head of the Plans and Policy section, were cryptic and to the point as always. They read:

> Hijacking of a U.S. flag airline flight is in progress. Aircraft will probably land in an African or Middle Eastern nation. Consider military solution options and political/military implications of alternative landing sites.

Rodgers glanced at his watch. 2:47. It took exactly eight minutes to get from his office to The Tank on the first floor of the Pentagon. He had five minutes before he absolutely had to leave. Time enough, he thought, to get this briefing to the typist. Five minutes and twenty-five seconds later, he rose, grabbed his cap, and walked rapidly down the aisle toward the hall. Dropping the completed briefing off on the desk of a civilian typist as he passed, Rodgers hurried down the corridor. The half-eaten cheeseburger lay forgotten on his desk.

He barely made it in time. When he slipped into the back of the large gold-carpeted conference room, which everyone called The Tank, an Army colonel from the Joint Staff was just standing up at the far end of the long dia-mond-shaped table that dominated the room. Recessed spot-lights in the dark-painted ceiling cast small overlapping pools of light over comfortable leather chairs at the table. The brownish drapes, which concealed maps and status displays on the walls, gave a somber and subdued tone to the room.

Rodgers dropped quickly into an empty chair and studied the faces of the fifteen or so officers seated in various attitudes of repose at the table. He recognized most of the younger men as being action officers like himself. In the past three years, he had sat in on hundreds of meetings with the same group. He nodded to Lieutenant Colonels Stanton and Lowell, the Air Force's experts on the African and Middle Eastern nations' air forces. They had worked with him on his first problem: the Israeli move into southern Lebanon. In the chair beside him, Colonel Mac Gelman, who was due for promotion to brigadier and then reassignment in two months, lounged with a large cigar clamped between his teeth. He had met Mac during the crisis brought on by the revolution in Iran when it appeared that U.S. troops might have to be used to evacuate American citizens. Gelman was the Army's specialist in counterinsurgency and a resident expert handball player whom Rodgers, no mean four-wall player himself, had yet to beat. He recognized Air Force Major Henderson from the Joint Reconnaissance Center and Lieutenant Commander Ferrar from Fleet Operations, whose office cubicle was next to his. Rodgers turned toward the head of the table as the colonel from Joint Staff began talking.

"All right gentlemen, here's what we've got. At approximately eighteen forty-five ZULU today, Pan World Flight two three one from London's Heathrow airport, bound for Washington, D.C., was hijacked by an unknown number of persons. The aircraft is a McDonnell Douglas DC ten dash thirty with two hundred eighty-three people on board. It is currently over the Bay of Biscay headed toward the Azores and is expected to turn eastward toward either the north or the west coasts of Africa. Its destination is unknown at this time. However, Pan World estimates it will run out of fuel at oh three hundred ZULU tomorrow morning. It is currently being tracked by air traffic control along its flight path. Brest, France has handed them off to Lisbon. We do not know the type or number of weapons aboard the aircraft or why this particular flight was hijacked. No communication with the aircraft has been made. We are expecting a passenger list momentarily."

The colonel paused for a moment, looking at the group of experts, before continuing.

"State has requested our immediate assistance in tracking the aircraft and our possible assistance in communications, rescue, and evacuation efforts after it lands. OK. Air Force and Navy Operations people, please remain for a meeting with J-three Reconnaissance types to get a preliminary tracking plan. J-six will coordinate a communications plan, and J-five will play mother superior to a joint set of rescue and evacuation contingency plans. For planning purposes, look at everything within a radius of forty-eight hundred miles from London. Any questions?" he asked, looking at the attentive faces before him. None was forthcoming.

"All right, that's it then. It looks like another all-nighter, gentlemen," he stated flatly in a tone that challenged anyone to argue the point. No one did.

As they stood up, Gelman turned to Rodgers.

"You wanna try for our game, or should I cancel us out?"

"Let's go for it. I'll be done with the first go 'round by seventeen-thirty."

"Me too. All I gotta do is issue a strike alert to the Blue Light Battalion in Germany. Besides, we'll be on the premises."

Gelman picked a piece of cigar off his lip, then growled, "See ya in the locker room, kid."

"Right."

Rodgers smiled as he walked down the hall. Gelman was largely responsible for the formation of elite forces known as Blue Light Battalions. They were specifically trained and equipped to rescue hostages being held on aircraft or in airports. These battalions were part of the Army's Airborne Special Forces and wore black berets. For years Gelman's super soldiers had been waiting for an American Entebbe situation to arise. No wonder Mac was happy, Rodgers thought.

Back in his office, Rodgers reached for the phone and dialed his home.

"Hello," came his wife's throaty voice.

"Honey, it looks like we've got an all-nighter going. Don't wait dinner for me."

"But I have a roast," she protested involuntarily.

"I know babe, but what can I tell you? I'll call around eight and say good-night to the kids."

"OK, honey," she replied soothingly, recovering herself. "If you do get home, nudge me. I was hoping for some loving tonight."

"That's a promise," chuckled Rodgers, hanging up the phone and pulling a lined pad toward him.

Although not as simple as Gelman's, the problem he set out to solve was still straightforward. First, he had to analyze the probable political and military reactions of the governments of various nations to the landing of the hijacked airliner within their borders. For every reaction that tended to frustrate the American objectives of speedy recovery of the hostages and the aircraft, he had to devise a series of political or military alternatives. His task was made easier because he only needed to consider those maritime nations that bordered on the coasts of North Africa and the Middle East, since only in such countries could the Navy play the prime role. The problem was further simplified by the fact that the basic position of each government was reliably predictable. Most were friendly and would cooperate with the United States. These governments he ignored, since it was axiomatic that the terrorists would not land within such a nation. There were, in fact, very few places the terrorists could land that presented difficult political or military problems to the United States, and an even fewer number that presented both. There were Tripoli and Benghazi in Libya, Latakia in Syria, and Assab in Ethiopia. If they pick one of those, Rodgers thought, I'll be here all night and then some. He continued writing steadily, covering the pages with his neat handwriting that reflected the orderliness of his thoughts.

Not far from where Rodgers worked, Fleet Admiral Swig Sauer, Chief of Naval Operations, had been waiting for a visitor. He stood up behind the broad expanse of his desk, which sat squarely in front of two large windows, and strode across the dark-blue carpet to greet the woman being shown into the large, comfortably furnished office by his secretary. Sauer was a thickset man of only average height. His energetic stride belied his fifty-eight years. With his short but unruly sandy hair and rosy complexion, he would have appeared cherubic but for his eyes. They were milky-jade in color and as cold as the waters of a northern glacier. Now they warmed with pleasure as he reached out his hands to the willowy, attractive woman coming through the door.

"Mary," he said with genuine affection. "You've gotten more beautiful with the years. Just seeing you makes me feel younger."

Mary laughed, her mouth and eyes carrying well the small lines that formed in her smooth skin. "Swig, you haven't changed a bit."

Without taking their eyes from one another, they sat down together. For an instant they paused as memories of their short but intense affair flooded back over them. Then they both started talking at once, stopped, and laughed together at finding that neither of them felt the slightest embarrassment or awkwardness in meeting again.

Still holding Mary's hand, Sauer leaned toward her. "When Tweedy died I had just about packed it in. Meeting you that summer made all the difference to me. What we felt in Boston I've had with me all these years. I've wanted to say that for the longest time."

He stood up and turned to the window, the pent-up emotions of a decade pouring out of him.

"It's hard to remember how urgent it all was then. When Kincaid took ill and I was transferred to Washington, I wasn't sure how you felt about my suddenly running out on you."

He spun around and looked down at her upturned face.

"I mean it was so damned convenient, my sudden leaving. You know, the older man, young girl story. It made me awkward when we said good-bye."

"I know," she said softly.

He sat down beside her, taking her hands in his again.

"When I got to the Pentagon, I got sucked up in the Vietnam thing. It was the biggest job I'd ever been given. I thought of writing or calling a dozen times. But before I got around to it, I heard you were engaged. I didn't know how to tell you without embarrassing you."

She put a hand to his face.

"Dear, dear Swig," she said shaking her head and smiling. "If I had known you'd worry so, I would have written. I wish I had. Meeting you got rid of all my hang-ups. I was a truly strung-out Irish Catholic lady, a real throwback, when it came to sex. I was twenty-eight and hiding behind a Ph.D. in psychology. When you made love to me in that hotel room, I was freed. You were so gentle, so sure, you made it seem so right. When I realized I could enjoy sex without feeling guilty, I was free. I couldn't believe it. You remember, I almost broke my neck trying to see everything you were doing. I loved it. What's more, when I saw that I could give you pleasure in return, I felt like a woman for the first time in my life."

"I'd hoped that's the way you felt, but I just didn't know," Sauer said.

"Well, I did. What's more, I'd wanted to marry Mike for years before you took me to Boston. I was afraid to. It almost drove him crazy. When you left, I walked around in a daze for weeks because the experience made that big an impact on my emotions. I was completely happy and felt good about the whole thing. As soon as I came to and realized that you were truly gone, I latched on to Mike as fast as I could." Mary's expression changed slightly. "Did you hear we lost Mike to cancer?"

"No!" Genuinely shocked, Sauer reached out and took Mary's hand in his. "When? I had no idea."

"A year ago last February. It was very quick. A brain tumor. We heard in November. They put him on chemotherapy, but it didn't help."

Sauer looked her full in the face. His eyes filled with pain for her and the memory of his own loss. "Mary, Mary. I know what you're going through. Are you all right?"

"*Went* through. I'm fine now, Swig. Really," she said patting Sauer's hand and smiling. "I mean, I'm thirty-nine. I had almost ten years with the world's best husband. I've got three terrific kids, and I'm recognized as one of the few nonweirdo psychologists. All because *you* taught me to screw the eyeballs out of a man. What more can a poor working girl ask?"

"Good for you," he said, matching her grin.

The phone on his desk buzzed. The warmth went out of his eyes as he moved to the desk and picked up the instrument.

"Admiral Courts and his team are on the way for their meeting at sixteen hundred," said his secretary Margaret's voice.

"Very well. Send them straight in," Sauer said, winking at Mary as he composed herself.

A few minutes later, the door opened and a group of eight officers came into the room. It was obvious that all but the tall admiral leading the way were experiencing varying degrees of stage fright at being in the office of the Navy's most senior officer—the degree being inversely proportional to the rank. Seeing the ensign who was nervously fumbling with the chart easel, Sauer remembered an experience of his own. Fresh out of the Academy, he had tripped over the coaming on the old cruiser *Lancaster* when he first reported to the captain.

He's got the leg set up the wrong way around, Sauer thought as he moved to meet the admiral who was advancing toward him.

"Avast setting up that easel, Mister," Sauer said quietly, but with a voice that could be heard anywhere. "We won't have time for it," Sauer explained, answering the admiral's questioning expression. Taking the man by the arm, Sauer led him to where Mary was sitting. She rose at their approach.

"Mary, allow me to present Vice Admiral Robert Courts, my Deputy CNO for Personnel and Chief of Naval personnel."

Mary extended her hand which was instantly taken by Courts.

"Bob, I'd like you to meet Doctor Mary O'Hegarty, Chief Scientist for DARPA's Motivational Research Group in New London and a longtime friend."

As the two exchanged how-do-you-do's, Sauer turned to the waiting officers. "Gentlemen, I believe you will find there are enough seats for you all.

"I had intended to hear your presentation, but I have a meeting on a more urgent matter starting in ten minutes. However, I did want to take what time remains to impress upon you personally the importance I attach to your appearance tomorrow before the Human Resources Subcommittee of the House Armed Services Committee." Sauer moved several paces to his desk, collecting his thoughts. Ready, he turned again to the room and smiled. "The situation is both simple and extremely sensitive. Without the draft and with a booming economy, the Navy does not now have sufficient eligible and available males to operate our fleet. We must, therefore, fill shipboard requirements with women. When Judge Sirica declared the law prohibiting women from serving in vessels other than transports and hospital ships unconstitutional, he opened the way for the assignment of women to all noncombatant vessels. Since that action, we have found that we are not getting sufficient numbers of women reenlist-

ments because career opportunities in noncombatant ships are
severely limited. In order to increase the billets available to
women, we need the law changed to permit women to serve
in any Navy ship without restrictions in combat roles."

Sauer paused, no longer smiling. Every officer in the
room was well aware of his position on women serving in
warships. That was not the problem. Slowly turning his head
as he spoke so that everyone present had to look him in the
eye briefly, he continued.

"The Navy does not need the law changed this year.
This is a presidential election year. God help the officer, beginning with me, who allows himself to get tagged by the
press as advocating the killing in combat of young American
women. I can think of nothing that would more surely
destroy a career. There is truly a season for all things, and
this summer is not the time for any representative of the
Navy to even appear to advocate such an historic social step.
And, gentlemen, the committee chairman, the Honorable
Ralph A. Dickerson damn well knows it. The Navy requested
the law be changed over a year ago. The subcommittee's decision to hold hearings on our request at this time was mo-
tivated primarily by political considerations. The chairman
hopes to generate publicity that is adverse to the present administration."

Sauer turned to Mary.

"What do you think, Mary? Your group's about as vulnerable to Dickerson's attack as the Navy."

"That's true. Although DARPA is part of the DOD, most
of the work done by my group is for the Navy with Navy Department funds. I'm sure Mr. Dickerson wouldn't worry about
fine distinctions."

Mary paused as if selecting her words.

She looked at Sauer and shrugged.

"Our findings on women in combat put us in much the
same position with respect to Mr. Dickerson. Our research
shows, and I plan to testify to this tomorrow, that the only
psychological problems associated with women serving uncon-
ditionally in combat are strictly societal. That is, the reactions
of women to the stresses of combat are expected to be identical to those of men. The primary problem is the traditional
cultural view of man, not woman, as the warrior. We have no
data on this since it involves the attitude of the nation as a
whole, rather than an individual Navy member. We can,

however, observe that traditional views have changed radically in the past decade. The second primary problem is the tradition of separation of sleeping and toilet facilities. Although mundane, this tradition, which our research shows must be continued, precludes women from serving in some older combat vessels in which the berthing spaces for men are already marginal. In such ships, there simply isn't sufficient space available to provide separate facilities for female crew members without degrading combat effectiveness. New construction isn't a problem, since the facilities can be designed in."

Mary looked around at the faces in the little group and smiled.

"I don't plan to stress the toilet habits of our American culture, but if Dickerson wants headlines, God knows the data is there for his use. My hope is that Representative Patricia Stratton and other members of the committee who are of the incumbent political party will temper the worst of Mr. Dickerson's thrusts. If not, then heaven help me," Mary concluded, raising her hands. A ripple of appreciative laughter passed through the group.

Relaxing, Sauer leaned back against the edge of his desk and smiled at the intense young faces before him. He knew Mary was a fine woman, now he knew she had an equally fine mind. He was impressed.

"Then we must all frustrate Mr. Dickerson's hopes. Any headlines resulting from these hearings must be generated by members of the subcommittee, not by testimony of Navy witnesses. Each of you will testify fully and completely to the facts of your individual area of knowledge. Stay with the facts. Constantly bear in mind that the decision to permit women to serve in combat is Congress', not the Navy's. Don't allow yourselves to be drawn into making that conclusion for them; leave that for the committee members. Present only the facts. Doctor O'Hegarty here is the nation's expert on human motivation in naval environments. Refer all questions that even imply motivational consideration to her. That's it. Leave me a copy of the briefing and good luck."

As the group began filing out, Sauer turned to Courts and Mary who had stood up.

"Bob, I'm worried most about you," Sauer said in a voice that only the three of them could hear. "You'll be under the most pressure."

"Thank you, sir," grinned Courts, "but I plan to give them the advanced idiot treatment. It's amazing how dense I can become when matters of opinion are involved."

"Exactly," grinned Sauer as he turned slightly to Mary.

"I realize Bob has a lot to discuss with you, but if you're free later, I'd love to take you to dinner. As you may have heard, a Pan World flight from London was hijacked this afternoon and is flying to God knows where. By tomorrow, the situation could be critical, and I might not have another chance to see you before you leave."

"I'd love to," Mary said putting her hand on his arm without the slightest embarrassment.

"Good. I've got a meeting on our contingency plans for the hijacking coming up now, but it should be over before six. I'll pick you up at Bob's office?"

"Perfect," Mary said, receiving a nod in answer to her questioning looks to Courts.

Mary turned and preceded Courts out of the office. Courts carefully kept any trace of the fact that he found this entire conversation between his boss and this striking-looking woman most unusual and interesting. He knew Sauer had been a widower for some time, but this was the first time he had ever heard of the admiral showing the slightest interest in a lady. He searched his memory. No, he thought as he pulled the door closed behind him, I'm sure there's never been even a hint of involvement. Not that it would be wrong if there were. Suddenly, he wondered just how long the admiral had known Dr. O'Hegarty and just as promptly castigated himself for holding an unworthy thought. Nevertheless, he turned to Mary with increased interest. She must be quite a woman if, as it seemed, the Old Man was attracted to her.

Sauer sat down at his desk and picked up the phone. His somewhat stubby finger shot out and punched the intercom button at the base of the instrument.

"Yes, Admiral?" questioned Margaret's cool and even voice.

Sauer fought down a sudden impulse to say something outrageous to his seemingly unflappable secretary; his spirits were that buoyant.

Instead, he simply said, "Margaret, when Admiral Anderson and his gang arrive, send them straight through."

"Yes, Admiral," came Margaret's voice, bringing a smile

to Sauer's lips. I wonder what she would say if I told her to skip down the hall in barefeet and fetch me a pail of water. You're getting dotty in your old age, he chuckled to himself, knowing full well his high spirits were due solely to the anticipation of having dinner with Mary. Shaking his head, he picked up Court's briefing and began reading.

He had not quite finished when the door opened and the tall, rangy frame of Vice Admiral Andy Anderson, DCNO Plans, Policy, and Operations appeared in the doorway followed by several officers, including Duke Rodgers.

Something about Anderson's expression brought Sauer immediately alert.

"What's up, Andy?" asked Sauer.

"We just got word from Norfolk. Brewer, Commander SubRon forty-two in Loch Tiree, called in a few minutes ago. Families of the *Montana* are on board the hijacked aircraft."

"How many?" asked Sauer in a flat voice.

"We don't know yet, sir. We have the passenger list from State and we're checking now. Brewer's estimate was over a dozen families including those of Commander Mawson, the captain, and Lieutenant Commander Edelstone, the XO."

"Mawson? Do the hijackers know who they've got?"

"We don't know that either, sir. Intelligence is working with the Agency boys both here and in London, but so far they say there's very little to go on. I've got an intelligence summary in our briefing, but there's nothing in it on why they picked Flight two three one. They say we probably won't know until the hijackers announce their demands. So far there's been no communication from the aircraft of any type."

Sauer leaned back in his chair and exhaled slowly through pursed lips as he considered Anderson's words. The news touched him personally. He knew the Mawson family well and had been with them all in their big Newport house only a few weeks ago. He made a mental note to call the old admiral and reassure him.

Reassure him about what? thought Sauer. I don't like it at all. It's starting out badly. Too complicated. Barbara, the children, and all the others are on that flight because of him, he realized guiltily. All because a year ago he had approved a new policy of rewarding the entire families of outstanding crew, rather than the ship itself as was done in the past. He had endorsed the policy change and sought the necessary funds from Congress. Research, Mary's research he supposed, had shown that such rewards would reduce desertion and lack of reenlistment, which was running at a peacetime high.

Suddenly he came full alert. Tomorrow morning Mary and Courts were appearing before the same subcommittee that had approved the extra funds a year ago. The situation was made to order for Dickerson's use. He reached for the phone.

"Sit down, gentlemen," he said as he punched his direct line to the phone on Courts' desk.

"Yes, sir," came Courts' voice.

"Bob, we've got problems with the hijacking situation that involve both you and Doctor O'Hegarty. I think it's best if you both hear Andy's briefing and become part of the team. Don't worry about your briefing tomorrow. I doubt if you'll ever get to give it. We'll wait until you get here before starting."

"I know. My boys just told me, sir. Give me five minutes to get my brains and we're on our way," Courts' voice said as the line went dead.

Sauer turned to the puzzled expressions facing him.

"Admiral Courts and Doctor O'Hegarty, a civilian psychologist, are joining us," he said to Anderson. "While we're waiting, I want you to consider the following point," he continued, turning and looking at Rodgers, but speaking to the group at large. "This is an election year. In all your planning, impact upon the election must be a primary consideration. Specifically, I want the potential for exploitation in the press by the opposition party to be assessed for contingency policies and plans. Let me say it more bluntly. We not only must play whatever role is assigned to us in successfully resolving the hijacking, but we must do it in a manner that presents the least opportunities for the Navy to become a pawn in the forthcoming election."

Sauer leaned forward and rested his arms on the desk top.

"I've made this speech twice today. Maybe it's time I set the record straight. As naval officers we are, in theory, not interested in politics as a group. However, the realities are such that our actions in an election year will be exploited by both parties for their own purposes, but not equally. If both the President and the Navy receive favorable publicity over the handling of some situation, well and good. If, however, the Navy receives unfavorable publicity over some situation and the opposition uses it against the President, then we are doubly damned, regardless of who wins the election. So, like it or not, the Navy is part of each incumbent President's team. During his term, our actions are intimately bound together with his, for better or for worse. The Navy's interests can never be served by causing embarrassment to our Commander in Chief."

The door opened. Mary and Courts, came in. Sauer waved them toward the settee near the coffee table.

"Let's have it now, Andy," Sauer said smilingly to Anderson.

Anderson stood up and walked to an easel set up where all could see. Turning back to the blank cover sheet, he began explaining the known facts of the hijacking, using charts prepared by Rodgers. Occasionally referring to a talking paper, also prepared by Rodgers' group, Anderson quickly presented a chart showing a map of the north coast of Africa and the Mediterranean and Red Seas.

"The aircraft is being tracked by military radar located here, here, and here," Anderson said, his pointer skipping lightly from place to place. "It was just crossing the Tunisian border when this chart was prepared. Its flight path will carry it over the island of Malta. As you can see, so far the track has been arrow straight, indicating that whoever's in command is probably following a definite flight plan toward a previously selected landing site."

Anderson turned and faced the group.

"As we see it, the hijackers had two critical tactical problems. The first was getting the needed weapons aboard the aircraft. We now know from a Scotland Yard investigation that weapons disguised in empty champagne bottles were placed aboard by an employee of the food service contractor. Fortunately, the size of the bottles limits the selection of weapons to handguns and grenades, probably fragmentation. There's no evidence that either heavy explosives or automatic weapons are on board."

Turning back to the chart, Anderson raised his pointer once again.

"Which brings us to their second tactical problem. The hijackers, if they have planned at all, and their flight path indicates they have, would realize that most of the possible landing sites are hostile to them. Only a few could be considered either neutral or friendly. Ideally, they would want to find another Entebbe. Of the possible landing sites along the coasts within the range of the aircraft, four are considered to be the most desirable from a terrorist's point of view. We have no indication that the terrorists aboard Flight two three one are aware of these sites. We have selected them purely for planning purposes. If they land at any one of them, we're faced with a worst-case situation."

Anderson's pointer came to rest on Tripoli.

"Tripoli and Benghazi would suit them. We believe the government of Libya would support the terrorists' needs to the point of giving them automatic weapons and high explosives. To a lesser degree, a landing at Latakia in Syria would also work for them. However, the Syrian government would probably supply automatic weapons only under severe duress. As we'll see in a moment, none of these three sites represents an overly difficult or high-risk military rescue operation, with or without the host country's cooperation. The fourth site, Assab in Ethiopia, is a different matter altogether."

Anderson's pointer jumped nearly a thousand miles to the tip of the Red Sea.

"The air strip at Assab is located on a Soviet naval base that was made fully operational seven months ago. The Soviet position, vis-a-vis hijackers of Western aircraft, has never been adequately defined. The few hijackings of Soviet aircraft have been treated as political defections by the Western nations. In almost every case, we've been supportive of the hijacker. Generally, we haven't accepted the Soviet view that these defectors were terrorists. It's possible that the Soviet might adopt a similar view if a terrorist group landed at Assab. The point is that, without Soviet cooperation, a rescue at Assab constitutes a significant risk to both the assault forces and the passengers since it's a fully operational military base. Fortunately, it is also equally probable that the Soviets will cooperate fully."

Anderson turned away from the charts and looked toward Sauer.

"Assab represents another significant risk because it lies at the extreme range of the DC ten dash thirty aircraft. We estimate that upon arrival over Assab, the aircraft would have no more than thirty minutes of fuel remaining, probably less. If the Soviets prevented the aircraft from landing, the pilot would be hard pressed for an alternate landing site within range of his remaining fuel. The nearest strip is at Obock in Djibouti, approximately eighty air miles away. It could be a very near thing. It could be a disaster."

Anderson turned back to the charts and began discussing the Navy's role in military rescue operations at the four candidate landing sites. As he was speaking, the office door opened and a female lieutenant from BuPers came in carrying a thick folder. She handed it to Courts as unobtrusively as possible. He glanced at the material in the folder and nodded to the lieutenant who turned and left.

Anderson's voice droned on. Duke Rodgers had trouble concentrating on the admiral. His mind kept going back to what Sauer had said earlier. Sauer's words had bothered him, but he could not quite put his finger on it. Ostensibly, it appeared that the realities of American politics during an election campaign would affect military planning only in minor ways.

The planning must be cautious but with a very high probability of success. With almost three hundred civilian lives at stake, there was a need to get in and get out quickly, to get the job done with precision and with few losses. But these factors were not political; they were already primary considerations from a purely military point of view. That was the nature of successful operations of this type. Politics had nothing to do with it.

What was it, then, about Sauer's words that bothered him? He didn't know. It had something to do with politics, of that he was certain. An important aspect they were missing. His brows came together in concentration, and he slipped lower in the deep comfortable chair, lost in thought.

Suddenly, Rodgers looked up coming completely alert. Anderson had stopped talking. Everyone in the room was looking at him, Rodgers. What had been said? he thought in panic. Goddamnit, why'd he always daydream like this? Fool, he thought.

He knew the rules of the game. As the junior officer who prepared the briefing, he was expected to be present and ready to field any questions that were beyond the senior officer's personal knowledge. That's it, he realized. Admiral Anderson had finished the briefing and Admiral Sauer had asked a question. Anderson must have referred it to him.

Involuntarily, carried by training alone, Rodgers began to stand up, his mind frantically trying to recall the admiral's question. He glanced at Anderson, who stood looking at him expectantly with absolute confidence in his ability to answer. Now he had it. Admiral Sauer had asked about the presence of Cuban ground troops at Assab. Rodgers began to relax, vowing never to dope off again during a briefing.

"Yes, sir," he responded carefully, keeping any hint of the relief he felt out of his voice. "There are approximately seventeen thousand Cuban ground troops in Ethiopia. The latest intelligence estimate divides this force roughly into thirds. About six thousand troops are deployed in the Ogaden region against Somalian guerillas. Another force of similar strength, headquartered in Asmara, is engaged with Eritrean rebels. The remaining troops are in reserve in Assab."

Sauer nodded.

"Good briefing, gentlemen. I'll approve that for JCS coordination. Andy, if you'll join us, I'll not detain the rest of you any further."

Anderson moved to the coffee table as the junior officers trooped out.

"Mary," said Sauer, "This is Admiral Andy Anderson, my Deputy CNO for Plans and Policies."

Sauer turned to Anderson.

"Andy, I'd like you to meet Doctor Mary O'Hegarty, Chief Scientist at DARPA, New London."

"How do you do," said Anderson, smiling as he sat down.

Sauer surveyed the little group around the low table. He pulled up a chair and sat down to join them. They were a good group. Each a first-rate mind and, except for Mary, personally selected for the job. It occurred to him he was glad that Mary was here. The next few days could get rough. It was good to have her near.

"What I'm concerned with is simply this," Sauer began quietly, "wherever the aircraft's coming down, it will be during the night. By the time the hearings begin tomorrow morning, the hijacking with the Navy families aboard will be the big story of the day. The Honorable Mr. Dickerson won't let an opportunity to participate in the headlines escape him if he can help it. He's certain to view the presence of Navy dependents aboard the flight as fertile ground for unfavorable publicity toward the President. What did we tell him last year regarding the use of civilian versus military transportation in implementing the new rewards policy?" Sauer asked of Courts grimly.

Courts, all eyes focused on him, put on a pair of reading glasses and shuffled through the thick file folder on his lap. He found what he was searching for and looked up.

"We requested military transportation."

The officers of the little group relaxed visibly. Mary's eyes were on Sauer.

"Did we make an issue of the use of military transportation because of security?" asked Sauer, not relaxing at all.

Courts handed the briefing chart copy he was holding to Sauer to read. "No. I'm afraid not. Security was listed as only one of several benefits derived from the use of military transportation. As you see, cost and availability are listed above security," pointed out Courts.

"Then why are we using commercial air and not MAC? Was that our decision?" Sauer demanded.

Courts dove back into the file and scanned the copy of the Congressional Record, a recording of the hearings. Again, silence descended on the room.

"Here it is," Courts said finally, his finger stabbing out at the text before him. "Chairman Dickerson made the use of commercial air a condition of budget approval. His statement at the time was that the government ought not to compete with private industry for holiday passengers. We're clean." Courts concluded, taking off his glasses, the relief obvious in his voice.

"Balls!" exclaimed Sauer roughly. "Excuse me, Mary," Sauer went on without stopping or noting Mary's smile. "That statement is going to act as a red flag to Dickerson."

Sauer paused, deep in thought.

"There's something about this situation that bothers me. I can't pin it down yet, but I don't like the way it's shaping up."

Sauer turned to Mary.

"Mary, what was your position on this question?"

Mary thought for a moment.

"If I remember correctly, our research showed that offering a MAC flight to a service family would not be viewed as a reward by the family. They always fly MAC. Offering them full-fare service aboard a commercial airliner would.

Our recommendation was to use commercial flights rather than military. I briefed the committee to that effect. Of course, factors such as security and costs were not considered since our study was limited to the motivational aspects of the problem."

Then, looking from Courts to Anderson, and finally directly at Sauer, Mary added.

"Excuse me for interjecting myself into the operational world, but my professional curiosity makes me itch to know. What're you going to tell the men of the *Montana* about their families? For that matter, are you going to tell them at all?"

Chapter 7

The vegetation closed around him like a cloak . . . thick, green, and damp. The sun broke through the tangle of plants overhead in occasional thin shafts of hot light. Small vines clung to his fatigues, impeding his cautious progress. The smell of decay and rot lay heavily upon the humid air. He stopped and listened. The VC were near. Very near. In the distance, he heard the cry of a bird. Of sounds moving along the ground, he heard nothing. Satisfied, he turned his shoulder against the jungle wall and pushed his foot out. His skin itched unbearably under the strap of his wristwatch. His heart pounded loudly in his ears. Through his half-opened mouth he took shallow breaths that could not be heard beyond a yard.

Captain Manuel Torres, Commanding Officer of Charlie Company, 1st Battalion, 9th Special Forces Group (Airborne), woke up. A dream, a stinking rotten dream, he thought with infinite relief.

He shook his head in the darkness of the small room and rolled over onto his back, his hands clasped under the pillow. The gold of the crucifix on his bare chest gleamed in what little light came from the open window by the narrow bed. The heavy, clean smell of newly cut hay from the German countryside surrounding the Army post reminded him of his home in east Texas. Within minutes he was again fast asleep.

Moments later the door of his room in the BOQ opened silently. The figure of the duty runner from Charlie Company headquarters was briefly framed in the light from the hall. The runner, flashlight in hand, took hold of one of Torres' feet, the only place a sleeping Black Beret can be safely awakened, and gently shook it.

"Cap'n Torres. Cap'n Torres. Wake up. We got an Ammo Alert goin' down."

Torres, instantly awake, threw back the light blanket and stood up dressed only in his shorts.

"What's up?" asked Torres, turning on the light.

"A hijacked airliner over the Mediterranean. The whole battalion's saddling up. Lieutenant Gorman said to tell everyone it's desert gear."

"OK," Torres said, waving the runner out.

He looked at his watch. 2313. He had been asleep an hour and had no memory of the dream that had awakened him such a short time ago.

Torres moved rapidly but purposefully through a well-practiced procedure, carefully planned to dress and pack him for combat in any part of the world within ten minutes. First he went to the closet of his small room and dragged out a large barracks bag on which the word DESERT was stenciled in white, ignoring the bags stenciled ARCTIC and JUNGLE. With his free hand, he reached up and lifted his personal weapon, a Heckler & Koch HK21 SAW submachine gun, from its hook.

He dragged the bag to the bed. The muscles of his wiry body rippled at the effort. Of average height, Torres was fighting trim. As did all Black Berets, he had not a spare ounce of either fat or muscle. Endurance, not brute strength, was the prime need of every member of this elite outfit. Each man had to be fully prepared to drop behind unfriendly lines within hours of receiving an initial strike order, march one hundred miles into combat, conduct a successful strike, and then either fight or infiltrate their way to a pickup zone.

The Black Berets had been formed after the Israeli raid on Entebbe and were trained only for desert and jungle strikes. After the Soviets shot down a Korean airliner, causing it to crash land on a frozen lake in northern Russia, they added arctic strikes to their mission capabilities.

First Battalion, known as a Blue Light Force, was specifically trained and equipped to rescue hostages being held by terrorists aboard commercial airliners. Alpha Company was trained to break into aircraft made by Lockheed, Bravo Company was trained to force its way aboard Boeing planes, and Charlie Company specialized in rescuing hostages being held aboard aircraft manufactured by McDonnell Douglas.

Both the Israeli and West German raids had shown that losses to both the hostages and the strike force could be minimized by attacking as soon as possible after the hijacked aircraft landed. The longer the assault was delayed, the higher the losses. To cut reaction time to minimum, two Blue Light battalions were rotated between duty in Heidelberg, West Germany, and Fort Bragg, North Carolina. All equipment needed to carry out the battalion's mission was pre-positioned on the Heidelberg post. The 1st Battalion trained constantly with practice alerts, identical to real alerts except that ammunition and live ordinance were never issued.

Torres leaned the SAW against the wall and opened his bag. Stripping off his shorts, he reached into the bag and took out a clean pair and a light weight T-shirt that formed the top layer of clothes. He dressed quickly, slipping into sand-colored combat fatigues on which multitoned camouflage patterns stood out boldly. He pulled out a helmet covered with cloth of an identical pattern and a pair of jump boots. Removing a pair of socks and a khaki handkerchief from the helmet, he sat down on the bed and put on his boots. Jamming the handkerchief into his pocket, he reached into the bag and took out a webbed harness. It was heavy with attached pouches that contained map case, binoculars, canteen medic pack, and combat knife. It also held an ammunition clip holder which, at the moment, held only a pair of sunglasses.

He wriggled into the harness and snapped the shackle in place. Reaching down into the very bottom of the bag with one hand, Torres pulled out his bulging field pack that contained everything he needed for five days. With his other hand, he stripped off the now-empty equipment bag. Stepping to the dresser, he distributed his wallet, change, notebook, and pen into various pockets. He jammed the helmet on his head, picked up the field pack and SAW in one hand, turned out the light, and left the room without a second glance. From the time the duty runner had first spoken his name to the time he softly closed the door to the room, only eight minutes had passed.

In the hall, other similarly dressed 1st Battalion officers were beginning to emerge from their rooms. Halfway down the corridor, Second Lieutenant Bo Johnstone, Leader of Charlie Company's 3rd Platoon, swung into step beside Torres.

"Did y'all heah what kinda plane, suh?" Johnstone asked, hitching his pack over his shoulder.

"No, Bo. I didn't," responded Torres looking at the lanky, blonde-haired youngster beside him. "All I know is that it's still in the air over the Med. We'll know soon enough."

"Yes, suh. I surely do hope it's a DC-ten. Then it's ouah bird fer sure."

Torres smiled. Johnstone was an avid, upland bird hunter. The two of them had discussed shooting many times. They felt much the same about the sport. The crisp fall air. The brilliant colors of the leaves after a hard frost. The eager working of a good dog. The sudden explosion of bird from cover, always unexpected however much anticipated.

As they neared the door of the building, First Lieutenant Al Lewis, Charlie Company's Adjutant, hurried down the stairs from the upper floor. A huge combat knife was strapped across his belly, lengthwise, to the webbing of his harness. The leaded hilt rested just below his navel where his right hand could draw it in an instant.

"Tanzola down yet?" Lewis asked. "Maybe just this once I could beat him."

"Speedy Tanzola?" Torres asked with a grin as the small group hurried out the door. "No way, Al. That guy uses magic."

"Or clones," interjected Johnstone laconically as he joined Torres in looking for their driver.

"Over here, Captain," came the voice of a very boyish-looking officer, standing by a jeep that was pulled up to the right of the BOQ entrance.

The group moved toward the jeep.

"What kept you guys?" asked Second Lieutenant Joe Tanzola, 1st Platoon Leader.

"Tanzola, how d'you do it?" Lewis asked with a grin. He

heaved himself up into the rear of the jeep and sat down with his pack on his knees.

Johnstone followed Lewis up while Torres settled himself in the front passenger seat and nodded to the driver. Tanzola handed Lewis and Johnstone his pack and weapon, then he quickly climbed up and squeezed himself between them.

"A misspent youth, Lieutenant," confessed Tanzola taking his weapon from Johnstone and turning to Lewis.

"Youth? Shit!" guffawed Lewis as he dumped the pack on Tanzola's lap.

"Go," said Torres to the driver.

The jeep moved rapidly away from the BOQ, which stood like a lighted oasis of activity in an otherwise still and dark post.

Second Lieutenant Paul Gorman, 2nd Platoon Leader, was waiting for them as they pulled up in front of Charlie Company's orderly room. All but Torres jumped out of the jeep to join their platoons.

While Gorman walked the few steps to the jeep, Torres turned in his seat and looked quickly but carefully at the scene around him. In the harsh glare of floodlights positioned high on wooden telephone poles, Charlie company was forming up. Under the urgings of the platoon sergeants who seemed to be everywhere at once, the three platoons were falling in. From the open window of the orderly room, came the voice of First Sergeant Mulaney as he directed the headquarters section.

Preparations are well in hand, thought Torres as he spied a radio operator with a field transceiver on his back, a runner, and Lieutenant Gorman all approaching on the double.

"Commanders' call in five minutes at Brigade HQ, Captain," said Gorman saluting. The radio operator and runner also saluted and climbed into the back of the jeep.

"I'm on my way," Torres replied, returning the salute. "What about transportation?"

"It's on the way, sir. And, for what it's worth, Mulaney says the aircraft is a DC-ten. I don't know how he knows," Gorman's grin seemed to float disembodied in the air as the edge of his helmet cast the upper half of his face in deep shadows so that only his mouth and chin were visible.

"Suits me," said Torres, twisting around to glance at the

two men in the back seat, who would now accompany him everywhere.

"Go," he said as he returned Gorman's salute.

Gorman barely had time to step back before the jeep started to move.

Twenty minutes later, Torres was back. He jumped from the jeep and moved quickly to the knot of officers awaiting him. With a quick glance he saw that the trucks had arrived and were being loaded with men and the company's few man-movable fire-support weapons. Nine M60 machine guns, two 60-mm mortars, and three M47 Dragon antitank missile launchers that had just recently replaced the older 90-mm recoilless rifles. Not much, but enough, thought Torres as he came up to the expectant-looking group.

"It's a DC-ten dash thirty. Load the assault kit," ordered Torres.

Second Lieutenant Johnstone let out a rebel yell that echoed down the dark and silent streets.

"Knock it off," demanded Lewis, trying to appear stern while grinning from ear to ear.

All of them felt the same way. Yet, had they been asked, none of them could have explained why they felt such pleasure. Part of the feeling was one of reward. They had trained long and hard for the job. Part of the feeling was the simple pride that has sustained elite groups of fighting men down through the centuries. They were the best, and because they were the best, the honor of the assault was rightfully theirs.

Upon hearing Torres' announcement, Second Lieutenant Tanzola left the group as Torres began briefing the others on what he had learned at brigade. Tanzola jogged toward the open door of the company supply room at the side of the headquarters building. There, men from his platoon stood waiting. The platoon sergeant, Too Quick Jones, a tall black man, stepped forward.

"Is she ours, Lieutenant?" asked Too Quick. The sergeant had gotten his nickname during an early training exercise when he found himself alone in the mockup, the others of his platoon having failed to break in at all.

"Ten dash thirty, Too Quick," shouted Tanzola.

"Alllrrright!" exclaimed Too Quick, preceding Tanzola into the supply room.

Much of the large room looked like any other supply

center. To one side, there was a counter behind which Charlie Company's everyday equipment could be seen. The opposite side of the room, however, was given over to the storage of what, at first glance, appeared to be slightly flattened, oval-shaped, plastic coffins resting in racks that reached from floor to ceiling. Farther into the room, one could see that the containers, which were coated with a non-reflecting black paint and fitted with six handles of nylon webbing, were much too long to be coffins.

Too Quick went directly to four containers stored one above the other in a rack near the door. Putting his hand on the uppermost, he said,

"These four."

Tanzola bent over the ends of the containers and forced all thoughts from his mind as he silently read the barely visible identification marks painted in a slightly lighter shade of black. Take your time and really read it, he told himself. Tanzola bent closer.

The containers held all the special equipment needed to break into the aircraft. Each set of containers covered a different airplane model. The equipment, therefore, was not interchangeable. During one early learning exercise, the 1st Platoon had brought the wrong set of containers, and the entire company had to wait while Tanzola and his men went back and corrected their mistake. There could be no going back this time.

Satisfied, Tanzola stepped back.

"OK. Go," he declared.

The words were hardly out of his mouth when six men slid the uppermost container out of the rack. At a jog, they carried the container to the waiting truck. Within moments, Tanzola was on his way to report to Captain Torres.

"Very good," said Torres, after hearing Tanzola's report. "Ride with me, and I'll brief you on the way to the airstrip."

Tanzola squeezed himself into the back of the jeep, the runner and the radioman making as much room for him as possible. Torres stood up in the front seat and raised his arm over his head to attract the attention of Lieutenant Lewis and the others.

"Move 'em out," Torres shouted, dropping his arm.

The trucks began to roll for the short drive to the military airstrip that was on the opposite side of the post. When his jeep had taken its place at the head of the column, Torres turned to Tanzola.

"Pan World Flight two three one out of London was hijacked this evening. Of the two hundred eighty-three people on board, one hundred seventeen are Navy dependents. The aircraft is over the Mediterranean and, at last report, was heading for the coast of Egypt. It'll have to land by oh three hundred ZULU when they estimate it'll run out of fuel. There've been no communications with the aircraft. It's known, however, that the only weapons aboard are 9-mm C-141 automatic pistols and fragmentation grenades. The number of terrorists is unknown. There was a report that they're an IRA group, but no one believes it. Charlie Company will make the assault, if there is one. Right now we'll load up in C-141 and stand by in Ready Alert status at the airstrip. We'll issue live ammo and ordinance while we're waiting. Any questions?"

"How come so many Navy families on the flight?" asked Tanzola.

"I don't know," replied Torres. "They're all from a single Trident missile submarine, the *Montana*. Maybe that has something to do with it."

"Anyway, that's a break we got on their weapons, huh, Captain? They won't do shit with those popguns. I hope there's not too many of 'em though. Takes too long to get at 'em."

Torres nodded and turned back to watch the street coming at him out of the night as the jeep's headlights probed the darkness. Ahead, he could just make out the tails of the C-141 aircraft silhouetted against the night sky. The interior lights of the aircraft glowed dimly through the open rear cargo doors. He breathed deeply. Tanzola was right, he thought, not having to deal with submachine guns makes the job a lot easier. But we aren't out of the woods yet, he cautioned himself. The terrorists still have a chance to get weapons and heavy explosives after they land. If they do, it could get rough.

Torres considered that possibility as the C-141's came nearer. Suddenly, he was glad he was a bachelor.

Chapter 8

Swig Sauer finished pouring two snifters of his favorite Armagnac brandy and stepped away from the small bar with a glass in each hand. Across the tastefully furnished living room, Mary O'Hegarty sat on a comfortable, beige-colored couch talking by telephone to her children in Connecticut. At one end of the long room, the sliding-glass door to a balcony stood open. Warm evening air permeated the room. In the dining alcove, an aging and devoted Chamorro houseboy with the improbable name of Old Nick cleared away the remains of an excellent, cold lobster dinner.

Sauer crossed the room and extended one glass to Mary, smiling. Mary, without breaking her conversation, looked up, took her glass, and returned Sauer's smile. He did not want to interrupt, so he walked out onto the balcony, idly swirling his brandy.

He stood for a moment at the railing that enclosed the balcony onto which both the living room and the bedroom opened. Sauer liked this time of day best of all. When evening was just coming upon the city, he could relax and regenerate. In the distance, the waters of the Potomac reflected a fiery red from the setting sun.

He turned and leaned back comfortably against the railing, sipping his brandy from time to time. Gazing fondly at the back of Mary's head, he noticed how the light played in her hair at the slightest movement. It's amazing, he thought, how her presence completely changes the place. There's warmth and graciousness that hasn't been in any place I've lived in since Tweedy died.

He remembered Tweedy and the old days with the quiet, resigned regret of a lonely but tough-minded man. His two children and numerous grandchildren all lived on the West Coast. As a widower, he had abandoned the large Navy-owned homes to which his rank entitled him for a series of bachelor apartments that he shared with Old Nick. Without

Tweedy, his work had become pretty much his entire life.

Sauer's mood grew philosophical. What're you going to do when you retire? he thought. You're on your last station now. But no answer came to him, for instead, he was pleasantly interrupted by Mary. She finished her call, stood up and came out to him, glass in hand.

"You OK?" she asked, stopping close beside him. "You seem a little down."

Sauer turned back to the river, leaning on the rail. He felt her turn beside him and smelled her light perfume. He realized suddenly that he wanted to talk to her . . . that he had wanted to talk to someone for a very long time.

"I feel old. Like a worn-out boxer who's got to climb into the ring one more time."

Mary turned to him, putting her hand on his arm.

"You? Old? Worn-out? Not you, Swig. I saw you today. You looked like there was an enthusiastic five year old trapped inside of you. Besides, I checked up on you. Bob Courts says you're a good skier and a terrific handball player."

Sauer took her hand in his.

"Yeah," he chuckled, her concern restoring his humor. "But skiing's all downhill."

"Nonsense," Mary responded, not recognizing the pun because of her preoccupation with his state of mind. "Bob says you terrorize all the junior officers on the handball court."

"Handball's got nothing to do with age. Like chess, it's all in knowing the moves. I was playing four-wall when those young fellows were having trouble playing jacks. As long as I can stand up, I've got a better than even chance of beating them. When I said I felt old, I didn't mean physically."

"What did you mean?"

"I'm in my last assignment now. What am I going to do when I get out? I can't ski all year, which is the only hobby I've ever gotten around to learning. Maybe I'll move to Hawaii in the summer and take up golf," he concluded mischievously. He turned to Mary smiling, his eyes flashing.

"Hah!" exclaimed Mary, poking him in the chest with a finger. "I remember that one. You hate golf."

"It's true," confessed Sauer with a laugh. "I tried when I was an ensign, but never could take the game seriously. I think it was the leisurely pace and sylvan setting. I mean, a handball court looks like a sweat box . . . the setting suits the activity."

Warming up to his subject, Sauer turned and leaned back against the rail.

"I feel the same way about a winter mountain slope. The runs and turns of the hill seem to match the easy fluid-like movements I make when skiing. Golf's not like that. For me, the lush green setting of a golf course is more in keeping with Platonic discourse than in periodically smacking the be-jesus out of an innocent, little, white ball."

Sauer took a sip of brandy. His eyes sparkled brilliantly as he gazed at Mary over the rim of the glass.

Mary reached up and gently pulled the glass away from his lips. She leaned close, their lips almost meeting.

"You always were a most charming man," she said softly and touched her lips to his. Twice she kissed him lightly as if summoning back memories of their time together. Old emotions stirred anew. Now awakened, suddenly urgent.

Sauer's free hand curved around her waist and pressed her to him. Their kiss hardened as she put her hand behind his neck.

"Oh, Mary," he managed finally. "It's been a long, long time."

"Shh," she said, putting her head on his shoulder. "That's all over now."

Without another word, he led her by the hand to the master bedroom, knowing Old Nick had retreated discretely to his room behind the kitchen.

Later, Mary awoke with the strange uncertainty of knowing she had slept, but not knowing how long. I don't care, she thought moving her naked body luxuriously under the crisp white sheets of the bed. God, I feel good. She put her hand out and found that she was alone in the bed. Swig was gone.

She rose up on one elbow and looked around the small room. The door to the balcony was open. In the darkness, she could see Swig's bathrobe-clad figure standing by the railing, his back to her. She watched him for a while, then swung her feet out of the bed and stood up to look for her scattered clothes. Almost immediately she saw a second bathrobe that Swig had laid out for her. Slipping into it, she went to him. Hearing her coming, he turned.

"Hi," he said quietly and reached out his arms to her.

"Hi yourself," she said and lay her head upon his chest. They stood that way for several moments, oblivious to the distant noises of the capital. Finally, Mary raised her head and looked up at him.

"What were you thinking about just before I came out? I watched you. You didn't move for several minutes."

Sauer sighed before kissing her lightly. The world had caught up with them. "You really want to know? It's not very romantic."

"Uh huh," she answered, still looking up at him.

"There's something about the Pan World situation that's bothering me," said Sauer. "I haven't been able to put my finger on just what, but it's important. You really want to talk about that stuff now?"

"Yep," Mary answered. She straightened up and led him to a couple of redwood deck chairs. Mary waited until they were both seated and then asked, "How exactly are you bothered?"

"Well, back in the office you raised the question of informing the *Montana* of the danger to their families. I said then that we would do so as soon as the plane landed, and we knew the full situation. Now, I'm not so sure that was the right decision. Maybe we should tell them everything as it develops . . . good and bad. I don't know why exactly, just a hunch. Seems only right. After all, the whole world knows what's happening to their families. If it were me . . . if I were in the *Montana* and my family was on that plane, I'd want to know everything that was going on."

"Then why don't you do it?" asked Mary.

"I'm afraid it might distract them from their duty. I know that sounds heartless, but like it or not, for the next seventy-two hours, the *Montana* is stuck with the duty. The problem is that there are a certain number of targets that have to be covered. The Air Force's B-52's and Titan missiles are so old they're being manned by men who weren't even born when they were made. Old weapons, like old cars, spend a lot of time being repaired. When they're in the shop, so to speak, somebody else has to cover for them. If I pulled the *Montana* out, the targets would be uncovered.

"My first thought when I heard there were *Montana* families on board the airliner was to take the *Montana* off the firing line," Sauer continued. "The men shouldn't do duty under those circumstances. My God! I know the Mawsons well.

The thought of Barbara and the kids going through this hell, well, it tears me up. Think what it would do to Doug Mawson. But I couldn't pull them out. For a few days, the *Montana* is the only game in town." He looked at Mary. "You're the expert. What d'you think?"

Mary spoke without the slightest pause. Her words leapt immediately from thought to lips, spoken the instant they were conceived.

"Tell them. The sooner the better. Start a dialogue with them now before you have more news. Bring them into it now. Don't let them feel isolated from you . . . cut off . . . alone out there."

Her voice ripped through the relaxed quiet of the evening. She stood up and paced to the railing, unable to contain the tension that suddenly rose within her. She was lost in thought and speaking more to herself than to Sauer.

"That's it, dammit. Dialogue. We've got to have dialogue." She spun around and faced Sauer, his oversized bathrobe swirling around her. A strange look came over her face. "Swig, I don't ever remember seeing a scenario covering this situation or any situation remotely like it. I've never seen a behavioral profile in which only the families of the *crew* were in jeopardy. All our studies assumed that when the families of the crew were in jeopardy from nuclear attack, so were the population of the entire country. We're breaking new ground, and it scares me."

"What are you talking about? What scares you?"

Mary caught the sharp edge to his voice and went to him. Kneeling down beside his chair, she took his hand in both of hers, the long sleeves of the robe falling back to her elbows.

"I don't know exactly, Swig. What I'm saying is that we've never looked at the stresses on a crew created by a hijacking of their families. I don't like not knowing their *probable* reaction because, offhand, I can think of several *possible*, very negative reactions. That's why I think it's so important to get a dialogue going. When you don't know where you're headed, dialogue is the only way to gain any measure of control. It would be better if you could pull them out entirely. But, failing that, communication is absolutely necessary."

Mary looked up at him and squeezed his hand.

"Does any of that make sense to you?"

Sauer heaved himself up from the chair, ignoring her hands. Mary's eyes followed him.

"No, frankly it doesn't." He moved to the doorway. "I mean, what the hell, Mary. Men have been doing their duty at sea for hundreds of years before fancy words like motivation and behavioral profile were invented. I don't see why they won't now, no matter what happens to their families."

The Admiral had spoken. Sauer had made his statement with a finality that only very senior military officers can deliver. He stepped toward her as if to soften the impact of his words.

"You're absolutely right, though, on pulling them out. I would if I could. But I can't. Not for at least another seventy-two hours. When it comes to nuclear equality, we live on the thin edge. The *Montana*'s targets are among those that must be covered to prevent the Russians from even thinking about a first strike. If we had newer bombers, it might be different, but we don't and I can't change it. Neither can the *Montana*. I agree with you on the need for starting what you call a dialogue. Unfortunately, it's impossible, if I understand what you mean by a dialogue."

"I meant simply talking to each other," interjected Mary.

"Right," said Sauer. "It can't be done. Once a submarine has left her base, she can't use her radios. It's too dangerous. Not only that, because of her great depth, we can transmit only very simple messages to her from land-based radios. We can't actually talk to her. We have to limit the message to simple word groups such as 'go here' and 'come home.'" In fact, it's one of the great ironies of our age that computers on the submarine and on land can now talk to each other with great ease and speed, but we humans can't. Ridiculous? But that's the way it is, Mary."

Suddenly making up his mind, Sauer reached down to Mary, who was kneeling beside his chair, and helped her up.

"Well, my dearest dear, I'm going to take your advice and get a message off to them now," he said. "Mind stopping by the office with me before I take you to your hotel?"

"Not a bit, you silver-tongued devil," laughed Mary. "Believe it or not, in all the years I've been coming to Washington, I've never been in the Pentagon at night."

*　　*　　*

The cabin was dark with the impenetrable, inky blackness of a subterranean cavern. A soft whisper of moving air came from vents in the overhead. From the deck, from the bulkheads, from the attractive furnishings of the cabin now concealed in the dark, from the very fabric of the ship itself, came the faint, all-prevailing vibration of the steam turbines as they thrust the *Montana* through the icy depths of the Norwegian Sea at a speed greater than thirty knots.

Commander Mawson lay on his side, deeply asleep. There was a faint glow from the digital watch on his wrist as his left arm curved upward, cradling his chin. His right arm held the pillow protectively beneath his head. He breathed lightly and evenly through his partially opened mouth. His face, could it be seen, had the look of youthful innocence.

The telephone handset on the bulkhead exactly sixteen inches above his head suddenly buzzed incessantly. Without moving his head or even seeming to come awake, Mawson's hand reached out and brought the offending instrument to his ear and mouth.

"Yes?" he said, not really awake.

"Eyes-only message from OPNAV on the way to you, Captain," said the voice of Lieutenant Perkins, the Launch Control Officer, who had the watch.

Instantly, Mawson was fully awake, making the transition from deep sleep to complete alertness without the slightest effort. The civilized practice of permitting one's mind to remain foggy and dull until the completion of some favorite awakening ritual, such as showering and drinking coffee, was a luxury totally unknown to him. Like all sea captains, he possessed the peculiar ability to wake up with his mental faculties operating fully. One moment he was asleep, the next, his mind was functioning as if he had been up for hours.

"Any change in alert status or operational orders?" he queried.

"No, sir. We're steaming as before."

"Very well," said Mawson and hung up the handset.

He looked at his watch as he stood up and stretched. The folds of his light-red pajamas with the distinctive Brooks Brothers piping fell easily over his muscular calves.

Two twenty-seven. It's almost twenty-one thirty in Washington, he thought, performing a quick calculation. That's late for OPNAV unless there's a crisis situation. He considered various possibilities that might require OPNAV to work late and send eyes-only messages to the commanding officers of submarines.

Absorbed with these thoughts, he stood up and walked to his desk in the day cabin. He turned on the light and stood looking down at the blotter framed in green leather that Robbie had given him last Christmas. There was a crisis somewhere in the world. It couldn't concern an immediate threat of nuclear war, or there would have been a change in alert status. It couldn't involve the use of the *Montana*, or there would have been a change in operational orders. Maybe the crisis wasn't military at all, but political. That's probably it, he thought. A political crisis somewhere that has the potential for possible military action. But then why an eyes-only message, and why to him? What role could the *Montana* possibly play in resolving a political crisis short of full nuclear war? He was intrigued, but totally relaxed as he stood turning this question over in his mind. No premonition of personal danger intruded on his thoughts.

A knock sounded on the cabin door.

"Come," said Mawson, turning toward the door.

Seaman Cale Medford, a signalman, entered with a serious and determined look upon his face. In his left hand, Mawson could see a message pad and a slip of folded, buff-colored paper. Across the fold of the paper the words FOR THE CAPTAIN'S EYES ONLY were stamped in large red letters.

Medford held the message out to Mawson as if he were discharging a sacred duty. In a sense, he was. It was a credit to Medford and to the system that trained him that he took the eyes-only stamp as a trust. The message was free of any sort of seals, merely folded in half. For men such as Medford, that was sufficient. If the Navy did not want anyone but the captain to read the contents, then, by God, as far as Medford was concerned, only the captain would.

"Message, Captain," announced Medford in a voice that matched the youthfulness of his face.

"Morning," acknowledged Mawson, his smile hiding the eagerness with which he unfolded the message. Now, he thought, we'll see what this is all about.

The fateful words stabbed at him like little knives probing for his vitals:

703750/2107
OPNAV–B124–mat–3
4 August

CNO
183589

Cmdr D. Mawson, USS *Montana*
Pan World Flight 231 hijacked. *Montana*
now over Med. Tracking.
Destination unknown Will advise.

S. Sauer

So unexpected were the words, so foreign to anything in his professional experience, that Mawson initially reacted as a husband and father rather than a naval officer. The faces of Kathy, Robbie, and Barbara momentarily appeared in his mind. For the first time in his life, a feeling of helplessness and inadequacy washed over him.

He stood immobile, like a rock being assaulted by storm-tossed waves, as emotions surged through him. Then his mind and his training began to exert themselves. He read the message again, this time analyzing each word.

Doesn't say how many dependents aboard. The list of names was too long to transmit. With the slow data rate of the extremely low frequency on ELF system, it could take hours, he thought. The men would know if their families were aboard. It's over the Mediterranean now. Probably headed for an African or Middle Eastern country. Apparently there's been no communication with the hijackers, and none's expected until after the plane lands. That means they don't know why the flight was hijacked. Jesus, what if it was hijacked because our families are aboard. Negotiating with the hijackers could be next to impossible. They might even single out the *Montana* families as hostages! The ship must be told. This thing could get really nasty before it's over.

Again, the unfamiliar feeling of helplessness swept over him. This time it caused a slight, unrealized resentment. The first stirrings of anger in his subconscious were born.

Mawson was a man of high intelligence from a rich and historically powerful family and the captain of the most destructive instrument ever devised by man. His career, his childhood, even his genes, if such can affect the behavior of a man, all mitigated against any feelings of inadequacy. Mawson was born and bred to lead men in the resolution of important issues. He had been trained and disciplined by a Navy which believes that opportunity has an uncanny way of coming to men who will make the most of it. He was a man who would render decisions promptly based on limited information and live with the consequences of those decisions. Mawson was the perfect product of a Navy tradition that was absolutely unchanged since John Paul Jones first forged the precept in blood and gunpowder. His background, therefore, was totally devoid of any preparation for a passive role.

Mawson turned to young Medford, who was watching him intently.

"My compliments to Mr. Perkins, and would he ask Chief Dacovak to come to my cabin," ordered Mawson, the ancient phraseology helping to keep any hint of emotion from his voice.

"Aye, aye, sir," replied Medford.

Mawson turned back to his desk and picked up the handset from its cradle on the bulkhead. Punching the buttons for Edelstone's cabin, Mawson turned and watched Medford leave.

Edelstone's gruff voice came to him before the end of the first ring.

"Edelstone."

"Harry, this is Doug. We've got trouble. Our families have been hijacked."

"Shit," came Edelstone's involuntary exclamation.

Mawson continued, ignoring the interruption.

"I want to discuss telling the ship and finding out whose families are on board. I've asked Dacovak to join us in my cabin."

"I'm on my way, Doug."

Mawson hung up the phone and went into his sleeping cabin. He dressed hurriedly and was just tying his second shoe when Edelstone knocked on the day cabin door.

"Come," said Mawson. Then, when he saw it was Edelstone, "The message is on the desk, Harry. Read it."

Mawson stepped into the small head and made his plans while quickly combing his hair. With a final glance in the mirror, he turned to join Edelstone. At the same time, a knock sounded on the door.

"Come," said Mawson.

The door opened and Dacovak's huge bulk ducked under the low doorway and came into the room. As always, Dacovak was parade ground immaculate.

"Reporting as ordered, Cap'n," said Dacovak. Then, seeing Edelstone, he said, "Good morning, Commander."

Edelstone grunted, pulling his pipe from his shirt pocket, and handed the message back to Mawson.

"Bad news, Chief. Read this."

Dacovak took a pair of glasses from a case in his shirt pocket, slipped them on, and slowly read the fateful words.

"What does it mean, sir?" he asked, handing back the message. "I know what it says, but what does it mean? My family's on board."

"It means our families are in some danger, but we just don't know how much and won't until the plane lands."

"What happens then, Cap'n?" Dacovak asked as if dreading the answer. The muscles of his neck stood out in knotted chords as he ground his teeth together from tension.

"I think that depends upon where the plane lands and what the hijacker's demands are. One way or the other, though, the passengers have always gotten out. They'll do it this time. And that's what I want to talk about."

Mawson turned to include Edelstone in his remarks and leaned back against the edge of the desk.

"Harry, I want to address the ship over both closed circuit TV and IMC. Set it up in the wardroom so I can hold an officer's call immediately afterwards. Then I'll meet with the chiefs in the CPO mess. I want every man in this ship asked if his family is on Flight two thirty-one and a list of dependents made up. Now, in about two hours we'll be making our arrival in Sigma Twenty-Seven. If we time this thing right, we'll finish the dependents survey and go immediately into countdown for Strategic Alert. That way the men will be kept occupied and won't have a lot of time to brood.

"The way I see it," he continued, "the thing we have to guard against is letting our imaginations run away with us. We have almost no information to go on. Speculation as to what might happen to our families can, at best, lead to unnecessary anguish for the individual and, at worst, a spreading panic among the crew. It must be discouraged at every level."

Turning to Dacovak, Mawson said, "Chief, I'm depending mostly on you to see that this is carried out. We must all try for a cheerful attitude. Our families are going to be all right. I believe that. We've all got to believe it. Whatever the means, they'll get out unharmed. Any questions?"

Mawson looked first at Edelstone and then at Dacovak. Both men shook their heads.

"OK. That's it then. I'll come as soon as you're set up," Mawson concluded to Edelstone.

As the door closed behind the two men, Mawson turned and sat at his desk. For several minutes he stared at the photographs of his family mounted in a small, three-fold, gilded frame. He looked at the message he still held in his hand.

Let's see, he thought. The plane took off around eighteen-thirty yesterday. It's now after two-thirty. It's been in the air for over eight hours and can't have much more fuel left. It's got to land soon. Which is good. Once the plane lands, steps to resolve the situation will begin.

Once again he stared at Barbara, Kathy, and Robbie. As he envisioned his family seated in the plane, fear began nibbling at his consciousness and intruding on his thoughts. He pulled himself up short. It's been so long I'd almost forgotten, he thought. It's like Vietnam.

That's what I'll tell them, he thought. Since there isn't anything we can do to help free our families, we've got to have patience and faith in the successful efforts of others. No, not *others*, that's too abstract to be of any comfort. I'd better say who. The State Department, for one. Who else? The Army. There was a classified briefing and film on the Army's special antiterrorist team. What was their code name?

He got up from the desk and went into his sleeping cabin to finish his toilet. While he brushed his teeth, the name came to him. Blue Light. He was comforted by the memory of the tough little cigar-smoking colonel who had given the briefing. Hodges, that was his name. Hodges knew what he was doing. If that man had to, he'd get them out safely.

Mawson's spirits began to rise. Without being aware of it, his subconscious feelings of isolation and helplessness subsided with the conscious realization that a man he had met and liked might already be moving to rescue their families. OK. He would tell the ship about Colonel Hodges and his Blue Light warriors.

Some minutes later, Tony Deville stood between Paul Schrader, his cabin mate, and George Robare. Across from them, Ross Wallstrom stood beside Edelstone. Knots of other officers were grouped around the wardroom table. Most had been off watch and asleep when an all-hands call summoned them to the wardroom where they now stood listening to their captain address the ship. Throughout the *Montana*, similar groups of men stood together, watching Mawson on a television monitor or listening to his voice from a loudspeaker. None among them spoke.

Mawson stood alone in the wardroom's lounge area, facing a small television camera manned by a technician. His face seemed pale in the bright lights set up on either side of him, but his well-modulated voice was strong, unwavering, and lent much to the reassurance he was expressing.

Deville's reaction to the hijacking was typical of his emotionally jumbled personal life. His initial thought was relief that his son Jamie was in Wisconsin and not on the plane. Of Jan, he experienced first fear for her safety, then anger because he did not know for sure if she was on the flight. But finally, Deville felt shame when he realized he would have to confess uncertainty to Edelstone. Some of what he was feeling must have shown on his face, for he noticed Wallstrom looking at him with concern.

Wallstrom's reaction was both direct and completely honest. He was relieved and grateful that his family was en route from California to their new home in Virginia and had not gone to Europe at all. Being the sort of man he was, his next thought was concern for the ship and her crew.

In the Maneuvering Room, Chief Engineman Ralph Ward looked up at the speaker, the ER log forgotten on the desk before him.

"Yeah. Them's the guys we need. Right, Mr. Vetta?"

Lieutenant Lou Vetta, who was leaning against the handrail of the Reactor Control Panel, nodded absently, his mind on his family.

"Uh-huh. They sound like the right bunch."

At the other end of the ship, Poley turned away from the loudspeaker in the Torpedo Room to send a stream of tobacco juice arcing towards his spitkit on the deck. Although he had never been married, he was thinking he'd like to have any three of them terrorists in the alley behind Rosie's Place for just five minutes. He ran the tips of his thick fingers over his lips. I'd fix their clock, he thought, a smile coming easily to his mouth.

In the CPO Mess, Dan Jackson sat across from Dacovak, watching TV in the overhead. Although his face gave not a hint, Jackson was worried. With an intellect that, except for acquired discipline, was the equal of Wallstrom's or even Mawson's, Jackson immediately saw the potential dangers of the situation. When it came to the well-being of Phyllis and his babies, he did not find the Old Man's discussion of the Blue Light forces reassuring. This thing could turn to shit quicker than ice cream in the hot sun, he thought. And there's not a fucking thing any of us can do about it.

Jackson tore his eyes away from the screen and glanced at his messmates. They're buying it, he thought. And why not? For the thousandth time, Jackson marveled at how the Navy system worked well for those who gave themselves up to it completely. He never had been able to bring himself to do that. As a consequence, he believed the system did not work as well for him as it did for men like Dacovak. With a smart-ass attitude, he successfully hid his feelings, but he cared and often longed for the simple faith of Dacovak.

Jackson looked across at his best friend with affection. It's a damn good thing that big turd does have faith, Jackson thought. God knows what would happen if he got angry.

Mawson was debating the same subject as he walked into his cabin forty-five minutes later. He had met with his officers and then his chiefs. Although it had gone off well enough, the buoyancy he felt earlier was gone. He was drained and depressed. At the moment, he regretted telling them. Why even bother them? he thought. None of us can do anything about the situation.

Mawson found his thoughts turning to Barbara. Images flashed up from his memory as he stood in the empty day cabin. Sparkling water and sails so white it hurt the eye to see them. Rail down and hard on the wind, the boat drove through the chop and set the spray flying. Barbara at the helm. Her hair flowing in the wind, her skin wet with salt spray, her fingers curved tightly over the tiller, as she took the big cutter to windward.

Unable to remain still any longer, he moved to the desk and slowly opened the center drawer of his desk. Taking out his journal, he began:

Monday, 5 August. At sea. I have just informed the ship of the hijacking. I told them, no, tried to con-

vince them, that speculation of the outcome is fool-
ish. Yet I fear for you . . .

As the powerful turbines thrust the *Montana* through
the dark, northern waters toward her launch area, Mawson sat
alone writing in his journal. Talking to Barbara.

Chapter 9

Flight 231 flew through a clear, night sky high above the
ancient sands of the Sudan. Isolated and alone, a tiny world
unto itself, it moved steadily eastward; its unswerving flight
delineated by a long, white contrail that followed in its path.
Within the plane, night lights glowed softly from the base of
the seats, illuminating the empty aisles. The distant rumble of
engines and the muffled roar of air rushing along the outside
of the fuselage was sonorous in its own fashion and thus
strangely soothing to the worried passengers within the dim
interior. They found in sleep both rest and escape from their
anxieties.

In First Class, Barbara slept in a window seat. Her head,
only partially supported by the hump in the seat back that
served as a pillow, slumped limply over her left shoulder. Her
raincoat, with which she had covered herself when the supply
of blankets ran out, had begun to slip down off her shoulders.
Beside her, Doris was reading in a pool of light that punc-
tured the gloom of the cabin, which, except for an occasional
murmur from one of the sleeping children, was still and dark.
In a seat on the far aisle, Carol Moore, her body shaking
with fever, slept fretfully under both her own and Doris' rain-
coats.

Back in Economy Class, Martin Schlosser sat in an aisle
seat smoking a cigarette, lost in thought. A dim light coming
from the center galley a few rows ahead was reflected in his
hard eyes. Beside him, Jan slept soundly with her head
resting lightly against his right shoulder.

Schlosser felt Jan stir and mutter unintelligibly. Without

breaking his train of thought or moving his head, he transferred the cigarette to his left hand. In the darkness that surrounded them, he smoothly slid his right hand over Jan's reclining body and began massaging her crotch through the blanket that covered her. Unconsciously responding to the stimulation, Jan rolled over full onto her back. Her full lips parted slightly and her feet drew in, spreading her knees as she elapsed contentedly into deeper sleep.

For the hundredth time, Schlosser reviewed their situation. He felt no fear for his personal safety. After all, he thought, they hijacked an American airliner. They must want something from the Americans. I am German. They want nothing from me. It was an essential part of his personality that he failed to recognize, much less consider, the arrogance inherent in such logic.

On the right aisle, almost opposite Jan and Schlosser, Harriet Edelstone sat in the darkness debating whether to go back to sleep or get up and brush her teeth. She had awakened a short time before and her mouth tasted ashen. She smiled as she recalled her encounter earlier with . . . what was his name? Ralph Albertson . . . that's it, she thought. It was the only light spot in an otherwise nightmare of a night.

From the moment she had left Barbara to join the throng of First Class passengers streaming back into the two Economy Class cabins, she had been totally absorbed in contacting other *Montana* wives and telling them not to reveal who they were. It had not been easy. When she entered the center cabin, she found herself at the back of the group shuffling aft along the left aisle. Ahead of her, frightened and unthinking passengers blocked her way. She had to get through and tell people from the ship, yet the scene was one of utter confusion. She looked around her, but saw no familiar face. The terrorists seemed to be everywhere, shouting and gesturing with their guns.

There must be *Montana* wives around me, she thought, feeling the first fingers of panic rising within her. She searched the face of each woman that came into view as she tried to push her way along the crowded aisle. Nothing. All strangers. Where are they? They must be here! I should have made more of an effort to know *all* the wives, she berated herself. Just as she was about to give up in despair, she saw Nancy Olsen in the far aisle. Without thinking of the possible consequences, Harriet turned and squeezed sideways through the row of center seats. Ignoring the protests as she trod on feet and ankles, she thrust herself into the right aisle next to Nancy.

"Don't let on we're from one ship," Harriet whispered urgently to Nancy.

"What?" Nancy replied, her eyes blinking rapidly, devoid of understanding.

Harriet's heart sank. Oh no, she thought, Nancy's panicked. Must make her understand. Harriet, now desperate, reached out and shook Nancy roughly by the shoulder, not caring whether she was seen.

"Nancy, listen to me! Don't let them know we're all from the *Montana*. Pass it on to whoever you can. Do you understand?"

Harriet looked hard at Nancy whose face reflected her struggle to regain control of herself.

Harriet glanced quickly around. The tall terrorist in the center galley was looking in their direction. Harriet turned Nancy around and pushed her up the aisle, closing the gap that had developed between them and the passengers ahead of them.

"Nancy, are you all right?" Harriet was beginning to panic herself now.

"Yes, I'm all right," replied Nancy. "Yes, I understand."

Nancy dropped into an empty seat beside a young woman, almost a teenager, who Harriet vaguely recognized as the wife of a man who had just joined the *Montana*. Harriet found an empty seat across from Nancy and was relieved to see the young wife slide crabwise past the occupied seats in the center section and speak hastily to someone hidden on the far aisle. A moment later the girl was back in her own seat and nodding to Nancy Olsen that all was well. Thank God, thought Harriet with a sigh. The word was getting around.

As it turned out, Harriet's initial anxiety and struggle to pass the word had been unnecessary. Once the terrorists had all the passengers seated, they withdrew to the center galley which marked the dividing line between Economy Class and First Class, leaving the passengers free to roam at will within the two aftermost cabins.

As soon as she realized they were permitted to move about, Harriet unobtrusively sought out Sally Bronick, Phyllis Jackson and some officers' wives. Between them, they made certain every *Montana* wife, including Jan, was told. That was how Harriet met Ralph Albertson.

When she finished her dinner, Harriet made her way through the knots of people talking anxiously in the aisles toward the lavatories to brush her teeth. She paused for a moment to talk to Sally Bronick. Just as she straightened up and turned to start back down the aisle, she bumped into a heavyset man just sitting down in his seat.

"I beg your pardon," Harriet said, noticing he also held a toothbrush in his hand.

Then, for she rarely spoke to strangers, she surprised herself by continuing the conversation.

"What a coincidence. I was just on my way to brush *my* teeth."

The man stood back up, his florid face breaking into a smile. "I don't brush my teeth anymore. Used to, but no more," he declared pausing for effect. "Now I've reached an age where I just just polish my investment."

His smile broadened into a huge, friendly grin that, because it totally ignored the realities of their surroundings, Harriet found very comforting.

"I'm Ralph Albertson from Minneapolis. What's your name?" he asked as he extended his hand.

"Harriet Edelstone," she replied, shaking his hand while she returned his grin.

"I think we must be the same age."

"Nah. Not you." he responded. "Where you from?"

"Vermont," Harriet answered, not untruthfully.

"There, you see," he beamed and spread his hands wide. "Not only do we have the same investments, but our weather's the same." Albertson turned slightly to include Sally in his question. "You ladies part of a tour or something? I see you all talking to one another. You school teachers?"

Harriet felt Sally's eyes on her.

"No," laughed Harriet lightly, "our husbands all work for the same company."

"Oh, yeah? Which one is that?"

Harriet darted a meaningful look at Sally.

"Tennco Shipbuilders," Harriet lied.

"In Vermont?" he asked incredulously.

"No. It's in Norfolk, Virginia," explained Harriet, earnestly wishing she had never started the conversation. "I just think of Vermont as my home."

"I know what you mean. When I worked in Cleveland, I always told people that I lived in Cleveland, but was from Minnesota. Let's see. Tennco in Norfolk. They make mostly ships for the Navy. Right? That's a third coincidence. I'm a sales rep for Minneapolis Ordinance Systems. One of the things we make is torpedoes for the Navy." He paused and looked up the aisle toward the Center Galley. "We also make grenades like the ones those punks are waving around."

Harriet looked at him with renewed interest. He may have useful information, she thought.

"You know about hand grenades?" Harriet asked.

"Yeah. Not only do I sell 'em, but I used 'em in Korea, and I can tell you the ones they're holding won't do as much damage in here as they think."

"What do you mean?" asked Sally, unable to contain her fascination.

"I got a good look at one when they first took over. It's an old case-fragmentation model. When it detonates, it throws out big, but slow-moving chunks of steel. That works fine in the open, but these here seats'll stop the pieces cold. Hardly anybody'll get hurt and even then they'll get mostly leg and foot wounds." He paused and looked hard at the two women, trying to judge the effects of his words. "You really want to know all this? I've lived with weapons so long, I sometimes forget it scares people."

"You're damn right I want to hear about it. They've got my kids up there," exclaimed Sally hotly.

"Yeah, I know. I been thinking about that. The kids'll be all right. What I mean is, we've been flying for a couple of hours now. That's a long way. They've got something big planned. They might be hijackers, but they're not crazies. So, I think the kids'll be all right."

"I hope to God you're right," said Sally, turning away to be left alone with her thoughts.

Albertson looked distressed, realizing he had managed to frighten the woman. Seeing his expression, Harriet laid her hand on his arm.

"I'm sure you are," Harriet said with a smile as she turned and walked back toward the lavatories.

That had been hours ago. Now movement in the center galley five rows ahead of her caught Harriet's eye. The male terrorist standing guard on her side of the plane straightened up from where he had been lounging against the side of the galley structure. Harriet's reassurance to Albertson had been solely for Sally's sake. I don't know about the rest of them, but the girl is scary, Harriet thought. She shot that poor man for no reason at all. Enough, Harriet pulling herself up sharply. You keep on like this and you'll upset yourself. With that, Harriet turned on her side and sought refuge in sleep.

In the clear space between the aisles in the center galley, Yonnie Trupp and Abdulla bin Salim lay sleeping on the carpeted deck that had been strewn with shreds of broken bottle until the stewardesses cleaned them up. On either side of Yonni and Abdulla, the Jadayel brothers stood watch, positioning themselves so they could see along the aisles into both the First and Economy Class cabins.

Hamed Jadayel yawned deeply and arched his back to stretch his cramped muscles. He was the smallest of the group, just slightly taller than Yonnie, Straightening up, he looked to the opposite side of the galley where his younger and much taller brother stood against the partition which marked the beginning of the First Class cabin. Mahmud, seeing Hamed's gaze, came erect with an impish smile spreading beneath his heavy black mustache. In silence, Mahmud extended his rather long neck and bowed his head toward the deck as if looking down from some great height.

Hamed's dark, thin face lit up with a smile of surprised delight. How like Mahmud to recall Saayed's wonderful story of the Americans. It's so true and so fitting. In a mock gesture, Hamed waved his hand for Mahmud to be quiet, but he could not stop grinning. His thoughts went back six months to Yonnie's apartment in Amsterdam and the night Saayed had told the story.

Her apartment on Thorbeckeplein Street was in a red brick building. Like so many of its neighbors, it was four stories high, but only one room wide. The ground floor of the old building was given over to a small cafe. The two tiny apartments on the second floor were rented by a seemingly endless succession of students from the university which was across the Amstel River.

Yonnie's apartment included the entire two upper floors. On the third floor, a fair-sized front room overlooked the busy street. A small kitchen and bath were located in the rear.

The bedroom, reached by a private continuation of the building's interior staircase, was on the top floor under the eaves of the steeply sloping roof that formed the ceiling of the small but bright room.

This apartment was as close as Yonnie would ever come to having a permanent address. She had moved in eight years before to use it as a safe house when she was the deputy leader of a very active Red Terrorist gang. At the time, she had told the landlord and everyone in the building that she was Swiss and was a field worker for the International Red Cross, which explained her long absences.

The rooms had served her well over the years. First, merely as a haven from the hard-pressed investigations by the police from three countries. Then, as the other members of the gang were hunted down one by one and she had to spend more and more time in the apartment, she came to think of the rooms as her home.

Hamed was last to arrive that cold winter night. When the pockmarked face of Abdulla cautiously peered around the door before finally admitting him, the others were seated on the floor in a rough semicircle around Saayed, who had returned from the United States a few days before. A great many pieces of notepaper and a map of Europe were spread out on the floor in front of them.

Mahmud looked up as Hamed came into the room.

"You're late. Did you have trouble?"

As agreed, Mahmud spoke in English which was both a convenient common language for them all and good practice for use later.

"No. No. I took time to be certain the house was not under surveillance before coming up," replied Hamed, struggling out of his heavy coat.

Yonnie smiled at Hamed and moved over to make room for him beside her.

"Hamed, the Cautious," she said, turning slightly toward Saayed. "Hamed was opposed to our holding this meeting. He felt it was too risky."

Hamed, who was seeing the room for the first time, tore his attention from the surroundings. "I didn't feel it was too risky. It's just that we have never before all come together at the same time. I felt the risk was unnecessary," he concluded, sitting down beside Yonnie.

"I know," said Saayed, who had visited each member

immediately upon his return. "Hamed mentioned his concern to me, but I think the meeting is necessary."

Abdulla resumed his place opposite Yonnie on Saayed's left, folding his long legs gracefully beneath him as he sat down.

"I think it is good that we all hear Saayed's plan together," interjected Abdulla. "We agreed after Stuttgart that separate meetings mean separate understandings."

"Besides," added Saayed, "in two days we begin moving to London. Soon we are gone from here, and Yonnie can have her refuge back."

Yonnie waved her hand impatiently. "Ach. I am not worried. Can we begin now?"

"Of course," replied Saayed, picking up a sheaf of papers from the carpet.

In a low, soft voice that was totally out of keeping with his words, Saayed began explaining his plan for the hijacking. Except for an occasional question or comment from one of the group, the room was still. The warmth of the good Dutch heater in the corner spread throughout the room, adding to the feeling of camaraderie felt by the group.

Sometime later, Hamed considered the roles each would play. He would be responsible for security. Mahmud, who had gone to school in England and understood their ways the best, would handle all contacts with the British. Abdulla would take care of communications with Beirut. Saayed would select the airlines and flight. And Yonnie, with her well-proven connections in East Germany, would be responsible for obtaining weapons and getting them aboard the aircraft.

Thoughts of Yonnie broke his concentration. Suddenly, he became aware of her nearness. Her right buttock was pressed lightly against his left hip. The clean scent of her body came to him. He knew she owned no perfume and found himself wondering what it was that smelled so fresh. Soap, he decided. Unscented, perhaps, but still a woman's bath soap. He was surprised to find there were aspects of Yonnie that he had never considered before. Yonnie, as did they all, spoke freely of her past and her family. From Mahmud, he also knew that she gave herself without hesitation to any member of the group who asked and seemed to enjoy the experience. She had never interested Hamed before, yet now his attention was so far diverted that he began imagining

Yonnie naked in her bath. He knew then that he wanted her, and he wanted her that night.

The realization shocked him. Hamed tried to force his attention back to Saayed's words. It's this house. It's because I've never been in her house before, he decided, trying once more to drive thoughts of her from his mind. Again he focused his attention on Saayed's words.

"I have said this before, but it is good to repeat it at this time," Saayed was saying. "It is inherent in the American political system that their foreign policy is reactive in nature. They are, thus, poor planners and rarely anticipate the actual results of the policies they put into effect. Yet, because of their childlike belief in themselves, they are always hopeful of success and willing to try again.

"While I was there this time, I gained a great insight into the American character. It was told to me as a simple joke by an American, but I think it is true wisdom. It is this: it seems a man fell from the twentieth floor of a tall building. As he fell past the tenth floor, a man stuck his head out of an open window and called, 'How are you doing?' The falling man answered, 'So far, so good!' "

Laughter exploded from the small group. Saayed smiled without humor, waited for quiet and then leaned forward.

"Although humorous, I think this little story expresses exactly the essence of the American attitude toward life. They can be made to pursue optimistically a course of action the end of which is not at all clear to them."

Saayed's eyes flashed with a strange light.

"For this reason, they will negotiate for the return of the hostages. When they do, we will use their inborn sense of optimism against them. It will be our strength and their weakness. In the end, they shall meet our demands."

Saayed sat back, supporting himself with his arms, his palms against the carpet.

The four looked at Saayed for a moment, considering his words. Yonnie was the first to speak, her voice intense.

"Oh, yes, Saayed. That is good. Very good. This will not be Munich. Not an Entebbe. With the Americans we will succeed. But we must have the right demands. We must squeeze them. We must squeeze them hard." Her hands closed in fists before her. Her eyes became slits. "I have spent too long striking mere blows. In the end, one's comrades are gone and the world forgets. This time I want something more lasting, something that lasts beyond a few days on the first pages of the newspapers. A victory! We must have a victory!"

Yonnie sat back on her heels, her hands upon her knees, her chest heaving rapidly. Mahmud and Abdulla, fired by her speech, were talking excitedly, each unaware of the other. Hamed, deeply touched, reached out and covered her right hand with his left.

Yonnie turned her hand under Hamed's, squeezed it tightly as if drawing strength from him and took a final deep breath. "Come help me carry in the coffee and cakes."

Still holding his hand, she stood up. He followed, delighted at this unexpected turn of events.

In the kitchen, Yonnie prepared the thick, sweet coffee the men liked and laid out rich, buttery Dutch pastries she had purchased that afternoon. Hamed stood to one side watching. Although he kept out of her way as best he could, it was inevitable that she brushed against him as she moved about in the small kitchen.

Desire rose within him. He admired Yonnie. She was tough-minded, loyal, and, above all, absolutely dependable. She was also, at this moment, very exciting. Unable to control himself further, he took hold of her shoulders as she again brushed past him, coffee pot in hand.

She stopped at his touch and allowed herself to be turned toward him. I should not do this, he thought as he bent and kissed her upturned face full on the lips. To his surprise, she responded eagerly. Her left hand curled around the back of his head, gently pressing it toward her so that their lips met more tightly. At the same time, her chin lifted slightly as she arched her back to press firm breasts against his chest. He embraced her tightly. His left arm was completely across her shoulders and his right hand pressed against the small of her back. It was a long passionate kiss, and when they finally separated, it left them both filled with desire for each other.

Yonnie looked up at Hamed, the coffee pot almost forgotten in her hand.

"We must go in now, but will you stay after the others leave?"

Her eyes, usually hard and cold, searched his and now seemed soft and liquid. He raised his hand to her cheek.

"Yes. Oh yes," he said softly. "I will stay."

"Good," she replied simply with a half smile, handing him the coffee pot. "You go in. I will bring the cups and cakes."

Yonnie turned away and picked up cups and pasteries from the counter. She looked up at Hamed and smiled again. Hamed, to show he was as much in control of his emotions as she, nodded with a smile and preceded her out of the kitchen.

Abdulla looked up as they rejoined the group.

"Ah. Coffee."

"And cakes," added Mahmud, who was well known for his sweet tooth.

That brought a laugh from the group and a general lifting of the tension. Hamed was gratified to find that he could participate fully in the discussion with only occasional thoughts of Yonnie intruding. In fact, so engrossed had they both become in the discussion that some two hours later, when the meeting began to break up, he was sure she had forgotten her invitation or had changed her mind.

Feeling somewhat sorry for himself, he stood with the others and began to move to the coat rack by the door. Yonnie took the tray of dirty dishes into the kitchen.

"Hamed," Yonnie said coming back into the room. "Would you mind staying a little longer? I would like to discuss some ideas I have concerning the security arrangements while the thoughts are fresh in my mind."

Carefully keeping any trace of the relief he felt out of his voice, Hamed answered, "I don't mind. It's better we do not all leave at once anyhow."

As soon as he said the words, he was afraid one of the others would agree and decide to stay also. Fool, he thought. Always you make the big pronouncement. Why not just keep silent?

But his fears were short-lived. After briefly reviewing the schedules for meetings between individuals, the others put on their heavy coats and left after saying good-night.

Yonnie closed the door and shot the bolt home. Hamed watched from the coat rack, suddenly wishing he had not stayed. He really did not know this side of Yonnie. What was worse, in the two years he had known her, he had really never before thought of her as anything more than a trusted comrade. The realization made him feel awkward and unsure how to begin.

Yonnie turned to him. She either did not see or ignored his awkwardness, for she linked her arm through his, covering his hand with hers and looking up at him.

"Come. We will turn out the lights and go to bed," she announced in a soft but firm voice.

Without letting go of his arm, she led him around the comfortably furnished room from one lamp to another. Not a word was spoken. Then, in the darkness, she turned to him and with both her hands upon his face pulled him down to meet her waiting lips in a hot and urgent kiss.

Hamed's awkwardness evaporated with the heat of his desire. He found the combination of her apparently cool and constrained exterior with her very real, inner passions to be extremely exciting. Without taking his lips from hers, he bent his knees slightly and wrapped his arms around her legs just below her buttocks. Lifting her off the floor, he carried her toward the stairway by the door. She put her arms around his neck.

She was heavier than he had thought. As he carried her, the body slipped slowly through his arms no matter how tightly he clasped her. He was afraid he'd drop her and make a fool of himself. By the time he deposited her gratefully on the bottom step, she was supporting herself more by her own arms than by his grasp.

His lips moved from her mouth to neck to right ear. Hamed glanced up the stairs. He would never be able to carry her to bed as he had originally intended. He thought he might lead her up the stairs when he felt Yonnie's hands leave his neck. As her lips sought his, one of her hands caressed his bulging penis through the fabric of his pants while the other tugged at his belt buckle.

He moved his hands, which rested one on each of her buttocks, in response. To his surprise, he found her skirt had slipped up, so he felt the smoothness of her skin and silkiness of her underwear. He slid both hands under the elastic waistband and pushed her panties down to her knees. Her buttocks were cool to his touch.

Yonnie pushed his pants and drawers downward with busy hands. Her lips worked against his. Waves of almost unbearable lust washed over him. He thrust his body against hers. His underclothes fell to the floor. He pulled back from her slightly and stepped out of his pants while he slid one hand from her buttocks to her pubis. He felt her take his straining penis in her hand.

She pushed her genitals against his hand, her breath coming in short heavy bursts in his ear. Without any conscious effort on his part, his middle finger slid between her labia and lingered momentarily at the entrance to her vagina. As if awaiting just such a move, Yonnie flexed her legs slightly and thrust her hips forward so that his finger moved deep into her.

Just as quickly, she wrapped her arms around his neck and her legs around his waist. Her hips moved in a slow, circular motion as she moved her vagina around his finger.

"Take me to bed quickly," her throaty voice whispered in his ear. "Hurry and I will give you this."

Hamed felt her deliberately contract her vagina. It was as if someone was sucking on his finger so powerful was the sensation. Suddenly wild with anticipation, he forced his free hand between her spread cheeks and grabbed the wrist of his other hand. She bit him painfully on the neck as he started up the stairs with her. At each step she moaned as his finger moved within her. She seemed lighter now and he had no trouble carrying her to the double bed he found behind a low railing at the head of the stairs.

Some hours later, he awoke from a deep, almost drugged sleep. The bed was soft and the thick blankets and coverlet smelled fresh and clean and were welcome in the chill of the unheated room. Beside him he felt the warm, naked presence of Yonnie. He lifted his head from the heavy pillow and gazed at her sleeping form.

She's amazing. I had no idea that such passion hid behind her unusually calm and restrained exterior. She had given him no less than three orgasms; he had given her four, the first with his shoes still on his feet and clothes still on their bodies. He rolled over onto his back and smiled in the darkness. He must finally be totally Westernized. What good Arab would make love with shoes on?

Hamed felt refreshed and, for the moment, fully awake. He slid out from under the covers and groped his way to the bathroom. On the way back to bed, he stepped to the window, his naked body oblivious to the cold of the room. The street was empty and the cafe long since closed. A gentle snow was falling in the still night air, covering everything with soft white powder. The scene seemed to be from another world.

He shivered but, lost in thought, continued gazing at the alien world outside.

How strange, he thought, that he and Mahmud, now sleeping in their apartment a few streets away, should be here in this place instead of in Cairo. Had any of them forseen this when they first talked of joining the fedayeen? Certainly neither he nor Mahmud had. Nor, for that matter, had his mother who was largely responsible for their being there.

Their father had been born in 1928 in the little coastal town of Ashkelon on the fertile coast of Palestine, which was then a British Mandate. In 1946, their father was sent on a British scholarship to England to become a pharmacist. When he returned in 1950, Palestine was no more. Instead, he found the young state of Israel flush with its first victory over the Arabs and filled with the conviction that the wandering Jews had at last come home.

Settling in the ancient city of Jaffa, neighbor to the booming Jewish Tel Aviv, Hamed and Mahmud's father opened a small pharmacy and married a local Palestinian girl whose family had lived there for centuries. But times were hard for Arabs living in Israel in those days. So, in 1951, the family emigrated to Egypt to escape what they considered to be economic as well as social persecution. The brothers' paternal grandparents chose to relocate from Ashkelon to a refugee camp in the Gaza Strip, rather than become citizens of Israel. Their mother's parents joined them in the flight to Egypt.

They were not alone. It was surely one of the most ironic twists of fate that the long-suffering Jewish people should regain their ancient homeland only by taking the Palestinians' land so that they, in turn, would begin anew the wanderings of an ancient people. It was sad. Always their mother and her parents would talk of the beautiful orange groves of Jaffa. They longed for them over the years until their Jaffa became a Paradise Lost. Neither brother had the heart to tell them that their house, the orange groves, and even the city of Jaffa itself were no more. All were gone. Instead, there was the ever-growing development of Jewish Tel Aviv.

Hamed shivered. The land my mother would have us regain exists no more, he thought. Then how can we win? We can't? Turning from the window, he walked back to the bed and slipped between the now-cold sheets on his side. Yonnie is wrong, he thought and turned on his side toward her. We will not find a victory, only death. Feeling a desperate loneliness, he slid his naked body against hers. Sleepily she rolled over and came into his waiting arms. He lay for some time with his chin buried in her hair, her breath warm against his chest. Finally he slept. Outside the silent snow fell, creating a fairyland.

After his night with Yonnie, Hamed walked around in a daze, so powerful was her impact on his emotions. Then, he slowly came to realize that Yonnie felt differently about the encounter. However much she was a passionate and eager sexual partner, so was she also totally unemotional about it. As she had pointed out the next morning, she enjoyed herself and she was very happy that he had enjoyed himself, but that was it. To her, sex was no more than one of many bodily functions, an important and powerful one to be sure, but still only the normal act of a healthy body.

He did not know why, but he realized that Yonnie was flawed. She could experience great passion, exhibit extreme loyalty, and enjoy all manner of social contacts with others, but she could not seem to form deep emotional attachments or show affection. The answer, he knew, lay in her childhood.

Yonnie's father had been born just before Hitler came to power. When the Third Reich was formed, his father and two uncles, all three professed Communists, went into hiding. Yonnie's father had been only a boy when he was taken to Gestapo headquarters and tortured to reveal their whereabouts. In the end, his right hand had been crushed and he confessed all that he knew, causing the arrest and ultimate death of the three fugitives.

After Hitler's fall, her father stayed in East Germany and became an important member of the Communist party. Refusing the excellent medical assistance of prosthetic devices available from the Russians, he had a ten-pound, wrought-iron hand made in the form of a clenched fist which he strapped onto the stump of his right forearm.

A cold and bitter man, Yonnie's father never overcame his feelings of guilt. He bore them throughout his life and they twisted his every waking moment. He was given to fits of rage, in which he would swing his iron fist like a sledgehammer at his wife, his children, and more usually, at the family's furniture. During one fit, while the family had all been at the dinner table, he broke a serving dish and all the plates he could reach, including little Yonnie's who was sitting beside him. After the family had fled the room, he then smashed the table top into kindling and with it, all chances of a normal life for Yonnie.

Abdulla stirred on the deck beside Yonnie. Hamed glanced at his watch. Almost time to wake them. I will give them five minutes more, he thought.

Hamed glanced at his watch again, bent down and gently shook first Yonnie and then Abdulla.

"It's time," he said softly.

A few rows in front of Hamed and the others, Barbara moved in her sleep. The raincoat had slipped further down, exposing her hands. The little finger of her left hand twitched slightly as consciousness, like the incoming tide crumbles a castle of sand grain by grain, slowly flooded her mind and eroded her shallow sleep.

She opened her eyes. In the gloom of the cabin, her window was transparent and free of glare. As her mind cleared, the now-familiar sound of the rushing air came to her, reassuring her. She remembered where she was.

Without moving her head, Barbara glanced forward. The top of Kathy's tousled head was just visible in the space between the side of the plane and the back of the seat before her. She listened for a second or two. From somewhere in the cabin came the sound of a child's cough. Nothing's changed, she thought drowsily, looking out the window.

Damn! she thought. Fully awake now, she looked at her watch which was set for London time. Twenty-five minutes of two. If we've been flying eastward, it could be almost dawn.

Suddenly anxious to confirm her suspicions, Barbara turned her head and leaned against the window, straining to see as far forward as possible along the plane's path. The plastic was cold against her cheek. I knew it, she thought with mixed feelings of triumph and foreboding. The sight of the first pale, bluish loom of light marking the beginning of dawn ahead in the blackness of the night sky was visible. We must be heading somewhat south of east, she concluded.

She turned back from the window. Doris' seat was

empty. Barbara moistened her lips with her tongue; her mouth felt dry and the cramped muscles of her neck ached. She unfastened her seat belt and rose up in the seat supported by her arms. Across the cabin she saw Doris bending over the seat in which Carol Moore lay. Barbara looked toward the forward part of the cabin where the girl terrorist had been standing. No one was there. Just as Barbara started to turn around, Yonnie went by and disappeared into the cockpit.

Barbara dropped back down into her seat. Let's see, she thought, doing some mental arithmetic, we've been flying for almost eight hours. That's a long way. Wonder where we are? She turned back to the window and looked straight down hoping to see the lights of a city. Only blackness greeted her. She turned her head and looked at the horizon once again. It'll be light soon enough, then we'll know, she thought. She felt Doris drop into the seat beside her. Barbara turned back from the window.

"Is Carol all right? I saw you over there."

"She's got a fever. Nothing serious. Flu, I think. She should be home in bed," replied Doris, yawning.

"We *all* should be home in bed," said Barbara flatly. "Did you get any sleep?"

"Some," smiled Doris. "I'm used to catnapping between rounds with patients."

"Anything happen?"

"Not much. The hijackers took turns sleeping on the floor of the galley behind us. They left one in the cockpit and then the rest stayed in the galley. I saw them when I had to get some aspirin for Carol. The one I talked to spoke very good English. They seem sure of themselves. Like they know exactly what's going to happen when we land. I don't mind telling you, Mrs. Mawson, it scares the piss out of me just thinking about it."

Barbara nodded her head. "I know what you mean. I'm trying not to think about it, but we've got to stay calm. They know the plane's been hijacked by now. They'll get us out; they always have." Barbara looked at Doris. "I keep telling myself that. Anyway, we'll know soon. It's almost dawn, and we've got to land pretty soon, I would think."

Unknown to Barbara, Pete Worthington was saying the same thing to Saayed Qabrestan in the cockpit.

"Damn it! Don't you understand? We've got to land.

We're on our reserve fuel now. The engines will flame out in less than thirty-five minutes. I've got to put her down now while I have power." Worthington twisted even farther around in his seat. His two hands, raised in the air before him, implored Qabrestan, who sat completely unmoved by Worthington's pleas. "If you wanted to commit suicide and take us with you, why have us fly all night?"

Russ Conrad and Charlie Wall, the flight engineer, turned and stared at Qabrestan. Except for the slightest whisper of air along the nose skin of the fuselage, silence enfolded the cockpit. The multicolored instrument panel light still glowed in the rapidly brightening cabin. Through the pilot's clear-view window, the skyline was now turning a pinkish yellow as the sun neared the rim of the earth in its ascent. The tiny world that was Flight 231 awaited Qabrestan's answer.

Qabrestan shook his head and pointed toward the copilot's window. "We do not plan to commit suicide unless *you* force us to." His voice was calm, almost soothing. "I told you at the beginning. There is only one airport at which we can safely land. If you have flown as I have directed, it will be below us when the sun rises. If you have deceived me, then *you* will have killed us all, not I."

The three American crew members strained their eyes to see the ground below them. Their search was in vain for night was still upon the ground.

"We flew her just like you said. Right, Russ?" declared Worthington.

"Right," confirmed Conrad, pointing to the flight computer. "We're coming up on Omega coordinates BH798 and AE979 now. We're there."

"This place got a name?" demanded Worthington again as he scanned the darkness below.

"Assab," replied Qabrestan simply.

Worthington looked at Conrad.

"I never heard of it. You, Russ?"

"Nope. What sort of runways does it have?" asked Conrad, turning to Qabrestan.

"I have no idea," replied Qabrestan evenly. "It's a Soviet military base in Ethiopia and can handle large aircraft. That's all I know."

"Shit!" exclaimed Conrad. "What kind of miracle workers d'you think we are? You don't know anything about the damn airport, and you run us down so low on fuel we can't climb out for a second go 'round." Conrad locked his hate-filled eyes onto Qabrestan's. "You bastard. I hope they kill your ass."

"Steady, Russ. Steady!" exclaimed Worthington, eyeing the terrorist's reaction. "Take it easy, man. Take it easy."

Qabrestan seemed unmoved by Conrad's outburst. His cold eyes met Conrad's stare without blinking. His masklike face remained unchanged and gave no hint to his inner reaction. Finally, Conrad broke away and turned back to stare morosely out the window.

The rays of the rising sun burst into the cockpit. At first there was a slow diffusion of light. Then, as the upper limb of the distant fiery orb climbed above the horizon, there was increasing brilliance until the cockpit was washed with eye-hurting light. For a few seconds, the earth below was still in darkness. Then, as sunlight flooded the land and a few scattered puffs of clouds came into view, Qabrestan stood up behind Worthington. All looked below. The blue waters of the Red Sea and the smooth, time-worn shores of Ethiopia stretched out before them. Just ahead lay two islands, on either side of which the shorelines of the great Arabian peninsula and Africa converged unmistakably to the narrow waters known as Bab el Mandeb or Gate of Sorrow. Conrad spoke first.

"What d'you think, Pete? Are we all right?"

"Beats the shit outta me. Where's the airstrip supposed to be?"

Qabrestan, who had been carefully searching the scene below and trying to relate it to the maritime charts he had bought and studied, was visibly relieved. It was right. They were approaching Assab.

"The field is just beyond the second island. You should come right about ten degrees." Qabrestan regained his seat and buckled his belt. "The Russians may try to stop us. You should land as quickly as possible."

Worthington, without taking his eyes off the surface below, asked in a tense, angry voice, "How much fuel we got, Charlie?"

"We're down to less than twenty minutes remaining. You don't have enough for a go 'round."

"There it is!" shouted Conrad, gesturing slightly to the right. Worthington rose up in his seat and followed Conrad's arm. "There. Just to the right of those islands forming a sort of hook."

"Got it," said Worthington. "A big one, too. I can grease her in there with no sweat. But I'm gonna have to dump her. Make the announcement."

Conrad turned and looked questioningly at Qabrestan.

"Gotta use the intercom to warn the passengers we'll be making an emergency descent. They could get hurt otherwise." Then, as an afterthought, he added, "Your people, too."

Qabrestan nodded his assent. For the first time since the terrorists had taken over the plane, Conrad lifted the handset from its cradle.

"This is the first officer. We have been ordered to make an emergency descent to an airport below. Everyone should return to their seats immediately and fasten their seat belts. We will begin the descent in one minute. That's Ethiopia below. We're landing at a place called Assab."

Conrad returned the instrument to its cradle and placed his left hand on the control that deployed the wing spoilers.

Worthington kept his eyes on the distant runway. Slowly he pushed the control column forward with his left hand. With his right, he eased back the three throttles on the center console. The nose of the plane tipped downward. As it began to drop, Worthington turned the control wheel so that the left wing started to come up and the plane turned to the right.

"Gimme the spoilers," commanded Worthington.

Conrad moved the control, actuating the spoiler motors in the wings.

All along the top of the wings, large panels driven by powerful motors rose up to 'spoil' the smooth flow of air over their surfaces. Instantly, the lift that had supported the plane since its wheels left the ground in London was destroyed. The plane dropped like a stone; everything not fastened down flew upward. Screams filled the cabins.

To all aboard except the three airmen in the cockpit, a crash seemed unavoidable with so violent a descent. Worthington, however, was more concerned with the reaction of the Soviets than with the fears of the passengers.

Chapter 10

The little port of Assab lay across the thirteenth parallel of North latitude as if impaled upon a spit. Warmth from the newly risen sun, reflecting off chalky cliffs that thrust steeply upward behind the town, was already driving off the night's coolness and hinting at a fierce noonday heat.

In the narrow streets between old houses built of thick stone, the ancient stench of putrid shark and fish oil from the old harbor mingled with the odor of crude oil from a new refinery just south of the village. Behind the houses, scrawny goats wandered in their pens with swollen udders tied up in dirty calico.

The dry, southwest monsoon wind that blew off the desert from April to November began to stir the waters of the harbor. Not until December would the cool, northeast monsoon wind begin. Since the days of Ptolemy, the life and pace of the village had been tied to these winds that brought commerce from the entire Arab world to tiny Assab. The shapely sailing booms, the impressive baggalas, and the swift sambuks had followed the seasonal monsoon winds for centuries bringing dates and sweet water from the Basara River in Iraq on the Persian Gulf, cloth from distant India, and timber from the forests of the Rufiji Delta in Tanganyika. In return for these precious commodities, the people of Assab traded bulk salt and dried shark meat.

Ancient salt pans still spread their briny surfaces under the hot sun, silently producing salt by evaporation. But gone were the numerous slaves that carried sacks of heavy salt into the ships. They had been replaced by a mile-long, aerial railway that extended over the shallows to a salt loading wharf. And, although the great Arab sailing dhows were gone from the sea, rusty tramp steamers found water deep enough for their keels and came in twice a month.

A few yards from the worn stones forming the corner of the southernmost salt pan, a new, twelve-foot high chain link fence enclosing the Soviet naval base slashed abruptly inland from the water's edge across the aged land. Some distance from the fence, across a dirt perimeter road, a single runway stretched two miles long in the precise direction of the two monsoon winds. Heat waves, beginning to rise from the white concrete surface, made the six-story control tower just beyond the runway shimmer in the early morning light. On the seaward side of the tower, hangers, administration buildings and naval shops were visible. Just beyond them, lay the double arms of the large breakwater enclosing the naval basin and drydocks. On the landward side, several three-story barracks that housed eleven thousand Cuban ground troops stood on the hard ground.

Beyond the barracks, in what was once an oasis, the officers' quarters stood among numerous shade trees. The individual homes of the senior officers were located in the thickest of groves around a cool, spring-fed pond.

In the bedroom of the largest home, the telephone rang. At the sound of the instrument on the desk, Rear Admiral Dimitri Kirsanov threw back the light bedclothes covering him and heaved his bulk out of his double bed. Hot rays of sunlight probed through a gap in the curtains of the air-conditioned room that, by Moscow standards, was comfortably furnished.

Kirsanov moved with surprising speed and grace for a fifty-two-year-old man, weighing two hundred pounds. His thick legs carried him quickly to the desk where he reached out a calloused, pawlike hand and lifted the instrument before it woke his still-sleeping wife.

He frowned at the early interruption, his thick black eyebrows coming together to form a line over the wide-set, dark eyes. He glanced at his watch, the dial all but lost in the black hairs that matted his wrist. 5:57. As he picked up the telephone, there seemed to be nothing but black hair from his head to the inside of his ears to the backs of his fingers. He gave the impression of a great, woolly bear in authority.

Two calls in the last hour. Too damn many calls, he thought. First, the report that a hijacked American airliner was heading down the Red Sea. Now, this.

"Yes," he growled into the telephone. His voice was an unusually rich basso and perfectly fitted the heavy features of his face. Even the pores of his cheeks, which now bristled with a night's growth of black beard, were large and prominent.

"Officer of the Day, here. Admiral, the large commercial-type aircraft we have been tracking now appears to be making an emergency descent toward our runway. We believe it is the hijacked American airliner of which Moscow advised. We have the aircraft in sight, but they do not respond to our calls. I request permission to block the runway."

Kirsanov considered this information. From long habit, he ground his teeth as his jaw muscles tightened and relaxed. The rhythmic rise and fall of his heavy jowels seemed to totally reject the note of urgency in the voice at the other end of the line. His lips compressed into a hard, thin line.

Kirsanov was a slow, methodical thinker and was incapable of making any decision without thoroughly examining all aspects of the problem. That is not to say he was slow-witted, for he was a brilliant engineer and a superb administrator. His unsuitability for handling fast-changing tactical situations had been recognized very early in his career, and his considerable natural talents had been channeled into the design and construction of naval ships, a process which, by its very nature, demands a conservative and evolutionary approach to change. After his abilities as an administrator and manager were recognized, he was promoted through a succession of assignments of increasing responsibility. He came to specialize in the operation of naval shipyards and was handpicked to head up the base at Assab. It was felt that his cautious and moderate nature was ideally suited to both the climate and the political realities of providing a host establishment for naval and ground forces in Ethiopia. As Moscow saw it, Kirsanov's job as commander of the naval base was to support Navy and Army unit commanders in carrying out Soviet military plans. Kirsanov, thus, provided only the home base from which others operated. He was, however, solely responsible for everything that took place on the base.

Now he considered his alternatives. If I let them land, then I will have to get involved. Moscow cannot desire such involvement. I will be criticized. On the other hand, he thought, if I prevent the plane from landing and it crashes or is destroyed by the terrorists, then Moscow will be criticized in the world press. That is not good. But, it could land somewhere else safely.

Recognizing certainty on one hand and only a possibility on the other, Kirsanov made his decision.

"Block the runway. Make no radio contact with them. Call out the base security force. If they do manage to land, isolate the aircraft until I get instructions. I want no contact. I'm on my way to the control tower in five minutes. Do you understand?"

"Yes, sir," said the voice just before Kirsanov hung up the phone to hurriedly dress. He cursed himself for not thinking to have had the runway blocked earlier.

Two minutes later, a large alarm gong in the hangar bay, housing three orange crash trucks, went off with a loud jarring sound as it began its deep-voiced beat. The three duty crews swarmed to the trucks in a well-disciplined rush as the great doors swung into the overhead. The crash team leader swung aboard his truck and spoke into the handset of a radio. His orders to block the runway went out even as the trucks began to roll out onto the sunlit hardstand.

When the plane first pushed over into a steep spiral, both Barbara and Doris were caught out of their seats trying to fasten the children's belts. Barbara was thrown to the deck, falling heavily against a seat back. Doris managed to get her foot around a seat leg and one arm around a seat back. With her other arm, she held tightly to two screaming children whom she was trying to strap in when the deck fell out from beneath her.

Barbara gritted her teeth against the pain coming from her side and held on to the seat in front of her. She raised her head and saw the sparkling waters below filling the window as the plane fell off on its right wing, rapidly losing altitude in its mad plunge toward the sea.

The five terrorists had quietly buckled themselves into seats when the sunlight first hit the plane's windows. Qabrestan had correctly anticipated the need for an emergency descent and had carefully instructed the group in how to prepare for it. Still, they, like every other passenger, gritted their teeth and gripped the armrests with white knuckles.

In the cockpit, Worthington concentrated on controlling the plane. As each spiral was completed, his head snapped around like that of a dancer in an effort to keep his eyes on the runway far below. Small beads of sweat covered his forehead. He had to judge it just right. They did not have enough fuel to climb out and go around again.

Conrad, his voice conversational from professional habit, called out the altitude:

"Sixteen thousand. Twelve thousand. Looking good, Pete. Passing ten thousand. Go for it."

Worthington made a final estimation of the distance to the near end of the runway. The tip of his tongue nervously explored the middle of his upper lip. Now or never, he thought.

"Close spoilers. Give me ten degrees of flap. Gear down."

Conrad moved the control to retract position. The powerful motors rapidly wound in the spoilers, leaving the curve of the upper wing surfaces smooth and fair again. Lift was once again restored to the wings, sustaining the plane in the clear morning air.

The engines' whine could be heard in the cabins as Worthington slowly advanced the throttles to gain power. Conrad's left hand moved over the flap control and pushed it downward to the ten-degree detent. Instantly, both the leading and trailing edges of the wings began to elongate as the hidden flaps began to deploy. The wings, now wider than before, were given added lift so that the engines could be throttled back for landing without losing control. Worthington made a long, curving approach to the runway below and off to the right side of the aircraft. Everyone in the cockpit studied the Soviet naval base that spread out before them for the first time.

Down on the concrete of the apron, the three trucks moved at a high rate of speed, speeding past parked aircraft. In the shadow of the tall control tower structure, they swung right and headed out to the central taxiway that led to the midpoint of the runway. The crash team leader looked upward toward the distant end of the runway. There, out over the Bay of Assab, sunlight flashed off the gleaming wings of the plane as it turned and leveled off onto its final approach. His eyes snapped forward as he judged the distance remaining to the midpoint of the runway. His hand clutched the side of the cab nervously. His heart began to beat faster. It was going to be very close. He watched the descending aircraft, now getting rapidly larger, and began to sweat.

* * *

Conrad was first to notice the activity on the field below.

"Look! They're sending out crash trucks!" he shouted, rising up in his seat and pointing to Worthington's left front.

Qabrestan leaned forward, straining against his seat belt, and looked in the direction of Conrad's finger. Three large, orange trucks were racing toward the midpoint of the runway. Why? Then it came to him.

"Get us down! Get us down!" Qabrestan screamed, beating Worthington on the shoulder with the edge of his hand holding the gun. "They're trying to block the runway!" Qabrestan twisted and turned in the seat, insane with excitement. His voice rose to a screech. "Get us down! Now!" The muzzle of the gun moved to the back of Worthington's head. "You'll be the first to die!"

Worthington, without taking his eyes off the runway or moving his head the slightest, momentarily removed his left hand from the control column and waved it impatiently in the air.

"Fuck you, turkey," he said with a sarcastic laugh. "We're all going together in this one. Either shoot or give Russ a microphone. It's a little late, but maybe he can call them off."

Qabrestan understood instantly and, reaching into his jacket pocket, passed a headset to Conrad who, with a grin, twisted around in his seat, obviously enjoying the terrorist's discomfort.

Conrad quickly slipped the band of the set over his head and reached forward to plug the end of the cord into a jack in the communications panel beside his right leg. He rapidly cranked the small handle of the VHF radio to an international calling frequency, not knowing the correct frequency for the tower at Assab.

"Assab. Assab tower. This is Pan World two three one. Do you read? Over."

Silence.

With his eyes drawn to the moving trucks before them, he repeated the message. "No answer, Pete. I'm not going to raise them in time."

"Forget it. Give me full flaps. I'm going in hot. If I yell, give me full power and yank the gear out from under the old bitch."

"Gottcha," replied Conrad grimly as he moved flap control.

"For God's sake don't turn after the pull up," said Wall, the flight engineer, looking at his instruments. "We're down to the nubbies now. Power can go anytime. Better figure on putting her straight on in."

"OK. Here we go," replied Worthington. He pushed the control column forward to fly the plane into the ground.

The line of three crash trucks had reached the taxiway and were making straight for the center of the runway. Beneath the nose of the steeply descending plane, Qabrestan saw the small islands in the bay flash by. The shoreline and the end of the runway were rushing up to meet the plane. The whine of the distant engines seemed to fill the cockpit. The crash trucks were almost to the runway. Qabrestan's eyes widened as if forced open by the extreme tension within him.

A heavy shudder ran through the structure of the plane as the wheels screamed briefly in protest to the overly fast contact with the surface of the runway. The plane, nose down but moving extremely fast, tore down the runway toward the Russian trucks. Large streams of smoke followed each tire as friction began to break down the casings.

Worthington judged the distance to the first truck, now only yards from the runway's edge. "Get ready. We're going to . . ." he paused, incapable of expressing himself as the leading crash truck flashed by his side window. "Made it," he continued, finding his voice. "Give me spoilers and full reverse thrust."

The engines roared as clamshell doors closed over the hot suctions to direct the power forward, slowing the plane. The brakes squealed and the nose of the plane bobbed up and down as both Worthington and Conrad guided the plane in its ever-slowing rush down the remaining runway.

Qabrestan had recovered himself by the time they reached the end of the runway. The excitement draining from him, along with his emotions, left him once again cold and distant. Only the insane light in his eyes revealed his inner tensions. He threw off his seat belt, stood up behind Worthington, and took the grenade out of his jacket pocket once again.

"Turn around and go back to the center of the runway," he ordered, prodding Worthington in the back of the neck with his gun. Turning to Conrad, Qabrestan gestured toward the radio headset. "You. Get them on the radio. Now."

Worthington began to crank the nosewheel around to turn the plane while Conrad tried to raise the control tower.

The Russian Officer of the Day stood watching the distant plane through powerful binoculars. He observed its turn around and movement back down the runway toward him. On either side of the plane, two armoured personnel carriers kept pace. Every one of the three men with him in the control tower also watched the plane. No one spoke. The three crash trucks were moving back along the taxiway when Conrad's voice came from the speaker in the overhead.

"Assab tower. Assab tower. This is Pan World Flight two three one. Come in, please."

One of the enlisted ground controllers turned and looked questioningly at the OOD. The officer lowered his glasses momentarily, turned to the young man, and shook his head.

"No. Do nothing."

"Assab tower. This is Pan World two three one. Come in Assab. I am directed to contact you by the hijacker in command of this aircraft. Please come in. This guy's getting nervous."

Just then Admiral Kirsanov, followed by two members of his staff and a senior political officer, came up the stairs and into the now-crowded room. Kirsanov was slightly out of breath from the long climb.

"I see they landed."

"Yes, Admiral. We were unable to block the runway in time." Looking up at the speaker, the OOD added: "They have been calling continuously. They say the terrorist leader insists."

"You haven't answered?" asked Kirsanov, looking at the younger man intently.

"No, sir."

"Good. I am waiting for orders. Until we receive them, we will do nothing," said Kirsanov, more for the benefit of the political officer than anyone else. "Let me have your glasses."

Taking the binoculars, Kirsanov stepped to one of the large, angled windows forming the tinted walls of the room and studied the aircraft now beginning to turn toward him at the midpoint of the runway.

"Assab. Assab. This is two three one. Come in. Come in. The leader of the hijackers demands to contact you. This is an emergency. Please come in."

Kirsanov stood immobile, as if the words meant nothing to him, yet he both spoke and read English fluently. *I made a mistake. I should have had the runway blocked at the time of the first report,* he thought. *I will not make another. This is a political thing. Let Moscow handle it.*

The plane came to a stop with its nose facing south and its fuselage blocking the runway. From where he stood, the entire left side of the aircraft was visible, with the cockpit nearest him. As Kirsanov watched, he saw the left forward loading door swing out and open wide.

Qabrestan stood framed in the doorway shouting in a black rage.

"Fools! Fools!" he shouted. "They won't answer. They think we came all this way to sit here and play games. I'll show them a game!"

Sweat caused by the hot sun pouring through the open door ran down his thin cheeks and sparkled in the bright light as he jerked his head about to emphasize his words. Beside him stood a young stewardess who had just opened the door at his command. With the swift motion of a striking adder, Qabrestan spun around and slammed the side of the pistol he was holding in his right hand against the girl's head. Stunned by the blow, the girl's knees buckled under her and she began to sink to the carpet.

Qabrestan's left hand stretched out and grabbed her right shoulder, spinning her around to face the open doorway. Extending the muzzle of the gun, he shot her in the back of the head. As the gun bucked upward, he reared and raised his right foot. Placing it carefully in the small of her back, he deliberately pushed her out of the door. Gripping the door jamb, he leaned out and watched her lifeless body fall to the hard concrete below.

On hearing the pistol shot, Worthington frantically shoved back his clear-view window and looked with horror at the girl below.

"Jesus, he's killed Helen!" he exclaimed in disbelief.

Conrad, who had been controlling his frustration and hate with great difficulty, could contain his rage no longer. Without thinking, he tore off his headset and launched himself out of the copilot's seat at Qabrestan.

Yonnie, who had taken over watching the flight crew when Qabrestan came out of the cockpit, immediately saw Conrad's headlong lunge and dropped into a squatting position. She locked both hands in front of her and brought her pistol to bear on Conrad.

"Saayed!" she screamed as she fired.

The bullet struck Conrad in the side and passed into his stomach. The momentum of his charge still carried him forward into the First Class galley where he fell heavily to the carpet.

With wide eyes and a strange grin upon his face, Qabrestan pounced on Conrad as he lay clutching his stomach. Grabbing the copilot under the shoulders, the terrorist dragged him toward the open doorway.

"You wanted this from the beginning! Now you have it!" he screamed, his voice contorted with the effort of pulling the semiconscious man across the deck.

With a final lift and a push, Qabrestan got Conrad's head to the edge of the door. Straddling his body, Qabrestan pressed the muzzle of his gun against Conrad's left temple and pulled the trigger. The copilot's head bounced once from the shock of the bullet, then, Qabrestan tugged and pushed until the body fell from the doorway, landing atop the stewardess below.

From the control tower, Kirsanov had had a perfect view of the two murders. Bile rose in his throat with the realization that two people had been ruthlessly murdered because he had refused to answer their call.

"Assab tower. Assab tower. This is Pan World two three one. For God's sake, come in!" said Worthington's voice from the loudspeaker. "If you don't answer, he's going to kill more of us. Come in Assab. Come in!"

"Answer him," commanded Kirsanov.

The controller quickly reached to his panel and threw a switch. "Pan World two three one. This is Assab tower. Go ahead," he said in good English, the language of international air traffic control.

Sitting in the pilot's seat, Worthington turned toward Qabrestan who stood behind him. "They answer."

Qabrestan pointed to the communications panel. "Connect it to a loudspeaker so I can hear without wearing that thing. Then both of you get out and go to the back."

Worthington quickly did as he was instructed, and with

Wall, he left the cockpit. As soon as they were gone, Qabrestan took up the headset and sat in the pilot's seat. From the inside pocket of his jacket, he pulled out a sheaf of neatly typed notes. Putting the papers and headset in his lap, he sat back and stared blankly for a long moment at the instrument panel before him.

Now it begins, he thought. I must be calm. My voice must be strong. They will judge not only the words but also the tone. He took out a cigarette and lit it, inhaling deeply. The smoke tasted good and steadied him. Feeling ready, he picked up the headset.

"This is the fedayeen group leader. Do you hear me?"

"This is Assab tower. We hear you. Go ahead," came the voice from the speaker.

Qabrestan chose his words carefully, staring at the tower. "As you have seen, we're in complete control of this plane and have no hesitation in using that control to obtain our objectives. We require your assistance. Any further attempts to withhold that assistance will only result in more deaths. Is that understood?"

After moments of delay, the voice came again from the speaker: "That is understood. What do you require of us?"

"You will relay our conditions for release of the passengers to certain governments. When you are ready, I will make a statement. Do you agree?"

In the tower, the controller looked toward Kirsanov at the question. Kirsanov lowered the glasses through which he had been watching Qabrestan and turned to speak to his political officer who also had binoculars.

"For the moment, we must do as he asks, but I think relaying and perhaps later negotiating his demands is not a naval problem. I would like to pass this fellow directly to Moscow where they are more prepared to deal with his kind. Once that is done, we can concentrate on taking him. What do you think?"

"Do you agree?" interrupted Qabrestan. "Answer!"

Kirsanov quickly instructed his controller, "Say to him that we agree and are considering how best to comply." Turning back to the political officer, he raised his thick eyebrows in anticipation of an answer to his question.

"Yes, certainly. We must give this to Moscow. Can it be easily arranged?"

"I'm sure it can," said Kirsanov, turning to the OOD.

"Get the communications officer here immediately. I want a direct line established between the radio in that aircraft and the Kremlin." He turned to a staff member: "Get me Admiral Vorozheykin in Moscow." Then, realizing the hour, he added, "Or the duty officer if the Admiral is not yet in."

Having gotten his staff working, Kirsanov turned back to the controller, "Tell him that we are making arrangements for him to communicate directly with the Ministry of Foreign Affairs in Moscow who can best take his statement and relay his demands. Tell him it will take at least half an hour to do this since it is an hour earlier in Moscow than here. Tell him that."

As it turned out, only twenty minutes passed before the harried communications officer turned to Kirsanov while holding a telephone handset to his ear.

"This phone line ties directly to the Ministry of Foreign Affairs. It is a secure link. We have also set up a link from the Ministry to the aircraft. You will hear both sides of that conversation through the tower speaker there. If you wish, you can speak on the link to the aircraft by using the controller's microphone. It is not secure, however."

The young officer handed the telephone to Kirsanov. "They ask that you get on the line, sir, to speak with a Deputy Minister of Foreign Affairs."

Kirsanov took the instrument. His stomach felt twisted and his mouth was dry. He'd have to answer for letting the plane land in the first place. He took a deep breath and squared his shoulders.

"Rear Admiral Kirsanov here," he said with his black eyebrows pulled down as if expecting a blow.

As he spoke, the "secure link" was established through a complex system of electronics in the base's main communications center which broke down his words into discrete pulses of energy. Some pulses were broadcast immediately. Some were held back so that Kirsanov's words were scrambled in a pattern that was meaningless to all but a similar set of electronics in Moscow. To Kirsanov, it was disconcerting to hear the last of his previous sentence as he spoke the beginning of a new one. Still, it had to be done.

"Good morning, Admiral. This is Viktor Skudny, Deputy Minister of Foreign Affairs for the Middle East. Please explain what is happening down there. I have just come in and been given only the barest information."

"Good morning, Deputy Minister. Yes, of course. The American commercial airliner, Pan World Flight two thirty-one has landed and is now blocking the center of our runway. It is in plain view of the control tower. The aircraft is controlled by an unknown number of terrorists, who have already murdered two people and thrown their bodies out of the aircraft to the runway. A male, who states he is the leader of the fedayeen group in command of the aircraft, demands to make a statement and have it relayed to unspecified governments. I felt the situation was clearly beyond my authority so I called Admiral Vorozheykin for instructions." Glancing at his watch, he continued, "It has been twenty minutes or so since we last talked to the terrorist leader. Nothing further has occurred that we can see."

"You say two passengers have already been killed by the terrorists? Did the leader say why?"

Kirsanov took another deep breath.

"Initially, I ordered that no communications take place with the aircraft until I had received orders. My thought was not to jeopardize any future dealings with the terrorists. I was wrong. I believe the two people . . . they appear to be members of the crew, not passengers . . . were shot in order to force me to communicate with the leader." Some of what he was feeling found its way into his voice.

"Admiral, don't be too hard on yourself. They probably would have killed those two in any event just to prove they mean what they say. They would have found any excuse. We are now in contact with the American Embassy here, and I have been given the details of the flight. I will speak to the terrorist leader in a moment over the other line. I understand that you will be able to hear both sides of that conversation. I ask that you personally stay on this line so that I can speak with you if the need arises. One last thing. You should be prepared to supply assistance that will make the passengers safer or more comfortable. The Americans have specifically requested this, and we want to grant it. I am talking about food, water, and such. Is this clear?"

"Yes. I will give the orders to prepare all ground services just as if it were an *Aeroflot* flight."

"Good. I will speak with the terrorist now."

Kirsanov handed the telephone to an aide and gave the necessary orders for preparing aid. Turning to the window, he used his binoculars to look at the plane again. A moment later, Skudny's voice came from the speaker.

"Flight two thirty-one. This is Moscow calling. Do you hear me?"

When the call came in, Qabrestan was standing with Yonnie in the First Class galley discussing the removal of Sam Samson's body from the nearby lavatory. Quickly, he broke off and strode rapidly to the pilot's seat. The interior of the plane had become almost unbearably hot. Even the open window beside the seat, as he slid into it, gave no relief from the vicious sunlight that poured through. He could feel the heat through his pants. The smell of vinyl lay heavy in the still air of the cockpit.

Qabrestan picked up the headset and his sheaf of notes. "I hear you."

"This is Viktor Skudny, Deputy Minister of Foreign Affairs for the Middle East speaking from Moscow. How may I help you?"

Qabrestan sat back in the seat, a smile of triumph on his face. They had done it. Just as he planned. The Soviet government itself was going to be the hammer with which he beat the Americans and Egyptians into submission. Yonnie would have her victory. They would all have their victory.

"I have a statement to be sent to the American and Egyptian governments. But first, we need to have the lavatories emptied and air conditioning connected. Also, the passengers need food and water. Will you arrange that?"

"Yes, certainly. How soon do you want it, and how do you wish us to go about it?"

"Immediately. Use one vehicle at a time driven by one person only. No tricks or more die." Qabrestan turned and shouted to Yonnie that the trucks would be coming.

"No tricks. We want no more deaths."

"Good. I will make my statement now, if you are ready to take it down."

"We are ready here. The services you asked for will begin to arrive shortly."

Qabrestan lit another cigarette and prepared himself for the statement which, to them all, was much more than simply a set of demands. They had labored over the wording for days. To them, it represented a declaration of the reason for their existence and the justification for their acts. Qabrestan picked up the headset and held the notes up before him. Smoke from his cigarette between the fingers holding the sheets of paper curled along the top page to rise upward in the bright sunlight as if the words themselves were on fire.

"We, the fedayeen of the People's Front for the Liberation of Palestine, greet the governments of the United States and Egypt," he read. "Since the year 1948, the government of Israel has systematically taken from the people of Palestine their ancient lands, their jobs, their homes, even their lives to make room for Jewish immigrants. These facts are well known to both of you. Yet, you made peace with Israel.

"The nations of the world assured the people of Palestine a homeland when, through the United Nations, they adopted a plan for partition in 1947. Instead of a homeland, the people of Palestine found refugee camps and forced immigration to other countries. Today, three million Palestinians are homeless. Yet, you enlarge Israel.

"Hundreds of thousands of Palestinian children, first born into refugee camps where they can neither work nor dream and must depend totally upon gifts of food and clothes from others for their existence, are still living in these wretched places, now surrounded by their children born into the same camps. Two full generations bred in hopeless misery. Yet, you trade with Israel.

"Israel grows by the day. The fertile fields and groves of ancient Palestine are no more. Great factories and buildings arise from the old lands. That which in living memory was Palestine is daily made less. Soon, only the memory of this land will remain. When that happens, the Palestinian people will be forever homeless. They will not be able to return to their birthplace anymore than the American Indian can return to Manhattan Island. Time is running out for the Palestinian people. Yet, you do nothing.

"You must be made to understand that there can be no peace until the free and independent nation of Palestine is brought into being within the existing boundaries of Israel. You must be made to understand that this generation of Palestinians must either secure the future for all generations to come or forever lose it. You must be made to understand that those who make peace with Israel, make mortal enemies of the Palestinian people.

"Heretofore, the Palestinian Freedom Fighters have made war only upon Israel. But the United States supplies Israel with arms and money that permit Israel to maintain the status quo. The United States is, therefore, allied with Israel against Palestine. Egypt, by making peace, provides Israel with the time necessary to make the creation of Palestine within Israel impossible. No longer can such situations be tolerated by the Palestinian people. The fedayeen now declare war upon the United States and upon its brother, Egypt.

"To that end, we have taken captive the passengers and crew of this aircraft. They will be released when the following actions have been accomplished:

1. The government of Egypt shall abrogate the peace treaty with Israel. A state of war will be declared between Egypt and Israel.

2. The government of the United States shall withdraw all assurance of the defense of Israel's borders against attack.

3. The government of the United States shall cancel all planned shipments of military equipment and supplies to Israel and shall forbid the solicitation of funds from the American people by Zionist organizations.

4. The governments of both the United States and Egypt shall jointly request United Nations intervention in Israel and call for the long-delayed implementation of the 1947 Palestine Partition Plan.

Until these four conditions are met, the lives of the passengers and crew of this aircraft are forfeit. We have the will and the means to kill them."

Qabrestan lowered the paper. There, he thought. It is done. I read it well, without stumbling over the words. Slowly he turned his head and raised his eyes to the distant control tower. Moments later, Samson's rigid corpse tumbled from the open door.

Chapter 11

Mary O'Hegarty squeezed farther back into a corner of Duke Rodger's small cubicle of an office. In front of her, Admiral Swig Sauer's, Rodger's and Admiral Andy Anderson's chairs were crowded around a table with the initial plan for Assab on it. They were oblivious to her presence. Mary looked at her watch and smiled. 10:10. They had been here almost an hour. Just for a moment, Swig had said. She looked at Sauer with love. He really hasn't changed, she thought. Still as enthusiastic as a schoolboy and twice as dear.

He had shown her the Pentagon at night just as he had promised. First, they had gone to the Navy Communications Center from which he had sent the message to the *Montana*. Then, he had taken her along one empty corridor or another, showing her the various military activities that never ceased. Finally, they wound up in Admiral Anderson's office just to see how "old Andy and the boys were coming along," he had said. The telephone on the desk rang, interrupting her thoughts.

Rodgers picked it up and identified himself. Then, "Yes, sir. He's right here." Rodgers turned to Anderson and handed him the telephone. "Colonel Drake in Joint Reconnaissance for you, sir."

"What's up, Johnny?" asked Anderson. He listened intently. After a moment, he printed the word ASSAB on a note pad. Sauer's and Rodgers' eyes were fixed on his face. From time to time he nodded in agreement with whatever was being said. "All right, Johnny. Odds are the Joint Chiefs will get a call from the White House within the hour."

Anderson hung up and turned to the two men beside him. "The plane disappeared from our radar tracking station in North Yemen at 2250 our time, twenty minutes ago, while on final approach to the Soviet airstrip at Assab. It's assumed to have landed. We've got a U-2 in the air now and should have photos within the hour. We'll fly as many missions as

144

needed. Situation maps of the Soviet base will be distributed in about two hours." Anderson paused and thought for a moment. "No. That's it. Except I think you'll get a call from the White House shortly, Admiral."

"Yeah," agreed Sauer, pushing back his chair.

In standing up, he brushed against Mary. Sauer turned.

"Mary!" he exclaimed. "I'm so sorry. Here, I offer you a tour of the place and wind up ignoring you. Will you forgive me?" he concluded as he gently took both her arms in his hands.

"Nonsense," replied Mary, smiling. "It's fascinating.

Sauer squeezed her arms and returned her smile before turning back to Anderson and Rodgers.

"OK. I've got it. It's a good plan. Even though it's not coordinated, package it up. I'll take it with me just in case I need it. Andy, I'll want you with me if I go." Sauer turned back to Mary.

"Mary, if you don't mind, I'll have a driver take you to your. . . ." Sauer paused in midsentence as he remembered something from Mary's background. She looked at him with interest. "I seem to remember reading that you did some work on terrorists. Is that right?"

"Well, yes, Swig. We've made several, extensive studies of the behavioral motivations of terrorists, mainly for the FBI. But I'm afraid that, except for a few basic conclusions, the results lacked much useful detail." Mary shrugged her shoulders. "We simply didn't have enough data. Why do you ask?"

Sauer smiled, his eyes twinkling. "I think you just became our resident expert on terrorists' behavior. How'd you like to go to the White House with me?"

Mary gasped. "I'd love it, of course. Do you really think I could?"

"Sure. The more I think about it, the more sense it makes. I'll arrange it when they call."

Sauer was as good as his word, and thirty-five minutes later Mary found herself following Sauer and Anderson into the Cabinet room in the west wing of the White House.

Mary felt excitement rise within her as a presidential staff member showed her to a seat in a long row of leather chairs along the side of the large room. Directly in front of her, Sauer took his customary place at the huge oval table.

Mary looked around, fighting to control her conflicting

emotions. Professionally, she felt secure. She had been dealing with the highest executives and officers of the Pentagon for years. Also she was accustomed to apearing before congressional committees. Yet, in spite of these experiences, part of her was still a middle-class mother from Mason's Island, Connecticut, who suddenly found herself rubbing shoulders with the President.

Mary looked to her left and saw a fireplace flanked by by two doors. Over the fireplace, the Stuart portrait of George Washington gazed sternly down upon the gathering. Behind her, the windows that formed the gold edging of the wall were draped in blue and held back by matching, tasseled, golden ropes. Mary could not resist the urge to reach behind her and feel the luxurious-looking material. Silk, she thought. My God, it's pure silk! Across the room, there were French doors draped with an identical material. Through them, she could see part of the Rose Garden, illuminated by light from the heavy gold chandeliers over the table. Similar chandeliers were located on the walls between the French doors and windows. Looking down, Mary found her feet resting on a deep pile rug of matching blue and gold which perfectly complemented the bone-colored walls. It's lovely here, she thought, and was glad she had come.

As Mary looked up, she noted that the room was now almost filled with men. There was a distinct division of how they were seated at the large table. All of the President's Cabinet were on the opposite side, facing Mary. All of his military advisors, the Joint Chiefs of Staff, faced them. Military versus civilians, she thought wryly. But they all had one thing in common. To a man, they all had the bearing and carriage that comes only to the very important and powerful.

She recognized both the Secretaries of State and Defense. She also recognized the Director of the CIA, who, according to the press, was suffering from emphysema. He does look pale, thought Mary as the tall man took a seat at the table directly opposite Sauer.

On Sauer's left at the very end of the table, the heayyset Commandant of the Marine Corps slipped into his leather chair with an ease that was surprising for such a large man. On Sauer's right, the Chairman of the Joint Chiefs, an Air Force general, sat chatting with the Chiefs of Staff of the Army and Air Force sitting down the table. Like Mary, the accompanying staffs of all these officers found seats against the window wall. The Cabinet aides were against the opposite wall.

The sound of small talk and good-natured banter rose as more and more men filed in and found seats. Mary was surprised to find the atmosphere was more like a men's club luncheon than a meeting on a serious, international emergency. An occasional burst of laughter could be heard above the hubbub. Yet, why not? she thought. Crises are their normal working environment.

The door at the far end of the room opened. A hush came over the room as all rose to their feet. The President entered smiling, but looking tired. As well he might, Mary thought, with him just getting back from a campaign in the Midwest. Mary liked the President, had voted for him in the last election, and intended to do so again in two months.

Followed by his staff, the President made his way directly to the center of the table with his back to the middle set of French doors. Pulling out his chair between the Secretaries of State and Defense, the President sat down. While everyone else resumed their seats, an aide whispered some last minute message in the President's ear. He nodded and turned to look directly at Mary. Mary felt her face grow suddenly warm at this unexpected attention.

"All right," the President began without any preliminaries. "It's late, and I've got to confer with both the president of Egypt and the Israeli prime minister when we're done, so let's make it as short as possible." With that he nodded to the Secretary of State beside him.

Stephan W. Boyd, a distinguished-looking, gray-haired man, looked around the table unsmilingly. As he did so, aides began passing out sheets of paper to everyone present.

"Flight two thirty-one has landed safely at the Soviet naval base in Assab, Ethiopia," Boyd began somewhat pedantically. "We have been fully informed of the situation in Assab through the Soviet embassy here. As you will hear later, our own intelligence sources confirm the information passed on to us by the Russians. Unfortunately, three persons, we believe them to be Pan World crew members, have already been executed by the terrorists. The Russians assure us that their personnel at Assab are doing everything possible to provide for the safety and comfort of the hostages. The Soviet Ambassador has delivered to us the full text of the terrorists' demands. This is being passed to you now." Boyd paused to take a sip of water from the glass at his elbow. He had had a long day during which his voice was in almost constant use. Now, at this late hour, it was beginning to fail him.

"The terrorists are Palestinian Marxists. What you have before you consists of a statement of justification followed by four demands. Looking at the justification, we can see we are dealing with an unusually sophisticated level of thinking. The statement is cleverly designed, we believe, to appeal to the media and, hence, to the average person who hears it. By this, I mean that, taken individually, every claim in the statement is true.

"In 1947, the UN did adopt a plan for the partition of what was then Palestine. Since that time, the borders of what was to have been the small state of Israel have been enlarged tremendously by the military efforts of the Israelis. Millions of Palestinians have fled the country. Time probably *is* running out for an independent Palestine within the borders of Israel proper. My own feeling is that it has run out already. The analogy to Manhattan Island is particularly shrewd and probably accurate.

"What is not stated, and I am sure it was deliberate, is that the entire situation in which the Palestinians unfortunately find themselves today, of which these facts are descriptive, is due solely to the Arab nations rejecting the 1947 UN partition plan and attacking the Israelis in 1948. Israelis accepted the 1947 UN plan; the Arabs did not. The Israelis have won every war since. The Arabs have not.

"The point is that most people either won't know or won't care what happened so long ago. We must, therefore, fully address ourselves to the history of the Israeli/Palestinian situation when dealing with the press." Boyd's voice was growing progressively fainter. He paused and took another sip of water. Putting on a pair of glasses, he picked up his notes from the table for the first time.

All the men at the table picked up their copies. "Turning to the demands, we find, again, an unusually clever approach to an embarassment of Israel and even a possible resolution of the Palestinian situation. First, the release of the hostages is made a condition of responses by both the United States and Egypt. If we both were to respond as demanded, Israel's most visible champions in both the Western and Arab worlds would be seen as taking joint action against her. Israel would appear isolated and bereft of friends.

"Second, the first three demands are of an entirely different magnitude than the fourth. Clearly, neither we nor the Egyptians are going to negotiate any of them. Although the first one does offer Egypt an excuse to abrogate the peace treaty should they now regret signing it. We believe the first three demands were included solely to be negotiated out so that all parties can agree on the real terms contained in the fourth demand. In negotiation, it is called the 'buried bone' technique, by which you purposely insert conditions into the initial discussion that during subsequent discussions you can allow the other party to negotiate out. In this manner, you appear to have given up something, when in fact you have given up nothing since the real negotiation has not yet begun.

"This brings us to the fourth demand which, frankly, is a brilliant thrust. Were such a joint resolution adopted by the UN, the Palestinian clock would be turned back to 1947 and all subsequent Israeli territorial gains erased."

Boyd took off his glasses. Leaning forward in his chair, he looked at the faces turned toward him.

"Make no mistake, gentlemen. We're dealing with a first class mind here. Perhaps more than one. When these demands are made known, Egypt will come under heavy pressure from the rest of the Arab world to introduce just such a resolution. The Soviet bloc members of the UN will not forego this opportunity to embarrass the United States and Israel. They will also press loudly for such a resolution. It is clear to me that some sort of resolution on Palestine will be introduced and most likely adopted by the U.N. General Assembly. The terrorists will accomplish that much since there is nothing we or Israel can do to stop it. We can, however, take a leading role in guiding the content and wording of said resolution. Therefore, since such a role also gains us the release of the hostages, we should assume it immediately and open negotiations with the terrorists. At the same time, we will, of course, begin close discussions with both Egypt and Israel. In short, I believe a political resolution of the hijacking is both possible and desirable.

"Specifically, I propose to immediately send Calvin Benson, our Ambassador in Djibouti, which is only eighty miles from Assab, to the Soviet control tower to begin negotiations with the terrorists. Benson will be instructed to discuss anything with the terrorists but to negotiate only the fourth demand."

Boyd sank back into his chair and looked to the President, who turned to Boyd, his face full of concern.

"If a resolution were to be adopted, essentially as demanded by the terrorists, what would that mean to Israel and to us?"

"Only embarrassment," replied Boyd. "It would, of course, be ignored by Israel since no sovereign state need follow any UN resolution."

"I don't know," said the President, his fingers drumming the table. "It would put Israel in the same position as South Africa. The next thing you know the Arabs or Russia would be introducing resolutions calling for economic sanctions against Israel and perhaps even us. I don't like it, Stephan." The President paused for a moment. "Besides, the Palestinians have only their friends the Arabs to blame for their present situation. God, the press would have a field day with me, not to mention the Jewish vote!" He turned to Richard Gibbs, the Secretary of Defense, seated on his left. "What does the military have to say?"

Gibbs, a bookish-looking man, cleared his throat loudly and spoke.

"Mr. President, I'm sorry, but we haven't had enough time. The Chiefs need a chance to resolve their differences on all military contingencies. However, we do have complete agreement on a primary plan that you can go forward with immediately. The contingency planning should be fully coordinated in a few more hours." Gibbs looked across the table at the Chairman of the Joint Chiefs of Staff. "General Mason, would you brief the President now?"

General John Mason stood up. The four stars on his shoulders glittered brightly in the light. Nine rows of campaign ribbons showed proudly on his breast under the silver wings of a command pilot. Below a balding scalp, his thin and sensitive face seemed more in keeping with the merchant of a small shop rather than with a veteran warrior.

"Mr. President, there are two things we have to do to solve this one. First, we've got to put an assault force on the Soviet naval airfield as close to the plane as possible. Second, we've got to hit the terrorists quick and neutralize them totally.

"Of the two tasks, the actual assault is militarily the simpler. We anticipated this situation a few years ago. The Army created a Blue Light Force within the Ninth Special Forces Group. It's battalion-sized and is 'specially trained for exactly what we've got at Assab." The General looked over to the President. "Mr. President, you saw a demonstration by members of the First Battalion last spring at Fort Bragg."

"Yes, I remember. Very impressive. These the same fellows?"

"Yes, sir," answered Mason. "They've been alerted, and they're standing by in Heidelberg. At this moment, the Blue Light Force is loaded aboard Air Force C-141's for the flight to Assab. These planes can land on a beach, highway, or even a goddamn soccer field. The Blue Light Force can't land at the Soviet airstrip itself; that'll probably alert the terrorists. But once landed, they'll wait until dark and then go in. They've got special equipment just to break into a DC-ten. We don't anticipate any problems in this attack. Should be a complete success with very few casualties to either hostages or assault team."

General Mason shot a glance at Admiral Sauer's upturned face. Sauer raised his eyebrows as if to encourage Mason.

"But now we come to the real problem: how to get the Blue Light Force on a Soviet airstrip. It would be optimum for State to get Russian permission. The Blue Light team would hand carry its equipment and make the assault from the edge of the airstrip. They'd only be on the base a few hours and then only at night. They wouldn't have the heavy weapons or sophisticated electronic equipment. They'd be absolutely no threat whatsoever to Soviet operations. The Joint Chiefs unanimously recommend that this solution be sought by State.

"Well, as I said, we're all in agreement over that phase. But we've got some problems over what to do if the Russians won't let us in."

Boyd, who had been idly toying with his pen, came stiffly alert and looked closely at Mason.

"We're considering several plans for employing air, naval, and ground forces in sufficient strength to secure the airstrip long enough to rescue the hostages. Also, our differences lie in estimates of the military consequences of such an action." Mason looked down at the Chiefs of Staff sitting on either side of him. "We agree, however, that we can get the job done." Mason leaned toward the President to emphasize his next words. "We can and *should* land the Blue Light Force to rescue the hostages with or *without* Soviet permission."

Boyd was now looking openly hostile to the military point of view. Gibbs' face was also grim.

Mason relaxed a little before he spoke again. "We need to control the airspace over Assab, so the Navy," Mason nodded at Sauer, "has ordered a task force consisting of," and here Mason looked at his notes, "the strike carrier *Hubert Humphrey* and the assault carrier *Veracruz* from the Fifth Fleet to steam toward Assab. They're currently in the Arabian Sea off the coast of South Yemen and will enter the Gulf of Aden shortly. They won't pass through the Straits of Bab al Mandab until so ordered." General Mason looked up at the President. "That's it from the military," he concluded, but remained standing.

"Is there anything unusual or provocative about the carriers' movements?" the President asked, sliding a glance towards Boyd.

General Mason looked down at Sauer.

"No, sir," replied Sauer. "The Gulf of Aden has been a regular part of their operational area since the Fifth Fleet was created after the revolution in Iran. Their movements will appear as precautionary deployment and strictly normal."

"In addition to aircraft, this task force also carries Marines. Am I right?" asked the President.

"That's correct, Mr. President," said Sauer. "The *Veracruz* carries eighteen hundred and there's a like number among the remainder of the ships. We can put over three thousand Marines ashore with armor, light artillery, and full air support any place they're needed."

Boyd, obviously worried, began to speak. The President caught his movement and quickly answered Sauer, "Let's pray they're not."

Boyd subsided angrily and Sauer started to sit down, but when he was halfway to his seat, the President asked him one more question, smiling.

"By the way, Admiral, are there any women sailors aboard those ships?"

Sauer returned the grin. So, he's heard already. "No, sir, not a one," he answered, finally sinking into his chair.

Now the President turned to Gibbs. "So, Defense says that getting the hostages out easily depends mostly on getting the Russians to let us put a few troopers on their airfield, which is still a political solution, not a military solution. Right?"

The Secretary of Defense turned to the President, sitting beside him. "That's right," answered Gibbs. "We only have a military solution if the base itself must be attacked. If this happens, we're going to get Russian casualties, not to mention our own. From the preliminary planning I've seen, I don't recommend such a course of action. I mean, we'll have the shit hitting the goddamn fan! There's got to be a better way."

"I can't agree with Dick more on this," Boyd broke in tensely. "In my opinion, it's absolutely vital that we move through diplomatic channels. If we take a military approach, we could have an uncontrollable situation. The middle east is too delicately balanced now. If we attacked Russian territory, we could have chaos."

Gibbs nodded and waved his arm towards Ken Thompson, the Director of the CIA, sitting at the end of the table.

"As Ken will confirm, there's about seven thousand Cuban ground troops with both heavy armor and artillery stationed on Assab at any given time, and there's another ten thousand not so far away. We could go in with a regiment and then find ourselves having to commit a full division to rescue the regiment. We could get into real trouble militarily. God knows what would happen to the hostages in the meantime. We might take a lot of casualties *and* lose most of the hostages. No, I don't recommend a military solution under any circumstances."

The President, his forehead wrinkled in a frown, turned to Thompson, "What d'you say, Ken?"

The CIA Director got slowly to his feet, his thin body seemed wasted and out of place in the room filled with healthy and robust people. Yet, his voice was strong when he spoke. It was flavored with the accent of Ochopee, Florida, his birthplace and home.

"Well sir, ah don't go along with all that. But 'fore ah explain why, let me fill y'all in on the background of the situation."

Thompson, who was the only CIA Director to rise from the ranks of the organization, was considered a character by most of the Capitol. He put his hands on his hips, revealing that he wore both a belt and plaid suspenders.

"Speakin' from an intelligence point of view, Assab was

the best Soviet base the hijackers coulda picked. We've had it wired for quite a spell now. Without goin' inta details, ah kin tell ya that *nuthin'* goes out over either the air or wire that we don't get. Our SIGNET posts in North Yemen've been operational since the Soviets first set up transits to survey the base."

Thompson paused and nodded to two aides, who positioned a large easel at the end of the table. One aide removed a cloth covering to reveal a large, three-by-four-foot, aerial photograph. Thompson stepped to the side of the easel and picked up a pointer.

"Y'all 're lookin' at the Soviet naval base at Assab."

Everyone at the table leaned forward to look at the easel.

"This photo was taken less'n two hours ago by a U-2, then relayed t'us by satellite. They're bein' sent to the Blue Light Force now." Thompson's pointer flicked from place to place on the photo as he spoke. "Heah's the Red Sea and the Straits of Bab al Mandeb. Heah's the civilian port of Assab and the town. These light areas heah 're salt pans, a majuh industry. You kin see the outline of a perimeter road heah markin' the boundries of the base. These heah whitish blobs're naval vessels within this breakwater. These heah're small patrol-type vessels. There're no majuh suhface units or submarines at Assab at this time.

"Heah, beyond these buildings is the runway. The control tower's off to the side about at midpoint." Thompson's pointer came to rest upon the center of the white streak that was the runway. "This object heah in the centuh of the runway is the airplane in question. As y'all kin see, it's within comfortable viewin' range of the tower for anyone usin' binoculars."

Thompson nodded to the aides, who came forward and removed the photo, revealing another beneath.

"This is a blowup of the aircraft area, usin' a more sophisticated version of the digital enhancement techniques developed by NASA for space work." The pointer began moving again over the image of what was now clearly a DC-10 parked across a runway. The aircraft filled the photo.

"Heah you kin see the op'n forward port loadin' door. These objects below the door're the bodies of the three murdered hostages. More on those inna minute. Heah, you kin see that the Soviets've hooked up an air-conditionin' cart and a ground power cart. This heah is a honey bucket inta which they're gonna flush the crap."

Stephan Boyd winced at Thompson's language, fastidious in everything. Sauer and the President, however, stifled appreciative grins.

" 'Cept for the door and pilot's window," Thompson continued, "all other openin's in the aircraft're still sealed."

Thompson nodded to the aides a final time, and the photo of the aircraft was lifted off. A murmur of shock went through the room as his final photo was exposed. In full color, it showed three bodies in an obscene pile. Helen Dupre seemed to sleep peacefully beneath the outstretched arm of Russ Conrad. Across Conrad's legs, the body of Sam Samson sprawled in a grotesque sitting attitude. The fancy scroll work on his boots was clearly visible.

"From the Pan World's Airline's uniform," Thompson continued, "we kin see that the girl, who was killed first, was a stewardess. She appeahs t've bin shot in the back of the head. The male body on top of her is a membah of the flight crew. We can't quite make out the numbah of stripes on his shouldah boards, but we know from radio transmission intercepts that he's the copilot. The second male body appeahs t'be a passenger. Looks like a cowboy t'me. From the stiff and contorted position of the body, representin' rigor mortis, we b'lieve he was killed first. Also he was obviously shot in the chest.

"Ah chose t'open mah briefin' with this photo in ordah t'remind all of us what we *are* about. What the real objective is. Ah, more'n most, realize it's difficult to remembah when y'all 're up to y'ass in alligators, that the objective is t'drain the swamp! Whatevah else is happenin', we always gotta beah in mind that ouah objective is to get those people out alive. A second reason for wantin' y'all to see these pictures right off is that this photo defines better'n any words of mine, the type of people we're dealin' with."

Thompson turned and looked at Boyd, whom Thompson considered to be a pompous ass. Since Boyd thought of Thompson as a country bumpkin, the dislike was mutual.

"Howevah *brilliant* or *clevah* these terrorists appeah t'be, they're first and foremost just plain killers. And from this photo alone, mah gut feelin' is that we're not gonna sweet talk ouah way outta this one. We've gotta go in and root 'em out. So, as I see it, the primary task is to get that Blue Light team on the airstrip real quick. With Soviet blessin' if possible, without it if necessary."

Thompson nodded to his two aides, who removed the photo and replaced it with a series of briefing charts.

"While mah boys're settin' up the charts showin' the Soviet strength at Assab, allow me t'digress for just a moment. We're monitorin' all transmissions 'tween aircraft and the tower at Assab. As a result, we're able t' confirm that the text of the terrorist demands delivered to State by the Soviet Ambassadah is a verbatim transcript. We're furthah able t'confirm it appeahs that neither the terrorists nor the Russians have any knowledge of the presence of large numbahs of *Montana* dependents aboard. We recommend that Ambassadah . . ." Thompson paused and looked down at his notes, "that Ambassadah Benson be cautioned against revealin' this very fact."

Boyd's mouth thinned into a hard line. He was extremely annoyed at being publicly, albeit indirectly, reminded of such basic procedure. He did not like making mistakes.

"To continue, ouah SIGNET station also locked onto a secure high-frequency radio communications link 'tween Assab and Moscow that was established shortly aftah the aircraft landed. By the timin' and the fact that they're employin' a tactical scramblah rathah than a naval or diplomatic ciphah, we conclude that the link is bein' used for real-time, two-way conversations 'tween Admiral Kirsanov, the commandin' officer at Assab, and Moscow . . . prob'ly the Foreign Ministry. Since there's no ciphah involved, we kin reconstruct the transmissions t'obtain the conversations. Howevah, since the signals 're spread randomly ovah several bands, it'll take at least forty-eight hours . . . maybe even seventy-two . . . t'obtain the data. Other'n this single link, military communications traffic to and from Assab is holdin' normal, indicatin' no change in alert status."

Thompson stepped to the briefing charts now in place and picked up his pointer. "Which brings us upta the military forces available to the Soviets at Assab."

The President stared at the briefing chart, lost in thought as Thompson's voice droned on. He had heard enough. The plan and its requisite decision was taking form in his mind. One corner of his mouth worked ever so slightly, revealing his annoyance. Damn, he thought. As usual, from a room full of advisors, I get no useful advice. The key thing here is that the election is less than ninety days away. Inflation and energy have really hurt me, so a good press on this thing could put me over the top. A bad press will kill me. One way or the other this is the issue the voters are going to remember at the polls. Mentally, he began ticking off factors for a sympathetic press.

Thompson's voice stopped, and there was silence in the room.

The President looked up and seemed to gather himself together as a swimmer might before plunging into an unfamiliar, dark, dark pool of water. When he spoke, his voice was vibrant and free of any trace of the fatigue that he had felt earlier. The making of the decision seemed to have refreshed him.

"All right. I'm going to speak bluntly so that there can be no misunderstanding later. If anyone in this room disagrees with what I say, for God's sake speak up now. I don't want anyone using leaks to a Washington columnist to fight their battles for them. It isn't necessary. I want your opinions tonight.

"OK. Here's what I think. We must free the hostages quickly and safely. However, like it or not, I'll be reelected or defeated mainly on how the press thinks I handled this situation.

"Now it seems to me that shooting your way onto a Soviet naval base is the most risky way of accomplishing either objective. Go ahead with your contingency planning, but let's not even discuss a military solution until we've tried every other approach. On the other hand, introducing a resolution in the UN that embarrasses and isolates Israel is not the answer either. In this case, Israel is an innocent bystander. We'll not be party to any resolution that isn't acceptable to the Israelis.

"For these reasons, we will adopt the following plan. State will open discussions with the terrorists on the fourth demand only. At the same time, State will also obtain permission for a Blue Light team to get on the base. I expect the Russians will demand something from us for that favor, so State will work up a list of concessions that we might be willing to accept. Defense will move the Blue Light team onto the base just as soon as permission is granted and then move to rescue the hostages. Defense will also continue to prepare contingency plans for a military solution. No deployments for carrying out such plans will be made other than the Naval movements already ordered. I'll speak with the president of Egypt and the prime minister of Israel immediately after this meeting."

The President paused. Both he and the room were filled with tension. "One more time. For Christ's sake, for once let's see if we can keep our plans out of the damn newspapers. You can release the text of the terrorists' demands, since the Soviets or Egyptians are going to do that for sure. But let's keep *our* policies to *our*selves. People's lives depend upon it this time. All right, gentlemen, thank you for coming."

The President turned and pushed his chair aside. Without another word to anyone, he left the room, followed by his aides and personal advisors. Everyone else in the room rose to their feet.

As soon as the President left, Sauer bent down hastily to write a short message on his notepad. He was tired. His mind was not focused solely on the task at hand, and so in his haste he scribbled:

Cmdr. D. Mawson, CO Montana:

Landed safely Assab, Ethiopia.
Negotiations begun. Will advise.
                              S. Sauer

And, without knowing it, Sauer caused an omission to occur that was so insignificant at its inception that it went tiredly unnoticed.

Finished, Sauer straightened up and turned to Anderson and Mary waiting patiently behind him.

"Andy, would you get this message off to the *Montana* when you get back to the Pentagon?"

"Yes, sir," replied Anderson, tucking the message in his jacket.

"I'll take you home now," Sauer said to Mary with a smile. Mary nodded and returned his warm look, but said nothing. The three went out of the Cabinet room, leaving it elegant but hollow in its emptiness.

Later, in the car as a Navy driver took them to Mary's hotel, Sauer asked, "What did you think of all that?"

"It was scary."

"You mean the photographs? It's always amazed me how they can blow up an aerial shot to that size. They say that if the entire image that's on the negative was enlarged to the same amount, the resulting print would be the size of the state of Ohio."

"No, Swig. Not the photographs particularly. The whole thing was scary. I thought it would be different. More organized, more agreement on things. But there were so many conflicting interests and personalities. Except for the subject matter, that sounded like a staff meeting of mine. It just scared me to find it's no different."

"I know what you mean," chuckled Sauer. "Everybody thinks there's some sort of excellence at the top. That somehow people become wiser as they rise in an organization. And, to some extent they do. But for the most part, I've found that no matter what the level, the decisions of the world are made by rather ordinary humans scratching their heads saying, 'Now what'll we do?' "

"I know that. Still, to actually see it at the very top is scary. I don't think I could take your job, Swig. I don't have your faith in humanity."

With that, Mary took his arm in both hands and rested her head on his chest. Her hair mingled with his campaign ribbons and curled possessively around a polished brass button with a fouled anchor embossed upon it. Outside a light rain began to fall. The amber-colored taillights of their car glistened in the newly formed puddles on the empty street.

Chapter 12

The amber-colored PROCESSING light on the NAVDAC display console stared back at the human. Mawson scanned the readouts. They were rapidly approaching the boundary of Sigma 27, their primary launch area. Since leaving the British frigates off the Shetlands, they had been steaming at deep submergence. They could come up any time. If I take her all the way up to periscope depth, he thought, before planing down to launch depth, we could pick up the BBC and hear something on the hijacking. On the other hand, it might be as much as a half hour before they run the news. That's too long; the Russian satellite sensors might lock onto our wake. Shit.

For a moment, Mawson continued to stare blindly at the glowing readouts while he balanced the risk of detection against his thirst for information. He ground his teeth, lost in thought. Not once did he consider that it would be violating orders to come up to periscope depth. Just the thought of deviating from orders was, for him, normally unthinkable and showed that the inner conflict between duty and family had unconsciously begun.

A few feet away in the command center, Edelstone watched the jaw muscles of his motionless captain move in rhythmic emphasis. He was worried about Mawson. Of all the men aboard, he was the only one who knew Mawson socially, free of the rules and professional restraints that help men live in harmony at sea. He and Harriet had been guests in the Mawson home many times and had come to know the family well.

He remembered one time in particular when he and his wife had joined the Mawsons aboard *Tranquility* for a leisurely cruise among the islands and coves of Maine. During the quiet, totally relaxed evenings, he had observed the depth of Mawson's feelings for Barbara and his children. He knew what the hijacking must mean to him and felt that Mawson suffered more than the others, although it would never be allowed to show. Good man that he was, Edelstone longed to ease his captain's mind.

Can't do it, decided Mawson finally. Too risky. Turning to Lieutenant Allen Olsen, the OOD of the watch, he said, "Engines one third ahead. Plane up to launch depth. Commence countdown to Strat Alert and rig for quiet running."

As Olsen in a low-pitched and calm voice began rapping out orders that were repeated throughout the ship, Mawson walked the few steps from the navigation center over to Lieutenant Ross Wallstrom standing in the fire control center.

"Ready for target tapes?" asked Mawson without stopping.

"Yes, sir," replied Wallstrom, running his eyes once more along the row of weapon control stations before turning to follow Mawson.

The six stations that made up the main fire control center stretched along the starboard side of the control room from the forward bulkhead back to the navigation center. They were now fully manned. The red lights that had dominated the weapons status display boards while they were moored in Loch Tiree had been released by green READY lights.

Below, the Tomahawk missiles nested in their thick-skinned torpedo tubes. They were ready. Within the guidance and control section in the very nose of each missile, tiny chips covered with thousands of digital integrated circuits pulsed with energy. They waited with timeless patience for a target assignment and the command to ignite the booster engine, thus beginning its flight to destruction.

Wallstrom was looking impatiently at the Weapons Summary Status board. Only three red lights remained below the green TACTICAL WEAPONS READY light. The red STRATEGIC WEAPONS STANDBY light showed that the Trident missiles were still in their transport and storage mode. In letters larger than any other display, the words TACTICAL WEAPONS RELEASE DENIED and STRATEGIC WEAPONS RELEASE DENIED glowed brightly red, indicating that the *Montana* was not authorized to fire any weapons of any kind. These two displays were controlled through digital links by machines in the Pentagon's National Command Center.

Just as Wallstrom was about to give up and follow Mawson, who had disappeared through a watertight door to the officer's quarters, the red STANDBY light went out. In its place, a yellow STRATEGIC WEAPONS SPINUP light came on. The Launch Control Officer, Lieutenant Charlie Perkins, and his men in the missile control center two decks below had begun a simultaneous countdown of all twenty-four Trident missiles.

Wallstrom spun on his heels and hurried after his captain, arriving just in time to follow Mawson into his day cabin.

Without pausing or speaking, Mawson crossed the cabin to a cupboard located beneath the coffee buffet that enclosed two squat, gray-green painted safes. Wallstrom, following behind, pulled a folded computer print-out containing a list of twenty-four numbers from his shirt pocket. Neither man spoke.

The safe on the left was fitted with a bank-vault-type combination lock and contained only the captain's sealed orders covering a number of different military contingencies. Instead, Mawson knelt before the slightly larger safe on the right.

Two separate latch handles and combination lock dials protruded from the otherwise plain face of the safe's heavily hinged door. Within this box were the magnetic tapes that programmed the twenty-four Trident missiles to hit specific targets. Without the tapes, the missiles could not be launched.

In order to guard against the unauthorized launch of a Trident missile by a crazed individual, no single person knew both combinations to the safe. Mawson knew only one combination as did Edelstone, his backup. Wallstrom, in turn, knew only the second combination; his backup was Charlie Perkins. Not only was knowledge of the combination kept separated on the *Montana*, but also ashore. There, each combination was changed at different times by different men in different chains of command who did not themselves know what the combination opened. For over twenty years, the system had worked without a hitch.

As regulations required, Mawson hunched over the upper lock, blocking Wallstrom's view of the dial. Wallstrom waited several steps behind Mawson, staring at the opposite corner of the cabin, precluding any question of his attempting to see the numerals Mawson was dialing. Reaching the final number, Mawson turned the latch handle. The first set of latches opened with a click that sounded unnaturally loud in the stillness of the cabin. Mawson stood up and made room for Wallstrom to come forward.

Wallstrom squatted before the safe. Shielding his hand from Mawson's view with his body, he quickly dialed in the second combination and turned the lower handle. As the final set of latches released, Wallstrom pulled open the thick door, revealing orderly stacks of target tapes that rested on hinged racks and looked much like ordinary music cassettes.

Wallstrom put his sheet of numbers on the deck beside him and peered into the safe. At the same time, Mawson pulled a small metal carrying case out of the cupboard beside the safe. Producing a computer print-out sheet identical to Wallstrom's, Mawson squatted beside the younger man. He looked at the list he held in his hand and read aloud the first entry.

"YZE dash zero forty-two CK."

For the first time since they entered the cabin, Mawson turned to Wallstrom. However, the other man, lost in thought, continued to stare into the safe unaware that the captain had spoken. Mawson knew immediately what was bothering Wallstrom.

Before them in neat rows awaited both the ultimate judgment of mankind and the end of the world as it has been known since the beginning of time. Each of the C-4 Trident missiles now coming to life in their launch tubes carried eight independent hydrogen warheads. Each of the innocent-looking cassettes before them contained magnetic swirls imposed upon their thin tapes that instructed the digital circuits aboard a missile to place the warheads on particular targets.

Wallstrom's hand was stayed by the realization that in selecting a single tape, he was choosing death for millions of people. By picking a different tape, those millions could live and others in another city hundreds of miles away would die in their stead.

It was not the thought of being directly responsible for the death of millions that stayed Wallstrom's hand. That came with the job. It was the choosing of life for some and death for others that got to him. That choice should be God's alone, he thought, and involuntarily withdrew his hand from the racks of cassettes.

"It's all right, Ross. It just means you're human. If you didn't hate to have to choose, you wouldn't be here. We all hate it, everyone, every time. No matter what others think, *this* is when you earn your pay. Do your duty, Lieutenant."

Wallstrom turned to his captain, steadied by Mawson's words. Wallstrom's mouth worked for an instant before he found his voice.

"What was the number, Captain?" Walstrom asked, swallowing. "I can't seem to remember the number."

"YZE dash zero forty-two CK," read Mawson gently.

"YZE dash zero forty-two CK," repeated Wallstrom, turning back to the racks of cassettes with identification numbers printed in orange on their black ends.

Wallstrom reached into the safe and took out the first tape. Mawson took it from him, confirmed the number, and placed it in the open case. Without waiting, Mawson read the next number and watched while Wallstrom, now in control of himself, reached in to pull it out.

And so they knelt beneath a coffee pot. A black man and a white man. Like Olympians, they selected life for some and death for others. They pulled twenty-four tapes out of the vault, enough to place a 100-kiloton hydrogen bomb on every major city in Russia.

Their task was supposed to be made easier by the meaningless of the numbers on the tapes. They would never know or find out the identity and location of the actual targets represented by the tapes. This was the second safeguard intentionally built into the system by the wise minds that devised it. By not knowing the names of the places targeted by an individual tape, they could not be influenced in its selection. Because one tape would be so much like another, this approach was also supposed to dehumanize the process. Thus, they were not selecting cities for destruction; they were only selecting numbered tapes. In this selection, though, the system failed completely. Mawson and Wallstrom knew full well what they were about.

The job was soon done and Wallstrom was on his way to the launch control center with the case of tapes. As Mawson reentered the control room, he felt tired and depressed. With Barbara and the kids being taken God knows where and him not able to do a damn thing about it, the business with the tapes had just added to his low state of mind. Some example you'll be if you keep on this way, he thought. Better lighten up, Douglas, my boy. With that in mind, Mawson turned to Lieutenant Olsen who was standing behind the planesman. Both were staring at the trim panel.

"Have you managed to find the surface?" asked Mawson in a loud voice, with a grin.

It was an old, well-known, and somewhat feeble joke referring to Olsen's training days. In a moment of confusion, he made the outrageous mistake of diving the school submarine toward the bottom of Long Island Sound rather than toward the surface as ordered. Yet, it was exactly the sort of remark needed now. For, as Olsen returned Mawson's grin, so did every man within the sound of their captain's voice. The tension lifted immediately, as if some transparent and invisible sheet that had been pressing down upon them all was suddenly whisked away leaving everything unchanged, yet somehow better.

"Yes, sir," answered Olsen. "We're at launch depth under automatic buoyancy control. We're grooving, Captain."

"Very good," laughed Mawson, pleased that Olsen accomplished the very difficult task of trimming out the *Alaska* so rapidly.

As Mawson moved to the plotting table, Dacovak finished plotting the ship's latest position.

"We on station yet?" asked Mawson.

"Yes, sir," replied Robare. "Just made our arrival."

Mawson looked down at chart 804. He knew it like the back of his hand. In one submarine or another, he had spent a good point of his sea-going career in this area of the world. Without looking he knew what he would see.

The gray-colored coast of Greenland formed the left side of the chart. The islands of the Svalbard spread out across the top of a white expanse that was the Norwegian Sea. The convoluted coastline of Europe ran diagonally from lower center to upper right-hand corner. In the lower left-hand corner, Iceland and the British Isles plugged the gap between Greenland and Europe like a cork in a bottle.

To the northeast of Iceland, a diagonally shaped area outlining launch area Sigma 27 had been penciled in just to the east of Jan Mayen Island. Like a kite string, a thin penciled line, showing the track of the *Montana*, ran from the Shetland Islands off Scotland to the lower left corner of Sigma 27. Along this line, hourly notations were printed neatly. The last notation showed the *Montana* to be just inside Sigma 27, seventy miles off Jan Mayen Island. The coast of Norway and the second alternate launch area, Gamma 9, lay some four hundred miles to the east.

Near Gamma 9, just to the east of the North Cape off Norway's Tonafijord, Dacovak was penciling in an "X" with the time 0420 noted beside it.

"What's that?" asked Mawson, pointing to the "X."

"That's our first sighting of the Soviet carrier *Riga* and her escorts. McKenna just got the data. He's waiting for confirmation of course and speed."

Mawson nodded and crossed the control room to the CIC where Lieutenant Terry McKenna, the CIC Officer and Oceanographer, sat at the head of the Tactical Display Table.

"What've you got?" asked Mawson as he looked at the huge circular display tube, glowing blankly from the center of the table top.

McKenna, who was as fussy over his work as he was careless of his personal habits, pushed his glasses farther up his nose with a pudgy finger. He shot a quick glance at the plasma screen that angled into the table in front of him before answering. The orange-colored characters displayed on the screen were changing. McKenna looked up at Mawson.

"The *Riga*, sir. Confirmation of course and force coming in now. I'll put it up for you. It's all we've got going of any interest."

Mawson looked at the table and the five young men that manned it. He considered this to be the most interesting area aboard. Of all the complex and sophisticated equipment on the *Montana*, this was the very latest. And, with the activation of the new seabed acoustic data-link system, for the first time they were tied into the worldwide Naval Tactical Data Acquisition and Processing System called TACDAPS.

The table, actually a flat surface supported by an enclosed pedestal, was star shaped. Each of the five stations was scalloped into the table so that the top extended around both sides of the operator when seated. In front of each position, a plasma screen was recessed below the level of the top so it would not block the operator's view of the central display tube. To the left and right of each station, located so that they fell directly beneath the fingers of a seated operator, were high-speed alphanumeric keyboards. McKenna's station was at the base of the star.

The men at the table neither fired weapons nor ran the ship. Their role was to analyze all information available concerning the defense of the *Montana* and to present the results on the central TV-like screen so that Mawson had a clear picture of the tactical situation. It was, at the same time, one of the most difficult and vital tasks on the ship. For one of the curses of modern combat is that too much is happening too fast for a commanding officer alone to assimilate and act on. These men and their sophisticated equipment relieved Mawson of the need for doing this work and left him free to devise winning tactics.

The group was like a small chamber orchestra. All of McKenna's men, Jennings, Roderiquez, Mejia, and Schwartz, contributed their own expertise. As though in recital, they now presented their information on surface sea combat, airborne combat, undersea activity, and any other communications that were occuring. All of these were then conducted by McKenna who blended and smoothed each man's efforts into a coherent and harmonious whole.

Now McKenna's fingers flew over the keys. Instantly, the data being received through the acoustic data link from TACDAPS appeared on the central screen. On the right, a green line simulated the coast of Norway. Next to this line, five yellow dots labelled 1, 2, 3, 4, and 5 appeared and from these dots, five parallel arrows extended.

Mawson bent over the table for a closer look. Jennings' fingers moved over his keyboard as additional information came in. On a blank portion of the screen, the numeric designators that Jennings had arbitrarily assigned were now identified as being the Soviet aircraft carrier *Riga* and her escorts.

"OK," said McKenna. "The *Riga*'s escorts are confirmed as consisting of a *Kresta*-class antisubmarine cruiser and three *Kashin*-class destroyers. As you can see, sir, their speed is twenty-six knots on a course to clear the North Cape. They should take a new heading after rounding it."

"What's the source?" asked Mawson.

Schwartz punched some keys and in white letters, the words SOURCE . . . NIGHT VISUAL, AIRCRAFT OVERFLIGHT appeared on the screen.

"They'll probably pass down the Norwegian coast," said Mawson. "What's the range?"

Jennings' finger moved. RANGE . . . 430 MILES appeared on the screen.

Mawson shook his head and turned away. Over four hundred miles away and we're tracking him. At half that range, I'd be only mildly interested. Yet, because they have the data, the machines have us plotting it. Ridiculous. Score another one for the machines.

In the meantime, Wallstrom had been watching the Summary Status board to which he had returned after delivering the target tapes. When the green STRATEGIC WEAPONS ENABLED light came on, Wallstrom turned from the board and called out, "Countdown complete, Captain. Ready to go to Strategic Alert."

"Very good," said Mawson, turning to Olsen. "Go to Strat Alert. Set the watch."

Below, in the communications center, Tony Deville watched as the radio operator sent a short code group over the accoustic data link, telling the National Command Center that the *Montana* was now covering her assigned targets and would launch when ordered. Minutes later, confirmation was received over the ELF strategic command radio system from an antenna wire that stretched out three miles behind the *Montana.*

Throughout the ship, men who were no longer needed began to return to their bunks. A few diehards made for the mess to have one last cigarette and coffee before turning in. Silence began to descend upon the ship.

In the missile compartment, the twenty-four launch tubes rose through three decks like leafless trees. Within the tubes, the Tridents stirred as each entire missile rotated to keep the axis of its inertial measurement unit on target azimuth. It mattered not that the target was thousands of miles away across distant mountains and plains, for in the strange universe of inertial space, huge distances are but small angles. Once the target tapes had been fed to the launch control computers and the inertial angles of the targets passed to the guidance system of each missile, the units would track that target, turning the whole missile in the process, regardless of how the *Montana* herself twisted and turned. To pass by and hear them stirring restlessly in their tubes like caged beasts was an unforgettable experience that would remove all doubt that in a very real sense, the missiles were alive and waiting to spring forth.

As Deville turned to go off watch, the ELF radio printer started to peck out an incoming message. Deville spun around, instantly alert. Another message on the hijacking, he thought. The duty radioman, whose family was also on board, hurried over to the machine.

Slowly, one agonizing clack at a time, with long pauses between letters, the message took shape as the long, sweeping radio waves were picked up by the *Montana*'s trailing antenna and sent through a receiver to the printer. Deville remained frozen at the door, waiting.

Finally, the radioman tore the message from the printer.

"Eyes-only message for the captain, sir," said the radioman. His voice seemed filled with concern.

"I'll take it up," replied Deville, watching the slip of paper being folded and stamped.

Moments later, Mawson stood by the bridge ladder in the center of the control room reading the message. Beside him, Edelstone waited. Everyone, even the helmsman, stole at least one glance at the captain. In fact, most of the watch stopped whatever they were doing and simply stared anxiously, wanting to know, yet not wanting to know.

Mawson did not keep them in suspense long.

"It's all right. They've landed safely," announced Mawson calmly, reaching for the IMC microphone to tell the ship.

"This is the Captain speaking. I have just received a message from the CNO. Our families have landed safely at Assab, Ethiopia. Negotiation for their release has begun."

Mawson paused. Although his thirst for news was momentarily satisfied, another part of his mind, which had been chewing on the message since he first read its words, rebelled against what he had just said. He opened his mouth to continue, but suddenly shut it. The hand holding the microphone dropped to his side. The muscles of his neck worked with tension. Sauer's omission had struck home. Assab? thought Mawson. Which Assab? Ethiopian or Russian? Questions tumbled crazily through his mind. Realizing he must say more, Mawson mechanically raised the microphone to his lips.

"As soon as I get any further word, I'll pass it on."

Mawson lowered the microphone from his lips and motioned for Edelstone and Wallstrom to join him. Stepping up into the circular command center where the low railing and periscopes provided a small measure of privacy, Mawson hung up the microphone and turned to the questioning faces of the men as they approached.

"Harry, Ross. Is there a civilian airstrip at Assab? I only recall a Russian one. Do you remember anything about a civilian strip? One large enough to take a DC-ten?"

Edelstone looked at Mawson blankly, trying to recall what he knew about Assab. Wallstrom, however, understood the import of Mawson's words immediately.

"The message doesn't say?"

"No," Mawson replied and handed the slip of paper to Wallstrom.

"The only airstrip I know of at Assab is the one on the naval base. It's the one Jacobs talked about in his briefing," said Edelstone, still not understanding. "What difference does it make?"

"It could make a helluva lot of difference," ground out Mawson. "If they're on the naval base, they've got to negotiate with both the hijackers and the Russians. It could get complicated."

Wallstrom looked down at the message. "The CNO doesn't say who they're negotiating with. Maybe that's why."

Seeing confusion in Edelstone's face, Mawson spoke quickly. "I don't know about that. Maybe we're borrowing trouble by analyzing his words too closely. . . ." Wallstrom nodded agreement. "But I'd feel a lot better if I knew there was a civilian field at Assab," continued Mawson, his thirst for news returning even stronger. "If we only could talk to OPNAV the way the damn machines can." Mawson looked at the two men. "Do we have anything aboard that would tell us?"

Both men thought for a moment and then shook their heads negatively. For a second more, the three stood silently. Finally, Wallstrom spoke, "Maybe we can get the machines to ask for us, Captain."

"Of course!" Mawson exclaimed. "We can phrase the question in operational terms and have Robare's Robot pass it stateside. Let's try it."

The three men stepped down from the command center and walked a few paces to the CIC. Robare looked up as they approached.

"Listen, George, we know there's a Soviet naval airstrip at Assab," said Mawson. "We want to use the TACDAPS to ask if there's also a civilian airstrip large enough to land a DC-ten. Can you access that information?"

"I don't know, sir," replied Robare, looking at Wallstrom. "But I can sure as hell try." There was nothing he liked better than to challenge his machines.

Wallstrom and Robare then held a short technical discussion after which Robare's fingers moved over the keyboard. The central screen went blank.

"Whatever we get will come up on the display tube, Captain," said Robare, sitting back in his seat.

The four men stared at the central display and waited. Minutes seemed to pass slowly in silence while machines relayed the question first along the seabed, then to a satellite, and finally by microwave link to a computer in Norfolk. The answer came back along the same route. Suddenly, the central display tube lit up with the words QUERY DENIED. SUBJECT AREA NOT WITHIN TACTICAL WEAPONS ENVELOPE.

Mawson stared dumbly at the words. Query denied? he thought. The machine declines to answer? Impossible.

"What the hell does that mean?" Mawson exclaimed in a sudden rage.

Wallstrom continued to look at the screen for a moment before answering. "Captain, it thinks we're after Trident missile target information and won't answer the question."

"But we specifically said tactical missiles, not strategic missiles," replied Mawson, stubbornly.

"Sir, I'm afraid it doesn't believe us. It's programmed to block the divulging of any information concerning strategic targets. Since Assab is so far our of our tactical range, the machine assumes it must be strategic missiles we're really interested in no matter what we tell it."

Mawson turned away in disgust. The strain was starting to show on him. His frustration bred tension and it was almost tangible in the air around him.

Chapter 13

It was high noon at Assab. The sun seemed to hang motionless in the cloudless sky, searing the land with a heat that shrivels will and reason and drives all creatures to seek shelter. From the coolness of the air-conditioned control tower, Ambassador Calvin Benson gazed down through the tinted window at the plane shimmering in the blazing heat of the runway.

Thin and gaunt, he was an unimpressive sort of man. In thirty years of Foreign Service, he had managed to neither distinguish himself nor offend a superior. His appointment as Ambassador to Djibouti was, therefore, due more to longevity and his lack of enemies than to anything else. Yet there was in the man, as there are in most men, a capacity for excellence that awaited only the proper situation. Many a man will go his entire life without the opportunity to have his best being tapped. For Calvin Benson, his time had come.

When Benson first arrived at Assab, he stood in his white linen, two-button suit waiting in the open doorway of the helicopter for its short flight of stairs to deploy. As he waited, he noticed a group of Soviet naval officers waiting to meet him. When he ducked his head to avoid the still turning

rotor blades overhead and walked the short distance to the
group with his hand holding down his old-fashioned, wide-
brimmed Panama, he saw that one of the officers was a rear
admiral.

Kirsanov, Benson thought. Knew him right off. Looks
just like his picture. I'll greet him in Russian. No harm in
that. As he came nearer, Benson carefully considered the
phrases he would use. He knew the language thoroughly, but
had not spoken it in several years.

One of Kirsanov's aides stepped forward to introduce
them. As Benson shook the Admiral's hand and spoke to him
in Russian, he heard Kirsanov greet him in excellent English.
Kirsanov was delighted and laughed for the first time since he
had been awakened that morning.

"You speak Russian well, Mr. Ambassador," Kirsanov
said in English as the group walked to the base of the central
tower. "Have you ever lived in Russia?"

"It has been my privilege to serve two tours of duty in
Moscow. Almost seven years in all," replied Benson in English. "Admiral, I must say, your English is excellent."

Kirsanov smiled. His career had not brought him into
contact with many Americans or diplomats. Benson, with his
spotless and well-fitting clothes and with his reserved but
courteous manner, was exactly how Kirsanov had envisioned
a foreign diplomat to be. Like engineers everywhere, Kirsanov was pleased when reality matched concept. He was
also impressed that Benson had brought only a two-man radio communications team with him and did not seem to need
either a staff or even an interpreter.

The two men made the long climb to the top of the control tower and stood looking down at the plane. While Kirsanov explained the situation to him, Benson began to
appreciate the Russian admiral. He seemed to be far more
open and free from the excessive caution that marked most
Soviet military officers when talking to a representative of the
American State Department. Kirsanov had already been most
frank in assuming the guilt for two of the murders.

That had been almost three hours ago. Now, from the
speaker overhead came the excited voice of Saayed
Qabrestan, the terrorist leader.

"No! Again, I say no! No hostages will be released until
all the demands are met. Do not mention that again. It is not
to be discussed. Is that clear?"

Kirsanov turned to Benson and raised his heavy eyebrows. Benson lifted the microphone to his lips. Earlier, he had been nervous and slightly hesitant in his dealings with the terrorist. Qabrestan had sensed this insecurity and had seized the initiative in their exchanges, refusing to discuss any alteration in his demands and even adding more conditions to them.

Perhaps it was the sight of the bodies, swelling grotesquely in the hot sun. Perhaps it was frustration: the culmination of thirty years of smiling when he wanted to spit. Perhaps it was rage: the realization that his career could end not quietly and honorably as he deserved. Perhaps in this land of original mysteries, it was simply fate. Whatever the reason, an inner door opened and to his own surprise, Benson found a new confidence rising in him. He felt cool. All nervousness departed, and for the first and only time in his life, his mind became free to concentrate on one objective. He was now totally focused on Qabrestan's words.

"Very well. If that is what you wish," said Benson in a calm and soothing voice. "We will not speak of it again."

Benson, keeping his eye on the plane, hitched himself up to sit on the edge of the table behind him. He was completely relaxed.

I must distract him from the central issues, he thought. Submerge him in details to slow everything down and chip away at his confidence.

Benson spoke into his microphone. "Of course, by not getting it settled, we make the chances of our mutual success very slim. Very slim indeed."

"What are you talking about?" queried Qabrestan.

"You have given us four demands to fulfill in order to gain release of the hostages. The first demand concerns the government of Egypt alone."

"That is not true!" objected Qabrestan. "You Americans put the peace treaty together; you can take it apart."

"Yes," replied Benson patiently, "but only if one of the two parties is willing. What I'm saying is that however much the United States might pressure Egypt, *we alone* cannot guarantee that your first demand will be met. Only Egypt can do that."

"So?"

"So, we come to the second and third of your demands. As you may know, the government of the United States is not a single entity. There is the President and then there is the Congress. The President makes policy, but only the Congress can make laws and treaties."

"I know that. I have lived in the United States. What is the point of all this?"

Benson turned and shot a meaningful look at Kirsanov while motioning to his two communications men. One was actually Benson's military attaché and a captain in the United States Army. He nodded his head in understanding and spoke into the radio handset he held, relaying the information that one of the terrorists had lived in the United States. This went directly to the embassy in Djibouti, and from there by teletype to Washington.

"The point is," Benson continued, "that if you know anything of our country at all, you know that the Congress and the President often disagree. The President, acting alone, can fulfill only your fourth demand. He will need the agreement of Congress to satisfy your second and third."

Benson leaned forward slightly and looked down at the microphone in his hand. His next words came slowly and with particular emphasis. "He will not get their agreement unless he can give them something in return."

"He will have the hostages in return."

Gotcha, thought Benson.

"That is precisely my point. He will *not* have the hostages because of the first of your demands. Because it rests on Egypt's action over which we have no control. The Congress will realize this and will not act. If, as I have suggested, you release some hostages as each individual demand is granted, then the problem would not exist. By not permitting us to discuss such a release, you are making it impossible for us to comply with your demands. I repeat: We wish to negotiate the release of the hostages. But your inflexibility in this matter, I fear, dooms them. In the end, this gains you nothing. Can we not at least continue to discuss it while we wait for morning to come to Washington?"

Benson straightened up and waited. No answer came immediately. As the pause lengthened, Benson looked at Kirsanov expectantly.

"Tell me what it is you want," came Qabrestan's voice. Benson smiled, as Kirsanov nodded in appreciation. He had done it. They were no longer discussing the terms of the hostages' release, but only the details, and he could haggle over details for days if necessary. But I'll have to be careful, thought Benson. Anything might happen if he thought I was just stalling for time. Benson took a deep breath and plunged into his first request.

"Release all the children in return for introducing the UN resolution."

"No!" Qabrestan's voice barked from the speaker. "The children will be the last released, not the first. Do you understand that?"

"Very well then," replied Benson, not the least put out. "In that case, suppose we. . . ."

And so it went. Back and forth. Proposal and counterproposal. With Benson giving as much substance and urgency to the discussion as he was capable of. Anyone hearing him would have thought he was unusually concerned over meaningless details. And he was, for they were the only cards he held. But as the hours went on, Benson knew that the game had to end soon. He could not hope to hold the terrorist's attention much longer. He needed new grist for his mill and feared what might happen if he could not continue to distract the terrorist.

Benson glanced at the clock on the wall. Almost four o'clock. That means 8:00 A.M. in Washington, he thought: Come on guys, give me some instructions. I've got him on the hook, now I need to know where to lead him.

However, something in Qabrestan's voice broke into his thoughts. Benson's entire attention was again concentrated on the terrorist. It was his tone more than his choice of words. Benson listened carefully. Yes, there was a new harshness, a new finality to it. As if the man had made up his mind on a new course of action.

"You talk and talk, but nothing happens," came Qabrestan's voice.

Benson cast about desperately for something to say, anything to interrupt this new train of thought.

"It is now eight o'clock in the morning in Washington," said Benson, his voice still calm in spite of his concern. "Within a few minutes, we will hear of the progress my government has made during the night towards satisfying your demands. If you will permit me, I will leave you for a few moments to talk to them myself and report our discussion."

Benson lowered his microphone and looked up at the speaker. He chewed his lower lip from tension. That wasn't very good, he thought, but it was the best I could think of. Maybe he'll take a break and do nothing. Maybe he'll just wait for me. Qabrestan's voice came through.

"You do that. And when you come back I will have some news for you, Mr. Ambassador," spoke the hard, flat voice from the wall, disembodied as if coming from some other world.

Benson gasped and raised the microphone to his lips, fighting to sound calm. "What do you mean?"

But the only answer from the speaker was the hiss of electronics.

Kirsanov raised his glasses and stared at the plane. Benson threw his microphone down, snatched up binoculars from the table beside him, and quickly brought the glasses up to his eyes. The cockpit window came into focus. Qabrestan was gone. But where? thought Benson. His hands were sweaty as he slowly lowered the binoculars.

Under the watchful eyes of the terrorists, the flight crew had finally begun to bring order out of chaos aboard the plane. With the help of the Soviet equipment on the runway, cool air once again flowed from ducts in the overhead, reducing the oppressive heat and humidity that had turned the cabin into a steam bath minutes after landing. Slowly, the flow of fresh air was also dissipating the sickening odor from the overfilled chemical toilets that were being drained into waiting service carts below. There was fresh drinking water flowing from the lavatory and galley faucets. Food from the Russian mess hall had arrived at last, and the first meal in many hours was being served to the passengers.

Abdulla bin Salim stood guard in the forward end of the First Class cabin. Idly, he watched as Barbara and Doris passed out box lunches to the noisy and hungry children who clustered around them. In the center galley, Yonnie Trupp stood watch while Hamed and Mahmud Jadayel ate their food. As always, Mahmud was eating his brother's dessert as well as his own.

Back in Economy Class, just a few feet from where Yonnie stood, Worthington and Wall sat eating in silence. Since leaving the cockpit, they had been quietly discussing the situation and had concluded that they could do nothing. They could see no way of disarming the terrorists. So they ate without appetite.

In the aisle seat behind them, Jan Deville was finishing her box lunch. She ate with an inconspicuous but persistent activity that satisfied her ravenous appetite as quickly as was humanly possible without, she imagined, making her appear unladylike. Jan's attention was focused solely upon the box and its contents. She sat bolt upright and neither talked nor looked about. Her hands made small, ferreting motions within the box, fingering the contents, then quickly darting to her mouth. Now and then, a small bit of food fell unnoticed from her mouth to her lap. Beside her, Martin Schlosser ate in a far more leisurely and dignified manner.

Jan's concentration was diverted by the appearance of a stewardess with a drink cart that now held only warm water.

"Would you like some?" asked the girl, reaching out a tray of empty, plastic glasses.

"*Ja*, dat vould be nice," answered Jan in a fair German accent.

Schlosser smiled in appreciation of Jan's attempt.

The stewardess filled the small glass from a pitcher and extended the tray to her.

"*Danke*," said Jan loudly, turning to Schlosser as his glass was filled. Just the idea of being his daughter turns me on, she thought. When we get out of this mess, we're really going to get down in Washington.

Yonnie, hearing the German, instinctively looked up. Seeing it was Jan who had spoken, her eyes narrowed.

As the stewardess straightened up from filling Schlosser's glass, Jan, excited by her fantasies of Washington, slid her right hand beneath the table covering Schlosser's lap and massaged his crotch. Schlosser leaned back in the seat and spread his knees slightly. As her fingers found the swelling lump of his penis trapped in his underwear, he turned his head toward her. She leaned toward him and their lips, covered with a thin film of grease from the military food, met in a long and passionate kiss.

Suddenly, the cockpit door flew open and Qabrestan strode into the First Class cabin, gun in hand. Strange fires burned in his eyes.

As Qabrestan came down the aisle, Yonnie started toward him. She motioned for Hamed and Mahmud to take over the guard.

"What is it, Saayed?" she asked as she reached him midway down the aisle.

"They play games, again. They talk, but do nothing. They think we are stupid. That we wait forever." He spit viciously into the aisle.

Out of the corner of his eye, Qabrestan caught sight of Barbara, who was just sitting down with her box lunch. He reached out, grabbed the front of her dress, and shoved his pistol into her neck. Then, he began to pull her up and out of the seat. Her lunch fell to the carpet, scattering its contents.

"They need another lesson," Qabrestan said from between clenched teeth.

Barbara, confused and startled by the suddenness of the attack, looked wildly about her. About this time, Robbie looked up and saw his mother being dragged down the aisle. He jumped up, latched onto the terrorist's pistol arm, and began kicking him in the shins.

As the nightmare escalated, Barbara found her voice. "No, Robbie! No!" she yelled. Her shout silenced the cabin.

Across the cabin, Doris had been kneeling among her own children. At the sound of Barbara's scream, her heavy body jerked upright. As she rose and saw the struggling group across the cabin, the pain-twisted face of the dead copilot as he clutched his stomach flashed into her mind. Without thinking, she extended an arm and called out. "Don't!"

Qabrestan let go of Barbara and, using both hands, shoved Robbie brutally back into his seat. The boy fell heavily against his sister who screamed in terror. Barbara quickly bent over the seat back and reached down to her two frightened children.

Qabrestan swung around and faced Doris. His breathing labored, his eyes insane. He pointed his pistol across the center seats and aimed at Doris' head.

Doris stood transfixed. Fear gripped her and set the large muscles of her thighs tingling deep beneath her skin. Yet, she met Qabrestan's look with unblinking defiance. For an instant they stood locked in silent confrontation.

Then, Yonnie's voice broke the tableau.

"Saayed. Saayed!" she said urgently, putting her hand on his arm. "Not these. I have the perfect ones. Martin Schlosser and his cunt. Come."

Saayed turned away from Doris and looked down at Robbie. Barbara tried to hide both of her children with her torso as Qabrestan turned away to follow Yonnie back toward the center cabin.

Jan was still kneading Schlosser's penis. Their breath was coming in shallow gasps as Yonnie and Qabrestan approached.

Without a word of explanation, Yonnie reached out and slowly ran the fingers of her left hand up along the base of Jan's scalp just behind one ear. Her hand closed over the thick brown hair and yanked Jan's head viciously forward and up. Jan's eyes opened wide with shock as she screamed in pain. Yonnie then extended her right arm over Jan's back and stuck her pistol into Schlosser's face.

Both Worthington and Wall started up out of their seats at the sound of Jan's scream. But Qabrestan was ready for them. At Worthington's first movement, he brought his pistol down across the pilot's face, splitting the skin between ear and mouth. Worthington collapsed back into his seat, blood running over the fingers that held his cheek.

"Don't move! Nobody move or the children die!" yelled Qabrestan as he backed into the galley entrance and motioned the brothers into the forward cabin with their grenades.

No one moved.

"Up," said Yonnie to Jan and Schlosser in a flat, tight voice. "You will both stand up and come with me."

Jan's eyes rolled like a frightened cow's. Desperately, she reached behind her with both hands and groped for the seat arms in order to relieve the terrible pressure on her scalp.

"Please. My hair," she begged. "You're hurting me."

Schlosser tore the little table aside and stood up. Bending over, he helped Jan slide out of the seat and onto her feet in the aisle.

"What is going on?" he demanded. "Don't hurt her. We'll come."

Without waiting or answering, Yonnie pulled Jan up the aisle by her hair. Qabrestan stood aside, allowing Schlosser to follow behind the struggling woman.

Jan, half walking and half running sideways along the aisle, tripped and lost a shoe as she bumped against a seat in First Class. Yonnie turned and struck awkwardly at Jan's head with her pistol. The weapon caught Jan a glancing blow on her temple, peeling off a small flap of skin that hung down partially covering her left eye. Blindly, she stumbled after Yonnie to the open loading door.

Goaded by Qabrestan, Schlosser followed. "What are you doing?" he demanded. Then, "Why? Why?"

"Why? You want to know why?" said Yonnie in German, her voice tense. "I will tell you why, Herr Schlosser, you fat bastard. We know you from old. How rich you have become at the expense of the Arab people!"

Schlosser looked shocked.

Yonnie's voice remained cold and flat. "For someone who was nothing in 1945, you have done well. Very well. So well have you done that the old Wehrmacht soldier can now afford an American mistress. That is rich indeed. Now, it is at an end. Finished. You pig."

At that moment, Qabrestan raised his arm and hit Schlosser in the head from behind with the butt of his pistol. The German, fighting for consciousness, staggered a half step forward and then sank to his knees. Without hesitation, Yonnie stepped behind him and placed the muzzle of her pistol against the base of his skull. She fired.

Jan screamed and screamed. Just when it seemed a though she would never stop, Yonnie turned and shot her through the mouth. Together, Qabrestan and Yonnie pushed the two bodies out of the door.

Benson lowered the binoculars, his face a mask of despair, and found Kirsanov staring at him in sympathetic understanding. Oddly, Benson felt a deep attachment for the hairy Russian who stood so solidly beside him.

Suddenly, the speaker on the wall came alive. Both men raised their heads to stare at it.

"Now, Mr. Ambassador, you have received my news for you! Until our demands are met, we will kill a hostage every six hours."

Chapter 14

Cool summer rain fell heavily from the dark, early-morning sky. Out of low leaden clouds, thunder rumbled ominously. Swig Sauer stood looking out of his Pentagon office window. Below him the commuter traffic splashed slowly by, and pedestrians delayed by the storm hurried to shelter and their jobs. In his hand, Sauer held a State Department message.

On the desk behind him, there were three folders. The red-bound OPERATION ASSAB folder with the seal of the Joint Chiefs of Staff on the cover contained the now-completed plan for an assault on Assab. The blue-bound SITREPS folder with the Navy seal contained reports describing the situation in Assab at six o'clock that morning. The plain, green-bound folder contained copies of stories concerning the hijacking that were appearing in the nation's leading newspapers. He had just finished sampling these PRESSREPS when he received the message that he was now holding. After reading it, he had gone to stand at the window.

He gazed unseeingly. Lost in thought, he tapped the paper idly against his leg. That tears it, he thought. The Russians won't let a Blue Light team on the base. Want us to request a negotiating team from the UN instead. Sauer shook his head disgustedly. They don't miss a trick, he thought. To hell with the hostages. The bastards are going to force us to the UN whether we like it or not. Not a bad shot, and it didn't cost them a thing. But it's going to cost us.

He turned from the window and stared down at the three folders on his desk. They were like three planets orbiting a single central issue: free the hostages without jeopardizing the President's chances for reelection. The SITREPS showed the results of the political solution now in effect. The PRESSREPS reflected the nation's opinion of the President's actions. As long as these two reports were favorable, the OPERATION ASSAB plan would be held at a distance. If one or the other of these areas weakened, then the military solution would move closer to the center.

Sauer pulled out his chair and sat down, fingering the blue folder. The SITREPS showed that the situation at Assab was stable. Discussions with the terrorists were underway. Food and water had been provided to the hostages, and aircraft comfort services had been restored.

Sauer picked up the green folder and began leafing through it. The PRESSREPS showed that, as usual, the reporting of the hijacking ranged from the factual to the absurd. With little hard news available to the press, the coverage had dwelt heavily on political aspects. The full text of the demands had been published together with extensive and conflicting interpretations. Sharing the front pages of most newspapers with other aspects of the hijacking were detailed reports on the *Montana* families together with extensive background material on Trident missile submarines and crews. The Palestinian question was discussed on the front pages, in numerous back-page articles, and, of course, in the editorial column. A surprising number of these editorial writers took the position that while they deplored the hijacking and killing the three hostages, it was high time the United States became involved in the Palestinian problem. Other columnists, by lauding the President's restraint and attempts to work through the Russians, made him appear to be committed to a political solution. Overall, the coverage was very favorable to the President. It presented a mature and thoughtful leader, carefully feeling his way through a complex and difficult situation.

Sauer threw down the folder and leaned back in his chair. He turned to look out the window once again. Good press. Good plan. The Blue Light team could have gone in tonight, and by this time tomorrow we'd have had the hostages back. Not now. If the President goes to the UN, it'll be days before this thing is resolved. Maybe weeks.

Sauer rocked slowly back and forth in the chair, thinking about the President's options. Time is the key. As long as the terrorists give him enough time, then the President will go to the UN. And why not? That's the wisest move politically, and it follows from the action he's already taken.

Sauer swung back to his desk and looked at the red folder. It'll take a radical change in the situation for the President to opt for a military solution.

The red phone on his desk suddenly rang.

"Sauer," he said.

The President's voice sounded calm, but tired. "Swig, get over here. The terrorists just upped the ante. I'm caught between a rock and a hard place on this thing, and I need you."

"Yes, sir. Can you tell me what's happened?"

"Yeah. The terrorists killed two more passengers, and they announced they'd kill one more every six hours until their demands are met."

"I'm on my way, sir."

"OK," said the President, then as an afterthought he added, "Oh, Swig. Bring that lady psychologist friend of yours. What's her name?"

"O'Hegarty, Mr. President. Mary O'Hegarty."

"Yeah. Get her over here too. I've got a feeling we may need her."

"Yes, sir. She's scheduled to testify before Dickerson's committee sometime today, but I'll take care of it. I'm on my way now."

"Fine,. Swig," the President rang off.

Sauer hung up his phone. Time, he thought. Time has run out already. Now everything's out of balance.

He stood up and started for the closet to get his raincoat and cap. Suddenly, Barbara Mawson and her children were in his mind. Then, halfway across the room, the conviction came to him that a political solution was no longer real. Like it or not, good press or bad, it's strictly a military problem now. I wish to hell I knew whether the President will see it that way, he thought shaking his head. He's going to have to as soon as possible.

A short time later, Sauer pulled out his usual chair in the Cabinet room and sat down. Noting the empty seats at the table, he shook his head. Washington, he thought wryly. God, how they flock to the glory meetings, the easy ones that are well covered by the press. They clutter up the discussion as well as the table, then after the meeting's over, spout some crap to a TV reporter waiting conveniently outside. But when it comes to the tough decisions, you're all alone. The great galloping horde has suddenly disappeared. Bullshit. This town runs on bullshit. And not just politicians either. The military are just as bad.

Sauer smiled, his sense of humor coming to his rescue. You're getting cynical, fella. It's a good thing the horde doesn't attend the gutsy meetings. If they did, you'd never get anything done. You can tell more about a man by the meetings he does *not* attend than those he does. Sauer looked around the room again. Thompson of the CIA now sat across the table. The other Chiefs of Staff along with Mason, their chairman, were just coming into the room. He could hear Secretary of State Boyd's voice coming from the office of the President's secretary. Sauer knew that Secretary of Defense Gibbs was in Chicago giving a political speech and would be absent.

Everyone stood as the President came into the room. He appeared rested, but his expression was grim. Behind him came Boyd, then Alexy Zhuravlev, the President's National

Security Advisor, and finally a small man that Sauer recognized as the President's chief political advisor.

"Sit down everyone. Let's dispense with formalities and get on with it," said the President, suiting his action to his words.

Just as Sauer was sitting, an aide led Mary to the empty seat beside him.

"Morning, Doctor," said the President, smiling for the first time. He looked around the table. "Gentlemen, this is Doctor O'Hegarty from DARPA. She knows about terrorists."

Mary produced a thin smile for the group and sat down. Sauer leaned over to her.

"Where'd Margaret reach you?" he whispered, squeezing her arm.

"In the shower, of course," she whispered back.

Sauer smiled. God, she smells good, he thought.

The President was speaking.

"The situation is this. The Russians have refused to allow us to land a Blue Light team on Assab. However, they will permit a UN negotiating team to land. The terrorists have murdered two more hostages and have stated that they'll kill one hostage every six hours until we meet their demands."

The President looked across the table at Mary. "Before we go any further, I'd like to confirm one thing. Doctor, is there any chance the terrorists are bluffing?"

Mary looked at the President, thinking back to last night's meeting "Let me make sure I've got my facts straight. These last two make it five people they've killed so far. Who were the latest victims?"

The President looked at Boyd, who responded.

"Passengers. A young woman and an older man. Benson saw the entire thing from the control tower."

"OK, then," said Mary, counting on her fingers. "That's three passengers and two crew. Of which two were young women, one a young man, and two were older men. If I've got it right, the random pattern leaves no doubt at all that they'll continue to kill hostages as it suits their purposes." Mary paused as another thought occurred to her. "Are there many children aboard?"

"Yes," replied Boyd. "I'm afraid there are. Most dependents of the *Montana* crew."

Mary sighed. "Then the next threat made by the terrorists will probably be the killing of children. Which, I'm sorry to say, I think they are perfectly capable of carrying out."

The room was totally silent. All eyes were on Mary. Everyone seemed stunned by her statement.

Feeling some further explanation was needed, Mary continued, "Mass killing is self-reinforcing. Once begun, the act loses all meaning for the killers and they act without emotion or feelings. Thus, atrocities such as the murder of children are not only possible but probable." Mary raised her hands in a gesture of helplessness and looked at the President.

"Thank you for your frank opinion, Doctor," he said in a calm voice. "It confirms my own suspicions." The President looked to General Mason. "Now I'd like to hear the plan for a military solution."

Mason stood up and moved to an easel that had been set up by an aide at the end of the table.

"As I indicated at our last meeting," Mason began, "we had several different approaches to the military solution. These differences have been resolved and the plan you are about to see has been unanimously approved by the Joint Chiefs. Essentially, it is the approach originally suggested by the Navy."

Mason nodded and an aide lifted the cover from the easel, revealing a military map of the Assab area. Mason picked up a pointer and continued.

"This, as most of you already know, is the Soviet naval base at Assab, and this is the town of Assab itself." The pointer moved from place to place as he spoke.

"This is the coastal road running northwest from the town. Three miles up the road from Assab, is Ras, or Point Dugai, with the island of Sanah Bar lying one and a quarter miles off it. Between Ras Dugai and the small village, here, of Maacaca, there are three miles of gently sloping, sandy beach with deep water within a quarter mile of the low-tide line. We will want our beachhead there." Mason paused to clear his throat and then continued.

"The assault will be made by approximately three thousand helicopter-borne Marines from the *Veracruz*, supported by aircraft from the strike carrier *Hubert Humphrey*. Once the beachhead is established, two companies of heavy armor and a light artillery brigade will be landed. The initial assault will, in addition to the beachhead, include vertical envelopment of hills five fifty-four, five eighty-four, and eight fifty-three, here, here, and here. They lie between the beachhead and naval base.

"No prelanding bombardment or air strikes are considered necessary or planned since no prepared defenses exist. Nor are any Ethiopian forces in the area. The major threats to the landing are from Soviet fighter aircraft based at Assab and from the eleven thousand Cuban ground troops housed there. No preventive air strikes upon the Soviet naval base are planned. Rather, an exclusion corridor extending southwest from Ras Lumah along the axis of the three hills will be maintained by fighter aircraft from the *Humphrey*, thus inviting the Soviet air and ground forces to stay east of the line of axis. Strikes against the naval base will be made only in the event the landing forces are jeopardized by the Soviets.

"The only possible threat to naval units is from the two OSA-class patrol boats that are armed with obsolescent Styx surface-to-surface missiles. They will be neutralized by jamming from continuous overflights of EA-sixB aircraft flying off the *Humphrey*, and we're not overly concerned with them."

Mason moved his pointer toward the dot representing the little town of Maacaca.

"Once the beachhead is secure and our eastward advance extends to the line of axis through the three hills, a defensive line to the west will be established. This line will be anchored in the town of Maacaca to the north and to hill nine eighty-four, here, in the center and, finally, back to hill eight fifty-three to the east. When this ten-mile perimeter is secure, heavy equipment will be landed from the *Veracruz* and a class B airstrip dozed, here, just east of Maacaca. The Blue Light Force will be airlifted in from Germany together with pioneer elements of the Hundred and First Airborne Division.

"Once possession of Maacaca with its airstrip and beachhead is an accomplished fact, the Soviet naval base at Assab will be neutralized. We feel that with no losses to them, the Russians will grant permission for us to put a Blue Light team on the airstrip at Assab. Upon receiving this permission, the Blue Light team will be immediately transported by coast road to the naval base. If Soviet permission is not granted, the entire Hundred and First Airborne will be airlifted into the defensive area during the night and an overland assault upon the naval base made at first light. At the same time, the

entire two hundred and fifty man Blue Light team will be airlifted onto the Soviet airstrip in the immediate area of the
airliner. Upon landing, they will carry out the rescue of the
hostages."

Mason looked directly at the President. "That's the basic
plan, Mr. President."

The President studied the map for a long time. He remained oblivious to Mason, who stood waiting expectantly
for his reaction. The room was still and silent, except for the
sound of rain lashing against the French doors and the
rumble of distant thunder.

I don't like it, the President decided. The odds are
wrong. Wanting to probe further, he turned to CIA Director
Thompson to his right at the end of the table.

"Ken, what are the chances the Russians will oppose the
initial landings?"

Thompson leaned forward and looked at the President.
"Well, suh, if we don't hit their base 'fore we go ashore, they
won't *have* a reason t'oppose us. In any event, very few of
the ground troops at Assab that're Russian nationals will
leave the base. In the past thirty yeahs, the Soviets've nevah
once used Russian nationals in ground combat in any country
not adjacent to their border. They always left the dirty work
and the dyin' to others. In this heah case, if anyone meets us
at the beach, it'll be Cuban troops with Soviet advisors. But I
don't b'lieve anyone will meet us. Why should they risk losin'
the whole damn' base for the sake of a few pisspot terrorists?"

The President nodded his head slowly as he considered
Thompson's words. Then he turned to Boyd.

"Any reason the Russians would want a confrontation at
this particular time and place?"

"Good God, no!" exclaimed Boyd. "Not at Assab. They
had to overthrow an entire government to get that base, and
they have only just made it operational. On this point, I agree
with Thompson. They simply won't risk giving us an excuse
to destroy it."

Across the table, Sauer leaned back in his chair and
watched the President in admiration. Sharp, he thought. If it
comes down to the crunch, he'll do fine.

The President turned back to Mason, who was still
standing at the map. "Suppose the landing is opposed by Cuban troops and we have to shoot our way ashore. Won't the
gunfire alert the terrorists?"

Mason raised both hands slightly and sighed. "That's a problem. A fire fight on the beach with air strikes against the approach routes would probably alert them. In which case, they would certainly begin executing hostages. The only way to prevent such murders is to put the Blue Light team in immediately. They would have to be parachuted onto the beachhead directly after flying in from Germany. Given the long flight time, it is very difficult to estimate the arrival of the Blue Light aircraft over the beachhead without incurring significant risk. Any delay in the landing schedule and the Blue Light aircraft would be orbiting the area, a helluva juicy target for a Soviet missile. If the Blue Light force can't get in, we plan to use Marines to make the assault on the terrorists. It's not optimum, of course, since the Marines aren't trained for such use, but it's a good backup plan."

Optimum? thought the President. What the hell kind of word is that when we're talking about children's lives.

"So, what's the answer!" asked the President. His annoyance with Mason was showing clearly in his voice.

"The answer, Mr. President, is to obtain permission from the Egyptians to use one of their airfields as a staging point. From there, we can bring in the entire Blue Light force now and have them standing by for an airdrop onto the beachhead. With their flight time cut to minutes rather than hours, they can be called in just as soon as the Marines are ashore."

Mason looked at the President. "We didn't include such a staging in our basic plan because it depends upon State obtaining Egyptian cooperation."

"I'm sure we can get that immediately, Mr. President," Boyd interjected.

The President stared at the map again before speaking. He was still not satisfied; he wanted to hear more. But from someone other than Mason.

"Thank you, General Mason," he said, making up his mind, but then he added one more question: "You say this is essentially a Navy plan?"

Mason nodded. The President turned and looked directly at Sauer.

"Tell me, Admiral. Is this plan identical to the one originally proposed by your people?"

"Identical? No, sir," replied Sauer. "As is usual, the original plan was changed during coordination. However, I have approved this plan and support it."

The President smiled. Team player to the end, he thought. "I understand, Admiral. Now tell me what you would put back in if you had all the votes."

Sauer stood up. As he made his way to the easel, he raised his eyebrows to General Mason in passing as if to say, "Don't blame me. The man asked." Sauer turned and picked up the pointer.

"Two things, Mr. President. First off, I believe that if Vietnam taught us anything, it proved that if you're going to seek a military solution to a political problem, you have to use overwhelming force for a quick win. The three-thousand-man Marine force proposed for Assab will do the job, but they're not, in any way, overwhelming. I'd like to see an entire Army division air-dropped onto the beachhead here, and once the Marines are ashore and across the coast road, here.'

Sauer turned back to face the President. "I'm old-fashioned. If you're forced to pay with the lives of young men for some piece of real estate that you didn't want to begin with, then you ought to damn well get as much back in return as possible. Therefore, if the Soviets oppose the landing at all, then we ought to go in and chew 'em up. Specifically, we should plan to destroy both the naval base and as many Cuban troops as we can get our hands on. The addition of an Army division to the Marine assault force will give us the weight necessary to do just that. I'm not suggesting we start the fire fight. Rather, we should offer the Soviets every chance to retire. But if it comes, then we ought to take advantage of this opportunity and reduce the Soviet/Cuban presence in Africa in a way they'll not soon forget."

From the end of the table near Sauer, came Thompson's drawl, "Mr. President. Ah couldn't agree more. If the oppuhtunity presents itself, we surely should hit the Cubans. But ah would also like to point out that whatevah happens, once we're in control of any part of that coastline, no matter how small, we should turn it ovah to the Eritrean rebels when we leave. Ah kin arrange for them to move inta the area whenevah you like. In fact, ah could have 'em on the beach to meet ouah boys when they land."

Boyd put his head into his hands and groaned, "Oh, God."

The President's face lit up. "I'm sure you could, Ken. But I'll have to think on that for a while." Then, speaking to Sauer. "Thank you, Admiral. I'm not convinced a military solution is necessary, even now, but I do agree that the planning should include the use of an additional division."

Sauer, still standing, was shocked at these words.

"Mr. President. There's no time for anything *but* a military solution. If you give the order now, the earliest we can get ashore is tomorrow morning. That means at least four more hostages will die. They may be children. We can't afford to wait."

The President nodded his head sadly. "I know. I know. On the other hand, the Middle Eastern situation is touchy. The Russians just might decide to make a fight of it and pour in forces of their own. They've done it before. I need support to prevent that. I have to go to the UN to get that support."

"Will you at least order the staging to begin now so that the forces are moving into position while you go to the UN?"

"Certainly. I'll leave now and get Egypt's permission to use one of their airfields. General Mason, you move the Blue Light team and the entire Hundred and First Airborne Division to Egypt. It won't hurt to let the Russians see us moving combat troops into the Middle East. Whether we use them or not remains to be seen."

The President stood up. Everyone else also stood.

"That's it. Thank you all for coming."

He turned and walked swiftly from the room, followed by his advisors and Boyd. Thompson did not join them. Passing the desk of the President's personal secretary, one of his aides paused before going into the Oval Office and asked her to place a call to Egypt.

In his office, the President sank gratefully into his large, executive swivel chair, welcoming the familiar embrace of its leathery arms. Boyd and the others found seats in the comfortably furnished room. Some stared at the carpet. Some looked at the President expectedly. All wore looks of concern. None spoke.

These men were the President's closest associates and friends. They not only worked together, but also played together. Their social poker games made up one of the President's favorite evenings each week. All were appointed by him personally; most had known him years before his election. During the past four years they had been forged into a tightly knit, hard-working unit. Each saw more of the President than they saw their families. His fears were their fears, his trials their trials. Now they all pondered the dilemma that faced them. It seemed that no matter what they did, they would get bad press.

Finally, the President spoke.

"What the hell are we going to do? We've got to get the passengers back quickly. You heard the man. Four will be dead no matter what we do, and those bastards are apt to start on the kids any time now."

The President stood up and began pacing behind his desk, turning now and then to look at the group.

"Landing troops solves the hijacking all right," he continued, "maybe even teaches the Russians a lesson, but it could also start a land war that'll cut off the world's oil. I've *got* to go to the UN before we hit Ethiopia. But, hell, the UN can't find its ass with both hands. It'll take days to get a resolution passed. Can't you just *see* the headlines! CHILDREN MURDERED WHILE UN STALLS. My God! Forget the election. I'd be lucky if I'm not lynched."

The President stopped pacing and stepped behind his chair. He looked inquiringly at the group. "So? What's the answer?"

From his seat on the couch, the political advisor looked at the door of the office to make sure it was closed before he spoke.

"There is only one answer to our problem. The way I see it, whatever we do we're going to lose some number of hostages. It can't be helped. Right?" he said looking to the group for support. "It seems to me the question then is not whether we save the hostages, but whether we save the election. If you look at it that way, the answer becomes clear." The aide looked behind him as if afraid someone was watching him. "An unsuccessful military solution will lose both the hostages and the election. On the other hand, an unsuccessful, but highly publicized attempt for a resolution through the UN will lose us only hostages. I say we go along with the Russians and work through the UN. At the same time, we'll crank up a really massive publicity campaign showing how hard you're working to recover the hostages without starting a war. We've got the people and funds available for that. Move the troops to Egypt, sure, that'll look good, but leave them there until this thing is over."

The President's jaw fell open slightly. An antique clock on the mantel above the cold fireplace ticked loudly as the political logic sought fertile ground.

Chapter 15

Mawson stood in the command center idly watching the activity around him. Now, in the entire ship, he was the only man with nothing to do. In order to keep the men's minds off their families, he had resorted to the ancient naval practice of exercising the crew. In the ship's control center behind him, Edelstone and Olsen had men scurrying from one end of the ship to the other in response to imaginary emergencies.

To his left, Mawson could see Wallstrom leading the ordinance division through simulated tactical defense exercises while Lieutenant Rossman moved from console to console developing various attacks. In front of Mawson, Lieutenant Robare observed as Dacovak led a group of quartermasters in plotting navigational problems. To Mawson's right, Deville sat at the main electronic countermeasures console, his battle station, engrossed with his two ECM operators in supporting Lieutenant McKenna and his section also supported the exercise. Throughout the ship, similar training evolutions were being carried out. The *Montana* buzzed with activity.

As he stood watching his "beehive," for the hundreth time Mawson wrenched his mind away from Barbara. He was like a sick physician who could prescribe the needed medicine of others, but had none to cure himself. His normally handsome and composed face appeared lumpish and gray. He had not slept at all after returning to his bunk. Instead, until the hours brought an unseen arctic dawn, he had tossed and turned, thinking only of Assab in spite of every effort to stop.

This lack of mental discipline was unheard of in him and indicated the extent to which his subconscious mind had become involved with the problem of freeing his family . . . an involvement that, unbeknownst to him, had already become an obsession.

Stripped bare of all the emotionalism that followed, the obsession would become the subject of endless, dull papers given at dry, medical meetings. It would become known as Mawson's Obsession, which was a misnomer since almost all the crew also came to hold the same compulsion.

Now, as he stood in the control room, all that could be said with certainty was that events over which Mawson had no control were focusing his thoughts into an ever-narrowing channel, a channel leading toward Assab. He could not stop thinking about the *Montana* families. He could distract the others, but not himself. Yet, because of his military training and experience, his mind did not dwell on imaginative fears for the plight of the families as a layman might. Rather, factor after factor concerning their rescue passed through his finely tuned, tactical mind.

He considered the effects the election might have upon the President's decisions. He recognized the need for obtaining Soviet permission to land an armed rescue force if the plane had indeed landed at the naval base at Assab. He considered the military options open to the President if the Soviets refused permission. Unfortunately, he had few facts to go on. The machines had frustrated every attempt to obtain factual news of the situation. This lack of communication heightened the built-in isolation felt by all strategic missile submarine crews, and Mawson began to fear that he was alone in wanting to rescue their families. Consciously, he knew that could not be true. Surely, he thought, the Navy's making certain everything humanly possible was being done to rescue them.

He tried to reassure himself. Yet deep in his subconscious, he knew that the President, not the Navy, was the key to the situation in Assab. Knowing that, his mind was no more able to forget about the problem than it was able to forget to direct his heart to beat or his lungs to breathe. Yet without hard facts, all he could do was ponder variables and construct hypothetical reactions to hypothetical situations. Isolation, hypothesis and gut-worry were eating away at him.

His thoughts were interrupted by the voice of McKenna at the Tactical Display Table.

"Captain, underwater sound contact bearing two three seven. Range twelve miles. Closing rapidly. Sound signature shows her to be a *Los Angeles*-class boat, sir."

Relieved to have something to do at last, Mawson did a quick mental calculation. She's on the right bearing for the *Tustin*, he thought. He looked at his watch. 1523. Right time too. Still, you never know, he thought, turning to Wallstrom.

"Secure from exercises. Track underwater sound contact. Mr. Wallstrom, I believe the contact is the *Tustin*."

The *Tustin*, Mawson recalled with mounting excitement, will have the latest news of the hijacking. He knew that as a regular part of their patrol routine, attack submarines periodically came up to near-periscope depth to record sea temperatures and salinity. At this relatively shallow depth, they could receive ordinary, civilian radio broadcasts. The captains of most attack submarines made a point of piping news broadcasts throughout their ships for the entertainment of the crew.

Mawson turned to the talker standing just outside the railing below him. "Communications. Standby to contact the *Tustin* on the underwater phone as soon as positive identification is made."

Seconds later the talker reported.

"Communications standing by."

Minutes later, the contact was made and Mawson stood conversing with the *Tustin*'s captain over the very short range underwater telephone. Turning aside from the phone, Mawson spoke to the ship's talker.

"Communications. Pipe this conversation throughout the ship."

In every compartment of the *Montana* overhead speakers crackled into life. From the speakers, came the voice of the *Tustin*'s captain, his words recognizable but tinny and inhuman due to the distortion caused by traveling through water rather than air.

"According to the last BBC broadcast we heard about an hour ago, the terrorists have killed five hostages and are threatening to kill another every six hours until their demands are met."

Mawson's voice was tense as he asked, "Have the five been identified?"

"Only as two of the flight crew and three passengers. Nothing more, I'm afraid."

"Are they at the Russian naval base?"

"Yeah. The Russians have refused permission for anyone but a United Nations team to come on base."

"What are we doing about that?"

"The BBC said we're moving an entire airborne division to Egypt as the first step in a possible assault on the base. Also, a strike force from the Fifth Fleet has been ordered to stand by off the entrance to the Red Sea. That, I can confirm. It's the *Humphrey* and the *Veracruz*."

"What else?"

"The President is flying to New York this afternoon to personally address emergency sessions of the U.N. General Assembly and Security Council. He's going to ask for super-quick action. 'Extraordinary' was the word the BBC announcer used."

"Have you had any change in alert status?" asked Mawson, his voice strangely tight.

"No."

"Neither have we."

The voice was getting indistinct now as the *Tustin* moved out of range.

"Hang tight, *Montanas*. We're pulling for you."

"Thanks. Good luck to you, *Tustin*," said Mawson mechanically.

In the control room, all eyes turned to Mawson. He stood immobile with the dead phone in his hand. He seemed not to see them, nor to be aware of his surroundings at all. To Wallstrom, he looked stunned. Deville thought Mawson looked preoccupied. He was both. For suddenly, into his conscious thought, burst the belief that the President was going to sacrifice their families to political expediency and take no military action. He knew this with a certainty that shook him to his very soul. Rage born of frustration rose within him and with it a plan. His subconscious thoughts had finally reached his conscious mind.

Out of the recesses of his mind came the full-grown conviction that the President would seek a swift military solution only if forced to do so by an outside, uncontrollable event. Mawson's mind, now leaping and tearing at the problem, stripped away the mists that had obscured the central issue because of lack of information.

And then he had it. The unthinkable happened. The unease that had bothered both Sauer and Rodgers thousands of miles away and then eluded them, now became substantial. Their sense of worry would soon turn to real and tangible fear. For, into Mawson's racing mind burst the singular thought: *I control the probability of nuclear war.*

Mawson seemed to gather himself. The distant look faded from his eyes. For the first time since he had heard about the hijacking, he was totally relaxed. For the first time, he was free of the unfamiliar feeling of helplessness, free of total dependency upon others. For the first time, the problem of rescuing Barbara and the kids was reduced to the simple choice between duty and family. Mawson's choice was made.

An on-the-spot recording of a world-shaking decision being made is the rarest of historical events. But Mawson was not thinking about history or his part in it. He simply wanted the facts straight for the court martial that was sure to come. He turned to Dacovak.

"Quartermaster," Mawson said, his voice calm to the point of being almost conversational. "Log the time and note the Captain addressed the ship."

Turning back, Mawson raised the microphone in his lips and in cold but persuasive tones destroyed his career for his family's sake. Again, the speakers came to life.

"This is the Captain speaking. We've all just heard the *Tustin*'s news. Three passengers are dead, but there's no reason to assume that any of our families are among them. The odds are against it. However, every six hours the chance increases that someone in our families will be killed. Time's working against them. For us, the question is simply this: how soon will our families be freed?"

Mawson's voice took on an unfamiliar edge, and his words, usually spoken with calm deliberation, now came more quickly.

"The fastest way to release our families is to send in the Special Forces team I told you about. As you heard, the plane landed at a Soviet naval base. It seems the Russians won't allow us to put a team on the base. They say we've got to deal through the UN."

Mawson paused. Throughout the ship, men waited expectantly. In the galley, a cook, chopping cleaver poised in midair, looked at the silent speaker. In the torpedo room, Jackson tore his eyes from the speaker and answered Poley's questioning glance with one word, "wait." In the engine room, the CPO mess, the wardroom, and even the pump room, the men were poised as if playing "statues."

And in the control room, Mawson's face was contorted with an inner agony. He turned his head and slowly looked around the compartment. Edelstone's homely face watched him calmly. Wallstrom looked puzzled and wary. Dacovak's eyes gleamed with a strange intensity in the light from the chart table. Deville returned Mawson's gaze with a distracted look that reflected his uncertainty of Jan's whereabouts.

No matter what they're thinking, decided Mawson, they're good men. They deserve a chance to judge for themselves and to make their own choice.

"The Russians know full well the UN would take a week to make up its mind. They've put international politics first. Time means nothing to them, *their* families aren't going to die."

Mawson's right hand clenched and unclenched in uncharacteristic tension as he spoke the next words. The microphone in his left hand pressed closely to his lips.

"And what is our government's reaction to this? What do *we* do? The President orders a concentration of forces for an assault on the Russian base, but then flies off to address the UN!

"When I first heard that, I was encouraged. I thought, how clever. Order the assault to take place while he's addressing the General Assembly. That's the way to play the damn game."

Rage welled up in Mawson. His jaw worked as he fought to control himself. The seconds ticked away. Finally, he regained control. When he spoke, his voice was icy calm and totally devoid of any emotion whatsoever. Each word was pronounced clearly.

"But there's been no change in alert status. No attack on a Russian installation, even one as remote as Assab, could begin without first alerting all submarine forces at sea. No alert, no attack. It's as simple as that. The force concentration is for show. The President's going the long UN route. Why? Because he's afraid. He's in the midst of a reelection campaign, and he's afraid of what the press will say if he uses force. How do I know this? I don't. That's the hell of it."

Mawson's eyes grew narrow and his voice seemed to growl from the speakers.

"But this I know. Time has run out and the odds are exactly even. Either I'm right and he's going to sacrifice our families, or I'm wrong and he's going to use the force necessary to get them quickly. Speaking only for myself, I can't leave it at that. Those odds aren't good enough for me. Nothing in my life or future is worth a one out of two chance of losing my family. I want to change those odds. I want to force the President to get our families out *now*. I don't want to wait two or three days while the damn politicians talk and our families die. I want action!"

Mawson's voice became low as he leaned forward with his right hand clenching the low railing. "And this ship holds the key. The President won't use force for fear of bad press. He thinks losing the election is the worst that can happen to him. Well, we know it damn well isn't." Mawson straightened up. His voice rang out through the ship.

"Nuclear war is the worst thing that can happen to him and everyone else. And this ship controls the start of nuclear war. *We* have the power, and *we* should use it. Dammit! They're willing for our families to be held hostage. Well, I'm willing to hold the whole damn world hostage! What difference does it make how your kids die? Shot in the head one by one or all together in an air burst? They're gone either way. I say we tell them we'll launch a missile unless our families are freed by midnight tomorrow. They want to play with terrorists. Well, we'll show them the ultimate terrorists!"

Mawson paused for breath.

"But no one need die. Just the threat of nuclear war is all we need. If we threaten to launch just one bird, the President and the Russians will have to settle their differences and get our families out in a hurry."

Mawson looked around the compartment, seeing only faces rather than individuals. Exclamations of agreement came back at him. The faces looked determined.

With a huge sigh, Mawson continued, "Of course, what I've just said means the finish of my own career. What you do and say in the next few minutes can have the same effect on yours. For me, the choice was simply between career or family. I'm convinced I can't have both now, so I chose family. But each of you will have to choose for yourself. Whatever you decide, my career's already over. You should understand that what I'm proposing is, at the very least, mutiny or maybe even piracy. I can go to prison for what I have just said to you. When you make your decision, you should consider that if enough of your shipmates don't join us, then you have thrown away your careers and possibly your freedom for nothing. This sort of thing can't be handled by ordinary Navy routine. So think about it privately. Talk it over. Make up your minds. Those who don't wish to participate, should go to their quarters and remain there. Whatever you decide to do, do it quickly. We don't have time to waste."

Mawson hung to the microphone and stepped down from the command center. For several seconds the men were silent and immobile like figures in a wax museum. Mawson started for the door leading to his cabin. He could not look them in the eye for fear he would see rejection. I've asked too much. I've thrown it all away for nothing, he thought.

Then, like the sound of a fast train coming through a tunnel, a swelling roar began to fill the ship. Through the loudspeaker from every compartment, the sound of a hundred or more men yelling came to him. Wherever they stood, they cheered. Some pounded each other on the back. Others shouted.

"Fuck 'em all!"

"Gettem, Baby. Gettem!"

"Right on, brother. Right on!"

And it went on and on. Mawson felt tears sting his eyes. He looked up and saw Dacovak grinning openly, his face reflecting admiration, almost worship. Edelstone stepped up, pride filling his face. "The ship's with you, Captain," he said, shaking Mawson's hand.

Overwhelmed by the reaction, Mawson continued toward the watertight door. But just before he reached the opening, Wallstrom stepped up to him and blocked his way.

"Request permission to speak with the Captain," said Wallstrom. His voice was tightly controlled, his face a mask of pain.

"What? Oh, yes. Of course," exclaimed Mawson, taken aback by Wallstrom's expression. "Go on to my cabin. I'll be there in a moment."

Wallstrom spun around without a word and stepped through the opening. Mawson stared after him. He didn't buy it, Mawson thought. He's not going to have any part of this.

Mawson turned to look at the excited faces still watching him. How many will join me only because they're afraid not to? he thought. How many more will want out once they realize what'll happen to them when this is over? Mawson turned to Edelstone. "Make sure no man is pressured into joining us against his will. Every man is to decide strictly for himself."

Edelstone listened to Mawson continue.

"It seems we've got more than enough men to work the

ship. Make sure Dacovak personally logs the names of all those who choose not to join us so that their record is clear. Prepare to stand down from Strat Alert. I'll have the message ready for broadcast in about fifteen minutes. In the meantime, start reworking the watch bills."

"Yes, sir," replied Edelstone absently. His mind was already occupied with the problem of running the ship with fewer men. Then, there was the problem of berthing and feeding the men who would be confined to quarters. What about security? he thought. Didn't he read somewhere about loyal men being duty bound to recapture the ship from a mutinous crew?

As Mawson started for the doorway, Edelstone looked at Dacovak who stood at the plotting table. There was a distant expression on his face, his eyes still glowing with dancing lights. A set of parallel rules lay crushed almost beyond recognition in the grip of his huge hand.

When Mawson entered his day cabin, he found Wallstrom pacing rapidly up and down. At the sight of his captain, he came rigidly to attention. Mawson gazed at him cooly, shaking his head.

"OK, Lieutenant. At ease. Quit choking on it and spit it out."

Wallstrom took a deep breath, but did not relax his cadet-like posture.

"Sir, it is my duty to tell you you are acting illegally and have given unlawful orders."

Mawson smiled.

"Very well, Lieutenant. You've done your duty. Anything else?"

"Yes, sir. I am bound to resist your unlawful orders and ask that you and Mr. Edelstone surrender yourselves to me so that I may restore lawful command of this ship."

Mawson's smile disappeared. His voice turned cold.

"You sound like a sea lawyer to me, mister. If you're trying to build a case for yourself, the record will show that you so requested and did resist to the best of your ability. Anything else?"

This last, cold thrust broke through Wallstrom's reserve.

"Captain, please don't do it. It's not right. You're threatening the entire country—the entire world!—for your own ends." He spun away. "I know that sounds callous since my family isn't on the plane." Wallstrom's deep voice wavered and almost broke with emotion. "I know they'll call me a coward, say I'm protecting my career since I've got nothing to lose. But so help me God, I would do no differently if they *were* on that plane. Duty comes first. It must. Otherwise there's nothing left but chaos. How many others will follow your lead and use their weapons for private purposes?"

Wallstrom, unable to contain himself, resumed pacing, waving his arms as he moved and continued with his tirade. Mawson watched him thoughtfully.

"Are my children going to grow up in a world that's a throwback to the Middle Ages? Armed factions, private wars, death and uncertainty everywhere?" Wallstrom took a step toward Mawson. With outstretched arms, he pleaded with his captain. "Please, sir. I beg you. Reconsider before it's too late."

Instinctively, Mawson took one of Wallstrom's wrists in both of his hands and looked full into the troubled man's eyes.

"Ross," Mawson said with deep conviction, "what you say may well happen. But if it does, it will have come from a madness that began long before. How could it be our duty to sacrifice our families for a Presidential election? For Christ's sake! We're not beginning or ending anything. We're just taking care of our own. And why the hell not? If we can't protect our own families, whose can we protect?"

Mawson looked at Wallstrom's troubled face. He felt tired and infinitely older. Dropping Wallstrom's wrist, Mawson put an arm over the younger man's shoulder and turned him toward the cabin door.

"I'm glad you're not with us. You're one of the best officers I've ever served with. I'm glad I won't be the cause of your throwing away your career."

Wallstrom looked at Mawson with pain in his eyes. "One question, sir?"

"Yes, of course."

"If your bluff is called, will you launch?"

Mawson looked at Wallstrom for a few seconds, not breathing. The cabin was deathly still. Only a soft whisper from the air vents and the gentle vibration of the turbines disturbed the silence. Finally, Mawson exhaled loudly and shook his head.

"I don't know. I just don't know." Mawson turned away and opened the cabin door. "Go to your cabin and stay there.

I'll put a boatswain's mate outside your door just to keep the record straight."

"Jesus, God help us all." Wallstrom turned and left without another word, closing the door after him.

Mawson stood and stared at the door. Could he really launch? he wondered. Could he kill a million people out of retribution? He knew he could kill a million people. He had known that for years. That was his job. Now the question was, could he do it solely because of his family? He thought about it for several minutes, but no answer came.

Several minutes after nineten hundred hours Greenwich Mean Time, the thin rod of a high-frequency radio antenna broke the cold gray surface of the Norwegian Sea forty miles off the barren shores of Jan Mayen Island. Sixty feet below, the huge black bulk of the *Montana* moved slowly through the icy waters like the biblical Leviathan who rose from the depths to feed upon little fishes.

From the antenna, stacatto pulses of Morse code began to broadcast the *Montana*'s ultimatum in plain language on 500 kilohertz, the international calling and distress frequency monitored by all ships and maritime governments. Because a radio telegraphist's patterns of keying are as distinctive as his signature, the radio room watch took turns sending the message. Deville began, using the urgency signal and general call to gain the attention of all operators.

"XXX XXX XXX CQ CQ CQ," he rapped out on the key, sending two thousand watts pulsing from the antenna.

Within seconds, a hundred radio operators around the entire Western Hemisphere jerked upright in their seats and pressed headsets closer to ears as the long powerful waves passed their stations and were detected by sensitive antenna. The *Tustin*, almost one hundred miles away, received the call first, although no human could sense the time difference. The duty operator aboard the *Woods* spilled his coffee in excitement as he tried to cut in a recorder and transcribe the message on his typewriter at the same time. The waves reached the government radio rooms in Oslo, Stockholm, and Murmansk simultaneously. An instant later, the message was recorded at the Admiralty in London as well as the Ministere Marine in Paris.

In the Communications Center, the Pentagon duty operator motioned frantically to his chief and cut in loudspeakers as the message began to pour in. Both men, in spite of, or perhaps because of, the terrible contents of the message, thought at first that some horrible hoax was being played. But when the unmistakable change in the fist of the sending telegraphist took place as the first radio operator smoothly took over from Deville, they and the entire listening world began to realize the deadly seriousness of the message. In hundreds of offices, the red telephones of both the Western and Eastern worlds began to ring as the full import of the message was realized.

At the newly relocated Soviet SIGNET center on the Kanin Peninsula, a team of experts frantically spun the controls that turned the large, high-frequency radio antenna atop their low building. Slowly it locked on to the *Montana*'s signal.

On the square-shaped cathode ray tube before him, a young blond Russian operator maneuvered two vertical lines of glowing green light one over the other so that they blended perfectly. He then spoke into the microphone on his chest.

In the center of the large semicircular room, a plotter stepped forward and used a glowing, yellow grease pencil to mark the resulting line of bearing on a large, transparent, edge-lit screen that displayed the entire Norwegian and Barents Seas. A few minutes later, the Russian plotted a second line of bearing received from a post on Franz Josef Land. He then drew a small circle around the intersection of the two lines and noted the time. With a grin of satisfaction, he stepped back from the screen and stared off into the back of the room where a group of intelligence officers sat at consoles in the semidarkness.

A buzz from their excited activity filled the room. The content of the *Montana*'s message was far less important to these men than its existence. During twenty years of constant listening, they had heard nothing. Finally, they had been rewarded with a message long enough for them to plot. When they had passed the exact location of the *Montana* on to their superiors, they allowed themselves a happy self-congratulation on a long and tedious job well done.

At that same moment deep beneath the silent seas, the *Montana* was already heading at her best speed toward the Vesteralen Trough and her alternate launch area Delta 3 off the Norwegian city of Tromsø some 440 nautical miles away. Between her and Delta 3 lay the *Riga* and her escorts like a trap across a forest game trail.

Chapter 16

The storm had moved northeast during the morning. By two o'clock, it was centered over Asbury Park, lashing the crowded New Jersey beach cities with unwanted rain and ruining the day for vacationers and businessmen alike. In the clear, sparkling air above thick storm clouds, the wings of an executive jet flashed in the sunlight. As the small plane banked to begin its descent to Kennedy International Airport some thirty miles ahead, the blue and white colors of the Presidential fleet stood out clearly.

Aboard the plane was a tiny but complete communications center. Crammed into a curtained space between the cockpit and the passenger cabin, a high-speed printer began ripping out an incoming message. As the clean-cut, young Air Force sergeant turned and bent over the printer, his attention was attracted by a red flashing light on the status panel. A call was coming in on a hot line that linked the President directly to the National Military Command Center in the Pentagon. The light stopped flashing and burned steadily when the phone was answered by someone in the cabin. At the same time, the printer fell silent.

The sergeant leaned forward and tore the short message from the machine. Sliding back his seat, he stood up and parted the curtain into the main part of the small cabin. The President was speaking on the red phone from a comfortable window seat. On the table before him, the remains of a late lunch were mixed with the clutter of papers that filled his working day. Across the table with his back to the cockpit, sat Alexy Zhuravlev, the National Security Advisor. Seeing the sergeant, the President motioned impatiently and held out his free hand for the message.

"Yes, Yes. It's just come," said the President into the phone. I'm reading it now. Wait a minute."

The President whipped the paper before him. His eyes narrowed to slits as he read the words:

TO THE PRESIDENT OF THE UNITED
STATES

BELIEVING THE SOVIET DEMAND THAT
NEGOTIATIONS AT ASSAB BE CON-
DUCTED ONLY BY A UNITED NATIONS
TEAM TO BE AN INHUMAN AND CRIM-
INAL POLITICAL MANEUVER PRE-
CLUDING SWIFT AND SAFE RELEASE
OF OUR FAMILIES, WE, THE MAJORITY
OF THE OFFICERS AND CREW OF THE
USS MONTANA DO HEREBY SERVE
WARNING UPON THE SOVIET UNION.
UNLESS OUR FAMILIES ARE RELEASED
UNHARMED BY 2400 GMT, 7 AUGUST,
WE WILL LAUNCH A TRIDENT MISSILE.
TO VERIFY RELEASE, PUT MY WIFE ON
22,105.0 KILOHERTZ.
                    D. MAWSON, COMMANDING

Damn, he thought angrily. Who the hell do they think they
are? I'll sink their ass if the Russians don't . . . he stopped in
midthought as the true reality of the situation struck him.
Now cold, sweaty fear replaced the heat of anger.

"The Russians!" The words exploded involuntarily.

Alexy Zhuravelev looked up in surprise.

The telephone in the President's hand sputtered unnoticed while on the other end General Mason responded to the
outcry. The Presidest handed the message on Zhuravlev and
shouted, "Turn us around. Now!"

Zhuravlev jumped out of his seat and bounded through
the curtain into the cockpit, the message still unread in his
hand.

The President raised the phone to his lips, calming himself by a tremendous effort of will.

"General Mason?" he asked in a tightly controlled voice.

"Yes, Mr. President. I'm here."

"I've just read the Mawson message. I'm afraid the Russians may launch an immediate preemptive strike. We've got
to reassure them that Mawson is acting alone, that he's not
part of some larger plan of ours. We must convince them
that we aren't taking advantage of this situation in order to
attack the Soviet Union. I now direct you to take all our

strategic forces out of alert status. Immediately! I want no weapons under our control aimed at Russia!"

"But Mr. President!" exclaimed Mason, shocked. "We just went to total readiness. The Airborne National Command Post just took off. We're ready."

"Well tell it to land, dammit!" snapped the President, his anger and frustration at Mawson finding a closer target. "It's just wasting fuel." The President took a deep breath. "Look, we'll talk about it when I get back. But first you order our strategic forces out of alert. I must have that when I talk to the Soviet president. Do you understand?"

"I understand, Mr. President," replied Mason in a grim voice. "I am to order the immediate stand down of all our strategic forces. I will do so but only under the strongest protest. Mr. President, we'll be without any retaliatory capability whatsoever. Why, we'll be . . ." Mason's voice failed him as he sought for the right word. "Why, we'll be defenseless," he declared incredulously, shocked beyond his wits at the thought of such a situation.

The President's face took on the studied blankness of a superb poker player when he has drawn the winning card. "Not quite, General. We still have the *Montana*."

"The *Montana*!" exclaimed Mason. He was unable to follow the President's cold logic. "Surely, Mr. President, you're not counting on them. Why, they're nothing but self-serving mutineers!"

"Why not? God knows, they're ready enough to launch: Whatever Mawson and his crew might be, the Russians will believe that if they attack us, the *Montana* will attack them."

"I don't understand. I thought our primary concern is to prevent the *Montana* from attacking Russia?"

The President shook his head. Mason's simply out of his league, he thought. Sauer's the man I need now. He'd understand.

"No, General," he answered patiently, "that's strictly a secondary problem. The first order of business is to prevent the Russians from attacking us. Listen, General, I'm on my way back now. Have the entire crisis team and Sauer's Doctor O'Hegarty in the Command Center War Room when I get in. The first thing I want to know is where the hell Mawson's damn missile will land if he does launch. OK?"

"Yes, sir. We'll be waiting."

"Fine. Thank you, General. You have your orders."

A white telephone by the window buzzed. Zhuravlev, who had returned to his seat and was intently following the President's conversation, turned and answered it.

"The Secretary of State, Mr. President."

The President nodded and held up a finger to wait. Zhuravlev took this moment to finally read the shocking message.

"Steve?"

"I'm here, Mr. President. Did you get my teletype?"

"Yeah. I read it. I'm worried about a possible preemptive attack by the Russians."

"Me too. It's a very real possibility. You must talk to President Gurinov just as soon as possible."

"I agree. I just got off the phone with Mason. I'm on my way back now and am going straight to the war room. I'll talk to Gurinov as soon as I'm briefed, so have my interpreter standing by."

"All right."

"In the meantime, you tell the Soviet Ambassador I'll be calling. Make him see that the *Montana* is acting alone. Tell him I've ordered the immediate withdrawal of all our strategic forces from alert status. Assure him we'll take care of the *Montana*. Urge him once again to grant us access to Assab, and you might remind him that the Soviet position on that issue was the direct cause of Mawson's threat. When you finish with him, pass on the same story to Benson in Assab, if you can still get through. Maybe he can do some good from that end. That's all I can think of at the moment. How about you?"

"No. You've covered everything I was going to suggest. Since I last talked to you, the Egyptians have agreed to a staging area and offered us the use of ground forces. The Hundred and First Airborne and the Blue Light Force are on the way there now. Also, the Egyptians have agreed to close the Suez Canal for seventy-two hours for 'repair' in order to prevent Soviet naval units in the eastern Mediterranean from passing into the Red Sea. That announcement is due any time now."

"Good work, Steve. That's beautiful. I'll see you in the War Room. I've got to think this thing out more, but I believe I've got a handle on it now. I'm convinced the Russians are the key to solving all our problems. Think about that."

The President hung up the phone and turned to look out

the window. Zhuravlev started to speak, but the President
waved his hand without turning his head. It was time to
think, not talk. God knows, there'll be enough talk later.

Chapter 17

Carol Moore opened her eyes and viewed the dimly lit
cabin through watery pupils. The human, particularly the sick
human, is an amazingly adaptive animal. In the almost
eighteen hours that had elapsed since the plane first landed at
Assab, Carol's feverish mind had accepted the cramped seat
in which she now reclined as completely as if she were in her
bed at home. Her aching, flu-ridden body had sunk gratefully
into the cushions as if they were the thickest of mattresses.
Three times she had made her way to the lavatory. To her,
the world seemed populated with unreal people and dream-
like situations. Three times she was made aware of the fact
that the plane was on the ground with everyone still aboard.
Three times she thought to rouse herself and investigate, but
fell back asleep before she could act upon her thought.

Now, as her consciousness registered the cabin around
her, the fever that had beclouded her thinking began to lift.
The cushions that moments before were a safe and comfortable haven, now became no more than a First Class cabin
seat. The thin, airline blankets that had once been welcomed
by her shivering body, now felt hot and oppressively heavy.

Where am I? she thought. Carol threw back the blankets. Raising her head, she fixed her gaze on the children
asleep in the seats across the aisle. Children! Why are all the
children here in First Class?

Suddenly her mind cleared completely. She looked
around at what she could see of the cabin. What time is it?
She pulled her left arm out from under her body and looked
at her watch. 11:52. We must have arrived while I was
asleep. She rolled her head to look out the window and saw
only the blackness of the desert night.

Where are we? she thought, sitting upright and looking full around the cabin over the tops of the seats.

At that moment, standing by the open loading door, Yonnie saw Carol's head appear. The terrorist turned and squeezed Qabrestan's arm to attract his attention. "It is time for the first." She raised an arm and pointed at Carol. 'We take that one? *Ja?*"

Qabrestan's cold, lifeless eyes followed the direction of Yonnie's condemning finger. For a moment he stared at Carol, who, not yet understanding the danger, returned his gaze with an expression of confused innocence.

It is just like when she spilled the water on my sleeve, he thought. Then, as he had done before with little Robbie, Qabrestan reacted to his own peculiar sense of humanity. It lay shriveled and stunted within the dark and twisted labyrinth of his mind, but it restrained him from killing anyone with whom he had had even the slightest personal contact.

"No. Take another," he replied without giving any thought to why he spared Carol.

Yonnie stared at Qabrestan for a moment, then shrugged and started down the aisle. On either side of the center galley, the brothers Mahmud and Hamed waited. The after cabin was a sea of grim faces.

This was the moment they had waited for since Jan and Schlosser's deaths. As the hour hands on their watches crept inexorably closer to twelve, the tension in her cabin mounted. One among them would die. One of them would feel the terrorists' hands and be led forward to be shot in the back of the head. Everyone, even the children, knew what was going to happen and were terrified. The terror of anticipation was laced with the panic of uncertainty as all had to come to terms with their fear in their own way: some behaved well, some badly.

Thomas B. Chandler of the Baltimore Chandlers was a coward, a fact he had learned to live with since his prep school days in New England. He did not enjoy being a coward, in fact he hated and resented it, and so he carefully hid his failing from the world. His family knew him to be a loving and attentive husband and father. His friends and business associates found him a warm and generous person. Yet through no fault of his own, he had somehow managed to reach manhood without acquiring even an ordinary amount of physical courage. Over the years he had learned to avoid violence, the mere threat of which made him ill. He had been violently sick when Sam Samson's body had fallen across his lap at the beginning of the hijacking. After he had been forced out of his First Class seat and herded aft to sit with the rest of the passengers, he had thought to disguise himself as a woman in the not unreasonable belief that the women would be safer and released sooner than the men. Before the long flight to Assab was half over, he had managed to buy a dress that fit his slight frame and steal some makeup and a wig. The remainder of the flight he skulked about the dark aisles, snatching the shoes from beneath sleeping women in a desperate search for a pair that would fit his size nine-and-a-half feet. Just before dawn, he had given up and settled for a pair of nylon stockings. These articles of clothing were now forgotten. He had stuffed them into the pocket of his seat six hours before when he realized that the sex of the victims was meaningless to the terrorists.

Now, a few minutes before midnight, he stood in a panic with his mouth pressed against the crack of one of the lavatory doors. Just minutes before, a young man with a backpack had beaten him to the door. He had rushed to the other heads, but they were also filled.

"Five hundred dollars cash if you let me in," Chandler called softly through the crack.

"Go away," came a muffled reply. "You'll ruin it for both of us."

"Five hundred for letting me in. You don't have to come out."

"Go away."

"A thousand. A thousand dollars cash."

"A thousand? And I don't have to leave?"

"Yes. Yes. Hurry. They'll be coming any minute."

"You got the cash on you?"

"I got it in my hand. For God's sake, open the door!"

"Show me."

The door opened a few inches, the light automatically going out when the locking bolt was withdrawn. Chandler took two five hundred dollar bills from his pocket and held them up in front of the narrow opening.

"I can't read 'em. It's too dark."

Chandler's voice rose to a panicked squeal. "Let me in, dammit! I'll show you."

The door opened wide and Chandler hurriedly squeezed

into the small compartment. The door closed and the bolt shot home. The words OCCUPIED glowed dully above the handle.

"For a hundred more, I'll let you blow me."

"Shit," answered Chandler.

At the forward end of the rear cabin, Sally Bronick bit down hard on the cuticle of her thumbnail. With an abruptness that reflected her inner struggle, she tore the finger from her mouth. A drop of blood welled up in the tiny strip of abused flesh. She wanted to be as far away from them as possible. Yet the fear of what might happen to her children gave her no rest. She was too far away. She had to get closer.

With that thought, Sally stood up and moved slowly forward along the right aisle. Past the partition marking the after end of the center cabin, she moved. The aisle was deserted.

Ahead, the figure of Hamed appeared in the light from the center galley. She was frightened. Yet a greater fear drove her to move slowly toward her goal. She was almost there. Empty, unwanted seats loomed ahead. She made it. Gratefully, she dropped into a seat behind the partition of the center galley. Hamed turned and looked at her. Sally buried her face in the seat cushion, unable to return Hamed's gaze. The terrorist turned away.

Sensing Hamed's lack of interest, Sally looked around. In the seats behind her, Worthington and Wall's white shirts stood out in the dim light. Reassured by the presence of the flight crew, she slowly rolled over on her back. Across the aisle sat an elderly couple with their heads touching as they stared past Hamed into the First Class cabin. Carefully, Sally leaned out into the aisle and attempted to follow the couple's gaze. Hamed's figure blocked her view. Frustrated, she fell back against the cushions and looked again at the elderly couple.

Russell and Agnes Wagner behaved well. The couple had been inseparable since they were married and moved into the spacious apartment above their newly opened drugstore on Scotia's tree-shaded Main Street. For over fifty years they lived a quiet life largely unaffected by the passing wars and changing fashions and moral attitudes of the world around them: Russell behind the glass partition of the pharmacy and Agnes behind the front counter. Their business prospered and their two sons grew tall, married, and did well in the community. Now, with the drugstore sold, the Wagners traveled during the summers to see the world they had never had time for during their working lives.

From their seats in the very front of the center cabin, the Wagners saw Yonnie start up the aisle on the opposite side. Directly in front of them, Hamed stood in the opening to First Class.

"They're coming," Russell said. "You put that nonsense out of your mind."

"No," answered Agnes firmly, the hat with the red cherries in her lap. She gripped his hand tighter and turned to him. He tore his eyes away from the terrorists and looked at her.

"If they take you, they'll have to take me too."

"That's ridiculous."

"No it isn't. Would you let me go without you?"

"Of course not."

"Well, there you are," she concluded, her plan firm in her mind.

He looked away, shaking his head. When she's like that there's no talking to her.

The old couple sat unflinching and watched Yonnie and Qabrestan move slowly up the far aisle. Their calm quieted Sally's fears.

Perhaps they've changed their minds about shooting people, she thought irrationally. It was just as well that she could not see into the First class cabin, for Yonnie's actions would surely have unhinged Sally's mind.

Eight-year-old Allen Olsen, Junior, was a beautiful boy. His face had a pristine, asexual loveliness that is sometimes seen in prepubertal children and is the rarest and most transitory of human perfection. He was also a happy boy with a sweet and loving disposition. His body was big for his age, and like his father, he looked forward to someday playing fullback at the Naval Academy. It was ironic that this interest in football should be the direct and immediate cause of his death.

His father's favorite team, and hence Allen's, was the Pittsburgh Steelers. One cold weekend last December the two of them had flown up to watch the Steelers win the AFC central title. After the game, his father, a friend of the backfield coach, had taken Allen down to the dressing room. When they left, Allen carried a tiny football with the autograph of a famous Steeler running back. Allen carried it everywhere. He even refused to go to bed without it.

Now as he slept in the seat across from Barbara Mawson, he turned slightly and the football fell off the seat and rolled into the aisle. Barbara, instinctively motherlike, leaned down to retrieve the wayward toy. But immediately she realized she was calling attention to herself during Yonnie's approach. She straightened up quickly. But it was too late.

Yonnie saw Barbara and then the ball wobbling across the aisle. She stopped and looked down at Allen. Qabrestan stepped up and thrust his gun toward Barbara's face, forcing her back against the seat so that her view of Allen was blocked. Hamed came down the far aisle and stood between Carol Moore and the front of the cabin. Abdulla came out of the center galley where he had been eating and stood behind Doris' seat.

The act of murder committed as a relaxed, effortless occurrence against a pliant victim is one of the greatest of man's obscenities. Yet there was little any of the hostages could do to prevent it. Barbara was immobilized by Qabrestan's gun. Across that cabin, Carol and Doris saw Yonnie bend down and lift Allen by the shoulders, setting him on his feet.

"Come," Yonnie said and pushed the sleepy child down the aisle toward the open loading door.

Qabrestan backed down the aisle after her, his gun ready.

Barbara half rose. Crying and slowly moving her head from side to side in anguish, she said, "Oh, no. Please don't."

On the opposite aisle, Doris started to her feet, driven upward more by instinct than by plan. But behind her, Abdula grabbed her shoulder and pushed her down.

"Sit," he commanded.

Carol Moore, restrained by Hamed's gun, watched Yonnie and the boy, not fully comprehending what was going to happen.

Russell Wagner, however, understood exactly what was going to happen. He could just barely see little Allen's blond head as Yonnie guided him up the aisle. The sleepy child leaned his head trustingly against Yonnie's hip as she led him toward his death. The sight enraged the peaceful pharmacist more than anything ever had in his long life.

"Stop!" he shouted and heaved himself upright.

The four terrorists turned.

"Take me. Leave the child alone and take me."

"And me," shouted Agnes, the hat in her hand. She also stood and placed herself close to her husband. They were one unit now.

The cabin became charged with tension. Captain Worthington's silver shoulderboards gleamed dully as he leaned out into the aisle to try to see past Mahmud. More heads went out into the aisle.

The Wagners' act struck Barbara like an electric shock. That was it, she thought. They *could* protest. She sprang to her feet.

"Take me! Take me!" she began to chant over and over again. Her voice gained strength and volume as she repeated the words.

Her protest was infectious. Hours of fear and frustration found release in this simple act. Doris and Worthington, at opposite ends, both rose at the same time and joined in the chant. Wall and Sally stood and took up the call. Within seconds, the protest spread aft through the cabins as dozens of passengers stood and shouted, "Take me!" They were transformed as the words united them and turned them from frightened individuals into an angry mob.

In the after cabin, Albertson stood beside Harriet. An idea was forming in his mind. As the shouting reached its peak, he began moving slowly up the aisle toward Hamed. Harriet was the first to follow him. Others joined behind her. Soon both aisles were filled with a shouting mass of people moving slowly forward.

Mahmud and Abdulla stood on each side of the center galley holding live grenades aloft.

"Sit down! Sit down!" they shouted but their voices were lost in the chanting.

Hamed ran back to join them and leveled his gun at Albertson who was at the head of the mob.

"Saayed!" he screamed over the noise.

Qabrestan reacted instantly. He bent over and grabbed up a three-year-old girl and ran past Barbara to stand next to Mahmud. Holding the tiny body to his hip, he fired four shots over his head. Those who were nearest to Qabrestan stopped their chanting immediately They stood transfixed by this new threat. Their silence was transferred to those behind them and receded through the cabin until it died out pitifully in the very last rows of the protesters.

Qabrestan lowered his gun and pressed the muzzle to the little girl's head. Her whimpers were the only sound in the cabin.

"Sit down and be still or I will kill this one also. Go back and sit down. All of you."

Qabrestan turned and walked back up the aisle, dropping the girl back into her seat as he passed. Yonnie herded Allen the last few steps to the loading door.

"Those old fools nearly spoiled everything," Qabrestan gestured toward the Wagners. "They're troublemakers and must go next."

"*Ja*," Yonnie agreed. She held Allen loosely by the shoulder. The boy stood quietly, rubbing his eyes with both hands, his blond hair shining in the glare of the overhead light.

At a nod from Qabrestan, Yonnie turned Allen toward the open doorway and thrust the muzzle of her pistol through the long hair at the base of his skull. Taking one step backward, Yonnie squeezed the trigger. Allen's head snapped forward against his chest and his body jackknifed out the opening from the impact of the bullet. Yonnie turned and slid the magazine out of the still-smoking pistol. Qabrestan, who had just finished reloading his own weapon, handed her a single round.

"I'm hungry," she said.

"I also," answered Qabrestan.

The two headed for the galley.

Chapter 18

The wooden door was ordinary and unguarded. It was set into the small, unmarked alcove. It seemed to crouch at the end of the obscure corridor on the Pentagon's ground floor. As the small group approached it, Admiral Anderson reached ahead and pulled the door open. Swig Sauer, grim and unsmiling, followed Mary O'Hegarty who stepped through. As Anderson began to enter, he collided with Mary who had hesitated at the unexpected sight that met her eyes.

She found herself at the top of a long, narrow, brilliantly lit tunnel. It angled so steeply downward that little wooden slats were fastened to the floor in order to help keep feet from slipping. The side walls were a cold, gray, hard-looking steel. Handrails of highly polished brass ran sharply downward along the walls. They seemed to converge in the distance below. Mary felt enveloped in strangeness.

Seeing her hesitate, Sauer leaned toward her. "It takes some getting used to. Put both hands on the railings and you'll be all right. Just don't catch your heel. When they built this twenty years ago, they weren't thinking of women's shoes."

Mary started down cautiously.

"Why is it so steep, and why are the walls made of metal?" she asked.

"Well, the Command Center has to be bomb proof and they wanted to get even the entrance underground as quickly as possible. The steel walls are for blast protection."

"Why didn't they use elevators?"

"Because this moves more people in less time and it can't jam or breakdown."

Looking down, Mary saw what appeared to be the bottom of the tunnel. "Well, if it's so important," she asked, slightly out of breath but moving rapidly, "why is it unguarded?"

Sauer smiled for the first time since hearing of Mawson's ultimatum. "It's not unguarded. You'll see. We're almost there."

Mary, with Sauer a step behind, reached a small landing at the bottom and turned to her right. On either side of a small chamber there were two, counter-high, armored positions angled so they could catch the landing in a cross fire. Behind the sloping front of each position, stood an unsmiling MP who held a submachine gun at ready. Between these two positions, a small ramp led into what looked to Mary like a doorway within a doorway. A smartly uniformed MP sergeant stepped out of the inner doorway holding a clip board.

Seeing the two men that approached him, the MP came to attention and saluted.

"Good afternoon. Admiral Sauer. Admiral Anderson. Your identification, please," he said politely to Mary and blocked any further progress. Mary produced her Pentagon identification card.

The MP clipped it to the top edge of his board and quickly found her name on the printed list.

"Dr. O'Hegarty. This way, please." He handed back her card, turned, and then walked through the inner doorway. Mary and the two admirals followed him.

As Mary stepped up to the ramp, she saw that the inner doorway was actually an airlock. Its heavily constructed doors now stood open, giving the visitors access into the side of a separate structure. Mary crossed the ramp ahead of Sauer and saw the dim outline of a huge coiled spring in the gap between the two structures. Why, that spring is as big around as a car, she thought, puzzled. What kind of place is this?

Coming out of the other side of the airlock, Mary found herself in a typical, office reception area. The floor was carpeted expensively and the walls were painted attractively in pastels. From panels in the ceiling, fluorescent lights lit the room evenly and gave life to a large rubber tree plant in the corner. Two desks faced her. To the left she saw a waiting area with an L-shaped couch and coffee table. Except for the unusual entrance, it could have been any office.

The MP sergeant went straight to one of the desks. "War Room," he said to a young MP.

The man reached into a drawer and produced a badge with the letters WR printed on them in red. Reaching again into the drawer, he came up with all-area picture badges for Sauer and Anderson.

"You know the way, Doctor?" asked the sergeant.

"We'll take her," replied Sauer and turned toward a hallway that led from the reception area. "This way, Mary."

As they hurried down the hall side by side, Mary turned to Sauer and Anderson. "It looked like we entered some sort of separate building back there. Why is it like that?"

"Besides being built of thick concrete to survive a blast of nuclear air above the Pentagon, the Command Center is also designed to withstand the shock of a ground burst. The whole thing is mounted on big springs. Hence, the door within a door. During an attack, the air lock would be shut to seal out radioactive air."

"I'll show you. We're here," he said, stopping in front of a door guarded by another armed MP.

The MP glanced at their badges and then opened the door. Mary stepped through the doorway, followed closely by the two men. A wide but shallow room stretched out before her. A large, triangular conference table dominated the center of the room. Along the walls on either side of the door, low counters stood against the brown, cork wall covering. Two large coffee urns and a deep pan of iced soft drinks rested on one of them. The floor was carpeted in a matching shade of brown. From the low ceiling, spotlights hidden in acoustical tiles cast dim pools of light over the comfortable leather chairs ranged along two sides of the table.

All of this Mary merely perceived rather than saw, for her attention was caught immediately by the far wall of the room which seemed to be entirely missing. Mary peered at it closely as Sauer led her forward.

Instead of a wall, there seemed to be a knee-high railing in front of a huge, brightly lit, open space. At the railing, groups of men stood talking and looking out into what seemed to be emptiness. Occasionally, one would point to something. She saw General Mason and Secretary of Defense Gibbs standing to one side deep in conversation.

As she came farther into the room, Mary realized the railing formed the bottom of a wall of glare-free glass that overlooked the Command Center proper two stories below. Four gigantic, lighted displays filled one end of the large room and rose up before the glass wall.

"Why, it's like a movie theater," Mary said to Sauer. "And we're standing in the projection booth."

"I hadn't thought of it that way, but you're right," He answered. Sauer looked toward Gibbs to see if he was needed: His superior was still conversing with Mason, so he led Mary up to the railing.

"I've got a few minutes yet. Look there," he said pointing. "Directly below us, where the audience would sit, are the Command, Control, and Communication consoles for the different force commanders. We call it the C-cubed area for those three sections. Under the Unified Command Structure, the most immediately critical forces needed to fight any size or type of war are under the direct command of the Joint Chiefs of Staff.

"That area there," continued Sauer as he pointed out a section of consoles below and to the left, "is for the JCS, deputy director of the European Command. Over there is the area that directs the Rapid Development Force. The Blue Light Team is ordered from it. That area there, with all the activity going on, is for the deputy director of all strategic operations.

"All those consoles in the front are used by the reconnaissance and the communications sections. OK?"

"Uh-huh," replied Mary, fascinated.

"Now, reconnaissance uses all kinds of world-wide, intelligence-gathering systems to find out what the Russians, Chinese, Cubans, Koreans, and so on are up to militarily. This raw intelligence data is analyzed and the results go up on those displays located where the movie screen would be. They show the entire world, although all of them can be used to show a single area, if necessary. Below and to the right of the Suez Canal, you can see Assab. It's a slowly pulsing, yellow light."

"Where is the *Montana*?" asked Mary, searching the huge lighted display covered with glowing symbols.

"Look at the middle of the very top and you'll see a pulsing, blue circle with a numbered blue arrow pointing to it. That's the *Montana*."

"I see it. You say it's moving from there?"

"Probably. They know that by making the broadcast they disclosed their position to the Russians. So they'll move."

"Will Russia try to sink the *Montana*?" asked Mary. Her voice reflected a sudden realization of the meaning of the pretty colored lights.

Sauer threw a quick glance toward Gibbs before answering. Thompson of the CIA had arrived and joined the group as had the Air Forces Chief of Staff. Their conversation was still intense, so he turned his attention once again to Mary.

"They might, but the urgent question is not whether they'll attack the *Montana* but whether they'll attack the United States."

"I know," Mary said quietly.

"Now, if you look at the red lights within the outline of the Soviet Union on the European display, you can see that the Russians are rapidly coming up to full emergency war readiness. I've never seen so many red pulsars. You know, Mary, by the President's orders, we're doing just the opposite. Look at the US display. You can see the Minuteman missile readiness lights going from green to yellow as they come out of alert. The same thing is happening on the Pacific Ocean display," he continued, pointing to the left, "as our Trident missile submarines operating from the West Coast come out of alert."

"Is this wise?" she asked, looking him full in the face.

Sauer felt her nearness as he returned her gaze. For the first time in many years, he felt protective of a woman. Something long dead was growing deep within him.

From the back of the room came the sounds of more men and conversation. The President, Secretary of State Boyd, and Zhuravlev, the National Security Advisor had arrived. Several ubiquitous Secret Service men followed closely. Sauer turned and, seeing that the group was making for the conference table, led Mary to some chairs at the left of the room.

The President went directly to his chair at the center of the table and sat down. Zhuravlev sat down beside him. Boyd, Gibbs, Thompson, Sauer and the other military officers all followed suit, each taking whichever seat was nearest. Without waiting for amenities or preliminaries, the President spoke.

"The Secretary of State briefed me on the diplomatic situation in the car. For your information, the Eastern bloc countries, France, and the OPEC nations have formally demanded we hunt down and destroy the *Montana*. The Soviets have declared a national emergency and have announced that for every nuclear warhead that falls within Russia, two will fall in the United States."

The President looked directly at Sauer, his eyes cold and unfriendly.

"OK. So much for the bullshit. Now, Admiral, suppose you tell me just where Mawson's warheads are going to land in Russia. I've got to tell Gurinov which cities to evacuate."

Sauer stood. "Mr. President, I'm sorry but I can't do that. At least not yet."

"Why not? You got a security problem or something?"

"I'm afraid so," replied Sauer. "You're the only one who can authorize the discussion of the *Montana*'s actual target assignments before this group. You'll have to come to the vault and personally authenticate release of the target list."

Minutes later, Sauer and the President stood on the lowest level of the Command Center. In front of them was a thick, bank-vault-type door, standing open. While two Secret Service agents waited, Sauer led the President forward to an inner door of gleaming stainless steel. Set into this second door, was a small keyboard above a horizontal, metal box whose top was made of optically clear glass. A thick cable dropped from the bottom of the box.

"Punch your social security number into the keyboard," explained Sauer, "then press the fingers of both hands down on the glass."

The President followed Sauer's instructions. As soon as his hands touched the glass surface, bright lights in the box came on to illuminate the sworls and ridges in the skin of his fingers. An optical scanner in the bottom of the box moved smoothly along its track, converting the President's fingerprint pattern into a unique series of digital, electromagnetic pulses. The cable carried these pulses to a simple computer that searched its memory for a previously stored identical series. Finding the required information and noting attached highest priority code bits, the processor sent a signal to the gate-actuating machinery. The door in front of the President slid silently open. Within, an officer waited, holding a manila folder.

"If you'll step in, Mr. President, the Major will instruct you on how to get the folder out," said Sauer as he extended one hand toward the open doorway.

The President moved through the opening, causing the door to shut behind him.

Moments later, the same door opened again, and the President emerged with the folder in his left hand, clutched against his chest and strode rapidly up the hall, leaving Sauer and his two bodyguards to hurry after him.

Back in the War Room, the President sat down in his chair and spread the contents of the folder out on the table. For the first time the nation's most secret information was in full view of outsiders. There were three, separate lists. Each, in turn, consisted of three sheets of red-bordered paper stapled together.

The President picked up the first list and ran his eyes

down its top page, looking at the column of target names opposite each tape number.

"There's a helluva lot of targets here, Swig. Which ones will be hit?"

Sauer did not answer immediately. The silence seemed to go on for a long time, so the President looked up, thinking that he had not been heard. But he had. For just a moment, Sauer wished desperately that he did not have to answer.

"There's no way to know," he answered quietly, his eyes never leaving the President. "It could be any eight from any list in that folder."

Almost everyone at the table gasped in disbelief.

"Please, Mr. President," continued Sauer. "We know the targets assigned to the *Montana*, but we don't know the targets they've selected. If I may explain, sir?"

"Please do."

"The *Montana* carries twenty-four Trident missiles. Each missile contains eight independent warheads each of which can be assigned to a separate target. The original operational orders sent out to the *Montana* covered one hundred and ninety-two individual targets. The list you picked up shows the geographical locations of those original targets. All are in the Soviet Union. The eight that are in jeopardy now depends on which missile the *Montana* launches. If you wish to advise them on evacuation, you'll have to give them the entire list."

"That's ridiculous! They can't evacuate a hundred and ninety-two cities any more than we could. It's impossible, dammit!"

The President stood up and shoved back his chair. He began to pace back and forth behind the table. Shit, he thought, everytime you get a hold on this thing, it snaps around and bites you on the ass. Sauer's urgent and pained voice intruded on his thoughts.

"There's more, Mr. President. I'm afraid the evacuation requirements are far worse than that."

The President spun around. "What?"

"The *Montana* carries three different sets of target tapes for each missile. One is a Deterrent Tape designed to protect us from nuclear war and essentially covering population centers within Russia proper. That's the tape we just spoke of. However, since it's impossible to get additional tapes to a fleet ballistic submarine while she's on patrol, the *Montana*, as do all Trident ships, also carried limited-land-war tapes. One is a European Tape designed to counter a Soviet advance into Western Europe. The other is a Middle East Tape designed to counter a Soviet advance through Iran into the Arabian Peninsula."

"I heard that four years ago. So what's the bottom line?" asked the President, exasperated.

Sauer drew himself erect, his ice-blue eyes steady and unblinking. "The bottom line, Mr. President, is the chances are two out of three that the eight war heads will explode over our allies rather than over the Soviet Union."

A murmur of disbelief went up from those at the table. The President looked stunned.

"Wha . . . what d'you mean . . . our allies? Why is that?" the President sputtered. "I've never been briefed on that possibility! What the hell's going on here?"

"What's going on, Mr. President," said Sauer in a voice as cold as his eyes, "is the inescapable result of holding to a strategic targeting policy that assumes overall military superiority while allowing the Soviets to get ahead of us in all but missile forces. Look," said Sauer hurrying on, "we've inherited the current targeting philosophy of deterring a nuclear attack upon the United States and of protecting our interests in Europe and the Middle East. Hell, that goes back to before Korea. All of us, myself included, agree with it. Militarily *and* politically it's a good and reasonable policy. But, with all respect, sir, since you took office four years ago, the Soviet forces in Europe have grown to a point where they now have a significant advantage over NATO's. We have ten thousand tanks; the Soviets have fifty thousand. The NATO plan for countering a Soviet attack accepts that its initial forces along the Soviet bloc borders would be overrun by the weight of a Russian attack. The plan envisions an attack upon the advancing Soviet forces by strategic nuclear weapons falling in a dead zone between the main NATO defense forces and the initial, trip-wire border forces.

"The problem is that with a five-to-one advantage in arms, the estimated depth of Soviet advance into West Germany is so great that the dead zone now extends into the borders of France, Belgium, and the Netherlands. The same situation exists in the Middle East. Without opposition by the ground forces of Iran, stiffened by US troops, the Soviets will be in possession of all Persian Gulf oil fields within two weeks of crossing the Iranian border. There is no one to stop them. In the event of such an advance, it is expected that only the Israelis and the Turks would be able to hold out until US forces arrived.

"The point here is this: as the Soviets became stronger and we became weaker, the target areas for our nuclear warheads became larger until they swallowed up the entire geographical area of our allies. We saw this coming several years ago. That's why we asked for production of a neutron bomb. We needed a weapon that would kill Russians without destroying our allies' countrysides. We were denied such a weapon. With no change in the strategic targeting policy, we had no choice but to aim hydrogen warheads at our allies. And that's where we are right now."

Sauer looked at the President who seemed lost in thought.

"Specifically, Mr. President, what this means is that if Mawson selects a target tape at random from those available aboard the *Montana* and substitutes it for a tape that is listed in his operational orders, he can, for example, launch a missile that will destroy eight bridges in France. With a different random selection, he might ensure complete destruction of the oil fields and ports of Kuwait."

"Does Mawson or anyone else aboard the *Montana* know which tapes are which?" the President's voice rang out like a pistol shot.

"No. And they can't find out," replied Sauer.

"Well, that's something. I'll say one thing, Admiral. When we fuck up, we fuck up royally."

"OK," the President continued, "here's what we're going to do. Dick, you and General Mason order the landings at Assab to go ahead as quickly as possible. As soon as you've got the hostages safe, put Mrs. Mawson on the air to the *Montana*."

The President turned to Boyd. "Steve. Get lists of targets that fall within the Soviet Union on the teletype hot line to Moscow. We won't release the remaining targets unless something goes wrong and we have to. I'm damned if I want to admit we're fixing to blow up our friends. Which reminds me . . ." The President looked unsmilingly around the table. "Don't anyone forget that targeting information is Top Secret. If I read about this meeting in the *Washington Post* tomorrow, I promise you I'll find the source and prosecute. And this time I'll get help, since every American will be

embarrassed by the disclosure. Speaking of embarrassment,"
the President continued, turning to Sauer, "what's the situation regarding neutralization of the *Montana*? Can you do it
without having to attack her?"

"Yes, sir. God must love us. The guided missile cruiser
Hawaii is in Trondheim for joint exercises with the Norwegian Navy. Not only is she within steaming distance of all of
the *Montana*'s launch areas, but she just happens to be one of
the few ships that can destroy the *Montana*'s Trident missiles
without destroying the *Montana* herself."

"How does that work?" asked the President.

"Once the *Hawaii* is anywhere within the *Montana*'s
launch area, a Trident missile breaking the surface to begin its
flight will appear to the *Hawaii*'s tracking radars as a large,
slow-moving target. It's a simple target for them since their
weapons are designed to hit supersonic missiles. Our problem
is to locate the *Montana*, so that we send the *Hawaii* to the
right launch area."

"What're you doing about that?" asked the President,
frowning.

"We've ordered the *Hawaii* and her two escorts to
proceed first toward the nearest of the three launch areas,
which is just off the Norwegian coast. I've done this because
it's more or less on the way and because I personally think
that's where Mawson is headed. Hopefully, we'll have the
Montana located before the *Hawaii* arrives at the nearest
area. We're working on it."

"You're sure they can launch from only three places?
It's a big ocean!"

"Absolutely. The inertial guidance systems in Trident
missiles must know exactly where they are when they're
launched. The submarine can go anywhere in the world
there's an ocean. To store every possible launch point, would
take a computer with an infinitely large memory. We get
around this by storing only three different sets of launch
points. We call each set a launch area. He has got to launch
from one of these areas, or the warheads on the missiles
won't arm."

The President nodded and glanced at his wristwatch.
3:40.

"Thank you. Gentlemen, I've run out of time. We'll forget the situation briefing. I've got all I need to talk to Gur-

inov." The President looked around the room. "Put the call through now. Is my translator here?"

A young, studious-looking man separated himself from the group of aides, some of whom were leaving, and made his way to the table. The President smiled warmly and stuck out his hand.

"What's your name? I haven't worked with you before. Right?"

"No, Mr. President, you haven't. I'm David Pritchard," said the young man, shaking the President's hand.

"OK, Dave. Only one rule. If you hear something in his tone or his selection of words that you think is significant, jot it down on this pad and show it to me immediately. OK?"

"Yes, sir. I understand."

The President sat down and turned to the small group around him while the communications team set up telephone equipment. He looked at his advisors.

"Any final words of wisdom?"

"Jes' one thing, Mr. President," answered Thompson of the CIA. "We be'lieve the Russians don't know how good our Tridents are, 'specially in a defensive situation." Thompson smiled. "In fact, suh, we've been goin' to some lengths to make sure they don't. If they tangle with the *Montana*, they're gonna take heavy losses, and they won't take kindly to that. You might warn 'em to stay clear of her."

"Good point, Ken. I'll do that. Anything else?" asked the President, looking at each face.

Everyone shook their heads in the negative.

It's late over there, the President thought, shifting his gaze to a clock directly above Moscow's location on the European display. 11:48. It's almost midnight there. Must keep that in mind, he thought, recalling that President Gurinov, although younger and healthier than his predecessor, was still under a lot of pressure. The late hour would not help.

The communications people completed their work. An ordinary white telephone was placed before the President. Pritchard put on a headset and adjusted the thin curved rod of the microphone to his lips. The others at the table put on simple headsets since they would not be speaking. The individual wires from the instruments trailed along the carpet away from the table to join in a thick bundle leading to a small portable telephone switchboard. This was manned by an Army sergeant, attached to the JCS Communication Section. A tall Foreign Service officer from the State Department stood beside the switchboard speaking softly in Russian to a Soviet counterpart on the other end. An Army captain hovered anxiously, overseeing the entire operation.

The room grew still as each man waited, retreating into his own thoughts. Mary observed them all carefully from her seat. She knew she had never been more fascinated or frightened in her life. The President picked up the white phone. He and the others quickly put on their headsets.

"President Gurinov, are you there?"

The sound of the President's question being translated into Russian was heard by all, then back came the strong and vigorous voice of President Gurinov, Brezhnev's handpicked successor.

"Of course," translated Pritchard. "I have been expecting your call for some time."

Pritchard scribbled the words "insulting tone" on his scratchpad and pushed it to the President.

"I'm sorry, but the delay was unavoidable," replied the President. "I am calling to personally assure you that the threats made by the officers and crew of the *Montana* are not part of some overall plan for an attack on the Soviet Union by the United States. As proof of our peaceful intentions, I have ordered every single strategic weapon we possess to stand down. I'm sure your sensors confirm this."

"Yes. Our detectors show that. It is well you did. At first we thought it was another one of those technical tricks you are so fond of. But you could not trick all our detectors, so now we wait." Gurinov's voice hardened, spitting out the words that lost none of the heat in translation. "But this I tell you. For every Russian city destroyed by your madmen, we will destroy two cities of yours."

Tough talk from a new leader, thought the President as he began to get the measure of his man. He sounds as if he's trying to impress a room full of people.

"President Gurinov," said the President, seizing the role of elder statesman, "let us not talk of destroying one another. That is an old threat. One that I have learned to live with. Let us talk, instead, of saving lives. I am sending you now a list of cities, any of which could be targets for a *Montana* missile. What I suggest is . . ."

"Good," interrupted Gurinov, the sarcasm evident in his

voice even before the translation, "and I will send you a list of cities. Washington will be at the head."

As Gurinov spoke, Pritchard leaned forward intently. Catching something in the Russian's voice, he wrote the single world "insincere" on his pad. As he translated. he tore off the page and pushed it to the President, who read it and nodded.

Why would he be insincere about that? he wondered. Unless. . . .

"What I was about to say," the President continued, deciding to play a hunch, "was that the entire affair can be resolved within six hours if you will permit our seventy-man assault force on your airstrip at Assab."

Gurinov's reply needed no translation.

"*Nyet.* You have already demonstrated your inability to control forces under your command. What assurance do we have that American troops would confine themselves to the airstrip?"

The President glanced at Pritchard with raised eyebrows. But the translator, unable to detect anything further in Gurinov's voice, merely shrugged his shoulders. Sauer, however, leaned over and pushed a note in front of the President. It read:

CRAP!

The president nodded. True, he thought, but why? What's Gurinov's game?

"We had anticipated that might be your position," answered the President smoothly. He decided to take another tack. "We have already dispatched the surface forces necessary to neutralize the *Montana*'s missiles. I assure you no warheads will reach Russia."

Gurinov rose to the bait. "We can protect ourselves," he snapped. "At this moment, our naval ships are moving to intercept and destroy your nuclear pirates!"

So that's it. They're going for the *Montana* themselves. He turned and looked at Sauer. But the admiral had twisted around in his chair and was waving a note to Anderson, who was hurrying toward the table. The President looked up at the huge War Room displays. Something bothered him. Are the Russians going after the *Montana* out of simple ignorance, as Thompson suggested, or is there something more to it? He decided to probe a little more.

"President Gurinov, the *Montana* is extremely well armed

with defensive weapons. I urge you to withhold your forces from the area and allow us to handle the situation."

The President glanced again at Sauer, who was now hunched forward over the table. Both of his hands held the earphones tightly to his head as he eagerly awaited Gurinov's response.

"No. *We* will take care of the Montana. But *I* urge *you* to keep out of the area to prevent another incident from occurring. We have been aware of your Trident submarine defenses for some time. I assure you our captains will overcome them."

The President looked around the table. Sauer, Gibbs, Thompson, Pritchard. All were jotting down notes. Time to wrap it up, he thought, an idea forming in his mind.

"I can only repeat my warning. If you attack the *Montana*, you will suffer grievous losses of men and ships. I urge you most strongly to allow us to handle our own problem."

"I do not agree. It is *our* problem. Since we are the target, it is for us to determine the outcome. We will attack and destroy your submarine. If you wish to escalate the issue, we are willing."

Again, the President looked at Sauer, returned his gaze with a steady eye, as he shook his head in a negative reply, a grim chilling smile on his lips. The President took a deep breath.

"All right. I will withhold our forces from the area and trust the *Montana* to look after herself. But I assure you that you are making a serious mistake if you attack her as you apparently are determined to do."

"We shall see who has made the mistake." The line went dead.

The President hung up and watched the small group at the table taking off their headsets, then he turned to the translator.

"OK, Dave, what've you got?"

"Mr. President. When speaking of attacking the *Montana*, President Gurinov was not only sincere but his voice sounded almost eager. At the last, when he was speaking of seeing who had made the mistake, he used an inflection that makes me suspect he may have been referring to something entirely different than the subject under discussion. What that might be I, of course, have no idea."

Alexy Zhuravlev, the National Security Advisor, who spoke Russian, looked up.

"I do," he said in a voice with only the slightest of accents. "He's referring to our SALT agreements."

"Of course!" exclaimed Sauer, slamming his hand down on the table top. "We went for the SALT treaty because the Soviets can't find and destroy our Trident submarines. If they destroy the *Montana* now, the survivability of the entire Trident force is open to question. Particularly since we were told in advance they would attack her."

"That's right," continued Zhuravlev, unperturbed by Sauer's interruption. "Having demonstrated the vulnerability of our prime deterrent, we would be forced to either unilaterally break the SALT agreements and deploy additional forces or accept the position of being inferior to the Soviets in the eyes of the world."

"Not bad," said the President, the poker-face smile coming to his lips. "No wonder he's willing to wager four or five ships against the outcome. It's a damn good bet." Then he turned to Sauer, his eyes cold and hard. "OK, Swig. This is where you earn all the pay you've ever collected. Put it on the line and tell me what you think we should do."

For a moment that seemed like an hour, Sauer returned the President's gaze steadily while he collected his thoughts. Then a light seemed to come into his eyes, a deep, blue flash like sunlight on an iceberg. He sat back in his chair and, for the first time, felt absolutely certain of the outcome.

"Regardless of what has gone before, the *Montana* still contains the best men and the best weapons on this earth. The Soviet Navy, for all its size and power, has never been tried in combat. Given the full use of its weapons, the *Montana* can send the Russians down to an overwhelming defeat that will lessen Soviet naval pressure in the world for decades to come."

Sauer threw a glance at Mary. She leaned forward, realizing that he was making the decision of his career, and nodded her head in unspoken support.

"First, I recommend," Sauer continued, "that we support the *Montana* through TACDAPS with real-time combat data links. To do that, Mr. President, I need your permission to order them to fire defensive weapons at the Soviets."

"I agree one hundred percent!" exclaimed Zhuravlev.

"Second, we must prevent the Russians from mounting a

large-scale follow-up attack on the *Montana* since she is only capable of surviving a single major encounter. Thus, I recommend that we position the attack submarine *Tustin,* which is in the area, to block the arrival of more Soviet ASW forces. If I'm permitted to issue these two orders, we'll defeat the Soviet challenge."

General Mason, who had rejoined the group during the telephone call, leaned forward.

"Mr. President, the Soviet attack on the *Montana* will take place in any event. I agree completely with Admiral Sauer. As much as we abhor their mutiny and blackmail, we've got to support them now."

The President turned to Thompson. "What do you say, Ken?"

"Gurinov's made a mistake. But now that he's called us out," answered Thompson, "ah say we have t'accomodate the gentleman."

The President turned back to Sauer. "Have you located the Soviet force that Gurinov mentioned?"

"We believe so, Mr. President. If you look at the European display, you'll see three red pulsers off the northern portion of the Norwegian coast. That's a Soviet task force consisting of the carrier *Riga* and a *Kresta* II-class ASW cruiser with three *Kashin*-class destroyers as escorts. We will, of course, confirm this immediately."

The President stared long and hard at the pulsing red circles, then he turned to the general.

"John, what's the status on the Assab landings?"

Mason leaned forward, his face serious. "It's under way. All units are moving toward an assault at oh six-fifteen Assab time tomorrow. That's ten-fifteen tonight Washington time."

"Any way to move that up?"

"No, Mr. President. We can't get the forces into position any sooner."

"Then we're going to lose four more hostages."

"I'm afraid so, if the terrorists make good their threat."

The President turned to Boyd. "Have they?"

"We don't know, Mr. President. We haven't heard from Benson since the Mawson ultimatum was broadcast. We assume they've taken away his transmitter until this *Montana* situation is resolved but are allowing him to continue discussions with the terrorists. That is, we hope to God they are!"

The President turned back to Mason. "Will we lose more than four hostages?"

"Only if the Blue Light assault on the aircraft is delayed beyond midnight tomorrow or if the terrorists become aware of the fighting on the beach."

The President thought for a moment then, making up his mind, turned to Sauer. "Admiral, you are hereby directed to order the *Montana* to defend herself from Soviet attack and support her defense with tactical data. Further, you are to deploy the *Tustin* to prevent further Soviet attacks upon the *Montana*. Also, you may so use the *Hawaii* provided the neutralization of the *Montana* is not jeopardized. Does that cover it, Swig?"

"Yes, sir. That's it exactly," replied Sauer. He turned in his seat and motioned for Anderson, who was hovering near the table for orders.

The President stood up, bringing everyone in the room to their feet.

"I'm leaving now to try to explain all this to our friends. I want hourly status reports on both the *Montana* defense and Assab landings. I'm going to try to hold off the press with releases until I can call a conference at nine o'clock tomorrow morning. By that time, God willing, we will have successfully resolved these issues. That leaves only the terrorist problem to be solved when it's dark enough in Assab." The President started to leave, but suddenly turned back and looked at Sauer. "If I had ordered the landings immediately, would it have saved the lives of the four hostages?"

"No, Mr. President. You've given the order in time. There never was any chance of saving the four."

The President nodded his head in sad understanding, then spun on his heel and strode quickly from the room followed by his staff. Before the door had closed behind them, Sauer turned to Anderson.

"OK, Andy. There's a couple of large assumptions in my discussion with the President. So, before we do anything else, let's verify the tactical situation. Put it up on the board."

"Yes, sir." Anderson moved quickly to a telephone.

Sauer turned to gaze at the displays, his thoughts on the hostages, not knowing or caring that his order was rippling throughout the command structure like the impulse from a distant brain to the eyes and ears of some huge beast.

* * *

As the signal was relayed through an uplink from the TACDAPS Command Center in Norfolk, Virginia, an ocean surveillance satellite in geosychronous orbit above the Barents Sea began radar tracking of all ships moving across the surface of the seas off the Norwegian coast. In the same satellite, a large infrared array sensed the heat signatures of the numerous targets detected by the powerful radar antennas. Through a series of microwave downlinks, the raw intelligence data was fed to the large computer in the TACDAPS Command Center. Within seconds, the raw data was compared with heat signatures stored in the computer's memory. The position, course, and speed of the *Riga* and her escorts were confirmed. Similarly, the position of the *Hawaii* was pinpointed.

On six-thousand-foot Mt. Jaeggevarne behind Tromsø, Norway, a large parabolic antenna slowly turned onto a bearing for the *Riga* in response to a command from the TACDAPS computer. Sensitive receivers patiently began sweeping the radio frequencies, searching for military transmissions. On 166 megahertz, a data link that contained a code usually used by the Russians for transmitting tactical information was discovered between the *Riga* and a Soviet military satellite. Although the code could not be broken in time to be of any use, the pattern and rate of data transmission was recorded by the TACDAPS computer in minute detail for future use.

Deep in the sea off the Norwegian island of Senja, large acoustic arrays of the Navy's most-modern passive-sonar system picked up all ocean sounds within hundreds of miles of their sensitive hearing elements. In a nondescript gray-walled building of the Naval Base at Tromsø, the largest, most-powerful digital computer ever produced sorted through the billions of separate sounds recorded by these sonar arrays and found faint patterns that matched the signatures of the *Montana* and *Tustin*, while at the same time verifying that no Soviet submarines were in the area.

When this last element of the tactical picture reached Norfolk, TACDAPS transmitted all the information it had acquired to the National Command Center beneath the Pentagon.

Sauer, who had not moved during the short time it took the machine to assemble the information, watched as the outline of the United States faded and was replaced by an enlargement of the seas between Tromsø, Norway and Jan Mayen Island. Before the outline had fully developed, five red circles, representing the *Riga* force appeared on the screen. From these circles, five parallel arrows pointed almost due west. A single blue circle, marking the position and course of the *Montana*, appeared with an arrow pointing due east straight at the red circles.

"Ah," said Sauer aloud. There was now no question that the two forces would meet.

Seconds later, blue circles representing the *Tustin* and the *Hawaii* force appeared on the screen.

Sauer stood up and moved to the window, followed by Anderson who held a handset on a long cord. For a moment Sauer stared at the display, looking at the area midway between the *Montana* and the *Riga*. Although it's always daylight up there, the water's damn cold, he thought. Anyone who goes in will probably die before they're picked up. Once again he considered all the alternatives available, but no better answer came. The ancient choice presented itself. Someone must die. Them or us? Sauer sighed and turned to Anderson.

"Order the *Tustin* and *Hawaii* into position. Issue the auto lockup signal. Tactical weapon release is granted for the *Montana* only."

Anderson repeated the order into the phone.

Sauer turned from the window with feelings that combined sadness with shame. He never had been able to accept the ordering of others to their deaths when he himself was safe. As he looked up, he noticed Mary sitting unneeded and unnoticed among the empty staff chairs. Suddenly, he hated the thought of her being alone. He walked rapidly around the conference table toward her.

Mary saw him coming and stood up, a look of concern on her face. Sauer knew it was for him. She knows what I'm feeling, he thought. He was deeply touched. His love for her was such a strong thing now.

"Mary. He never called on you and this thing won't be over until well after midnight. So, I can't . . ." Sauer hesitated. You're asking too much of her, he thought. You're being a fool. Close to despair, he threw his hands up and shook his head. Mary looked on, a small smile hovering about her lips.

"Oh, hell, Mary, there's no other way or place to say it. I love you. Will you marry me?"

A great wave of emotion surged through Mary. He wants me, she thought. And oh, she realized, do I want him!

"Oh, yes." Her voice was so low that it was almost inaudible, but he heard her. She laid a hand tenderly on his arm. "I'll be waiting at your place, dearest. Whatever time you get back. I love you, Swig."

Sauer covered her hand with his and squeezed it.

"I'll have someone take you." He led her towards the door, his eyes warm and, for the first time in over ten years, tender.

As he and Mary spoke, the auto lockup signal was already being transmitted to the network of self-powered acoustic transceivers covering the cold, barren seabed beneath the dark waters of the Norwegian Sea.

Chapter 19

Chief Dan Jackson glanced over the head of the duty fire control technician. The digital clock readout on the face of the Weapons Summary Status board read 2255. Thank God. Only an hour to midnight and the end of the watch. He felt awkward in the spacious quiet of the control room and missed his normal watch station. His home was the crammed confines of the Torpedo Room, filled with the hissing of highly compressed air and Poley's curses.

Watch bill's scrambled all to hell, he thought. Mr. Rossman taking Mr. Wallstrom's place. Charlie Duncan standing Mr. Rossman's watch, me standing Charlie's and Poley standing mine. Jesus! Jackson smiled at the thought of Poley finally finding himself in complete charge of the Torpedo Room. His cursing would be something to hear. Jackson started to turn away when he noticed the fire control technician in front of him suddenly stiffen as if struck in the face.

"What's a matter?" asked Jackson anxiously, turning back to look at the board.

"An attack alert's coming in." Unbelievingly, the technician pointed to a red pulsing ALERT light on the board."

Jackson bent over to see the board better. As he watched, the red TACTICAL WEAPONS RELEASE DENIED light went out to be instantly replaced with the green, glowing words TACTICAL WEAPONS RELEASE GRANTED. The soft but unmistakable sound of a slow chiming bell came from the board, calling the operator's attention to the change in status.

"What the hell does that mean?" demanded Jackson, totally out of his element.

"Get the OOD. We're gonna be attacked and they want us to shoot back," answered the younger man excitedly. His hands flew over the controls on the console, bringing the other stations alive.

Jackson spun around immediately to Deville, who was standing at the plotting table of a few yards away.

"Mr. Deville," Jackson called in a steady voice, "we have an attack alert coming in. It's the real thing."

In two steps Deville, who happened to be OOD, was beside Jackson peering at the board.

"Damn!" exclaimed Deville, spinning around to face the CIC hidden behind the bulk of the Command Center island. "What've you got, Jennings?" called Deville. He leapt onto the island and stared down at the Tactical Display Table. The center display was pulsing slowly, flooding the entire CIC section of the control room with a hideous, greenish-orange light.

Jennings, the sole CIC watch stander, turned his head and looked up, his cheek bathed in the ghoulish glow.

"We have auto lockup. It's not a drill. Our acknowledgement has gone out. First tactical data's coming in now, sir."

As he spoke, the central display stopped pulsing. Jennings' fingers moved over the keyboard under his hand. Instantly, five-yellow dots appeared on the display besides the green line of light that represented the coast of Norway.

"It's the *Riga* force. They're confirmed as moving to attack us," said Jennings, the excitement evident in his voice in spite of his attempt to appear calm.

"Attack us!" repeated Deville, still not believing. "Are you sure? How soon?"

"Don't know. We dropped out of the system when we came out of Strat Alert. I can compute it, but it'll take a few minutes to get everything lined up."

"Do it." Deville turned quickly to the duty talker.

"Captain to the control room," ordered Deville. He stood for a moment debating with himself. Should he sound General Quarters? The attack might be hours away and the captain would be here in a moment. If he sounded the alarm now, he'd rob the men of much-needed sleep. On the other hand, it's just possible the attack might be minutes away so that seconds counted.

As he thought out the situation, Deville was surprised to find himself perfectly calm. Jan was forgotten along with the old feeling of inadequacy associated with thoughts of her. He had gone along wih the mutiny without thinking much about it. Later, he realized he was again just drifting along with events making no effort to control them. He had cursed himself for being weak. But when the TACDAPS was reactivated and he realized the Navy was giving them full support, it was as if he personally was being given one final chance to straighten out his life. This time it would be different, he vowed.

"Sound General Quarters," barked Deville, mashing his thumb down on the switchbox mounted to the railing.

Jackson looked around at the new sound of authority in Deville's voice.

Throughout the ship, the measured beat of the general alarm gong sounded. From the IMC speakers came the voice of the talker.

"General Quarters! General Quarters! All hands man battle stations. General Quarters! General Quarters! All hands man battle stations."

Instantly, the quiet and darkened ship, guided by isolated groups of watchstanders, was transformed into urgent and highly organized activity as each off-duty man rolled out of his bunk, dressed, and rushed as quickly as possible to his battle station. The methods and routes used by the men to gain each station in the least time were highly individualistic, each man working out the best routine for himself during countless drills.

In response to the phone call, Mawson was already out of his bunk and tearing off his pajamas when the first sound of the gong came. Ninety seconds later, he was out the door of his cabin heading for the control room. Crowding right behind him was Edelstone.

McKenna, who slept in his skivvies, heaved his bulk out of his bunk. While groping frantically for his scattered clothes, he stubbed his toe on the desk leg. Moments later he joined the other officers in the passageway looking as untidy as every and smelling slightly from a sour uniform. Below in the chief's quarters, Dacovak awoke, crossed himself, and dressed quickly in the clean and freshly pressed uniform he had laid out before turning in.

When the alarm sounded, Wallstrom was pacing his cabin fully clothed, tormented by his decision. At the first sound of the gong, he turned instinctively to the door. Pulling it open, he started out when the startled boatswain's mate guarding his cabin turned toward him, not knowing what to do. Wallstrom hesitated, his handsome face a mask of pain.

Damn. Damn it to hell, he thought as he backed into his cabin and closed the door. I can't help without becoming part of the mutiny. Wonder what's going on? Suddenly his knees went weak and he thought he was going to be sick. My God, he thought, maybe we're being attacked by American forces. He dropped down on the edge of his bunk and buried his head in his hands, his elbows resting on his knees. But they couldn't, he thought, raising his head in hope. Mawson, Edelstone, all of them making a threat is one thing, but firing on our own ships is something else. They couldn't do that, he thought with conviction. Feeling better, he started to stand up when a single knock sounded on the door and it swung open. Mawson stepped into the cabin without waiting for an answer.

"What's happened, sir?" Wallstrom asked.

"According to TACDAPS, we're going to be attacked by a Soviet ASW force in about three hours and forty-five minutes."

Wallstrom, bewildered by the news, stared in silence.

Mawson took him by the arm. "Don't you see? We have both auto lockup *and* permission for weapons release. Only the President can grant that. For some reason they're backing us all the way in this fight. You're free to join us. For now, anyway." Mawson looked full into Wallstrom's eyes. "What d'you say, Ross? Come on out and help us sink these bastards. We'll be using your tactics."

"We really have weapons release granted?" asked Wallstrom. His mind was struggling to grasp the sudden change in the situation.

"Yeah. And nobody was more surprised than I was to see it," replied Mawson, shaking his head. Mawson stepped forward and put his arm around Wallstrom's shoulders. "I don't pretend to understand it. I'm just going to run the play they sent in," giving Wallstrom's shoulders a squeeze. "What d'you say? You going to stay in here or you going to come out and put it to these guys?"

Wallstrom thought for a moment. Arguments for and against poured through his racing mind. Mawson waited patiently.

"Fuck it, Captain!" exclaimed Wallstrom and gave up trying to find the answer, "I'm coming!"

"Good man. Wait till you see the plot. You won't believe how close it is to your model."

Mawson led Wallstrom out of the cabin. As he stepped through the door into the passageway, he turned to the boatswain's mate.

"Return to your station. You're no longer needed here."

"Aye, aye, sir!" replied the man happily.

In the control room, Wallstrom's appearance brought cheers from the men. As the hurrahs died down, Mawson approached Edelstone.

"Harry," he said quietly, "take Dacovak from his plotting table and both of you go and explain the situation to the men who haven't joined us. Tell them it's up to them, but we'd like to have them with us just for the fight."

"Aye, aye, sir."

Mawson joined Wallstrom at the Tactical Display Table, now fully manned.

"OK. Mr. McKenna, let's go over it again for Mr. Wallstrom," ordered Mawson, as he looked at the central display with its five yellow dots off the green-lined coast of Norway.

"Yes, sir," answered McKenna, who began keying the necessary instructions.

Instantly, the five yellow dots grew short, parallel arrows that pointed almost due west. The yellow glowing numerals 1 through 5 appeared beside them. To the right of the green blob that was Jan Mayen Island, a blue dot appeared with its arrow aimed directly at the five yellow dots in the east. The glowing numeral 1 appeared beside the blue dot. A second blue dot with its arrow pointed toward a speck of green light labeled Norway's North Cape appeared to the northeast of the five yellow marked Soviet ships. This dot was labeled with a blue-colored numeral 2. Three additional blue dots appeared off the Norwegian coast with arrows showing that the force was moving northward along the coast from Trondheim toward Tromsø. This force was labeled with the numerals 3 through 5.

Wallstrom bent over the table as McKenna began talking.

"We're Blue One. Range to *Riga* force, Yellow One through Five, is three hundred twenty miles. At our present speed, they're closing at combined speed of seventy knots. We'll be within the anticipated Soviet engagement range of sixty miles in four hours and twenty-four minutes."

Who's Blue Two and Blue Three?" interrupted Mawson. "They're new."

"Yes, sir. They've just come up. Blue Two is the *Tustin*, which you can see is moving to block any reinforcement of Yellow One by offshore Soviet units."

"And Blue Three through Five?" queried Wallstrom.

"That's the guided missile cruiser *Hawaii* and her two escorts, the frigates *Hale* and *Gates*. They're moving into position to block reinforcement of the *Riga* by Soviet surface units hugging the Norwegian coast."

Wallstrom shook his head. "I see it, but it's hard to believe. You say we have permission to fire?"

"Hell, yes. You can see for yourself," replied Mawson, gesturing toward the fire control panels. "What's more, we have confirmation of Soviet intentions to fire on us. There's no question of what's going to happen. Only how."

Wallstrom shrugged his shoulders, a wry smile on his face. "Christ, we're going to war and I almost missed it! So be it." Wallstrom's normally deep voice seemed to grow stronger as he changed mental gears. "OK. Let's see the tactical picture at a range of one hundred twenty miles."

The colored images on the display faded in response to McKenna's commands and were replaced by the same images projected forward in time. The *Montana* and the *Riga* were now much closer to one another.

"What time will that be?" asked Mawson.

"At oh two forty-two, sir," McKenna read as the numerals appeared on the display in response to his query.

Two hours and twenty-five minutes from now, thought

Wallstrom, opening his mouth to speak. Plenty of time to check out their assumptions.

Mawson, however, beat him to the same thought. "Let's check their actual response time. It may have improved significantly from our last input." Mawson turned to Olsen, who stood behind the helmsman. "What're you steering?"

"Steering one zero zero, sir," Olson replied promptly.

"Come right to one one five," ordered Mawson and then turned back to McKenna.

"Start the clock, Mr. McKenna."

McKenna punched a button causing the numerals 0000 to appear on a digital timer in the corner of the central display.

"Clock started, sir," said McKenna as Olsen's voice came from the ship's control center saying,

"Steering one one five."

Mawson and Wallstrom stared at the central display.

"What do we need, Ross?" Mawson's voice was hushed, his eyes glued to the yellowish dots.

"Twelve minutes minimum, Captain," answered Wallstrom.

Silence descended upon the control room as all waited for the Soviets' tracking systems, now locked onto their wake, to respond to the *Montana*'s course change. The seconds of the digital display appeared and disappeared one after the other, each old number blending into the new. Minutes passed. Five, ten, twelve. No one in the small group took their eyes off the display. This was the final piece in the puzzle. Wallstrom's attack plan depended upon a period of twelve minutes during which the *Montana*'s movements would be unknown to the Soviets.

"There they go, sir," McKenna said in his carefully expressionless voice. "They've altered course fifteen degrees to port. Clock stopped at nineteen minutes, seventeen seconds."

Mawson straightened up as his mind made the simple calculation. "Allowing three minutes for our own delay, that makes their actual response time a bit over sixteen minutes," he said. A grim smile hid the relief he felt.

Wallstrom nodded absently while watching as the parallel arrows leading from the yellow dots changed direction slightly. His smooth brown skin appeared lamp black in the greenish light.

"We got 'em, Captain," Wallstrom said thoughtfully. "No question of that." It's strange, he thought still gazing at the display. Both governments seem to be using Mawson's ultimatium as an excuse for the two of us to meet in combat. It's as if they're settling their differences in medieval combat.

Wallstrom's thoughts were interrupted by Mawson turning to Olsen.

"Return to course one zero zero."

Mawson stepped up to the Command Center island. Ever conscious of the crews' needs, he picked up the IMC microphone and put it to his lips. Once again, his voice came over the loudspeakers. This time it was cool and free of any hint of passion.

"This is the Captain speaking. A Russian ASW force is moving to attack us. In about two and a half hours we will engage them at a range we hope will catch them unprepared. All of you, I know, will be glad to hear we are no longer acting alone and contrary to orders. We are now receiving full tactical support and are ordered, I repeated ordered, to resist the Soviet attack."

The sound of scattered cheering caused Mawson to pause. Fools, he thought angrily. They think they're going to get away with it. Waiting for the noise to subside, Mawson continued, his voice becoming warmer.

"Although it is not clear just why Washington is supporting us, you can be sure it's out of need, not forgiveness. It would be a mistake to think our future at home looks any brighter." Enough, he thought, searching his mind for something more positive with which to finish. He continued, his voice becoming warmer.

"Set Condition Two. Those not on watch should try to get some rest. We must survive the coming fight for our families. In this, at least, our own and our country's interest are identical. Good luck to us. We've earned it!"

The speakers went dead as Mawson hung the microphone up. For several seconds there was a pause like a wave gathering itself as it rears with foaming crest before crashing down on the bench. Then, cheers from every throat like the roaring of surf broke upon Mawson's ears as he made for his cabin.

Below, once again in the bottom of the ship, Dan Jackson stood staring at the loudspeaker. He was oblivious to the noise created by Poley and the men around him. You're wrong, skipper, mused Jackson. His own thoughts mirrored Wallstrom's. This is going to be exactly like an ancient trial by combat. If we pull it off, we're going to be treated a lot better back home than we deserve. With that thought in mind, he turned to the group around him.

"All right. All right. You heard the Old Man. Those not on watch turn in and get some shut-eye."

Turning to Poley, Jackson continued,

"I'll be in the CPO mess spreading a little joy."

"Huh," responded Poley dully, but with a broad grin lying heavily upon his thick features.

"Never mind, Poley," responded Jackson kindly as he started for the watertight door. "If anything, you're too damn ready to fight."

"Ah, Chief," pleaded Poley because he misunderstood Jackson, "I never start them brawls. I just finish 'em."

"Like this one?"

"Yeah, like this one here," grinned Poley as he slowly turned his head aside and sent a thick stream of tobacco juice into his personal spitkit.

Two hours later, Mawson was back in the control room bending over the Tactical Display table. Wallstrom, who had remained on watch, was beside him. The tactical situation had devleoped exactly as TACDAPS predicted. The five yellow dots were now much closer to the *Montana*. The blue dot off the North Cape showed the *Tustin* was already in position. The three blue dots off the Lofoten Islands showed that the *Hawaii* force was still hurrying north along the coast.

"How long until engagement range?" asked Mawson as he stared at the three blue dots.

"Twenty-eight minutes, Captain," answered McKenna, who also had remained on watch.

"The *Hawaii* group isn't going to make it. They're still too far south. They'll be in the middle of Delta Three when this is over."

"Hmmm," murmured Wallstrom. He wondered if the *Hawaii* was moving at her best speed, but did not want to ask.

"Not that it matters," continued Mawson, his thoughts solely on the coming engagement. "Verify hostile intent."

McKenna's fingers moved over the keys, sending pulses

containing Mawson's query out through the long series of links to the National Command Center. Within seconds, the red-lit words IMMINENT ATTACK VERIFIED appeared on the screen.

"Verify tactical weapons release," ordered Mawson in an emotionless voice.

Again, McKenna's fingers moved over the keys. Again, red words that foretold the death of hundreds of young men appeared: TACTICAL WEAPONS RELEASE GRANTED.

Mawson stood as still as stone, his eyes fixed upon the five yellow dots of light. For the first time he realized the true meaning of the phrase "political animal." Political games can't be stopped, he thought, shaking his head. All I've done is substitute one set of pawns for another. Soviet sailor for our families. Insatiable insanity. And I'm part of it. Hell, I'm the one that's going to kill them. Suddenly, he knew his career as a naval officer was truly over and that he was glad. Mawson took a deep breath, held it a moment, and let it out. So be it, he thought and turned to the talker. Mawson's voice sounded unnaturally loud as his orders poured out.

"Sound General Quarters. Plane up to launch depth and stream the XBT."

Again, the general alarm brought grim and determined men quickly to their stations. The deck beneath their feet slanted upward as the bulbous bow of the *Montana* began to rise from the depths of the Norwegian Sea.

McKenna looked up as Petty Officer Mejia, the Subsurface Integrator, slid into his seat at the Tactical Display Table.

"Steam the XBT," repeated McKenna. "Sweep from sixty to six hundred feet."

Mejia's fingers moved over the keyboard beneath his hand. In response, a door in the after exterior superstructure of the *Montana* slid open and a large torpedo-shaped device rose into the dark cold waters at the end of a thick towing cable. It moved slowly aft as the cable unreeled until it was well above and behind the thrashing propeller. From the side of the device, an expendable bathythermograph, XTB for short, that looked like a football with movable fins, was ejected and rose immediately on the end of its own cable to begin its first sweep.

As controlled by Mejia, sensors in the XBT monitored water temperature and salinity from the surface to a depth of

2500 feet. McKenna, aided by a highly specialized computer, used this data to locate areas of poor acoustic performance, called shadow zones, which would hide the *Montana* from the probing Soviet sonar systems. Some minutes later, the *Montana* leveled off as her rise toward the surface was checked.

"Launch depth," announced Edelstone from his position in the ship control center.

"Sonar report," called out Mawson, stepping up into the Command Center island.

"Negative contact all around," reported the young sonarman sitting in front of the circular scope of the AN/BQQ-6 sonar set.

"ECM stand by," ordered Mawson looking aft to the compartment where Deville sat at the center ECM console between two ratings. His back was to the Tactical Display Table.

Without turning his head, Deville sang out, "ECM standing by."

"Target bearing three five zero. Range one two zero miles," called out McKenna from the CIC.

"Torpedo Room stand by. Tubes One, Three, and Five," said Wallstrom coming up to the ordinance talker in front of the Weapons Summary Status board.

Below in the Torpedo Room, Jackson stood in front of the tube control panel.

"Tubes One, Three, and Five. Open outer doors."

Poley reached up and turned the valves that opened the doors at the exterior ends of the three tubes. Jackson watched the indicator lights on the control panel illuminate.

"Tubes One, Three, and Five ready!" announced Jackson. His hand moved upward to hover above the three starboard tube manual firing valves. His eyes remained fixed on the squawk box, awaiting the next order.

In the already hushed control room, a strange new silence descended as each man waited for Mawson to speak, knowing full well what he would say. The kaleidescope of lights winked and glowed, flashing into eyes staring unblinking on the edge of history. Time itself seemed to hang back as if reluctant to begin a series of events the end of which no one could foresee.

Deville licked his lips nervously. Say it, damn it, say it!

he thought impatiently, wanting and yet not wanting
Mawson's order to come. He squirmed in his seat and stared
unseeingly at the three display screens in front of him. They
glowed blankly, also waiting. He was experiencing exactly the
same fears that a novice actor does, waiting anxiously in the
wings to make a first appearance upon the stage. That he
knew the role he was to play in the coming battle, Deville
was certain. That he would remember the role, he was not so
sure.

He stole a sidelong look at Sheldon on his right. He
could see the ECM operator's calm and impassive profile out-
lined against the gray, equipment cabinet, forming the outboard side of the space. I should be like that, thought Deville.
But the weight of his responsibility bore down on him. The
Montana's success was in his hands. He had to do this one
right. If he fucked it up, they were all dead.

Deville's bladder felt as if it would burst. He was on the
edge of panic. He had never been able to face up to important situations. Never had he stood toe to toe with trouble
and slugged it out. In the end, he always ran away. Not from
fear, although sometimes he called himself coward, but from
a deep-rooted desire to remain a child by avoiding adult decisions and confrontations.

As it must come to all young men, events had finally
forced him onto the threshold of manhood. Either he faced
up to his responsibilities now, or someday he would find himself a bewildered, forty-year-old child, wondering where his
youth had gone. His life hung in the balance, waiting. But it
was fate, not himself, that decided the issue. For, just as the
tension in him built to the breaking point, young Seaman First
Kofsy on his left spoke out in fear.

"I'm scared, Mr. Deville," said the high-pitched, boyish
voice. "I ain't never done this for real. What if I fuck it up?"

Deville started to turn toward the voice, his body rigid
with tension. But in that instant, he felt the horrible sensation
of warm urine against the skin of his crotch.

"Ah, shit," he groaned aloud involuntarily.

"Sir?" came Kofsy's surprised voice.

Deville looked down at the spreading, damp area between his legs. Goddamnit! he thought. I don't believe this is
happening to me. When I stand up, everyone'll see. He shook
his head in disbelief. He could not run away. He had to face
it.

Deville turned and met Kofsy's stare, a smile spreading slowly over his face.

"You think you're scared of fucking up! I just wet my pants. Ain't *that* a pisser!"

Deville had been hauled screaming into manhood by an infantile act.

Mawson's voice, calm and free of any expression, came at last. His were simple words, spoken in forceful tones that ranged throughout the compartment.

"Launch Mark Two's."

"Fire One! Fire Three! Fire Five!" ordered Wallstrom.

A slight tremor through the huge bulk of the *Montana* as the missiles, together weighing almost five tons, were ejected from the starboard tubes by thousands of pounds of compressed air. In the nose of each missile, an accelerometer sensed the sudden motion and sent a pulse of energy to the waiting integrated circuits of the guidance and control systems. Instantly, explosive bridge wires buried in the solid propellant of the boosters vaporized in a burst of heat, thus igniting the rocket motors in a muffled explosion of steam and bubbles.

To Jackson in the torpedo room, the explosions which were distorted by the steel of the hull, sounded like firecrackers going off inside tin cans. One, two, three, he counted the distinct sounds coming easily to his ear. Jackson grabbed a stancheon for support as the ship turned sharply to a new course.

"Tubes One, Three, and Five fired electrically," he shouted into the squawk box. "All boosters ignited."

"Very good," came Wallstrom's voice from the box. The deck became level again as the ship steadied onto her new course.

Jackson turned to watch Poley, who was directing the preparations for reloading the now-empty tubes with standard Tomahawk missiles.

"Move it!" shouted Poley to no one in particular. They only had twelve minutes to accomplish the reload, which meant four minutes for each tube.

Outside the hull, the three missiles angled steeply upward toward the surface, driven by the booster engines. Because oxygen was part of the solid propellant in the engines, they were as at home in water as in air. Within seconds of being launched, the missiles burst from the calm surface of the sea in a cloud of smoke and steam. Even as the last sea water cascaded from their smooth skins, watertight coverings were explosively stripped from the sides. The missiles sprouted tail fins, stubby wings, and air inlet scoops. Moments later, the booster engines fell away and the sustainer engines roared into life.

A small dish antenna linking the three missiles to Deville's ECM consoles broke the surface of the water and quickly locked onto the tracking signal emitted by a tiny powerful transmitter in each missile. Below, eyes glued to his console, Kofsy depressed a switch and watched the resulting three green lights appear.

"Uplinks and downlinks verified," he announced in a squeaky voice. "Tracking transmitter disabled."

"Clock started," came Sheldon's contribution.

"ECM standing by for terminal maneuver," Deville called out to Mawson.

The missiles, with transmitters shut off, rose vertically over the launch point to a height of several thousand feet. As they rose, the belly of each missile rolled slowly until it was pointing directly at the distant *Riga*. When the guidance systems sensed the belly was on the target azimuth, the missiles pitched over and descended to within a few feet of the water as they began their long, one-way flight.

Cold wind quickly dispersed the clouds before the missiles disappeared into the pale light of the artic night. As the clouds blew away, the small dish antenna waited patiently for the now-departed missiles to reappear above the radio horizon.

The five Soviet warships tore through choppy, green-gray seas at full speed. In the center of their loose battle formation, the soaring bow of the *Riga* threw out a smother of foaming water for a hundred yards on each side of its rushing hull. Four great propellers under its stern converted the full two hundred thousand horsepower of her engines into forward motion. Throughout the ship, men stood quietly at battle stations waiting. On the flight deck which angled from the port side of the ship, crewmen bustled around the seven

Kamov KA-25 ASW helicopters, hurrying to complete arming and fueling the aircraft.

One thousand yards to starboard of the *Riga*, the large ASW cruiser *Admiral Arbatov* kept precise station. A huge array of redundant radar antennas towered one above the other over the enclosed bridge and formed the central superstructure of the ship. Now, the rushing wind caused the wire mesh of the antennas and the open supporting girders to whine and moan in a whole chorus of sounds. Ahead and to either side of the two large vessels, the three sleek destroyers formed a protective screen. High above the formation, a Yakovley Yak-36 fighter circled endlessly on combat air patrol.

Seen from without, the warships formed an impressive force. The high bows and sweeping deck lines that were the mark of the new Soviet Navy lent grace to the powerful blocks of soaring structure, bristling with rocket launchers and automatic, rapid-fire guns. Yet, this outward appearance was deceiving. For within, the ships were flawed. At the same time, they represented both the best and worst of the Soviet system.

This exact problem was occupying the thoughts of Captain Leonid Borosky as he balanced himself on the *Riga*'s bridgedeck. He was looking past the *Admiral Arbatov* to center the image of the destroyer *Rossiya* in his binoculars.

There, he thought, as the almost invisible stream of black smoke from the *Rossiya*'s after stack momentarily thickened into a hard flat line. They won't be able to maintain this speed much longer. She's straining now.

He lowered the glasses and glanced at the bridge clock. Only twenty-three minutes more, he thought reviewing the plan in his mind. We'll launch the Kamovs at a range of ninety miles. With an airspeed of one hundred eighty knots, they'll be over the target area just as the American Harpoon missiles are coming into striking distance of us. Close, he thought, turning to gaze down at the flight deck with hard brown eyes. If only the KA-25 had more range or the Yak-36 better sensors.

The thought of sensors caused him to look to the foredeck, cluttered with missile launchers and both 23-mm and 76-mm guns. He knew that more weapons were mounted above his head and in the after portion of the ship, all made blind by jamming, for the lack of a computer. He thought of the bulbous, electronic, countermeasure antennas on the superstructures of both the *Riga* and the *Admiral Arbatov*. Beautiful designs. As good as anything the Americans had, but they lead only to manually operated stations designed twenty years ago. The spaces in both ships for the digital computers that completed the system remained empty.

Borosky shrugged his thin shoulders in the distinctive gesture of the great Russian people that for time immemorial had signified an individual's apathy toward that which appeared unchangeable.

Borosky's thoughts were interrupted as the speaker above his head suddenly came to life.

"Bridge. CIC. Three low-flying targets bearing zero one two. Range twenty-two thousand meters and closing. Speed nine two six. Altitude three meters."

"Missiles? At this range?" asked Borosky aloud in great surprise. Recovering himself quickly, he turned to the navigation officer and the bridge talker. There was not a moment to lose. At nine hundred and twenty-six kilometers per second, they'll be here in one minute. They must be the new Tomahawks. But why only three? he wondered even as he spoke.

"All units. Turn three points to port. Engage missile targets to starboard."

Borosky paused while the talker transmitted the order to the other ships before putting the order into effect.

"Execute!" he barked and then turned to the window.

The deck beneath his feet tilted as the *Riga* began a high-speed turn. Borosky watched with satisfaction as the three ships within his view turned smoothly with the *Riga*. His small, but not unhandsome face relaxed slightly. But the frown that darkened his prominent forehead remained as he turned his attention to the crowded flight deck.

"Prepare to engage missile targets," came the voice of his Starpom or executive officer from loudspeakers along the deck.

Hurry, thought Borosky. Must get the helios away. A single hit on the deck now would be disastrous. He raised his binoculars along the bearing of the incoming missiles, his eyes straining to see them among the wind-tossed sea. Nothing.

Why only three missiles? he thought again. His native distrust of all foreigners was aroused. The Americans must know that three subsonic missiles, even the new Tomahawks, would be simple targets for our antiair defenses. If they had supported them with a jammer aircraft, that would be different. Jammers, Borosky thought as doubt nibbled at the edge of his mind. Could those missiles contain jammers? Could the Americans have jammers small enough to put in a missile? He spun around and pressed the switch on the squawk box.

"ECM. This is the Captain. What do you show on the screens?"

"Bridge. ECM. The screens are blank, sir. We are not picking up any jamming transmissions."

Just then the speaker in the overhead crackled.

"Bridge. CIC. Three targets executing high-G turns and climbing steeply. Two to port. One to starboard."

Shit! thought Borosky as Wallstrom's trap sprung.

The three missiles, now widely separated, clawed their way skyward with incredible speed. At an altitude of 47,000 feet, they leveled off and began circling the five ships. From each missile, a single burst of coded tracking data was broadcast as each transmitter came on again.

At his console, Sheldon watched the digital timer as it counted to zero.

"Stand by," he said, hunching forward. "Five seconds to acquisition."

Deville and Kofsy were poised above the many controls on their consoles, eyes fastened on the three blank display screens glowing in front of each of them. Above them, the dish antenna received the coded tracking signals and moved slightly as it locked onto the exact bearing and altitude of the distant missiles.

"Aquisition!" shouted Sheldon, finally showing excitement as one of his three screens suddenly showed a thin, bright spike of green light. It rose high above the glittering, waving mass of tiny spikes that filled the bottom of the display and formed what is known as grass.

"I'm hot!" exclaimed Sheldon.

With his left hand he twisted a knob on the console and deftly brought a second shaft of light, appearing on the screen in response to a switch depressed by his right forefinger, directly over the quivering spike. As soon as the two were superimposed, he depressed another switch with his right thumb, entering both the frequency and the characteristics of the Soviet transmitter represented by the light spike.

From now on, each time that particular transmitter came on, a coded signal would be sent through the dish antenna to the circling missile. This would cause a jammer aboard the missile to broadcast an interference signal that destroyed the usefulness of the Soviet transmitter.

Although the system was capable of jamming a great many transmitters, Deville and his assistants had to be very fast in acquiring each new transmitter as it came on. Not only were there dozens of radar transmitters aboard the Soviet ships, but also the Russian antiaircraft missiles carried two or sometimes three of them. These operated in varying sequences on differing frequencies in an attempt to circumvent the American jammers. The spikes of light from such missiles appeared to hop about the screen, sometimes tall in height; sometimes almost lost in the grass.

It was a difficult and exacting task, requiring absolute concentration and extraordinary hand/eye coordination. It was a young man's job.

Kofsy's hands moved rapidly across his console as a short spike rose up out of the grass on a screen.

"Up your ass, grass!" he shouted happily, his earlier nervousness forgotten.

Deville waited with a detachment and calmness that was new to him. He liked the feeling.

At that moment, the squawk box on the *Riga*'s bridge came alive again.

"Bridge. ECM. We're getting jamming on both air search radars."

Borosky grasped the tactical picture instantly and spun around to his Starpom or Executive Officer. His shocked look was beginning to be replaced by one of a grim determination.

"CAP to engage high-climbing targets. They are jammers for the main attack and will orbit the area. We must destroy them."

Borosky turned back to the window and stabbed at the squawk box switch with a surprisingly long and delicate finger. He performed the necessary calculations in his mind.

"Flight Control. This is the Captain. Get the helios away. Then launch the fighters. You have ten minutes before the American missiles arrive."

Above the task force, the YAK-36 pilot cut in his afterburner and pulled the nose of his fighter into a steep climb.

From behind the plastic nose of the aircraft, twin radar antennas sent out wide-sweeping cones of energy to find and track the Tomahawks.

In the *Montana*, a screen in front of Deville came alive with twin spikes that were as clear as the air in which the Russian pilot's radars searched. In an instant, Deville was on them with a shout that was straight out of Southern California.

"Adios motherfucker!"

Moments later all nine screens went wild.

On the *Riga*'s bridge, Borosky had barely straightened up when the results of Deville's unseen efforts were announced.

"Bridge. CIC," came from the speaker. "CAP reports search and fire control radars jammed. Unable to acquire targets. Attempting visual acquisition."

"Very good," replied Borosky, pounding the fist of his right hand slowly into the palm of his left. His eyes blinked and flashed as the flare from the firing of twin SA–N–3 surface-to-air rockets on the bow lit up the bridge. Borosky followed the rockets with his eyes as they streaked skyward to port at three times the speed of sound. Instantly, they were out of sight leaving a long, curving trail of smoke behind. A moment later, a second pair arched upward to starboard.

Borosky raised his head and stared at the gray-grilled speaker in the overhead. Report, dammit! As if hearing his thought, the speaker came alive.

"Bridge. CIC. All rockets missed. Fire Control reports unable to maintain track due to jamming."

Borosky punched the squawk box switch viciously and shouted, "ECM! Captain. Report!"

"Bridge. ECM. They are too fast for us, Captain," came the youthful voice almost sobbing with frustration. "They are on us as soon as we switch frequencies. We cannot hold lock long enough for a kill!"

"Do the best you can," Borosky responded.

Borosky took a deep breath and exhaled slowly as he turned over the options once more in his mind. Four more SA–N–3 rockets streaked upward from their launchers. This time he did not bother to look up; he knew they would miss. Instead, he looked across the choppy water to the towering superstructure of the *Admiral Arbatov* now almost hidden in smoke as an entire salvo of SA–N–3 rockets lifted off her deck.

He noticed the rows of radar antennas sticking out of the cloud of rocket exhaust like shrubs out of a snowbank. Junk. All of it useless junk, he thought. Without being able to lock the tracking radars on the targets, hitting the incoming missiles with antiair rockets was more a matter of luck than skill. A few might go down but most would get through, leaving only the close-defense guns. The guns must not use radar. No, he thought, coming to a decision. In this case, the human is better than our machines.

Borosky turned to the Starpom. "All guns to optical sights and local control."

As if fate was rewarding him for a bold decision, the first KA-25 helicopter rose from the deck, followed immediately by two more. As they cleared, the crew began to jockey the fully manned Yak-36 fighters into the vacated takeoff spots.

"Request permission to turn into the wind and launch fighters," asked the Starpom.

"Granted," answered Borosky and carefully kept any feelings of relief from his voice.

Again, the deck tilted as the *Riga* turned. Borosky watched the three helicopters settle on a bearing that led to the *Montana*. For the first time since the engagement began, a smile broke across his face. Now I have you, he chuckled, thinking of the nuclear depth charge in the belly of each helicopter, as you have me.

The wakes of the five ships traced a set of beautiful curves as they turned. Above them, the three jammers continued to circle. The *Montana*'s second flight of six standard Tomahawks came over the horizon. Unlike the jammers, these missiles contained hundreds of pounds of high explosives. In the lead missile, moving at almost Mach 1 a few feet above the water, an infrared sensor in the nose cone scanned the space ahead seeking the largest source of heat. Instantly, it caused the terminal guidance system to lock onto the boiler rooms of the *Admiral Arbatov* which lay between it and the *Riga*. Pulses from the sensor caused the flight control system to turn the missile so that it was aimed directly at the bulkhead between the *Arbatov*'s No. 1 and No. 2 Boiler Rooms.

One hundred yards away a six-inch diameter cover in

the nose of another Tomahawk slid smoothly back to admit light to an optical sensor. Like a human eye awakening from sleep, the entering rays of light took an instant to resolve themselves. But as they did, the image comparator in the terminal guidance system sensed that it was viewing the super-structure of a large cruiser-type warship. From the memory of the on-board computer that was no larger than three slices of bread, came a short series of digital pulses. This machine-stored human thought said that forward ends of superstructures are more important than after ends. When the terminal guidance system received these pulses, it queried the intertial measurement unit to determine which direction was forward and caused flight control to turn the missile until the optical scanner was centered on the *Admiral Abatov*'s bridge.

Of the remaining Tomahawks, another one was equipped with an infrared sensor and the other three were fitted with optical sensors. The infrared-equipped missile locked on to Boiler Room No. 1 of the *Riga*. The image comparators in the optical-equipped missiles sensed they were viewing an aircraft carrier. From the on-board memory came the stored thought that flight decks are the most important target aboard aircraft carriers. In these missiles, the guidance systems aimed for the after end of the *Riga*'s superstructure and prepared the flight control system for a special high-G terminal maneuver.

As the Tomahawks bore in just above the waves, splashes from the 76-mm shells began to fall around them. In and out of the splashes moved the missiles, ever closer. Denied the use of radar, the *Riga*'s guns were almost useless. As the Tomahawks bore in, their images of the ships grew larger and larger until they filled their optical scanners. Now the spinning barrels of the Riga's 23-mm Gatling guns, spewing out six thousand rounds per minute, added their roar to the din. It sounded as if the ship herself was being torn apart like an old cloth. But the rushing missiles were hidden in a continuous splash of water that moved inexorably closer. Along the *Riga*'s decks, brave men held their breath and waited. Time was running out.

From the center of one splash, a red ball of light appeared as the warhead, aimed at the *Riga*'s boiler room, suddenly exploded from a hit. A cheer went up from the *Riga*'s gunners. At that same instant, the three optically guided Tomahawks made a two hundred-G pull up to turn again and plunge vertically down into the flight deck.

The first missile hit a girder which supported the flight deck itself. The force of the impact cause the instant vaporization of the entire guidance section. The warhead continued to penetrate into the hangar deck before detonating directly above a loaded and fueled YAK-36.

The second and third warheads encountered only deck material and so plunged deeper into the ship. One exploded in the aviation machine shop beneath the hanger deck. The other penetrated three decks below to detonate among the jet fuel tanks at the ship's water line.

The YAK-36's handling crew was engaged in moving the aircraft to the elevator when the warhead exploded a few yards above them. One instant they were sweating, breathing, thinking humans; the next they were nothing.

The explosion in the machine shop found no human victims, all the men being at their battle stations topside. So, the warhead turned its fury on the fabric of the ship itself. It detonated just two feet off the reinforced steel deck amidst the heaviest machinery. Unable to penetrate the deck, the force of the explosion turned sideways and rolled along the compartment. Huge pieces of equipment, some as hard as armor-piercing shells, were hurled with express train speed at the ship's plating and bulkheads. Their bodies changed instantly into free molecules, joining and mingling with those from the aircraft.

From his position on the bridge, Borosky could not see the gaping holes that that were torn in the port side of the *Riga* just above the waterline. But he could feel them. Up from the deck and through the fashionably thin soles of his shoes came the sickening impact of the hurtling pieces of steel as they tore the ship apart. One piece the size of a grand piano cut through the sea water piping that provided the main source of water for fire fighting in the after portion of the ship. Another piece, deflected when passing through the after bulkhead, tore a hole in the deck forty feet long and six feet wide. Thus, the fourth deck was opened up.

The third warhead detonated just above the fourth deck alongside the starboard jet fuel tanks. The first obstacle the explosion met was the steel bulkhead forming the inner wall of the tank. As this steel bent and then shattered under the tremendous force of the expanding fireball, the pressure was

transmitted through thousands of gallons of kerosene jet fuel.
Below the water, the ship's plating that formed the outer wall
of the tank gave way, rupturing outward as the explosive
force lost itself in the sea.

For two thousandths of a second, the outer wall of hot
gases from the explosion kept the Norwegian Sea out of the
jagged hole in the *Riga*'s starboard side. Then, the cold water
lowered the gases' pressure. In the next instant, water flooded
into the ruptured tank and forced the fuel out through the
hole and onto the deck, above which the fireball still roiled.
As the raw fuel gushed from the tank, it immediately caught
fire. Within seconds, the in-rushing sea bore the flames to the
furthest corner of the compartment.

The *Riga* listed to starboard and began to settle slowly
by the stern. On the bridge, Borosky turned to the Starpom,
his face a mask.

"All engines stop. Counterflood. Little boys come assist
me."

As the *Riga* lost headway, the counterflooding gradually
brought her back onto an even keel. Now however, with the
stern lower than ever, the burning fuel found its way up
through the torn third deck so that the flames roared into the
hangar. Borosky was thrown violently to his knees as heavy,
secondary explosions rocked the ship. As he regained his feet
and looked aft, he saw the entire stern of the ship covered with
smoke and flames. A huge plume of black smoke rose obscene-
ly thousands of feet into the crystal-clear air. From both quarters, he could see the destroyers curving in to help fight fires
and take off the wounded. With a final effort, he looked across
the water at the battered hulk of the *Admiral Arbatov*.

The *Arbatov* was already lying almost on her side from
the huge hole at her waterline. With both her boiler rooms open
to the sea, she could not long stay afloat. Where her bridge and
forward superstructure had been was now a mass of twisted,
blackened, wreckage. In one corner, the captain and his entire
bridge watch lay mashed together in an unrecognizable
bundle of flesh and bones. When the warhead had detonated
in the conning tower below, they had been unmercifully
destroyed by a freak upward curl of the bridge deck. Blood,
bearing bits of flesh and cloth, ran down the steel plating to
drip into the flaming wreckage below.

Alongside the sinking ship, the *Rossiya*'s captain bravely
risked everything to rescue what was left of the *Arbatov*'s

crew. He lay his stern beneath the projecting superstructure of the heavily listing hulk. Hundreds of men crawled out on the nearly vertical decks and dropped to safety. Those that hesitated died in the cold arctic water.

Circling above the ships, the three jammer Tomahawks continued their vigilance. Like eagles with magical powers, they were still unseen in spite of the frantic searchings of the lone YAK-39 pilot. Now, he wept with frustration as he broke off to make for land.

Aboard the *Montana*, Wallstrom turned from the Weapons Summary Status board and called out to Mawson who was in the Command Center.

"All tubes reloaded!"

"ECM clear. No transmissions being received," reported Deville, his voice edged with excitement.

At the same time, McKenna sang out from the Tactical Display Table:

"Target ships dead in the water! TACDAPS reports three helicopters launched."

Mawson swung around toward McKenna, "Source?"

The CIC officer punched his buttons.

"Voice intercept between pilots and *Riga* flight control."

Our turn now, thought Mawson calmly. He began to go over the plan in his mind one last time.

It depended upon one simple fact: in order to destroy the *Montana*, even with atomic depth charges, the KA-25 pilots first had to find her. And, the need to find her made their actions predictable. Thus, Mawson knew the Russian pilots would fan out from the *Riga* toward the *Montana* on slightly diverging courses like the spokes of a wheel, steadily increasing the area covered. When the pilots reached the distance at which the submarine was believed to be, they would hover their helicopters, lower a sonar probe, and listen for the *Montana*. It was while they hovered that the KA-25's were vulnerable to attack by the *Montana*'s self-initiating antiaircraft missiles or SIAMs. These had acoustic sensors that were designed to lock onto the distinctive sound of whirling rotors, which can be heard underwater. The *Montana* would launch a spread of SIAMs that would fan out to meet their adversaries.

In execution, the plan was not at all simple. The range of the missile's acoustic sensors was limited so that success depended upon correct estimation of the helicopter's positions. These were analyzed through such diverse and complex factors as relative speeds and courses, flight times, and sea and air temperatures. The computation was made by machines, but the subjective inputs were made by the men of the *Montana* who acted as a team.

One thing, thought Mawson, we got a break on the small number of choppers. Seven of them with six missiles would have been a real problem. He now gave his orders.

"Set up for a three-helio target speed."

At the order, McKenna and his crew set to work determining the most probable position of the KA-25 helicopters. The result of their work would be fed automatically to Rossman and his men at the fire control consoles. They would, in turn, use the data to program the flight of the six SIAMs that lay ready for launching in their torpedo tubes. Wallstrom moved back and forth between the two teams, directing the overall effort.

"Assume a fifteen-degree spread," McKenna ordered without the least fear of selecting the wrong figures.

Seventeen minutes later the battle was over. The three KA-25s were destroyed by SIAMs that rose without warning from out of the sea and blew the hovering aircraft into thousands of pieces.

Two of the helicopters immediately became fire balls. From their centers, bits of radioactive material joined the other debris and sank slowly toward the dark sea bottom like leaves falling from a tree. Out of the remains of the third helicopter, a depth charge tumbled into the sea intact.

Seconds later, the sea surface rolled under the impact of a nuclear detonation. From the depths came an incredibly bright flash of light as the process of the sun itself was duplicated within the ocean. Then, a huge column of water rose hundreds of feet into the air as a small part of the tremendous energy of the explosion found release. Most of this energy moved outward in the form of an ever-expanding wave of pressure.

Not many miles away, the *Montana* rolled sharply onto her side as the awful shock wave passed. Through her thick steel hull, she felt the energy and force of the wave. Light bulbs and glass-covered instruments exploded from the shock. In the galley, pots and pans rang in discordant tympany, as if being struck by a mad drummer.

The *Montana* was designed to survive exactly such a shock wave. All her vital machinery and electronics were isolated from the hull by thick rubber mountings. Only her single propeller shaft which had to be free to turn could not be protected.

For years, Chief Engineman Ralph Ward had been preparing for this moment. He had been aboard the old *Tullibee* when she was partially flooded while submerged by a broken propeller shaft. It was he who had squeezed his thin body into the shaft alley in order to stop the flooding. He had done it with a large wrench. His report to the subsequent investigating board had led directly to the development of the pneumatic seals used on the *Montana*. It had been the high point of his career, and so he had talked about it until the story was a joke to most of his mates. But joke or no, Ward knew his shafts.

When the shock wave hit the engine room, Ward was standing above the shaft alley. Clinging desperately to a handhold that was welded to the bulkhead, Ward watched anxiously as the two spinning turbines swayed in their heavy beds.

No sweat there, he thought as the glass globe of a waterproof light fixture in the overhead shattered.

But just at that moment, the long propeller shaft running aft outside the pressure hull, whipped as the wave of energy traveled its length. The outer-bearing seals ruptured. Highly pressurized sea water burst around the still rapidly turning shaft and flooded the alley, spraying violently up from the floor plates under Ward's feet.

Ward reached up and spun open a valve that admitted air into the emergency seals around the shaft. With his other hand, he held down the squawk box switch and yelled.

"Maneuvering room! Shaft alley. Outer seals ruptured. Emergency seals inflated."

The engineering officer's voice came back to him.

"All ahead slow. Start ER drain pumps." And then, because the man could not resist, "Ward? Now I suppose we'll have to listen to how you saved us all on the *Montana*?"

"Noooo suh," Ward answered. "No suh. Only one man save dis boat and dat de Cap'n."

In the control room, Mawson regained his footing as the *Montana* righted herself. Edelstone turned with a sound-powered phone still in his hand and triumph in his voice.

"Engine room reports emergency shaft seals inflated. Ready to make revolutions for thirteen knots. All other stations report only minor damage. You've done it, sir!"

Mawson only nodded in a preoccupied way.

"Resume course for Delta Three."

In the Communications Center, the code computer's high-speed printer started up. Moments later, Mawson stood reading the cryptic message from Sauer.

Congratulations. Surface Delta Three. Surrender command Hawaii. Marines landing Assab 0330 ZULU.

"It's over, Harry." Mawson handed his XO the message. "We did it. They're going in to get our families out." Mawson fought for self-control as he stepped down from the island. "You tell the ship, Harry. I just can't do it."

As Mawson headed to his cabin, Edelstone turned to Wallstrom, "Look after him, Ross. I'm worried about him."

Wallstrom found Mawson sprawled facedown on his blankets fully clothed, his left foot dragging on the deck. With a tenderness that was new to him, Wallstrom bent down and gently lifted Mawson's leg onto the bunk.

"Sleep well. God knows, you've paid for it."

At the door, Wallstrom paused and switched off the lights. On impulse he turned back and stared for a moment at the dim form of the sleeping figure.

"I love you, Mawson," he said simply before turning and leaving the man to the reassuring vibrations of the turbines.

Chapter 20

Ambassador Calvin Benson slid off the tabletop that was littered with the remains of food and half-empty coffee cups. His white linen suit coat hung limply over the back of a chair. He gazed with reddened eyes out of the control tower window.

Only a few minutes ago, he had watched the execution of the dawn victim. An elderly man. He had been unable to discern the age or sex of the midnight victim. Now, as the details of the DC-10 were revealed in the early dawn light, he raised the binoculars from where they hung against his rumpled shirt and scanned the pile of bodies, distorted and askew in the early light.

He squinted in concentration as he focused on what seemed to be a pair of sticks protruding from the pile. Then he had to swallow quickly to suppress the sour taste that rose in his throat as he realized he was staring at a thin pair of small, bare legs sticking out from beneath the uppermost body."

"They're killing children!" he exclaimed aloud. Rage choked him as images of his own grandchildren flashed across his mind.

He picked up his microphone from the table top and screeched into it. "Can we not at least have the child's body?"

Qabrestan left the cockpit and stepped to the open doorway. A lighted cigarette dangling from his lips, he looked down at the bodies unemotionally.

The hot sun and humid night had done their work. Towards the bottom of the pile, the body of Sam Samson was badly bloated. The skin of the torso, unable to contain the noxious gases that formed in the stomach cavity, had split open from crotch to breastbone.

The cloying, sickening death smell assailed Qabrestan's nostrils. He seemed to be taking inventory, then he turned away and reentered the cockpit.

A few moments later his voice came over the tower's loudspeaker, "Take them all away if you want. But send only two men at a time and no tricks!"

Benson turned to the Soviet officer in charge who stood talking on the telephone. He was staring at Benson with a peculiar look on his face.

"Would you please make arrangements for removal of the bodies from the vicinity of the aircraft?"

"*Nyet!*" barked the officer, his young face grim and unyielding.

"No? In heaven's name, why not?"

At that moment, a burly sergeant of the Soviet Naval Infantry, followed closely by two heavily armed men, came pounding up the stairs. They leveled their assault rifles at the three Americans.

"You two. Move away from the radio," ordered the sergeant in Russian, gesturing with his weapon.

The two startled radio operators understood the gesture if not the words and joined Benson at the table.

"What's happened now?" demanded Benson in Russian, looking from the young officer to the sergeant. "Why the weapons? We're not armed."

"As if you did not know! American troops are landing at Maacaca just up the coast."

"Put me through to Admiral Kirsanov immediately," Benson demanded.

"The admiral is busy and cannot be disturbed," answered the young officer. He turned and hung up his phone without meeting Benson's eyes.

"You take too much upon yourself, Lieutenant. Since when does one of your rank speak for an admiral?" Benson's finger jabbed the air in front of the officer. "*You* put the call through or *you* will be responsible for the murder of more children!"

The dart struck home. The young lieutenant picked up his phone and dialed Kirsanov's headquarters. Benson waited with studied impatience, until a moment later he took the instrument from the officer's outstretched hand.

"Admiral Kirsanov, I assure you I had no prior knowledge of a plan to land American forces at Assab. I say this because I feel it is important that you understand that I have neither deceived you nor withheld any information from you. . . ."

Benson spoke in Russian calmly and soothingly. He put forth his most persuasive arguments for continued Soviet support in dealing with the terrorist situation regardless of what might be happening elsewhere. At first Kirsanov was reluctant, but Benson's well-reasoned pleas for the safety of the children finally won the admiral over with the single provision that the American radio not be used. To this restriction, Benson readily agreed.

And so it happened that, while the United States Marines swarmed ashore from both amphibious craft and helicopters and the entire 101st Airborne Division parachuted onto the beachhead, a masked and gowned team of Russians approached the aircraft. Oblivious to the frantic activity around them as the naval base prepared to defend itself, they labored to remove the bodies of the murdered hostages.

Shortly before noon, the C-141 aircraft carrying the Blue Light team from the Egyptian staging area landed on a temporary runway that the triumphant Marines had bulldozed. Clouds of dust from this maneuver blew across the littered beach to the waiting *Veracruz,* anchored off shore.

In the lead aircraft, Captain Manuel Torres stood with his back braced against the cold aluminum of an armored personnel carrier. The machine and the man, secured in the center of the long and windowless cargo compartment, waited for the plane to stop. Behind him the men of Charlie Company stood swaying as the plane taxied over the uneven surface of the runway.

After a series of bumps and turns, the plane came to rest with a final squeal of brakes. As the sound of the jet engines slowly faded away, the remotely operated latches on the pressure door in front of Torres opened suddenly with an unexpectedly loud CLACK. A high-pitched whine filled the air as hydraulic motors began raising the pressure door that had sealed the after end of the compartment during the flight.

An ever-widening bend of brilliant light appeared at Torres' feet as the door came open, flooding the gloomy compartment with sunlight. Torres, momentarily blinded, slipped the pair of sunglasses he held in his hand over his eyes. Heat, like that from an open furnace, hit him in the face when the pressure door opened fully. Although his eyes had not fully adjusted to the light, Torres stepped carefully down the short ramp to a small group of men waiting on the ground. A young second lieutenant from the 101st Airborne Division Headquarter's S-3 Section stepped forward.

"Charlie Company?"

"Right," answered Torres. He stepped off the ramp and looked around at the desolate expanse of empty desert.

"Captain, our division Command Post is set up behind that hill there," stated the lieutenant and pointed to a spot in the low ridge one-half mile away.

"By that microwave tower?" Torres asked as Lieutenant Al Lewis and First Sergeant Mulaney came down the ramp to join him.

"Yes, sir. That's the place. We've got tents ready for your men and hot chow. Control says to disembark as quick as you can. We want to get these birds outta here in case of counterattack."

"Doesn't look like you met much resistance," noted Torres.

The lieutenant pushed the edge of his helmet up and smiled. "Hell, Cap'n, I've had more excitement at Fort Benning!"

"No bombardment? No fire fights?"

"No bombardment. A Marine squad took some automatic weapons fire from some Cuban skirmishers but the Cubans pulled back before the gyrenes could engage 'em. You guys'll have a nice, peaceful rest until it's time to hit the DC-ten."

"Are the Russians going to let us on the base?"

"I don't know, Cap'n. You'll have to ask at headquarters. I heard they're working on it, but that's all."

"Yeah? Well, they better work it out before dark. We're gonna take that plane before midnight if we have to infiltrate the fucking base alone." Torres' hand moved unconsciously to the receiver of the SAW hanging muzzle down from his right shoulder. "Two more hostages are all those bastards are gonna get." Torres turned to Lewis and Mulaney.

"OK. Send 'em after me in open column as they come off." With that, Torres spun around and set off on foot in the direction of the Division Command Post, his pack and SAW swinging easily with his loose stride.

At a shout from Mulaney, Torres' runner and radio operator dashed from the belly of the plane and sweated to catch up in the hot sun. Their feet raised small puffs of dust on the loose, parched soil.

Lewis' voice range out in the superheated air, "Charlie Company will dismount by files! Left file HAAAAH!"

Sound is a peculiar phenomenon. In the steep-faced, hard, rocky canyons of mountainous country, sound can travel for great distances so that in some places a whisper can be heard with perfect clarity miles from its point of origin. In desert terrain filled with soft-sided hills and the dry dust of centuries, sound is sucked up as greedily as water. Thus, Agnes Wagner and everyone else aboard the plane was unaware that help lay just beyond the barren hills. It was just as well, for as she stared out of the plane's window, she knew she was about to die. She had known it for six hours now. Ever since they came and took Russell away and shot him as he stood with quiet dignity in the dawn light. Now, it was almost noon. They would come any minute and then her wait would be over.

Agnes turned from the window. Her oddly youthful eyes, set in old wrinkles, were clear and untroubled. She thought of Russell and their wedding night, of how they came to open their own store, of their children and grandchildren. For no reason at all, the image of Russell sitting proudly in his shiny new Buick Century formed in her mind like an old photograph. The musty smell of the summer cottage on Galway Lake and the echo of a screen door banging in the warm, afternoon came to her as if she were there once again. All the memories of a long and happy life welled up now from the storehouse of her mind to sustain and comfort her, to make her unafraid of death and its companion pain. She smiled and fingered the old hat in her lap. The two terrorists were moving up the aisle toward her. It was time.

A few feet from where Agnes Wagner sat, Ralph Albertson was engaged in a desperate conversation with Pete Worthington and Charlie Wall.

"Come on," he urged in a hoarse whisper. Albertson was leaning over the back of Wall's seat. Worthington looked up with interest. "They're coming up the right aisle. They'll stop here. It's perfect. We'll be on them before they know."

Pete Worthington leaned toward Albertson, his mouth a grim and hard line that pulled at the Bandaid on his cheek. "How many are there?"

"Only three. Come on! You take the one in the galley. We'll take the two in the aisle."

Worthington stood and turned to Wall, "Come on, Charlie. Let's end this thing."

Walls nodded grimly. But just as Albertson started out into the aisle, he felt his left wrist grabbed and held tightly. Surprised, he looked down into the face of Sally Bronick.

"No," she croaked in a vicious whisper. "The others will kill our kids. You can't do it."

Albertson twisted his wrist free of Sally's grip. "We've got to. They're killing the kids anyway."

"No! Please don't!" she cried, her voice trembling and

tears starting from her eyes. Now Sally clutched at Albertson's shirt.

Just then, Hamed's voice rang out in a high-pitched scream as he stepped into view from around the far side of the galley partition.

"Stop, or I'll throw it!" he shouted. Hamed brought his left arm back behind his head, a grenade clearly in his hand.

The three men froze in their tracks.

"Sit down! Sit down!" screamed Hamed, his voice trembling with excitement. "You do anything and they die!" He nodded towards the passengers who were cowering in their seats around him. Yonnie and Qabrestan appeared beside Agnes, their weapons ready.

"OK. OK," answered Worthington, raising his hands in the air. "We're sitting down." Then to Albertson, "Forget it."

Albertson backed slowly into a seat. A few moments later, they heard the muffled sound of a single shot from the forward cabin.

President Gurinov leaned forward in his chair, his thick, stubby finger, stabbing impatiently at the pile of reconnaissance photos. The *Admiral Arbatov* lay on her side, sinking; the *Riga,* at that very moment limping slowly toward Murmansk, was photographed half-covered by the heavy black smoke from her many fires.

Across the table were his closest advisors, men with whom Gurinov shared the uppermost power of the Politburo. Pavel Kondratiev, the Minister of Internal Affairs broke the silence. "Three hundred and thirty dead, two ships sunk, and now this massive landing at Assab. That is provocation enough. We should strike now while they are defenseless. Be rid of them once and for all."

Gurinov's eyes narrowed, "Always with you, Pavel, your answer is the same. 'Destroy the Americans.'"

"But it is true, Sergy," Kondratiev's tone of voice as well as the use of Gurinov's first name asserted his right as head of the secret police to argue with his superior.

His patience at an end, Gurinov shoved the photos toward Kondratiev. "But at what cost? Look what a handful of American missiles did. Are they truly defenseless or will the next photos show our cities burning also?"

The normally expressionless face of Viktor Mishuk, Minister of Defense and a Marshall of the Soviet Union, clouded. "That is exactly the point. They are *not* defenseless. And now a third British Polaris submarine has just put to sea. We would lose tens of millions of our people, would take years to repair our cities."

"But we must meet force with force!" persisted Kondratiev as he shoved the photos back to Gurinov. "Can we not at least go after the American submarine that attacked us?"

"We could. Our units in Murmansk are waiting for orders to do just that," said Mishuk.

"Then what are you waiting for?"

"For *my* decision," interjected Gurinov, staring directly at Kondratiev who shrugged his shoulders and sat back in his chair.

Ever patient, Mishuk continued, "The question again is one of cost. Norwegian naval units have sortied and right now are reinforcing the American surface force off Tromsø. I have just learned that elements of the British Home Fleet have put to sea. It seems the Americans and their allies are willing to allow this affair to escalate into a major sea battle. But are we?"

Gurinov's fist came down hard on the tabletop. "No, we are not!" His cold eyes swept the five men in front of him. "Whatever the outcome, we gain nothing from such a battle. If we fight, we will fight in Assab."

Igor Shilov, the Foreign Minister and next to Gurinov the most powerful man present, broke his silence.

"That too has little to recommend it. At this moment, the Americans are content to merely sit within their beachhead. Their ambassador assures me that they are determined to free the hostages immediately. I believe him. After Iran, what else could their response be? If we fight, our men will die, as will the hostages. And what do we gain from all this? Nothing. Absolutely nothing. Assab is the wrong place to fight. We have Afghanistan. Why stir up new trouble? I say allow the Americans access to the base so they can free their own people."

"What is the status of the reinforcements for Assab?" asked Gurinov.

"All is ready," answered Mishuk. "Ground and Air Force units are standing by. The first can arrive at Assab within three hours of receipt of the deployment go ahead."

Gurinov nodded his head, an idea forming in his mind. "Are you sure the Americans know about our preparations?"

"Oh yes, Mr. President. We made certain their sensors detected both our troop and aircraft movements. They know what we are doing."

The telephone rang on the desk behind Gurinov. He spun around and answered it. It was the President of the United States.

"We regret most deeply the loss of your men and ships in the Norwegian Sea. A most unfortunate incident."

"Your condolences would carry more conviction had you not deployed additional naval forces into the area. Your submarine attacked our vessels without any provocations and at an extremely long range."

"True," acknowledged the President of the United States. "The *Montana* launched upon my orders because your statements convinced me that the *Riga* was sent to sink her. It is over and I assure you that we seek no further engagements or escalation of the situation."

"Your deeds do not bear out your words! You have landed the entire Hundred and First Airborne Division on our doorstep at Assab. Two can play at escalation, you know."

"Now, Mr. President. I know you have massive reinforcements ready to send to Assab. We appreciate the restraint your local commander and troops have shown thus far at Assab. But we must have the hostages freed immediately. Another Iranian situation is intolerable to us. Other than this single objective, we desire no confrontation at Assab. We have, as I am sure you have also concluded. decided that it is the wrong place and time."

"So, you think because we see areas of mutual interests, I am to swallow our losses and suffer your threats? Without so much as an apology?"

"We are prepared to formally apologize for the action of the *Montana*."

"You mean you will accept the responsibility for the attack *and* our losses?"

"Yes. We are prepared to do that in exchange for giving our assault team access to the hijacked aircraft."

"You will pay for our losses?"

"Yes, certainly."

"Will you lift the trade embargo and grant us most favored nation status?"

"We will vigorously pursue those goals in Congress."

"Will you keep the details of the sea battle and our losses out of your newspapers?"

"That I cannot promise. You must know I cannot control the press. But I can promise not to release any official details of the battle."

"What about the men of the *Montana*? Will they talk?"

"Probably. I have no power to prevent them."

"In the interest of international security and in the true spirit of detente I will issue the orders. Instruct your ambassador here to issue the apology and your acceptance of full responsibility."

"It will be done."

"Then it is over."

"Yes."

"Thank you, Mr. President."

"Thank you, Mr. President.'

Gurinov reached for the phone. "I want to speak with Admiral Kirsanov," he ordered.

The first sign Ambassador Benson had that the situation was changing was when he found the security guards gone.

"Why have the guards left us?" he inquired in Russian.

The young officer lowered the binoculars through which he had been observing the plane and turned at the sound of Benson's voice.

"Orders."

"Well, then, if there is no objection, I'll reestablish contact with my embassy," continued Benson.

The air controller looked at the two Americans sitting idly beside their radio and shrugged.

Interesting, thought Benson as he faced the two men who, although they spoke no Russian, were rising to their feet.

"Put me on to Washington as quickly as you can," he ordered, keeping his voice conversational and free of the urgency that he felt.

As the two men bent to their task, Benson turned at the sound of footsteps on the stairs behind him. A moment later Admiral Kirsanov climbed slowly into the control tower.

"Ah, Mr. Ambassador," said Kirsanov, smiling but winded from the long climb. "You must forgive me for not joining you sooner, but the landings by your countrymen detained me."

Benson returned Kirsanov's smile with well-practiced ease. First the guards are removed, then we're permitted to use the radio. Now, the smiling Admiral himself leaves his command center to join us. We've won this round.

"I trust our two forces did not clash," replied Benson as he tried to feel his way into the discussion.

"No. No," Kirsanov tried to find the right English expression. "It was once or twice close but at the end, there was no fighting. We have no casualties or damage. I would think that your troops have none either."

"Good. Then perhaps we can now work together to free the hostages before more are murdered." Benson gestured to the window.

Kirsanov stepped forward and gazed down at the single body resting on the stained runway beneath the open door of the plane. "I have already given orders to admit your special assault force to the base," said Kirsanov, turning from the window. "Do you know when they will be ready and how many there will be?"

"I'll have to confirm the arrangements," replied Benson, gesturing toward the radio. "But I believe it will be an infantry company. They will come at sundown and make the assault as soon as it is dark enough to hide their movements."

Kirsanov nodded as he again turned to stare at the body. "Then one more will die," he said sadly.

Benson joined him at the window. "I'm afraid so."

Chapter 21

Captain Manuel Torres watched with keen interest as the main entrance of the Soviet naval base came into sight. He stood in the open commander's hatch of the lead M113 armored personnel carrier. Behind him stretched a column of carriers that held the rest of Charlie Company. The Soviet jeep in front of him, which had provided escort through various road blocks, slowed as it neared the gate. In the fading,

red light of the setting sun, Torres could see a small knot of
men waiting at the entrance.

The jeep stopped just inside the gate. Torres held up his
right hand in the timeless cavalry signal to halt. At the same
time, he used his left foot to tap his driver on the shoulder.
The M113, its tracks squealing, turned onto the side of the
road and came to a stop in front of the waiting group.

Torres spoke into the microphone of the headset he wore
beneath his helmet. The vehicle's radio carried his voice to
the other officers of Charlie Company, who stood in the commander's hatches of the M113's behind him.

"OK. I'm going to palaver with these guys just ahead.
Open the personnel compartment doors, but keep everyone
aboard till I find out the score."

Without waiting for confirmation, Torres lifted his helmet and removed the headset. Replacing the helmet, he
heaved himself out of the hatch.

A slight man in a white suit stepped forward as Torres
scrambled over the top of the M113 and leaped lightly to the
ground.

"Good evening, Captain," said the waiting man. "I'm
Calvin Benson, the American Ambassador to Djibouti."

Torres shook the outstretched hand. "Captain Manuel
Torres, Mr. Ambassador. First Battalion, Ninth Special
Forces Group. I'm ordered to report to you, sir."

"Yes. Well, the situation here was quite sticky as you
can imagine, but it's cleared up now." Benson took Torres by
the arm and led him toward the waiting group.

"Admiral Kirsanov, may I present Captain Manuel
Torres of the United States Army."

Kirsanov and Torres shook hands, each looking at the
other with interest. Kirsanov had never seen an American in-
fantryman. Torres, in turn, was having his first view of a
Russian military officer.

"Captain, please explain to the admiral how you will deploy your men for the attack on the plane and any support
you may need from the Soviets. I'll translate for you." Benson turned toward the admiral, then turned back as he
remembered something. "Oh, yes. The admiral has had a situation map specially prepared for you and will present it to
you for your use. He also has some rather good photographs
of the terrorists. You understand, this is a rather extraordi-

nary gesture of cooperation," Benson concluded, watching Torres' expression closely.

Torres smiled and nodded slightly to Kirsanov. "Please thank the admiral and tell him the photographs will be real helpful and the map is appreciated, but *you* should know we have our own maps prepared from a U-2 overflight a few hours ago."

"Captain," interjected an embarrassed Benson, "I should have mentioned that the Admiral speaks excellent English."

Several hours later, Torres stirred himself from the side of the M113 against which he was resting and glanced down at the luminous numerals of his watch. Because of the black greasepaint covering his hands and wrists, it appeared to float disembodied in the air. 9:45. Time, he thought as he rose unhurriedly to his feet.

Beside him, the First Lieutenant Al Lewis stood also, his eyes and teeth appearing unnaturally white against the black greasepaint covering his face. Both men were dressed in coveralls made of a lampblack material. The same material also covered the surfaces of their helmets.

"Form 'em up, Al," ordered Torres, holding his SAW submachine gun lightly in his left hand.

Lewis went down the line of M113s and quietly roused the men. As they rose silently, their black clothing and skin made them appear as mere shadows in the darkness. Out of the night, First Sergeant Mulaney appeared at Torres' side.

"Ready for equipment inspection, sir."

"Yeah. We'll begin with the First Platoon," replied Torres as he started off down the line of waiting men.

From the gate, the Soviet officer who would accompany them part way stood watching with interest.

When Torres was satisfied, he raised his SAW over his chest with his right forefinger on the receiver.

"Load and lock. Safety all weapons," he ordered in a low but far-reaching voice. Along with his men, he pulled back his receiver and then released it. The clacking sound of a hundred bullets being stripped from the top of their magazines and rammed home into a hundred breaches rippled through the night.

With a glance down the file of men, Torres turned and faced the gate. He raised his right arm over his head and then suddenly dropped it.

"Move out!"

The captain led the long column of his men through the gate. The Soviet officer, a captain also, fell into step beside him. Torres, his eyes upon the distant lights of the plane, led the column in a circuitous route across the perimeter road and over the arid soil surrounding the runway. When they were one hundred yards from and directly behind the tail of the plane, Torres turned to Lewis just behind him and whispered.

"Column halt."

Torres stepped aside and stopped. The Soviet officer also stopped as the word was passed quietly down the line. From habit, Torres listened carefully. Not a single sound came from the long line of men. He smiled in the darkness of the moonless night, remembering how hard they had all worked to first find and then eliminate the thousands of clicks and squeaks emitted by equipment and even clothes when in movement.

Torres turned his attention to the plane. The vertical stabilizer with the bulging aft engine was silhouetted against the lights of the hangars. The sound of the plane's auxiliary power generator came pulsing through the night. All was well.

Torres led off at a jog. At the head of the column, he kept his eyes on the plane's tail as he ran over the uneven ground. Hold the pace down, he thought. Don't spread them out. The tail loomed larger against the night sky. Almost there.

Out of the darkness came the stubby shape of one of the lights marking the edge of the runway. Torres stepped aside without breaking stride barely in time to avoid tripping over the unlit light. Jesus, he thought, as he felt the tarmac under his feet.

The tail of the plane filled the sky now. He was there. Torres stopped. Above his head the aftermost portion of the fuselage blocked out the sky. The sound of the generator was loud now. On either side, the plane's horizontal stabilizers spread out, casting the runway around him into even greater darkness.

Torres stood motionless and listened. A pool of light from the open loading door illuminated the concrete ahead and to the left of the fuselage. He moved carefully forward under the left wing. Something in the air caught his attention. He stopped and sniffed the night. Cigarette smoke. Someone's standing in the open doorway smoking.

He placed one foot carefully beside the other and edged out. He stayed within the darkness and well away from the pool of light that was now before him. There. The bottom of the doorway and two pairs of legs came into view. Torres slowly sank to a half squat as he brought the entire scene into view.

Qabrestan and Yonnie stood talking, framed in the lighted doorway. Torres' heart beat faster. He recognized them instantly from Kirsanov's photos.

Seconds later, he was under the tail. In turn, he took Lewis and Mulaney by the arms and pointed out the patch of light. With gestures, he warned them to keep away from that side of the aircraft. When both men indicated that they understood, Torres motioned them forward.

Without waiting an instant, Lewis and Mulaney turned and moved quickly beneath the right side of the fuselage. Close behind them, Lieutenant Bo Johnstone led the 3rd Platoon. Next, came Lieutenant Paul Gorman leading the 2nd Platoon. All disappeared toward the wing and front of the plane. Finally, the thin figure of Lieutenant Joe Tanzola came out of the darkness followed by the men of the 1st Platoon. Sergeant Too Quick Jones brought up the rear, standing beside Tanzola who was peering anxiously, head thrown back, up at the right side of the plane. Tanzola shuffled his feet, moving sideways first one way then the other, as he sought to position himself directly beneath a certain point on the fuselage. He needed to be just under the lip of the aft engine's air intake. On the runway beside him, six men assembled a black, foam-covered scaling ladder that was especially designed to fit the DC-10-30 model aircraft.

Satisfied, Tanzola raised both arms above his head like a referee signaling a goal. His SAW hung heavily from the strap over his shoulder. The ladder was raised quietly. The instant it was in position, Torres stepped up and adjusted his pack and SAW. He then tested the ladder with one foot. It gave slightly under his weight and then stabilized. Good enough. Now if the damn thing just won't squeek. Torres looked up once, then began climbing. Over his boots he wore elastic coverings of half-inch foam. He had taken them out of his belt and slipped them on while waiting for the ladder to be assembled.

Behind Torres, Too Quick Jones climbed with the speed and grace of a panther. Tanzola, meanwhile, steadied the ladder's base as the remainder of the platoon prepared to mount. All wore the sound-deadening slippers.

Up in the darkened control tower, Benson lowered the binoculars with which he had been studying the two terrorists in the plane's open doorway. Earlier he thought he had detected movement around the plane's tail, but he could not be sure. He took a final look at his watch. It was time. According to Torres' plan, they should be scaling the plane now.

Holding the binoculars in his left hand, he picked up his microphone from the table with his right. At the same time, he raised the binoculars to his eyes. He knew exactly what he was going to say. The truth was, he had thought of little else since Torres had asked for his help.

"Are you there?" he asked, peering through the glasses.

He saw Qabrestan's head snap around. The terrorist turned unhurriedly from the opening, flipping his cigarette away. Benson watched its red glow arc into the night.

"What do you want now? Have you heard from Washington?" Qabrestan's voice came from the tower loudspeaker.

Benson smiled. It was easy, really. There was only one subject that was guaranteed to hold the terrorist's attention.

"Yes," replied Benson smoothly. "I have received my instructions and am now ready to discuss all of your terms."

As he spoke, Benson continued to watch Yonnie through his glasses. She moved toward the cockpit door. Good. Good, thought Benson excitedly. She wants to be able to hear me better so she's moved closer. Perfect.

"I am waiting." Qabrestan prodded wearily.

"Sorry," said Benson. "I had to get my notes out. Now then. . . ." he continued to speak as though the United States had accepted the first of the terrorists' conditions, subject to only minor changes.

Qabrestan turned and gave Yonnie a grin of triumph. "Victory! Yonnie, it is victory! Do you hear what he is saying?"

Yonnie nodded, wanting to believe but not daring. She grew quiet. Maybe it *was* victory she wanted. Her mouth felt dry. She moved into the forward galley to get a drink of water.

At the top of the ladder, Torres paused. With his left hand, he felt for a small inspection door in the side of the air inlet. Finding it, his finger pushed in on the release, allowing the door to spring outward. Using both hands, he quickly attached it to one end of a thin, braided Dacron line from a reel clipped to his harness. He gave the line a light tug. Satisfied it would hold, he climbed onto the upper surface of the fuselage, being careful not to allow a knee to bump against the plane's skin.

Torres steadied himself on the smooth aluminium and faced forward. Before him, the fuselage gleamed dully in the lights from the distant airfield buildings. From here, he could see the control tower clearly. Slowly making his way forward with a peculiar shuffling walk, he wondered if Benson could see him from the tower, and whether he was keeping the terrorists talking. From the reel on his belt, the Dacron line silently spun out.

Too Quick Jones followed slowly three steps behind Torres. The line ran loosely through his right hand. As he shuffled along, he counted the small plastic balls that were pressed onto the line at regular intervals.

Behind Too Quick, the men of the 1st Platoon climbed the ladder in teams of two. Then he moved forward, counting the balls that marked each team's position. Tanzola was the last to mount the ladder. As he began to climb, he saw Gorman lead the 2nd Platoon back beneath the tail.

Tanzola strained to hear any unusual sounds; because from his position, he was best able to detect unexpected movements by the terrorists. But only a slight rumble from the auxiliary generator below and behind him came to his anxious ears. He had just placed his foot on the fourth rung of the ladder when over the generator rumble came a sound like the loud SCREEEEEEEECH of chalk against a blackboard. The ladder had shifted slightly against the smooth skin of the plane.

Tanzola froze, as did the men above him. No one dared move for fear of causing another squeak. On top of the fuselage, everyone stood motionless, waiting. Shit, thought Tanzola, his face pressed against the ladder. If they didn't hear that, they're deaf! Again, he listened carefully.

At the head of the line of men, Torres had halted in midstep, one foot in front of the other. He too was listening for any reaction to the sound. He was just a few yards shy of the open door in which he had seen the terrorists standing only minutes before. Torres waited, prepared for anything.

A full minute passed. Nothing. Nothing at all. Tanzola

slowly raised his right hand and gently tugged three times on the leg of the man above him. He waited while this signal was passed along. Tanzola sensed, rather than felt, the man above him move upwards. With infinite care, he slowly followed, letting the cool aluminum rails of the ladder slide loosely through his sweaty palms. Moving at exactly the same speed as a slow motion film, his body rose smoothly with the freedom and effortlessness of a superbly conditioned athlete.

On the other side of the skin directly beneath the ladder, Harriet Edelstone straightened up from the washbasin as she finished brushing her teeth. She was just reaching down to dry her mouth on her skirt, the towels having run out, when she received the distinct impression someone was looking over her right shoulder. Instinctively, she straightened up and spun around. She looked toward the outer wall, then up at the curved ceiling. Nothing. A chill ran down her spine. God, you're getting jumpy, she thought.

With a sigh, she started to turn back to the mirror, but again some indistinct sound, something different caught her attention. She stared at the vinyl-covered surface. The toilet. Something *was* there. Faint and formless, but there nevertheless.

Intrigued, she closed the toilet cover and knelt on it to put her ear against the vinyl. Did she hear something? Yes! No! Maybe? She couldn't tell. She reached up to grasp the handhold over the toilet to steady herself as she rose. It quivered in her hand ever so slightly. She was right! Something was moving along the outside of the plane. Suddenly, she was anxious to be out of the place. She scooped up her things and shot back the bolt on the door. Pushing it open, she hurried back to her seat.

Torres stopped again. Just ahead of him the skin of the plane angled sharply downward to the cockpit windows. To his left, he could see light from the open door flooding the concrete below. Directly beneath his feet was the forward galley.

From the open pilot's window Torres could hear Benson's voice coming from the loudspeaker. The smell of cigarette smoke came to him again. He stood motionless for a moment, listening and waiting for the rest of the platoon to reach their positions on the fuselage. He began to sweat and rubbed one hand on his pants leg as he listened.

I'll have to be damn careful. But it looks good. The ambassador's got him talking in the cockpit.

Too Quick reached out and tapped Torres twice on the shoulder. The platoon was in position. Torres straightened. Too Quick reached into Torres' pack and took out a long sausage of plastic explosives. Torres then turned, opened Too Quick's pack, and removed a string of detonators and a three-eighths-inch thick sheet of Kelvar cloth.

Too Quick bent and carefully formed the explosive into a rectangular shape three feet square. Torres bent down and, using the plastic balls as guides, aligned the charge precisely over a carefully calculated spot on the skin.

All along the fuselage, the two-man teams of the 1st Platoon bent to their work. Each rectangular charge was positioned over a section of the plane that was free of any secondary structure and was directly above an aisle.

Satisfied with the positioning of the charge, Torres inserted some detonators into the side of the explosive and handed the remaining ones to Too Quick. The latter then passed them to the next team, while Torres connected the free end of the detonator wire to a hand generator he had taken from his belt. While Torres connected the wire, Too Quick covered the charge with the Kelvar cloth.

They stood up and swung the weapons from their backs. Torres looked back toward the nearest team, barely discernable in the darkness. In a moment, he saw all the men raise an arm and step aside as the signal was passed up the line from the team nearest the tail. They were ready.

Torres raised his SAW and then lowered it. At that signal, each man lowered his arm and turned his back to the explosive. Torres paused for an instant and listened one last time, the generator plunger in his hand. Benson's voice came from the open window. The sound of someone in the forward galley drifted up from the open loading door.

"Madre de Dios," whispered Torres as he quickly withdrew the plunger and pushed it home. A pulse of electrical energy shot to the detonators. The bulletproof Kelvar cloths leapt upward as all the explosive charges went off with a sharp sudden clap that echoed across the airfield. Their force cut through both the skin and ribs of the aircraft as neatly as a saw. The rectangular plug of skin in the center of each

charge came free and fell onto the top of the vinyl inner ceiling of the cabins, leaving gaping holes in the fuselage. The kelvar cloths sagged and disappeared into the holes. .

Too Quick brought his feet together and jumped into the center of the still-smoking hole, protecting his face with his weapon. Torres followed him.

In the forward galley, Yonnie, deafened and disoriented by the explosion, fought to regain her senses. As she straightened up, the ceiling bulged and then burst apart as a solid, rectangular plug of metal skin came down under the weight of Too Quick's body. A sharp corner of the metal caught her on the shoulder, tearing through her blouse and causing a deep gash down her right arm. An instant later, the soles of Too Quick's jump boots knocked her pistol from her grasp and sent it flying to the far side of the galley. As Yonnie's knees made contact with the carpet, she broke her fall with her hands and scrambled desperately on all fours across the galley towards the pistol.

Too Quick rolled to his right to absorb the shock of his fall as his feet came into contact with the carpet; at almost the same time he opened fire on Yonnie from a range of three feet. Too Quick shot a half a clip straight up her anus. The steel-jacketed military slugs, tumbled by the soft organs in her belly but unchecked in speed, passed completely through Yonnie's torso into her brain to slam against the inside of her skull. Yonnie's head exploded in a fine mist of red that ran in obscene streaks down the cream-colored vinyl fabric of the forward bulkhead.

Just seconds behind Too Quick, Torres landed and rolled forward over Yonnie's twitching legs. With the SAW hugged to his chest, his left shoulder slammed painfully into the deck, breaking his fall. He twisted quickly onto his side so that he faced the open door to the cockpit and began firing.

At the sound of the explosion, Qabrestan had dropped the microphone and grabbed his grenade. He turned toward Torres' dim figure and yanked at the safety ring. Torres, lying on his side, kept his fingers clamped down on the trigger. The bullets plowed into Qabrestan's genitals and lower stomach.

Tanzola had dropped to the deck on the right side of the plane between a lavatory and the after galley. His teammate landed at the same position, but on the opposite side. Even as they fell to the carpet and rolled on their sides, they could see there were no terrorists in the area. Both men stood up, guns at ready, and heard the unmistakable CRUMP of exploding hand grenades followed by the sound of submachine guns coming from forward.

Tanzola looked up the aisle. Several passengers in the last row of seats stared back at him. Tanzola flashed them a smile that was meant to be reassuring but only looked hideous under the streaked, black grease covering his face. Without a word, he spun around and went to work.

Covered by his teammate, Tanzola went from lavatory to lavatory and methodically yanked open each door, jumping aside each time to give his partner a clear field of fire. At the third door, Tanzola's hand met resistance. The door was locked. He glanced at his teammate and then, keeping most of his body to one side, raised his foot and kicked in the door handle and slide bolt. As his heavy jump boot smashed the frail locking mechanism, a high-pitched scream came from the lavatory. Tanzola yanked open the broken door, revealing Thomas B. Chandler.

Chandler, beside himself with terror, stood with his hands covering his face, his body shaking with fear. Behind him appeared the frightened face of a young man.

"Don't hurt me," whimpered Chandler, still holding behind his hands with his eyes tightly shut.

Tanzola's arm shot out and plucked Chandler from the tiny room, fully revealing the long-haired youth behind him. His partner's finger tightened on the trigger. Tanzola's trained eye flicked over the young man.

"Hold it. He's OK." Then, gesturing to the young man with the muzzle of his weapon, "Out. Down on the deck." Tanzola patted him down for weapons and then said, "He's clean." Then, he pushed Chandler to the deck.

As Chandler took his hands away from his face, he asked, "Is it over?"

"All over mister. Just stay down low here and you'll be OK."

Chandler looked up gratefully and nodded.

Tanzola then jumped up and checked out the last of the lavatories. Finding no one, he ran quickly up the right aisle. His team mate paced him up the left aisle.

When they reached the partition, they turned and looked back over the seated passengers. Tanzola's eyes swept the sea of faces warily.

"Any terrorists back there?" he shouted. "Sing out if there are."

Phyllis Jackson looked up from where she sat. "None here! They're all in the front." As she finished speaking, she was startled to see Tanzola suddenly appear beside her, his eyes cold. The muzzle of his wicked-looking SAW was inches from her chest.

"Sorry. Just checking, ma'am," he said and flashed his hideous smile.

"I should hope so," answered Phyllis with relief.

When the explosions first occured, Hamed had been asleep on the deck of the center galley. His brother Mahmud was standing guard nearby in the left aisle, while Abdulla watched over the right. As fate would have it, none of them was directly under an explosion point. When they heard the charges going off somewhere above them, both Abdulla and Mahmud instinctively ducked forward a step or two into the center cabin before spinning around to see what was happening. Seeing two troopers dropping from the ceiling, both turned and ran aft. As they ran, they frantically pulled out the pins in their grenades. Abdulla dropped his pistol.

But at midpoint in the center cabin, another two more troopers dropped into the aisles. One was directly in front of Abdulla. The terrorist, seeing he was cut off, raised his arm to throw the grenade. At the same time, the trooper from the center galley shot him in the back. His arm, lifeless from shattered bone and muscle, crumbled in a wide arc as his body sank towards the carpet.

Mahmud got only half as far as Abdulla before he was cut down in an crossfire. As he fell, his live grenade rolled under a window seat before exploding. The white hot fragments ripped Mahmud's body apart and almost severed the legs of the passengers in the seat under which it detonated. Worthington and Wall, sitting across the aisle, were also wounded in the lower legs with shrapnel from the same grenade.

At the sound of the explosion, Hamed woke with a start. He rolled over and grabbed his pistol and grenade from the carpet where he had placed them before going to sleep. As he scrambled to his knees, he saw a trooper come through the white smoke covering the ceiling to his right. Raising his pistol, he fired three times at the indistinct form. The bullets missed. Now on the deck, the trooper was turning toward him. With a curse, Hamed dropped the grenade, its pin still in place, and grasped the pistol with both hands. As he raised the pistol again, a trooper behind him brought the butt of his SAW down on Hamed's skull.

The firing stopped as abruptly as it had begun. Except for the moans of the wounded and the cries of children, the cabins were still. Everywhere, passengers raised their heads and looked about them. Without exception, each felt the most secret, most selfish joy in finding himself alive.

Tanzola, his weapon still at ready, stepped to the rear of the First Class cabin.

"Two dead. One prisoner, Cap'n!" he shouted.

Torres stepped out from behind the forward galley, his dislocated shoulder hanging useless. "Two dead up here," he replied. Then, to the sea of children's faces around him, "It's all over, kids. No one can hurt you anymore."

"We've got wounded back here," called Tanzola.

Torres stepped over Yonnie's body and leaned out the open doorway.

"Lewis!" he bellowed into the darkness. "Get the medics up here on the double. The plane's secure."

Lewis, Sergeant Mulaney and the radio operator appeared below. More men ran forward with a second boarding ladder, and two Army medics, who had accompanied Charlie Company from the beachhead, rapidly climbed it.

"Back aft," said Torres.

On the ground, Lewis handed the radio handset back to the operator and called up to Torres.

"Medevac choppers on the way from the *Veracruz*. They'll be here in six minutes. A Russian ground crew and transportation for the passengers are coming. And, Cap'n, the ambassador's on his way." Then, almost as an after thought, Lewis added, "The colonel says 'well done'."

Torres looked down at Yonnie's bloody body. "Yeah," he said simply.

When Benson appeared at the entrance to the First Class, he hesitated. The cabin was filled with people. Barbara Mawson, I don't know what she looks like. He looked at his watch. Eleven o'clock. Not much time.

He was about to start down the aisle and call out her name when Carol Moore came out of the cockpit with the crew's flight bags and papers.

"Can I help you?" she asked.

"Yes. I need to find a Mrs. Douglas Mawson."

Carol put the bags down and pointed. "There. The blond woman standing in the window seat behind the two children."

"Thank you," Benson answered over his shoulder as he moved down the aisle. "Mrs. Mawson!" he called.

Barbara had finished packing their few things and now stood talking to Harriet Edelstone. She turned at the sound of her name.

"Yes? I'm Mrs. Mawson."

"My dear Mrs. Mawson. You've no idea how glad I am to see you," announced Benson with relief. "I'm Calvin Benson, U.S. Ambassador to Djibouti. I must speak with you."

"Has something happened to the *Montana*?" asked Barbara worriedly.

"No. No. Nothing's happened to the *Montana*, but a very dangerous situation has come up and you're needed in the control tower immediately."

"Dangerous situation? Me? What are you talking about?"

Benson made a determined effort to pull himself together. "Forgive me. I'm very tired. Let me explain. We have very little time." Benson paused, collecting his thoughts. When he spoke, he chose his words carefully.

"Yesterday, your husband and the crew of the *Montana* decided that the rescue of the passengers on this plane was not progressing swiftly enough."

Barbara started to interrupt, but Benson held up his hand.

"Wait, I beg of you. So," Benson continued, "they gave the world an ultimatum. If you do not call him on the radio by midnight tonight and tell him that you and the passengers are safe, the *Montana* will launch a missile at Russia."

Barbara's jaw dropped open in disbelief. "That's impossible! Doug couldn't do such a thing! They . . ." She stopped in midsentence. "What do you want me to do?" she asked.

"Come with me to the control tower. We have a radio waiting. It's eleven-fifteen. We must hurry." He held out his hand to her.

Barbara ignored the hand and bent over to wake the children. This was too much for Benson.

"For heaven's sake! Leave them! We're coming right back," he exclaimed in exasperation.

Barbara straightened up, her eyes flashing. "I'm not leaving this plane without my kids. You carry Kathy," she commanded. "No use trying to wake her now. You have a car?"

"Yes. Yes," answered Benson, sounding more like a grandfather now than a harassed ambassador. He bent down and gently picked up the sleeping child.

Barbara turned to Harriet. "Stay with Nancy Olsen. She'll need you."

When they reached the base of the control tower, Robbie and Kathy were left sleeping in the big Soviet car. The Russian driver watched over them. Wearily Barbara and Benson climbed the long stairs to the top. When they were nearly there, Benson called to the waiting radio operators.

"Mrs. Mawson's here. Put the call through." He hurried over to them, leaving Barbara alone.

She went to the window facing the runway. Bright work lights now illuminated the plane. The last of the wounded had been flown to the hospital on the *Veracruz* some time ago, including Hamed who had been severely concussed. Now, Soviet trucks and buses were being loaded with the passengers and their baggage for the eighty-mile trip to a hotel in Djibouti.

Benson came back from the radio. "They're just about ready to try the call. Be another minute or so. Do you want some coffee or tea, Mrs. Mawson?"

Barbara shook her head slowly, her voice cold wirh rage. "No. I want to know just how long you stood here and watched us being killed. You saw everything. You knew all along exactly what was happening." Her voice grew harsh in accusation. Her eyes flashed with almost uncontrollable fury. "Why did you wait? Why didn't you get us out the first night? What the hell kept you?" Her chest rose and fell with shallow, emotional breathing. She felt light-headed and dizzy, yet she waited for an answer, her chin thrust forward aggressively.

Benson answered with diplomatic precision.

"The hijacking caused a major confrontation between our country and Russia. We almost went to war over the issue. As it was, your husband's ship fought with a Soviet force. The *Montana* survived, but the Russian losses were heavy."

Barbara was dumbfounded. "Over the rescue of a plane full of women and children . . . all that occurred? That's insane."

Benson was almost unable to answer, but finally he felt compelled to speak his mind.

"I know."

"Circuit's ready, Mr. Ambassador," came the radio operator's voice.

Barbara turned toward the voice, eager to speak to her husband.

Chapter 22

Tony Deville bent over the table in the Navigation Center and watched Dacovak plot the *Montana's* latest position on the chart. A long row of identical plots, reaching back almost to Jan Mayen Island, marked the ship's hourly progress toward the coast of Norway. In another two hours, judged Deville, they should be inside launch area Delta 3. As he watched, Dacovak penciled in the time. 2030. Dacovak's huge, usually awkward, hand now formed each numeral perfectly with the painstaking labor of a lifetime's practice. The world might be going to hell around him, thought Deville, but no one could find fault with Chief Dacovak's plot. As if to confirm his thought, Deville glanced back along the course line on the chart to the entry labeled 0300. Sure enough, he thought, it was as perfect as any of the other lettering.

Deville glanced up at the gyro repeater readout on the NAVDAC. They were right on course. All was as it should be. He turned and looked down at the plot once again, his mind on Jan.

Twenty-thirty, he thought as Dacovak completed his work. It's been almost seventeen hours since they landed at Assab. Why haven't we heard anything? It must be plenty dark there by now. It occurred to him that he did not know which time zone Assab was in. Maybe it wasn't dark there at all. He looked up at Dacovak, who stood staring down at the plot, lost in thought.

"What time is it in Assab, Chief?"

Dacovak's face twitched once at the sound of Deville's

voice, showing just how far away his thoughts had wandered. It took a second before he was able to answer.

"I'm sorry, Mr. Deville," Dacovak responded finally. His troubled eyes looked down at the young officer. "I was thinking the same thing. Assab's three hours east of us, so it's twenty-three thirty there now. The sun set at eighteen thirty-three, their time. I looked it up." Dacovak's big hands moved restlessly at his side. "It's only half an hour from midnight. I know the Captain said they had to wait till dark to get our families out, but Mr. Deville, it ain't gonna get no darker. We shoulda heard by now."

"Us not hearing doesn't mean a thing, Chief. Maybe they had to wait for the terrorists to settle down for the night. Everything's going to be OK. Your family's probably walking off the plane right now." Deville kept smiling as he searched Dacovak's face, judging the impact of his words. They seemed to have the desired effect.

"Yeah. You're right. I worry too much," Dacovak seemed to pull himself up. "Thanks, Mr. Deville," he concluded with a wry smile.

"Thank *you*, Chief."

Deville started for the CIC to have a look at the display table. As he moved across the compartment, Deville realized that he actually believed what he had told Dacovak. He wasn't worried. Either Jan would make it or she wouldn't. There wasn't a damn thing he could do about it either way. He couldn't save her from the terrorists any more than he could save her from her own weaknesses. It was out of his hands and it always had been. The events of the last seventy-two hours had finally forced him to understand that. At last he was able to think of Jan without guilt or shame.

He was still deep in thought as Seaman Medford stepped in front of him with an ELF radio message. It was from the CNO.

COME UP ON 22,105.00.
RESCUE COMPLETED.

Deville was barely able to suppress a whoop of joy. Only the thought that it was the captain's privilege to make the announcement restrained him from shouting aloud. Even so, as he reached for the phone to call Mawson, he was unable to prevent himself from giving a thumbs up gesture to the entire Control Room watch. That gesture and his wide grin were enough.

The long awaited news spread quickly through the ship.

Mawson was pacing the deck of his day cabin when the phone on the bulkhead buzzed. He snatched up the phone. He had been waiting for this call for the last hour.

"Yes?"

"Captain, OOD. We've just received the following message from OPNAV," said Deville. He read it, familiar routine helping to keep the excitement from his voice. "Congratulations, Captain. You've done it!" concluded Deville, his enthusiasm finally gaining the upper hand.

Mawson, thinking of the charges and trial that they would all soon face, sighed. He felt no elation, only relief.

"I'm on my way," said Mawson, carefully keeping any hint of his thoughts from his voice. "Plane up to periscope depth. Raise the HF antenna and come up on the frequency."

"Aye, aye, Captain," answered Deville.

Mawson shook his head as he hung up. I'll have to try to give them some idea of what lies ahead before they take me out of the ship. As he stood up, his eye caught his photo of Barbara. He paused for an instant, a wry smile forming on his lips. Then he spoke his thoughts aloud.

"It's OK, babe. Whatever happens, it's been worth it."

Minutes later, Mawson stood in the Command Center with a radio microphone in his hand.

"Pipe this throughout the ship," he ordered.

Soon the entire ship was listening intently to Mawson's conversation.

"*Montana. Montana.* This is Assab. Do you read me?"

"Assab. This is the captain of the *Montana.* Go ahead."

A new voice came over the speaker.

"Captain Mawson. This is U.S. Ambassador Calvin Benson. I'm going to put your wife on in a moment. Before I do, I am instructed to ask you if you will now surface and surrender your command?"

Mawson's voice was steady as a rock as he answered, "That is my intention. We will rendezvous with the *Hawaii* force within two hours. At that time, I will surface and await the pleasure of the senior officer present."

"Thank you, Captain. Here is your wife."

"Doug? This is Barbara. They've told me what you and the *Montana* did. Are you all right, dear?"

Barbara's words were exactly what was needed. Had it been planned and carefully calculated, nothing could have done more to instantly restore the men's sense of pride and faith in themselves. Her simple, heartfelt question had moved the entire situation beyond shame or guilt. Unknowingly, she had given them all absolution.

"I'm fine, dear. We're all fine. Are you and the kids OK? How about the ship's families? Are they all right?"

"Everyone came through OK except Jan Deville and little Allen Olsen," said Barbara, plainly thinking she was speaking only to Mawson. "They were killed by the terrorists."

Mawson spun around and looked at Olsen, then Deville. He was shocked as much by his failure to warn Barbara that everyone was listening as by the impact of the words themselves.

Olsen stood stunned. His jaw worked grindingly as he fought to control himself, his fists clenched into tight balls of flesh. Mawson turned to Edelstone and motioned him in Olsen's direction. The XO led Olsen unseeing from the control room.

Mawson turned toward the Navigation Center. Deville stood staring at the speaker from which Jan's fate had just been pronounced. Jan gone. Gone. The soft clinging warmth of her. The sloppy, little house and his unwashed uniforms. The shame of Frank and others. All gone. It was over. All of it finished. Every single, knotty, emotional problem that had so occupied his mind. The dread he felt at seeing her again. All of it suddenly solved.

Mawson's voice recalled him to the present.

"You're relieved, Mister."

Deville straightened up, his face impassive. There was no need to fake grief he did not feel. Not now, not ever. He was free of all that.

"No, sir. If you don't mind, captain, I'd rather remain on duty," he replied evenly.

Mawson looked long and hard at Deville. Deville returned the look. His eyes were steady, almost defiant.

"Whatever you say." Mawson turned away.

Two hours later, the glassy eye of the *Montana*'s little-used attack periscope broke the surface of the sea. Sixty feet below, Mawson sat on the edge of a hinged stool in the Command Center, hunched forward peering into the instrument's fixed eyepiece. His hands rested lightly on the dual control handles. All about him the watch stood silently waiting.

As the seawater ran from the lens and the field of view cleared, Mawson set the internal optics of the periscope traversing to the right. The watery horizon spun slowly before his eyes. The utilitarian bulk of a *Perry*-class frigate came into view.

"Mark target bearing. An escort frigate," ordered Mawson, depressing a switch on the handle with his thumb. "Range one thousand."

At the Tactical Display table, one of the blue dots of light appearing on the central screen pulsed briefly as Jennings entered Mawson's sighting into the TACDAPS. From his seat at the table, McKenna noted with satisfaction that green dot of light representing the *Montana* was well clear. Beside him Edelstone looked on, checking every move, making certain that the always hazardous business of surfacing within a force of moving ships was carried out safely.

The horizon continued to swing before Mawson's eyes as the periscope traversed to the right. Three more times Mawson called out the position and range of escorts before the stern of the *Hawaii* came into view.

"Mark target bearing. The *Hawaii*," ordered Mawson, pressing the button for the last time. "Range five hundred. Prepare to surface."

"Sonar plot confirmed," called out McKenna.

For one moment longer, Mawson continued to peer at the *Hawaii*. It was the last maneuver of his career and he wanted it right. They were on perfect station off the starboard side of the large cruiser moving along at the same slow speed. Mawson turned from the periscope, hitting the switch that would retract it. Well, he thought, nothing left to do but surface and get it over with. As he opened his mouth to give what would be his last order, he remembered it was Olsen who had the conn and had made the tricky underwater approach.

"Well done, Mr. Olsen. We're right on station."

Mawson looked around the control room. The rock-steady eyes of the watch met his gaze. They would follow him anywhere. Even now, they would follow him. Mawson looked down, embarrassed at this naked loyalty. He had done them false. With a deep sigh that was almost a sob, a single word exploded out of him.

"Surface!"

Epilogue

THE WHITE HOUSE

Pursuant to resolutions of the House of Representatives, its Committee on the Judiciary conducted an inquiry and investigation into the actions of certain officers and men of the United States naval vessel *Montana* during a four-day period in August of 198–. The hearings of the committee and its deliberations, which extended for more than three months and which received wide national publicity over television, radio, and in printed form, resulted in votes adverse to the said officers and men on recommended Articles of Indictment.

As a result of certain acts or omissions occurring before the voluntary resignation or discharge from naval service, said officer and men have become liable to possible indictment and trial for offense against the United States. It is believed that the trial of these officers and men, if it became necessary, would not be in the best interest of this nation.

NOW, THEREFORE, I, President of the United States, pursuant to the pardon power conferred upon me by Article II, Section 2 of the Constitution, have granted and by these presents do grant a full, free, and absolute pardon unto the officers and men of the USS *Montana* for all offenses against the United States that they have committed or taken part in during said period.

IN WITNESS WHEREOF, I have hereunto set my hand this 8th day of February in the year of our Lord nineteen hundred eighty—.

ABOUT THE AUTHOR

F. ROBERT BAKER has considerable experience in weapons systems technology: From 1956-1959 he worked on the first of the nuclear fleet and ballistic missile submarines at the Electric Boat Division of General Dynamics. From 1959-1965, he was a Project Engineer with the Atlas missile program. From 1965 to 1970 he was at Lockheed. And since then he has provided personal consulting services to several major high-tech corporations as well as to a number of foreign governments. He is also a contributing editor to *Motor Boating and Sailing* magazine.

The wonderful new novel by the author of
KRAMER VS. KRAMER

Steve Robbins has a heart-wrenching dilemma.
His wife has found a satisfying career of her own.
His kids have grown up. And the job he is so good
at has lost its challenge. Caught in the mainstream
of modern marriage and success, Steve wakes up
one morning to realize that his dreams—everything
he's longed for—have come true...and they're not
what he really wanted at all. So Steve goes back to
where the dreams began. And he starts searching for
the one thing he left behind...happiness.

THE OLD NEIGHBOR-HOOD

By AVERY CORMAN

(14891-5) $2.95

Available September 1, 1981,
wherever paperbacks are sold or directly from Bantam Books.
Include $1.00 for postage and handling and send check to
Bantam Books, Dept. ON, 414 East Golf Road, Des Plaines, Illinois 60016.
Allow 4-6 weeks for delivery.

This offer expires 1/82.   7/81

THRILLERS

Gripping suspense...explosive action...dynamic characters... international settings...these are the elements that make for great thrillers. And, Bantam has the best writers of thrillers today—Robert Ludlum, Frederick Forsyth, Jack Higgins, Clive Cussler—with books guaranteed to keep you riveted to your seat.

Clive Cussler:

☐ 14455	ICEBERG	$2.75
☐ 13899	MEDITERRANEAN CAPER	$2.75
☐ 13880	RAISE THE TITANIC!	$2.75
☐ 12810	VIXEN 03	$2.75

Frederick Forsyth:

☐ 14765	DAY OF THE JACKAL	$3.50
☐ 14863	THE DEVIL'S ALTERNATIVE	$3.50
☐ 14758	DOGS OF WAR	$3.50
☐ 14759	THE ODESSA FILE	$3.50

Jack Higgins:

☐ 13202	DAY OF JUDGMENT	$2.75
☐ 13848	THE EAGLE HAS LANDED	$2.75
☐ 14054	STORM WARNING	$2.75

Robert Ludlum:

☐ 14300	THE BOURNE IDENTITY	$3.75
☐ 14733	CHANCELLOR MANUSCRIPT	$3.50
☐ 14775	HOLCROFT COVENANT	$3.50
☐ 13098	THE MATARESE CIRCLE	$3.50

Buy them at your local bookstore or use this handy coupon:

Bantam Books, Inc., Dept. TH, 414 East Golf Road, Des Plaines, Ill. 60016

Please send me the books I have checked above. I am enclosing $_____ (please add $1.00 to cover postage and handling). Send check or money order—no cash or C.O.D.'s please.

Mr/Mrs/Miss_____

Address_____

City_____ State/Zip_____

TH-5/81

Please allow four to six weeks for delivery. This offer expires 11/81.